Joan Jonker was born and bred in Liverpool. Her childhood was a time of love and laughter with her two sisters, a brother, a caring but gambling father and an indomitable mother who was always getting them out of scrapes. Then came the Second World War – a period that Joan remembers so well – when she met and fell in love with her late husband, Tony, while out with friends at Liverpool's St George's Hotel in Lime Street.

For twenty-five years, Joan campaigned tirelessly on behalf of victims of violence, but she has recently retired from charity work in order to concentrate on her writing. Joan has two sons and two grandsons and she lives in Southport, where she is busy working on her next bestselling saga. Her first book, *Victims of Violence*, is the moving and compassionate story of her fight for justice for victims; and her previous novels of life in Liverpool's backstreets have won her legions of fans throughout the world:

'Wonderful characters and humour' Mrs Ivy Deeks, Essex

'The characters were so believable – I really got the feeling of being there with them' Mrs B. Webb, Suffolk

'Great books. Once I start reading them I can't put them down' Mrs R. Crow, Eltham

'I really enjoy your books. They are so funny, I find myself smiling when I'm reading them' Susan Fretwell, Western Australia

'You've done it again! Molly and Nellie are so funny, I love the bones of them' Jean Breward, Norfolk

'When I'm low and feeling sorry for myself . . . all I need is to pick up one of your books . . . and I'm soon feeling better' Marion Carver, London

'Molly and Nellie a⎯⎯⎯⎯⎯⎯⎯⎯⎯⎯⎯⎯⎯⎯⎯⎯⎯ ⎯en for more new titles

D0733755

The Sunshine
Of Your Smile

Joan Jonker

headline

First published in 2002
by HEADLINE BOOK PUBLISHING

First published in paperback in 2003
by HEADLINE BOOK PUBLISHING

10 9 8 7 6 5 4 3 2 1

ISBN 0 7553 0317 2

Typeset in Times by Avon DataSet Ltd,
Bidford-on-Avon, Warwickshire

Printed and bound in Great Britain by
Clays Ltd, St Ives plc

HEADLINE BOOK PUBLISHING
A division of Hodder Headline Limited
338 Euston Road
London NW1 3BH

www.headline.co.uk
www.hodderheadline.com

I dedicate this book to every one of my readers;
for the lovely letters, for stopping me in the supermarket or
street to say how much you enjoy my books, and, of
course, for your loyalty in buying them when they come
out. We share the same sentiments in life and enjoy the
same sense of humour. As one of my characters would say,
I love the bones of yer.

Dear readers

This is a 'Molly and Nellie' classic, which I really enjoyed writing, and which I know you will get great pleasure from, plus lots of chuckles and fun.

Take care.

Love

Joan

Chapter One

Nellie McDonough faced her friend across the dining table and, pressing her finger on the raised chenille of the cloth, made a fabric tunnel towards the middle of the table. While her finger was busy, her legs were swinging under her chair. 'Ay, girl, there's not much doing these days, is there? Life is very dull.'

'Dull! Did yer say dull?' Molly Bennett's voice went up two notes as she gazed in disbelief at her friend. 'In the name of God, Nellie, don't yer think I've had more than my share of excitement over the last thirteen months? Our Tommy, me only son, got married three weeks ago, and twelve months before that I had a double wedding on me hands when Jill and Doreen got wed. I would have thought that was enough excitement for anyone, but that wasn't all, was it? Our Doreen has a four-month-old baby, and didn't I worry meself to death the whole time she was carrying? Then, to top it all, our Jill tells us at Tommy's wedding that she's pregnant, so I can start worrying over *her* now for the next six months. I'm made up for them, of course, and I love me grandson to bits, the same as I'll love Jill's baby when it comes. But yer must admit I've had a hectic, money-worrying thirteen or fourteen months. And you above anyone knows how much running around I've had to do, so how the hell yer can say life is dull, well, that's beyond me.'

'All right, girl, keep yer hair on!' Nellie's chins swayed in all directions as she wagged her head from side to side. 'I don't know why yer had to bite me head off, I was only passing a comment.'

Molly couldn't help grinning. 'Is that why ye're wagging yer head – to make sure I didn't bite it off? I know I've been a bit short-tempered lately, sunshine, but letting go of three children in a year is pretty hard going. It was bad enough for me and Jack when the girls left home, but it's ten times worse now Tommy's gone. Oh, I know I see the girls every day 'cos they only live in the street, and Tommy calls every night as he still walks home from work with his dad. But the house isn't the same and I get emotional at times.'

Nellie could feel herself getting on her high horse, and her whole eighteen-stone body was bristling with injustice. 'It's no wonder I've been feeling miserable for the last three weeks, it's *you* what's causing it. Every day I'm having to listen to yer bragging about yer grandson, or moaning 'cos yer miss the kids. I'm not surprised I've been feeling down in the dumps, ye're enough to make anyone want to stick their head in the gas oven. In fact I have thought of it, but I never seem to have a penny handy for the meter.'

'Nellie, to put yer head in the gas oven, yer have to get down on yer knees, and yer'd never make it, sunshine. I mean, the penny is no problem, I'd lend yer one, but the knees would let yer down.'

'Yer'd be daft to lend me a penny, girl, 'cos yer wouldn't get it back. I'd be sitting in the front row of the stalls in heaven, next to Saint Peter, and we'd be laughing our cotton socks off when we looked down and saw yer trying to get the penny off George. Now my feller isn't what yer'd call tight, but he definitely wouldn't fork out a penny after the job was done. He might have lent yer one before, but not after. He's not that daft.'

'This is not a very pleasant subject, sunshine, so can we talk about something else, if yer don't mind? Something that won't give me nightmares, like seeing you laying on the kitchen floor with yer head stuck in the gas oven. It doesn't bear thinking about, and it's not a sight I'd like to see.'

'I wouldn't show yer up, girl, I'd make meself presentable first. Yer wouldn't have to worry about calling the police out, 'cos I would have put clean knickers on.'

'Oh, yeah, I can see it all now,' Molly said. 'I call the police and tell them I lent yer a penny so yer could gas yerself. But before yer passed away, yer'd left instructions to say I wasn't to be embarrassed 'cos yer'd changed yer knickers.'

'D'yer know what, girl?' Nellie leaned forward and rested her mountainous bosom on the table so she wouldn't keep banging it. 'Yer've not half cheered up, yer've got a smile on yer face and a twinkle in yer eyes.'

'I might look better, but I can't snap out of me sadness just like that.' Molly snapped a finger and thumb. 'I miss me kids and that's all there is to it. We used to have a good laugh around the table eating our meal every night, and now there's just me and Jack and Ruthie. Thank goodness she won't be getting married for at least six years.'

'Don't bite me head off again, girl, but I've got to say what's in me mind whether yer like it or not.' Nellie lifted her bosom from the table and sat back on the wooden dining chair. The chair wasn't very happy about this, and made its complaint known by creaking loudly. 'Yer were moaning about yer children leaving home, but yer never think about whether I miss our Steve or not. And yer go on about Jill being pregnant, and how yer'll worry about her. Yer seem to forget it was my son what put her in the family way, she didn't manage it all on her own. So I have as big a stake in the baby as you have, and I'm entitled to worry as well.'

The emphatic nodding of Nellie's head had the chair creaking and groaning and her chins trying hard to keep in rhythm. 'Of course yer have as much right as me, sunshine, and I wouldn't leave yer out for all the money in the world.' Molly bit on the inside of her lip to stop herself laughing in Nellie's face. 'And while I'm on the subject of money, there's no way I can afford to buy a new dining-room suite in the foreseeable future, so would yer transfer yer backside to the chair what I bought especially for yer? It's stronger than these, yer see, and it's used to your bottom now.'

Nellie scratched her head. 'We weren't on the subject of money, girl, it was you what brought it up. And d'yer have to use long words just to make me look ignorant in front of people?'

Molly let her eyes roam the room. 'Which people, sunshine? There's only me and thee here. And what word are yer on about?'

'If I knew it, I wouldn't be asking, would I? I can't even say it, but I remember yer won't be able to buy a dining-room suite in it.'

Molly narrowed her eyes. 'Sometimes I think yer act daft when all the time yer know far more than yer let on. Everyone understands what "the foreseeable future" means, so if I was going to try and trick yer I'd be more inclined to interject a word like "assiduously".'

Nellie could feel her tummy shaking, lifting the dining table from the floor, so she stood up quickly and leaned on the table with clenched fists. 'A tanner says yer don't know the meaning of that last word what yer just came out with.'

'Don't waste yer money, sunshine,' Molly said. 'Yer'll only lose.'

Nellie pursed her lips and, nodding knowingly, folded her arms which disappeared from sight beneath her bosom. 'Not this time I won't lose, girl, so the tanner bet is on. Say that word again, then tell me what it means. And don't forget Corker's home now, so I'll be asking him for advice.'

'Yer can write to the King for advice for all I care, sunshine, but I won't take a tanner off yer. If yer lose yer can buy me a cake. Is that all right with you?' When Nellie nodded, Molly felt a pang of guilt and almost owned up to truth: that she'd been going through the dictionary last night expressly to find a word she could use to pull her friend's leg. 'The word is assiduously, and it means carefully and regularly.'

It's a good job Nellie was standing because the chair wouldn't have stood an earthly under her huge body which was shaking with merriment. There wasn't an inch of her that wasn't in motion. 'Careful and regular! Oh, yer mean like going to the lavvy every day?' In between hoots of laughter, and bending down to try and get her breath, she said, 'I'll have to ask George about that tonight. How can I put it now? Shall I ask if he's been assiduously to the lavvy, or if he's been to the lavvy assiduously?'

Molly looked at her mate's face which was creased into a huge grin. The devilish merriment lurking in those hazel eyes made Molly want to round the table and hug the woman who had filled her life with laughter for the last twenty odd years. The four-foot-ten, eighteen-stone bundle of happiness whom she loved like a sister. But if she told Nellie that now her mate would stop every person they met on their way to the shops, and with head held high and breasts standing to attention would repeat the compliment Molly had paid her. And the shopkeepers wouldn't be left out, they'd get action as well as words. But Nellie always got a smile of welcome when she entered any shop because the assistants knew her antics would brighten their day.

'Well, sunshine, it's nice to sit and have a natter, but I think it's time for us to get our messages in.' Molly pushed her chair back. 'I want to stop at Doreen's to see if she needs anything, save her going out.'

'Ah, ay, girl, we've only had one cup of tea! Let's have another.'

'It won't be fit to drink, it'll be stiff.'

'It'll be wet and warm, and that'll suit me fine.' A glint came into Nellie's eyes. 'And I know yer've got a couple of custard creams left, so they'd go down a treat with the tea.'

Molly gasped. 'How d'yer know that?'

Not in the least embarrassed, Nellie grinned. 'I sneaked a look in yer pantry when yer went down the yard for a quick one. So it's yer own fault for leaving me.'

'No, it's not my fault, Nellie McDonough! I don't expect me friends to go snooping as soon as I'm out of the room. I wouldn't have the nerve in someone else's house.'

'Ah, yeah, but you're not like me, are yer, girl? I'm a different breed to you. I mean, yer don't tell lies, only now and again a little white one, and yer don't really swear. Me now, I tell whopping big fibs and swear like a trooper.'

'Yer wouldn't be bragging about telling lies and swearing, would yer? 'Cos I don't see anything to brag about, yer should be ashamed of yerself.'

'I'll make a deal with yer, girl. If you'll pour the tea out, while we're drinking it and eating our custard cream, I'll tell yer all about how ashamed of meself I am.' Nellie sensed a weakening and added a little bonus. 'And I'll mug us to a cream cake when we get to Hanley's.'

Molly's resistance faded as the thought of a fresh cream cake had her mouth watering. And if Nellie didn't mind drinking tepid tea, who was she to argue? 'That sounds very appealing, sunshine, and I'm not going to refuse. But remember, I can't return the favour because I've only got Jack's wages coming in now while you have three.'

'Holy suffering ducks, girl! Have yer found something else to moan about? Ye're turning into a right moaning Minnie.'

'Oh, I have no qualms about letting yer buy a cake for me, sunshine, I don't feel obligated to return the treat. Not after the thousands of cups of tea yer've had in here. And the sugar and milk on top. It'll take yer a lifetime to pay all that back.'

Nellie didn't turn a hair. With a look of pure innocence on her face, she moved to where the carver chair stood and carried it to the table. It was a strong chair, with polished arms, and well able to support her ample proportions. When she plonked herself down, there wasn't a peep out of it. 'Yer forgot to mention the biscuits I've had, girl, so I'd better remind yer in case ye're making a list of the debts I owe yer.'

'Yer've well paid yer debts, sunshine. Yer paid them with all the fun and happiness yer've given me and mine over the years.' Molly pulled a face as she poured out the lukewarm tea. But as much as she loved her friend, she had no intention of making a fresh pot. There was shopping and work to be done. 'Yer've paid up in full, Nellie, account cleared.'

Nellie jerked her head back, throwing her chins into turmoil. 'Thank God for that!' There was more than a hint of sarcasm in her voice. 'I don't need to stay awake every night, worrying about when yer going to send the bailiffs in.'

Molly handed her a cup, saying, 'I can't see anything keeping you awake at night, sunshine. Yer wouldn't worry if yer backside was on fire.'

'Nothing would keep me awake all night, girl, but there's a feller laying next to me in bed, and he sometimes keeps me awake. He can't resist me voluptuous body.'

'Right, that's it!' Molly glared across the table. 'Once we get to talking about your bedroom, then it's time to call it a day. So get that tea down and let's be on our way.'

Like a little girl doing as she was told, Nellie lifted the cup to her lips. Loudly enough for Molly to hear, she muttered, 'I feel sorry for her feller, he picked a real cold fish when he picked her.'

* * *

7

Doreen greeted her mother and Nellie with a smile and a kiss. Motherhood suited her, she looked the picture of health and prettier than ever. 'I'm glad yer called, Mam, 'cos I'd like yer to get some shopping for me, if yer don't mind.'

'That's what we've called for, sunshine.' Molly crossed the room to where a frail old lady sat in her rocking chair, a smile of welcome on her face. Miss Victoria Clegg was ninety years of age, and although she could no longer get around as she used to, she still had all her faculties. A spinster, she was loved by everyone, especially Molly's daughter and her husband Phil whom she had taken in and given a home to. And when the baby came along, it seemed to have given the old lady a new lease of life. With no family of her own, she considered God had been watching over her when she was befriended by the Bennetts and McDonoughs. They had made her part of their families, and she thanked the Good Lord for it every night.

'How are you this fine day, Victoria?' Molly had a hand on each of the wooden arms of the chair and smiled down into the old lady's faded blue eyes. 'I've got to say yer look good, so my daughter can't be such a bad cook.'

'She's a marvellous cook, Molly, and a marvellous housewife and mother.' The old lady looked past Molly to where Nellie was standing. 'And what has Mrs McDonough been up to so far today?'

'I haven't been up to nothing, girl, it's me mate what's been playing up. She was in a right miserable mood when I called for her, and all the time I was in her house she did nothing but find fault with me.'

Doreen leaned back against the sideboard and waited to be entertained by the woman she'd always known as Auntie Nellie, and who was like a second mother to all the Bennett children. 'Oh, aye, and what's me mam done now?'

'Well, it's difficult to know where to start, girl, 'cos according to her, I've got more things wrong with me than I've got right.

But I won't burden you and Victoria with me woes, except to tell yer that two of her complaints were I swear like a trooper and I've got no sympathy for her in her time of sadness. Oh, and I'm a nosy poke into the bargain.'

'Are yer cut to the quick, Auntie Nellie?' Doreen asked. 'Has me mam upset yer?'

'Oh, yer'll never know how much, girl, never. She's me mate, but sometimes she can be a right cruel cow.'

Victoria was used to this sparring; in fact she looked forward to it. She'd never known a day when these two friends hadn't brought a smile to her face and filled her room with laughter. 'I don't think Molly was far wrong when she said yer can swear like a trooper, Nellie. Not that I've ever heard a trooper swear, mind, but I have heard you forget yerself sometimes and come out with the odd swear word. But I have to admit I don't see enough of you to know whether ye're nosy or not.'

Molly jerked her head at Nellie. 'Explain to them the reason I said yer were nosy. Go on, tell them and see what they think.'

'All this because I was truthful with her.' Nellie's nodding head set her layers of chins jiggling up and down in harmony. Until she changed tactics and began to shake her head, then they decided it was every chin for himself. 'I'll tell her lies in future, it's easier.'

'Don't be shy, sunshine,' Molly said. 'Tell them why I said yer were nosy.'

When Nellie let out a deep sigh, it was as if her bosom had been blown up by a bicycle pump. 'Honest, talk about making a mountain out of a molehill isn't in it. All I did was look in her pantry to see if she had any biscuits to have with our cup of tea. That's all I did, yet to hear the way she took off on me, anyone would think I'd killed the cat.'

'Me mam hasn't got a cat, Auntie Nellie.'

'I know that, girl, but I was just supposing.' Hitching her bosom, Nellie came up with a thought. 'If yer mam did have a cat, girl, I would have trod on it and killed it ages ago. Yer see, I haven't seen me feet for years, so I can't see where I'm putting them.'

'Nellie, will yer stop prevaricating and get on with it! The day will be gone before we get to the shops.'

'All right, girl, whatever you say.' With that, Nellie folded her arms and clamped her lips tightly shut.

Molly looked confused. 'What are yer doing now?'

'Yer told me to stop it, so I've stopped!'

'I told yer to stop prevaricating, not to stop talking!'

'I didn't know what that word meant, girl, but I do know the meaning of the word stop. Yer see, big words are all very fine, but what use are they if nobody understands the bloody things but yerself? Yer could have a fine conversation with yerself, but it would be very one-sided and there'd be no fun in that.' Nellie's head went back and she looked up at the ceiling. 'It's no good me asking her to repeat the word so I can tell my feller tonight, 'cos it's taking me all me time to remember assiduously.'

Oh, dear lord, Molly thought, we'll be here all day at this rate. It would suit Nellie fine because she never worried about whether the dinner was ready for her family coming in from work. If it wasn't then it was just too bad and they'd have to wait. 'Nellie, will yer tell Doreen and Victoria where I was when yer went snooping in my pantry?'

'Yer'd gone to the lavvy, girl, I thought yer knew that. I mean, yer wouldn't have let me snoop if yer were there, would yer?' Then she said in a defiant voice, 'I don't think that was being nosy. We've been friends long enough to do what we like in each other's house.'

'Oh, so I can go in your house, wait until yer go down

10

the yard, then sniff around to see how many biscuits yer've got?'

Nellie didn't answer but dropped her head and gazed down at the floor. After a few seconds the three women could feel the floorboards move beneath their feet, and they were ready when Nellie burst out laughing. The sound ricocheted off the walls, and although Nellie was the only one who knew why she was laughing, it was so infectious the others joined in. Rubbing a chubby hand across her eyes, she gulped, 'Oh, dear, oh, dear, oh, dear! Molly, girl, I'll tell yer something to save yer the bother of searching me pantry for biscuits. If yer searched for a month of Sundays yer'd never find any, 'cos there's never any there, not even a crumb.'

'Who are yer kidding, sunshine? Yer forget, I'm always with yer at the shops, and when we get biscuits at the corner shop, you get exactly the same as I do. So don't be pleading poverty because I know different.'

'Oh, yer see me getting them, girl, I'll grant yer that. But yer don't see me eating them, do yer? And cross my heart and hope to die, I'm telling yer the truth. Any biscuits I get are eaten the same day. None over, all gone.'

'Are yer telling me that you and yer family can polish a pound of biscuits off in one day? That's greedy, that is.'

'No, not me family, girl, they haven't got a sweet tooth like me. George might have one with his cup of tea before he goes to bed, but that's all. I'm the guilty party, I eat the blinking lot. All by meself, on me tod.'

Molly's hands went to her hips and her head tilted. 'Are yer telling us, Nellie McDonough, that you go through a pound of biscuits, on yer own, in one day? I don't believe yer! No one can be that greedy, especially when they're so hard to come by.' Another thought struck her. 'And yer have the cheek to come to my house and cadge whatever I've got! That is downright cheeky, that is.'

'I can't help it if I've got no willpower, girl! I do try, honest I do, but while I know there's biscuits in me pantry, I can't leave them alone.' Then came Nellie the drama queen. 'They seem to draw me like a magnet.' She stretched out her arms and grunted as she drew them slowly back, as though from the effort of pulling a heavy weight towards her. 'It's just like that, girl, honest! I try to take me mind off them, but like I say, it's as if I'm being drawn to them like a magnet. Even at two o'clock in the morning I can't resist the pull. Many's the night I've crept down the stairs while all the family were asleep, and scoffed the last two ginger snaps. And yer'll never believe me, but once I know there's none left, I can creep back up the stairs, climb into bed and go fast asleep.'

Molly didn't believe her for a second, but had to admit her friend could be very entertaining exaggerating any situation. 'Oh, and George didn't feel yer getting out of bed, didn't hear yer going down the stairs, and climbing back into bed? He must be a very heavy sleeper, your feller. Or deaf.'

'I have woke him up a few times, but I tell him I've been down the yard. And he believes me when he feels me cold feet on his back.'

'Nellie,' Victoria said, pressing a hand against the stitch in her side, 'yer definitely should have got a job on the stage or the films 'cos ye're far better at acting than most of the big stars. If only you'd been seen by a talent scout they would have snapped yer up. Oh, yes, fate has definitely been unkind to you.'

The little woman rose to her full four foot ten, for this was praise indeed. 'Thank you, Victoria, you're the only one of my friends to recognize talent when they see it.'

'Shush!' Doreen put a finger to her mouth and strained an ear. 'There's Bobby crying, it must be time for his feed.' She made haste to the stairs, saying, 'Yer can tell the time by him, he's every three hours on the dot.'

'We'll wait for Doreen to come down and tell us what she wants from the shops, sunshine. And after I've had a cuddle from me grandson we'll be on our way.'

'Oh, ye gods and little fishes, she's going all soppy again.' Nellie tried hard to put a look of disgust on her face. 'It's enough to make yer sick.'

'Wait until Jill and Steve have their baby, then yer'll be just the same,' Victoria said. 'Your first grandchild . . . you and George will be over the moon.'

'Of course she will! She just likes to play the tough guy, that's all. It's these gangster films she sees. One day she's Edward G. Robinson, and the next James Cagney.' Molly glanced out of the window. 'It's a nice blue sky, a good day for washing.'

'Is it nice out, Molly?' Victoria asked. 'It seems to be, looking out of the window, but sometimes looks are deceptive.'

'Yeah, it is nice, considering we're into October.' Molly smiled down at the old lady, and suddenly, without any warning, it was as if someone had switched on an electric light in her head. She could see Victoria walking down the street with Doreen holding the ninety-year-old firmly by the arm for support. They never walked far, just down to the shops and back, but the old lady liked the fresh air, and stopping to chat to neighbours who made a fuss of her. There had been no walks since the baby arrived, though, and Molly was now cursing herself for being so thoughtless. How could Doreen take Victoria out and push the pram at the same time? It was impossible because the old lady had to be supported. This was something Molly should have seen. She probably would have realized if she hadn't been so busy, but that wasn't a good enough excuse.

She closed her eyes briefly. How could she have been so thoughtless that her neighbour whom she loved dearly was now reduced to asking what the weather was like outside? Victoria would never ask to be taken out, she'd consider that to be imposing herself. But she shouldn't have to ask, and wouldn't have needed to if Molly had given her a thought. It was time to make up for her lack of care and concern. 'Would yer like a short walk, Victoria, to get some fresh air? Me and Nellie would be only too glad to take yer, and we'd walk yer nice and slow.'

'No, that's all right, sweetheart, yer've got enough to worry about without me adding to it. It was kind of yer to ask, though.'

Doreen came down the stairs holding the baby close in her arms. 'I heard that, Aunt Vicky, and ye're telling fibs 'cos I know yer'd love to go out for a little walk. So don't be so ruddy stubborn and go with me mam and Auntie Nellie. I'll have finished feeding Bobby by the time yer get back.'

Nellie had been pondering while this was going on. Like her mate, she loved the old lady to bits and would do anything for her. And it would be a bit of a bonus as well, 'cos Molly couldn't blame her when people stopped to chat to Victoria. 'Don't take no arguments from her, just tell her to get her coat on.' She winked at the old lady whose eyes were looking decidedly brighter. 'We'll run yer down to the butcher's and back. That should be no problem to a spring chicken like yerself. In fact, if my corn starts playing me up, yer could give me a piggy-back.'

'If you hold the baby, Mam, I'll get her coat,' Doreen said. 'And she'll need a scarf, even though yer say it's nice out. We can't have her getting a cold.'

Molly held her grandson, and when she heard him gurgling, and felt his feet and arms waving about, all the love she had for this tiny scrap of humanity welled up within her. 'Ooh, I love yer that much I could eat yer!' She bent and kissed his forehead. 'I'm sure he knows me, Doreen, he's smiling at me.'

'Oh, my gawd, she's off again.' Nellie sighed and tutted. And because she didn't know whether to shake or nod her head, her chins were allowed the freedom to do as they pleased. 'If yer ever hear me getting as soppy as that when my grandchild arrives, tell me to put a sock in it, Victoria.'

Doreen was helping the old lady on with her coat while she grinned at the woman who was like a second mother to her. 'Yer'll be singing a different tune then, Auntie Nellie. As soon as the baby is put in yer arms, yer'll be hooked for life. And I promise yer, yer wouldn't have it any other way.' After she'd fastened the buttons on the coat, she looked into her old friend's lined face and gave a conspiratorial wink. 'Jill and Steve were only wondering the other night, if they had a baby girl, would it take after you?'

'Not on your life,' Molly said. 'The world is not big enough for two Nellie McDonoughs. And seeing as the baby will be my grandchild as well, can yer 'magine what I'd have to put up with? No, if it resembles Nellie in any way, I'm going to ask our Jill to send it back 'cos I can't afford to keep two of them going in biscuits.'

'Have yer had the wireless on this morning, Mam?' Doreen asked. She waited until Molly shook her head, then said, 'Sweets have come off rationing from today. So yer can go in any shop and buy as much as yer like.'

Nellie punched the air for joy. 'Yippee! I'm going to buy meself a slab of Cadbury's from the corner shop, and eat the whole lot on the way to the butcher's.' She glared at Molly, daring her to comment. 'And I'm not going to share it, so there!'

'I don't care if yer make a pig of yerself, sunshine, but don't ever again come crying to me because yer can't bend down to fasten yer shoes. Yer'll never lose that tummy if yer carry on eating biscuits and sweets.'

'Yer can't shame me, girl, 'cos when it comes to chocolate there's no shame in me. If I had to choose between a slab of Cadbury's or being able to fasten me shoes, then I'd go ruddy barefoot.' When Molly shrugged her shoulders as if to say, 'What can you do with her?' Nellie turned away and muttered, 'Miserable cow! She's only jealous 'cos she hasn't got a voluptuous body like mine what has all the men chasing after me. Even Tucker the coal man told me last week he'd lusted after me for years.' She turned suddenly to face Molly, her grin spreading from ear to ear. 'He offered to give me a ride on his horse if I'd meet him down the side entry one night, when it's dark.'

'Oh, and was he going to bring a ladder with him?' Molly asked. 'Yer'd need one to get on the horse.'

'Nah! He said he'd give me a leg up.'

Molly was looking down at the baby, and when she burst out laughing she spluttered all over him. 'Oh, I'm sorry, Bobby, but yer can blame yer Auntie Nellie. And I only hope to God she's learned how to control her tongue by the time ye're old enough to understand her.'

Nellie waddled over to gaze down at the baby. Rubbing a chubby finger over the soft, smooth skin, she said, 'No, ye're laughing, aren't yer, son? And who made yer laugh? Why, yer Auntie Nellie, that's who. You and me are going to get on just fine 'cos yer've inherited my sense of humour, not yer other grandma's.'

The other three women looked at each other with raised brows. Then Molly said, 'How can he have inherited your sense of humour, sunshine, when he's not even related to yer? You are not his grandma!'

Nellie shifted position to stand with feet apart. Folding her arms, she glared at Molly. 'Let me get this straight before I clock yer one. When my Steve has his baby, you'll expect to be its grandma, won't yer?'

'Well, I *will* be his grandma, 'cos it's my daughter what's having the baby! So naturally I'll be its grandmother.'

But Nellie wasn't going to budge. 'Then how come I can't be

a grandma to Bobby? Doreen's your daughter, same as Jill. So if you can be grandma to my son's baby, why can't I be grandma to your daughter's?'

As she handed the baby over to her daughter, Molly was shaking her head. 'If I give her an answer to that, she'll keep it up and we'll never get out. So from this minute, Helen Theresa McDonough is your son's grandma.' She winked before going on. 'I'm not doing the poor child any favours, but it'll stop me from having to listen to yer Auntie Nellie bringing the subject up every ruddy day.'

Molly spun around to see a smile on her mate's face. 'Did yer hear that, sunshine? You are now a grandma to my grandson, and that means watching what yer say in front of him when he gets a bit older, buying him an Easter egg every year, and a birthday and Christmas present. Is that understood?'

Nellie tried to click her heels together as she stood to attention, but there was too much fat between them. So she settled for a smart salute. 'Aye, aye, sir! Understood, sir! I am to watch me language, never mention me voluptuous body what the men crave for, never, ever mention the antics me and my feller get up to in the bedroom, and spend all me money on presents! I'm beginning to wonder what I'm letting meself in for.'

'Please yerself, sunshine, it's no skin off my nose.' Molly looked over to where the baby was beginning to whimper. 'Bobby wants his feed and we're stopping him. So if yer tell me what yer want from the shops, Doreen, me and Victoria and Granny Grunt will be on our way and leave yer in peace.'

They set off down the street, Victoria in the middle being supported on either side by Molly and Nellie. Coming towards them they saw Nellie's next-door neighbour. The Mowbrays hadn't lived in the street long so Beryl had only spoken to Victoria on the odd occasion when the old lady had been standing at the front door for a breath of fresh air, but she knew of her great age and good standing in the community. 'It's not often we see you out, Miss Clegg, and it's good to see yer looking so well.'

'Thank you, that's very kind of you.' Victoria had never let her standards slip and was always gracious, as her parents had taught her to be. 'That's because I'm very well looked after by my adopted family and my friends. I am indeed very lucky.'

'How's the family, Beryl?' Nellie asked. And then before the woman could answer, she went on to say, 'I wouldn't have to ask yer if yer talked a bit louder, 'cos I'd be able to hear yer through the walls. But we seldom hear a sound. Is that because you and your feller aren't speaking, or because yer've knocked each other unconscious?'

Beryl chuckled. 'Could be one or the other, Nellie, except my feller never falls out, he says life is too short. And he'd never dream of raising his hand to me or the kids.'

Molly knew they couldn't keep Victoria out long, she'd soon get tired, so she decided to cut things short. 'I'm sorry, Beryl, but I'm afraid it's hello and goodbye. We don't want to be out long so we'll be on our way. We'll see yer later, probably. Ta-ra for now.'

'Well, that was nice, I must say! Yer did that on purpose, Molly Bennett, so I wouldn't be able to tell Beryl about me being a grandma.'

'Yer can talk to her to yer heart's content when we get back, sunshine, but right now we're taking Victoria to the butcher's. So if we meet any more neighbours, it's just a nod and a smile. Then, later on, yer can go round knocking on doors to tell them yer news, if yer like. But don't be surprised if they look at yer funny, and ask how yer can be a grandmother to my daughter's son. Mind you, they'll understand if yer explain to them how yer've worked it out.'

'If I thought yer were being sarky, girl, I'd belt yer one.'

Molly feigned surprise, while Victoria looked in bemusement from one to the other. 'Me be sarky with you! Ye're imagining things, sunshine. How could I possibly be sarcastic with me very best mate? Why, we're almost like sisters!'

Nellie walked on without saying a word, her brow furrowed in thought. Then she said, 'That's right, girl, of course we're sisters! Remember how years ago we cut our arms like the Indians do, and held them together so our blood would mix? Don't yer remember that day, girl, 'cos I do. There was blood all over yer tablecloth while we pledged to be sisters for life.'

Molly gasped. She knew Victoria was wise to Nellie's tales and took them with a pinch of salt, but although this one was too far-fetched to be true there was just a chance the old lady would believe it. 'Nellie, yer imagination is certainly working overtime today. Victoria must think yer've flipped yer lid. Blood all over me tablecloth indeed! That's a new one on me. As for slitting our arms with a knife . . . huh! That would be over my dead body.'

'No, yer didn't die, girl, I wouldn't let that happen to yer. I tore up yer tablecloth and made bandages, and yer were soon sitting up and taking notice. Yer were too weak to do a war dance, though, so we had to wait until the next day when yer were feeling better.'

They were standing outside the butcher's shop by this time, and Molly said to Victoria, 'Have yer ever known anyone like my mate for telling tales?'

Victoria shook her head. 'I really don't know how she thinks all these things up. She amazes me, but it's a good job I know her and don't take her seriously. Otherwise I might have dreams about being initiated into the sisterhood of squaws.'

The three women were laughing when they entered the shop. The owner, Tony, excused himself from the customer he was serving so he could welcome Victoria. His assistant, Ellen, who was Molly's next-door neighbour, followed him out from behind the counter. Pleasure at seeing Victoria could clearly be seen on their faces, an indication of the high esteem in which she was held. 'It's wonderful to see yer, Miss Clegg, looking as sprightly as ever,' Tony told her. 'You're as welcome as the flowers in May.'

Ellen gave her a gentle hug. 'Tony's right, yer do look well. And it's lovely to see yer out and about.'

The two customers in the shop weren't going to be left out. It was ages since they'd seen the old lady, and they greeted her warmly. 'It's nice to see yer looking well, queen, yer don't look a day older than the last time I saw yer.'

'Cissie's right, and it must be over a year since we last saw yer. I look like an old hag compared to you.'

Victoria delighted in the fuss being made of her. 'It's lovely to be out, and it's all thanks to Molly and Nellie. They're angels, both of them.'

Nellie was preening herself. 'Angels and grandmothers, Victoria, or did yer forget?'

Ellen frowned. 'You can't be a grandmother yet, Nellie, Jill's only about three months.'

Molly took a deep breath and blew out slowly. 'Ellen, take a bit of advice from me and let the matter drop. Unless yer want you and the customers still to be here when it's time for yer to close up for the day.'

Tony chortled as he went back to serving his customer. 'Oh, what's she been up to now? Come on, give us all a laugh.'

Nellie knew she was getting cow's eyes from Molly, but she didn't care, it was only for a laugh. 'What shall I tell him, girl? About me being a grandma, or your tablecloth being covered in blood?'

Tony's customer's mouth dropped open. The tablecloth covered in blood! My God, this should be worth listening to. So she waved aside the parcel Tony was handing over the counter to her. 'I'll get me purse out in a minute, you finish serving Irene. I don't mind waiting a while.'

'I wouldn't waste me time if I were you, Cissie, 'cos she's only pulling yer leg.' Molly was eager to be served in case Victoria became tired. 'Nellie, will yer tell the ladies yer were only acting daft?'

'Oh, about the tablecloth yer mean? It's a few years ago now, but it's still fresh in my mind. Yeah, Cissie, me and Molly had been to see a cowboy film the night before, and we decided we'd like to be squaws. And to be sisters, yer have to mix yer blood. But Molly hasn't got much sense of fun, and she wouldn't let me nick her arm with the carving knife. So to make it look real, I got a bottle of tomato sauce out of her pantry and poured some on our arms. But yer know what it's like getting sauce out of a bottle – yer wait ages for it, then it comes all in one dollop, and it went all over her cloth. And it didn't half look like real blood after we'd tried to wipe it up.'

Cissie knew when she was being taken for a ride. With flared nostrils and a look of disgust on her face, she paid Tony, grabbed the meat with one hand, her friend Irene with the other, and marched out of the shop. They could hear her saying: 'Silly buggers! It's about time they grew up.'

Victoria was thoroughly enjoying herself. It was a long time since she'd mixed with these people she'd known for years, and she'd laughed so much this morning she felt a lot younger than her ninety years. But when Molly had bought two lean breasts of lamb for her and Doreen, and Nellie had wormed extra lamb's liver off Tony, the old lady agreed that to carry on to the cake shop would be too much for her. 'Tomorrow's another day, sunshine,' Molly told her, 'and weather permitting me and Nellie will take yer to the cake shop then. It would give Edna Hanley a surprise, she's always asking about yer. I can just imagine her face when we walk yer into the shop.'

'What about our spuds, girl, are we coming out again when we take Victoria home?'

'We'll have to, sunshine, 'cos I need spuds and bread. It won't take us long if you walk with yer eyes closed and don't see no one yer know. When we come out shopping, it's the same every day. We spend more time gabbing in the streets than we do getting our shopping in.'

'I can't help it if I'm popular, girl, now can I?'

'No, sunshine, and yer can't help having a voluptuous body, what no man can resist. And I know ye're telling me the truth about that, because Tony has never taken his eyes off yer since we came in the shop.'

His face red with laughter, Tony flicked his straw hat further back on his head. 'It's a good job my missus isn't here, she'd wring me neck. She's no sense of humour, my wife.'

Her face deadpan, Nellie said, 'Mmm, she must be like Molly then. She's got no sense of humour either.' Then she grinned at her friend. 'Okay, girl, keep yer hair and yer knickers on, I'm coming now. And I'll keep me mouth shut until we get home. But I ain't walking with me eyes closed, just to please yer. I know what ye're after, yer want me to get run over 'cos yer can't stand me being more attractive than you are. I don't blame yer, mind, 'cos I'd be the same. Jealousy is a terrible thing, and I know yer can't help it. So to please both of us, I'll walk home with one eye open and one eye closed.'

They managed to get through the shop door, and were standing on the pavement when Nellie stepped back inside and shouted, 'Remind me to tell yer how I became a grandma, Ellen, yer'll find it very interesting.'

Molly gritted her teeth then said, 'Forward march, Nellie, or I'll not have time to stuff me breast of lamb and get it in the oven to do slowly.'

'Speaking of breasts, girl, did yer see the way Tony...'

Molly pulled the trio to a halt and put a hand over Nellie's mouth. 'That is going too far, sunshine, I'm sure Victoria is disgusted with yer.'

But that wasn't true. The old lady was keeping her laughter back until she could tell Doreen and Phil. They would really enjoy hearing what it was like to spend an hour in Nellie's company.

Chapter Two

Molly opened the oven door to make sure the breast of lamb wasn't being done too quickly, and the smell that wafted out brought a blissful smile to her face. 'Ooh, that's just what the doctor ordered,' she told the empty kitchen. 'Jack will be over the moon, it's one of his favourite meals.' She closed the door and turned to wash her hands at the sink. 'I'd better put a move on and make meself presentable before Jill gets here.'

This was the time of day Molly looked forward to most. Her eldest daughter called in every night on her way home from work, and although she only stayed five minutes because she wanted to be home in time to see to Steve's dinner, those five minutes meant a lot to Molly. A glance at the clock told her it was just about time, so she took off her pinny, folded it, and threw it into the kitchen where it landed on the draining board. 'Good shot, Molly.' She smiled at her reflection in the mirror over the mantelpiece. 'Yer should take up darts.'

Then came the knock, and she nearly fell over herself to get to the door quickly. 'Hello, sunshine.' Molly opened her arms and Jill walked into them as she'd been doing since the day she took her first steps. 'Yer look the picture of health. Being pregnant suits yer.'

'I feel fine, Mam, I'm not even sick in the mornings any more. But I'm beginning to show and the girl I work with passed comment this morning.'

'It's got nothing to do with her, sunshine, so take no notice.'

'Oh, she wasn't nasty or anything, just said I was blossoming. She's got two children herself, so she understands.'

Molly gazed at her first-born. Jill took after her for looks, as did Doreen and Ruthie. They were all pretty, with long blonde hair and vivid blue eyes. Except that Molly's hair was now peppered with white and she was no longer the slim girl she'd been before having the children. Jill was the gentle one of the family and would never raise her voice in anger, unlike her two sisters. In fact, Molly couldn't remember Jill ever answering her back. 'Have yer set a time for packing in work, yet? Yer don't want to carry on too long.'

'As soon as I start to feel uncomfortable, I'll hand in my notice. But me and Steve have got a nice little sum in the Post Office now, and it makes us feel better to know we've got something to fall back on when we get a house of our own. Not that we're thinking of leaving Mrs Corkhill because we like it there, and she wants us to stay. But sometime in the future, if we have more than one baby, then it'll be a case of having to.'

The front door had been left ajar. Now they heard it being pushed open so hard, it banged against the hall wall. 'In the name of God, do yer have to do everything so quick, Ruthie, can't yer think before yer act?'

'I didn't mean to push so hard, Mam, but I was in a hurry 'cos I thought I might miss seeing me big sister.' Ruthie put her arms around Jill's waist and hugged her. 'We don't half miss yer, yer know. Me mam wouldn't say nothing in case it upset yer, but the house is like a morgue with you and Doreen and Tommy gone.'

'I miss you too,' Jill said. 'But it's not as though I've gone to live miles away.' She put a hand on each of her sister's arms and pressed her away so she could see her properly. 'Good grief, Ruthie, ye're nearly as tall as I am! A few more inches and our eyes will be on a level.'

'Ooh, don't tell her that, sunshine, she already acts like an old woman. She can't wait to leave school so she can go out with boys.'

'I thought yer were keen on Gordon Corkhill?' Jill's smile was teasing. 'Or has someone else knocked him off his pedestal?'

'I think she's torn between Gordon and Jeff Mowbray,' Molly said. 'She can't make up her mind, but I've told her not to worry because she's got quite a few years yet before she even thinks of courting.'

The young girl's chin came out in a show of defiance. 'Our Jill started courting Steve when she was only fifteen, didn't yer, Jill? So I've only got about sixteen months to go. And that's not long, 'cos I'll have been working for a year by that time.'

'Listen to me, sunshine. No matter how old yer are, ye're not too old to smack, so don't be giving me any old buck. I like Gordon, he's a nice kid, but he's not old enough to be thinking of girls even though he has been working for a year. And the same goes for Jeff Mowbray. We don't know that much about the family, they're new in the street, but he seems a nice enough kid. Still, no matter how nice they are, yer can forget about boys for a while, and I mean that. Yer dad would have a fit if he knew his youngest daughter had an eye for the boys.' Molly couldn't keep her thoughts to herself. 'I know what yer Auntie Nellie would say, too. She'd say yer take after yer me, 'cos she's always telling me I'm man-mad.'

Ruthie pursed her lips and nodded knowingly. 'Oh, aye, so what does Auntie Nellie know that we don't? She must have some reason. I'll have to ask her some time when she's on her own.'

'Don't you dare ask Nellie!' Molly was sorry now she'd mentioned her friend, because after an hour in Nellie's company, Ruthie wouldn't need anyone to tell her about the birds and the bees. 'Ye're thirteen, sunshine, so don't be trying to grow old before yer time.'

Ruthie had been a surprise, coming seven years after Tommy was born. And of course she'd been spoilt, being the baby of the family. She was far more advanced than her sisters were at that age, and certainly not afraid to speak her mind, even if it did mean a slapped bottom. Then again, all the local kids seemed to be advanced for their age. It must be due to the war years when there was less discipline.

'Yer dinner smells nice, Mam.' Jill's nose wrinkled as she sniffed up. 'It's not half making me feel hungry.'

'Why don't yer stay and have yer dinner with us, Jill?' Ruthie missed her sisters more than she would ever admit, especially Jill who never shouted at her and was always ready to wipe away a tear. 'Me mam could make it stretch to another one, couldn't yer, Mam?'

'Of course I could, sunshine, but Jill has a husband to look after, and he'll be in from work soon expecting her to have a dinner ready for him. And I know yer've got a soft spot for Steve, so yer wouldn't want him to go hungry, would yer?'

Ruthie sighed and shook her head. 'No, I know I'm being daft. But I don't half miss yer, and so do me mam and dad.'

Jill put an arm across her sister's shoulders. 'And I miss you. I love the bones of all of yer. But Steve is my husband now, and yer know I've always been crazy about him. And if I don't make an effort to get home now, I'll worry meself sick that his dinner won't be ready to put on the table when he comes in.'

'What are yer having, sunshine?' Molly asked. 'Anything nice?'

'Mrs Corkhill is cooking tonight. I told her she shouldn't, but yer know how stubborn she can be. It's an easy meal, though, we're having corned beef hash. It's one of her favourites and she makes it nice and tasty with plenty of onions in.'

'It's a few days since me and Nellie called in to see her, she'll think we've forgotten her. Tell her we'll nip up tomorrow for a cup of tea and a natter.'

'She knows yer've had yer hands full, Mam. She said she doesn't know how yer've managed everything so well, with the three of us getting married and Bobby's christening in such a short space of time. And yer don't have to worry about her, she's fine. Considering her age, she does very well. I mean, Uncle Corker is in his forties so she must be near the seventy mark. Yet she keeps the house spotless, does her own washing and ironing, and always looks neat and tidy. I keep telling her to leave the housework, me and Steve would do it over the weekend, but she insists on doing it herself. She says it keeps her young, and if she sat all day doing nothing but twiddling her thumbs, she'd end up like a cabbage.'

'I can't imagine Lizzie sitting all day doing nothing, it's not in her nature.' Molly cast an anxious eye at the clock. 'I don't want to throw yer out, sunshine, but yer've been here longer than usual tonight, and Steve will be home before yer.'

Jill smiled as she nodded. 'I'll blame it on Ruthie for keeping me back, telling me about her love life. Anyway, I'll be on me way now so give us a kiss, Mam, and you, Ruthie.'

As Molly held her tight, her mind went back to the day Jill was born. How happy she'd been, and Jack had strutted around like a peacock he was so proud. It didn't seem like twenty-one years ago. 'I love yer, sunshine.'

Ten minutes later, Molly was setting the plates out on the draining board when she heard the key in the door. Wiping her hands down the front of her pinny, she rushed through to the living room for the next joyful part of her day. That was seeing her son Tommy for a few minutes before he set off home to his new wife. He was a handsome lad, taller than his dad, who had followed him inside, and with a face that was never far from a smile. 'Hello, Mam.' He put his arm across her shoulders and planted a noisy kiss on her cheek. The face she turned up to him reflected the love she felt for her only son. She'd thought of him as a young, easygoing lad when he went into the army, without a care in the world. But he came home a mature man who had seen things that had made him grow up quickly. Things that were so bad they still gave him nightmares. The only person he ever talked about the war to, though, was Archie Higgins, who was now going steady with Lily, Nellie's daughter.

Archie had been a corporal in the same regiment as Tommy. When the war in Europe was over, about thirty men from the same regiment were on a mopping-up operation in Germany. They'd seen the horrors of a prisoner-of-war camp which they would remember until the day they died and were moving forward, alert for any German soldiers still in the area, when two men at the front stepped on a hidden landmine and were blown up. It was Archie who ordered the others back and remained calm, showing no emotion, even though he must have felt as bad as any of the frightened soldiers. His composure helped to restore the men's confidence and enable them to cope with the horror they had just witnessed. The two men who were killed had been close comrades, and more than a few tears were shed for them.

After a while Archie led them back through that minefield, walking ahead so that if he came upon a mine he might be killed but the rest of the men would be safe. He became a hero to all of them men that day, and was a hero to Tommy still. He had been awarded a medal for his bravery but no one had ever seen it apart from his mother, he was too modest. When he met and started courting Lily, he had made Tommy promise never to tell his family, or the McDonoughs, about what had happened. Tommy wanted to tell the world he owed his life to this man, but kept his promise. Now, when Rosie or his family mentioned his time in the army, all he would say was that Archie had made a man of him.

'Something smells good, Mam.' Tommy reckoned he had the best family in the world, and he adored them. 'A smell like that makes me wonder if I did the right thing in getting married. Perhaps I should have stayed at home.'

'Away with yer!' Molly said 'Rosie is a smashing cook and you know it. Besides, yer wouldn't last a day without her.'

His handsome face lit up at the mention of his wife's name. 'I know, I fret for her when I'm in work.'

'That's the way it should be, son,' Jack said. 'I've felt like that about yer mam since the day we got wed. In fact, I'm counting the days until I retire. To my reckoning, I've got seven thousand three hundred days to go.'

Ruthie hung on her father's arm. 'I'm counting the days too, Dad. In one hundred and twenty-three days, I'll be leaving school.'

Jack ruffled her hair. 'I know that, love, 'cos I'm counting those days, too! Then yer'll be getting a job and bringing a wage packet home. Me and yer mam will be a lot better off.'

'I hope ye're not expecting me to hand me whole wage packet over.' Her chin jutted defiantly. 'Because that wouldn't be fair.'

Tommy put his hands on her shoulders and turned her around. 'That sounds like mutiny, little sister. But before yer go on strike, I want yer to look back and wonder where the food came from to feed yer all these thirteen years, and the clothes to keep yer warm? The pennies for sweets and the presents at Christmas and birthdays? And who read yer stories in bed until yer were ready to go to sleep, and then kissed yer and tucked yer in? And remember when yer were little and yer got the measles, who was it sat up with yer every night until yer got better? And never complained because they were all acts of love.'

Ruthie dropped her head, shame bringing a blush to her face. Then she looked up into her brother's eyes. 'I didn't mean I wanted to keep all me wages! Just enough for me to buy long stockings for when I get a job, and some scented soap.'

His hands circling her waist, Tommy lifted her high, until her head was inches away from the ceiling. 'I know yer didn't mean it, little sister, 'cos ye're a Bennett and we share and share alike.' He spun around and was pleased when she began to chuckle. He hadn't meant to upset her, just to make her think a little about the sacrifices their parents had made to give them as good a life as they could. 'I can see yer now, in yer long stockings and smelling of scented soap. Yer'll look so pretty, and smell like a rose garden, yer won't have no trouble getting a job. The bosses will be forming a queue with offers of work.'

Ruthie laughed down at him. 'Then I'll choose the one who pays the best wages. And I'll demand me own office and secretary.'

Tommy had touched a chord in Molly's heart and she was feeling very emotional. But she didn't want to spoil her son's visit by blubbering like a baby. 'D'yer know, that little madam kept our Jill late tonight, and she's doing the same with you. I think she's hoping yer'll both get thrown out and will come back here again to live.'

Tommy lowered his sister to the ground. 'Yeah, I'll get a move on.'

'Yer better had, or Rosie will have the police out looking for yer.'

'I'll run all the way, Mam. If I'm lucky, I'll be greeted with a kiss. If I'm unlucky, she'll be standing on the second stair with the frying pan in her hand, and I'll get a wallop on me head.'

'Well, I'll find out later what happens,' Molly told him, 'because I'm coming round to see me ma and da.'

'That's good, Mam! If I'm not confined to bed with a lump on me head as big as a football, we can have a game of cards.'

'I might walk round with yer, Molly,' Jack said, 'if Ruthie is going over to Bella's.'

'That would be nice, sunshine, and make a change. It's not very often you and me go out arm in arm. And Bella could come over here if yer like, Ruthie. It would give Mary a break because ye're over there every night. You run over and ask if she can come, and tell her mam I said we won't be late back, and yer dad will make sure she gets home all right.'

Like a streak of lightning, Ruthie was gone. Her father shook his head and chuckled. 'I think your suggestion met with her approval, love. So will yer tell yer grandma that Mr and Mrs Bennett will be paying them a visit later?'

'I'll tell them if I'm not in bed waiting for the doctor to come.' Tommy moved towards the front door, grinning. 'I'll see yer both later, ta-ra.'

Nellie happened to be looking towards the window when Molly and Jack walked past. She moved the curtain for a better view, and tutted. 'Well, the flaming underhanded so-and-so! There goes Molly, arm in arm with Jack, just like a ruddy courting couple. And she never said a dickie bird to me about going out. How's that for a best mate?'

George peered over the top of the evening paper. 'Nellie, she doesn't have to tell yer everything. When she saw yer, she probably didn't know she was going out. Not that it's got anything to do with you anyway!'

But Nellie wasn't to be pacified. 'She must have known five minutes ago, and she could have given us a knock on the wall. I've a good mind to put me coat on and follow them.'

Her son Paul burst out laughing. 'Mam, even you wouldn't have the nerve to do that. Auntie Molly would clock yer one!'

'She'd have to get past my tummy first, and no one's ever been able to do that.' When Nellie nodded for emphasis, her chins did a quickstep. 'I can't get over the cheek of her! And where does she think she's off to, this time of night, that I couldn't have gone with her?'

Paul shouted to his sister who was getting washed in the kitchen. 'Can yer hear that, Lily? Me mam's got a right cob on 'cos Auntie Molly and Uncle Jack have just gone past. She wants to put her coat on and follow them.'

Lily came through, drying her face. 'Yer can't do that, Mam! I mean, what's it got to do with you where Auntie Molly goes? Yer don't knock and tell her when yer go to the corner shop some nights, do yer?'

'Ah, well, yer see, girl, that's different. When I go to Maisie's, I have a natter with all the women and get all the gossip – which I pass on to me best mate the next day. She wouldn't know what was going on in the neighbourhood if it wasn't for me keeping her up to date. But Molly never stands listening to gossip, and when she does hear anything she forgets it right away. Never thinks of telling me. That's why I've got to be with her all the time, so I know what's going on.'

Paul, a black-haired, brown-eyed handsome lad of twenty, thought his mother was hilarious, the things she said and got up to. And, thank goodness, she'd passed her sense of humour on to her three children. 'Go on, then, Mam! Put yer coat on and hurry after them, they can't have gone far. And if Auntie Molly pulls yer up about being so nosy, yer could always say yer'd run out of sugar and were going to the corner shop.'

'Ye're right, lad, I could.' Nellie was on her way to get her coat off one of the hooks behind the door when George growled, 'Don't even think of it, Nellie, because the only way yer'll get over that doorstep is over my dead body. So sit down and listen to the wireless, and let me read me paper. I don't know why I

33

bother buying one because it's just a waste of money. Yer never give me the chance to read it.'

Just then there was a knock on the door, and Lily passed the towel to her brother. 'Here, Paul, I'll get it. It'll be Archie, and he's ten minutes late.'

'Perhaps he bumped into the Bennetts.' Paul winked at the sister who was a year older than him, had inherited her mother's colouring and sense of fun, but thankfully not her eighteen-stone build. Then, out of devilment, he added, 'I bet he did, and he's been standing nattering to them, getting the low-down on all the news.'

The new arrival came into the room then and smiled to see them all.

'Good evening, I hope everyone in the McDonough household is well and happy.' Archie was so tall and broad he seemed to fill the room. He was nice-looking, too, with the black hair always immaculate, not deep brown eyes, a good set of white teeth and a ready smile. The only thing that stopped him from being really handsome was his nose, which was rather on the large size. But his other features and his caring nature more than made up for it. He cocked his head as he eyed Nellie, standing in front of the fireplace. 'Are yer going out, Mrs Mac? Yer look as though ye're set for the off.'

'Oh, don't get her going, Archie, or we'll miss the start of the big picture.' Lily was struggling into her coat. 'If I were you, I'd leave well alone.'

But Archie knew Nellie inside out now, and thought she might be up to one of her tricks. If she was, he could do with a good laugh. 'Now yer know I'm always ready to listen to yer mam if she's in a dilemma, and we've got loads of time to get to the Astoria before the big picture starts. So tell me what's up, Mrs Mac, and I'll give yer my undivided attention.' He pulled out a chair and sat down. 'Fire away, I'm all ears.'

Nellie sat on a chair facing him, rested her bosom on the table and clasped her chubby hands together. 'My lot don't take me serious, Archie, and it doesn't half make me mad. Yer see, I saw me mate Molly going past the window just before you got here, and she was arm in arm with Jack. They looked like a courting couple, and it made me blood boil because she never said a word about going out with him. I've been with her all day, she had plenty of time to tell me. So I wanted to go after her and ask her what she was playing at, but my feller wouldn't let me. And Lily and Paul are just as bad, 'cos they agreed with him.'

Archie was by this time convinced Nellie was having them all on. But he managed to keep his face straight. 'Why did yer want to go after them, Mrs Mac?'

'Well, it's like this, yer see, Archie. Molly's me best mate and we tell each other everything. But she never breathed a word about going out with Jack tonight, and I think that was very underhand of her.' As Nellie nodded and wagged her head her face was doing contortions, and each layer of her chins gave up trying to keep in step and went their own way. 'If I was going out I'd tell her, I wouldn't keep her in the dark. And I wouldn't sneak past her window, hoping she wouldn't see me either!'

With the evening paper lying on his lap, still unread, George growled in disgust. 'The next thing, yer'll be saying they crouched down so yer wouldn't see them! Some mate you are, Nellie McDonough.'

But Archie looked as though he found the conversation really interesting. 'And yer wanted to go after them to see what they were up to?'

'In a nutshell, lad, in a nutshell.'

'Wouldn't yer get yer eye wiped, though, if Mrs B turned around and said they were only going to her ma's?'

'That wouldn't surprise me, lad, 'cos I know she's going to Bridie's.'

Paul's dimples always appeared when he smiled. They were in evidence now as he crossed his legs and sat back waiting for his father to erupt. And he didn't have long to wait.

'What the hell are yer talking about, woman? Are yer saying that yer knew all along where Molly and Jack were going, and yer've just been taking us for a ride?'

'Ah, now that's not true, George. I knew Molly was going, but she never mentioned Jack was going with her.'

'There's something wrong with you, woman, ye're not right in the head. Yer've wasted half an hour talking a load of rubbish, and we've been daft enough to listen to yer.'

Lily stood behind her mother's chair and put an arm around her. 'What made yer think that up, Mam? For the sake of something to do?'

When Nellie's body moved, her chins were the first to go into action, followed by her bosom and tummy. 'Oh, not just for the sake of something to do, girl, no! I mean, if I just wanted something to do I could go out and brush the yard. No, there was a method behind me madness. It might sound drastic to yer, but only something drastic would take yer father's eyes off the ruddy paper. Every night he sits there with it in front of his face, reading every bloody word. Sometimes I walk past his chair, just to make sure he's still alive and breathing. If I talk to him, I only get a grunt, never a whole sentence. So I thought I'd liven him up a bit, and it worked, 'cos he got all red in the face and het up. And he's still only on page ruddy five of the *Echo*! But yer've no idea how bored stiff I get every night, he drives me mad. From the front page to the back, he doesn't miss a word. And then he starts all over again from the front page again, only this time he's standing on his head and reading it upside down. I've never told you children before, because I didn't want yer to know yer father was going ga-ga. I'm just waiting for the day when he takes it up to bed with him and lays it down between us.'

George's laughter started as a low rumble in his tummy, then grew louder until the room was filled with the sound. It drowned the laughter of the other four people who were doubled up and wiping away the tears. It wasn't all caused by what Nellie had said, but the way her hands and face acted out her story too. 'Now what would I want to take the *Echo* up to bed with me for, Nellie, when I've got you? I couldn't handle both of yer at the same time.'

Archie pushed his chair back and stood up. Leaning across the table, he cupped Nellie's chubby face in his hands. 'Mrs Mac, ye're a hero. Yer didn't fool me for a minute, like, but yer played yer part well, as usual. And now I'd better take yer daughter out, 'cos if we miss the beginning of the big picture I'll never hear the end of it. It's Errol Flynn tonight, in one of those swashbuckling things, and he's so brave he makes Lily go weak in the knees.'

'I'll come out with yer,' Paul said, 'or Phoebe will have a right cob on.'

'She only lives next door but one!' Nellie shook her head. 'When me and yer dad were courting, he had to travel six stops on the tram. You don't know ye're born, having a girlfriend living a few yards away.'

'I didn't know I was born when I was going those six stops on the tram every night,' George said. 'If I'd known what I was letting meself in for I would have been better keeping me money in me pocket.'

'Yer can say that now, lad, but yer certainly weren't thinking it when we were courting. It was you what did all the running.'

'I'm going,' Paul said. 'Phoebe won't believe I've been listening to me mam telling me how me dad stands on his head to read the *Echo*. That's one excuse she'll never swallow.'

Lily and Archie followed him out. 'Oh, Phoebe will believe it all right. She's known me mam long enough to expect anything from her,' Lily said. 'But how the heck she can come up with all these weird and wonderful tales is beyond me. All our lives we been listening to her, and never once has she repeated herself.'

'My mam's a bit like that, she likes a good joke,' Archie told them as they stood outside the Corkhills' house. 'But she's not a patch on Mrs Mac for dreaming things up.'

Paul's eyes were bright with laughter and his dimples were deep. 'D'yer know, I've spend me whole life crying, like most other kids, but while they were crying 'cos they'd been smacked, I've been crying with laughter.' He heard the door behind him opening and turned to see his girlfriend Phoebe. 'Yer won't believe me excuse tonight so I'll tell it to yer mam and dad instead.'

Phoebe smiled at Lily and Archie before putting on a stern face for Paul. 'Two doors away, and yer still can't be on time.'

'When he tells yer his excuse, believe him, 'cos it's true.' Lily was pulling on Archie's arm. 'It's me mam's fault, she's made us late for the pictures. Come on, Archie, if I miss the start of the picture, I can never get into the plot.'

When they'd gone, Phoebe leaned forward from the top step. Puckering her lips, she said, 'Yer can give me a kiss for keeping me waiting.'

Paul was all for that. 'Oh, yer deserve more than one kiss, babe, after me keeping yer waiting at least ten minutes.' He kissed her waiting lips. 'How about a kiss for every minute?'

'Later.' Phoebe jerked her head towards the house. 'Come on in, and yer can tell us all what Auntie Nellie's been up to now.'

Paul breezed into the living room and was surprised to see there was only Phoebe's mam and dad in. 'Where is everyone?'

Her dad, well, he was really her step-father, stood up and gestured for Paul to sit on the couch. At six foot five, built like a battleship and with hands the size of shovels, the man who was now Phoebe's dad, and had always been Paul's Uncle Corker, was a man you couldn't miss seeing. A seafarer all his life until just a few weeks ago, his weatherbeaten face was hidden behind a broad moustache and beard. He was a gentle giant, loved by his family and friends. The kids in the neighbourhood called him Sinbad because he looked so much like the character in their story books. 'Well, if we're to believe what they told us, Dorothy has gone to the pictures with a girlfriend from work, Gordon has also gone to the flicks with Jeff Mowbray, and Peter is in his mate's having a game of cards. Gordon and Peter I believe, but Dorothy I have me doubts about. I think she's got a boyfriend on the sly. Anyway, sit yerself down, son, unless you and Phoebe are going straight out?'

'If I don't tell yer me reason for being late, and if yer don't believe me, then Phoebe will get a cob on with me and we won't be on speaking terms for a few days.'

Corker had known the Bennett and McDonough families for as long as he could remember. When he wasn't sailing the seven seas, he'd lived at the top of the street with the widowed mother he adored. That was long before he'd married Ellen after her first husband died. He'd been a rotter, had Nobby Clarke, a violent, gambling drunkard, who treated his wife and children like animals. He was his own worst enemy, and on VE Day went on a drunken binge while his wife and children starved. But he got so drunk that day, he walked in front of a tram. He wasn't killed, but very seriously injured and never came out of hospital. Ellen was left penniless, and would have been thrown on the streets with her children but for Molly and Nellie. They did everything they could to help her, even getting her the job in the butcher's. And Molly had been instrumental in bringing her and Corker together, for which he would be eternally grateful. The three families, the Bennetts, McDonoughs and Corkhills, had grown closer still, when Jill Bennett married Steve McDonough and went to live with Corker's mother until they could afford a home of their own.

Lowering himself into a fireside chair, Corker lit a cigarette. 'Come on then, son, but if this has anything to do with yer mam, then I believe yer before yer start.'

Ellen, a quiet, gentle woman, leaned forward. 'We could do with a good laugh, so give it to us word for word, and with the actions if possible.'

'Ooh, I don't know about that, Auntie Ellen, 'cos I haven't got me mam's – er – me body isn't like me mam's. But I'll do me best.'

Paul stood up for better effect, and started the tale. He did a pretty good impersonation of his mother, bar the mountainous bosom. As the tale unfolded, his audience of three were in stitches, but when it came to his father standing on his head to read the *Echo*, Ellen and Phoebe were bent over having convulsions, while Corker's loud guffaws could be heard by people passing in the street.

Paul was very pleased with his own performance when he saw the reaction of his girlfriend and her parents. 'So, am I forgiven for being ten minutes late?'

Phoebe had to swallow hard before she could speak. 'Yes, I forgive yer for being late, but look what yer've done to me face. Me eyes are all red, me powder's come off on to me hankie, and me lipstick is ruined.'

Paul held his open hands out to Corker. 'See what I mean, Uncle Corker? I can't win. And it's all me mam's fault. In future I'll leave the room when she's having her funny half hour, then I can't get into trouble.'

Then Phoebe, who like her mother was shy, did something she'd never done before in front of her parents. She put her arms around Paul's neck and kissed him. 'No, yer must never do that, 'cos I look forward to hearing what Auntie Nellie's been up to. I don't mind yer being ten minutes late, but if it ever gets to eleven minutes, then ye're in trouble, Paul McDonough.'

Chapter Three

Molly handed her coat to Tommy before pulling a chair from under the table and sitting down. 'I won't ask how yer are, Ma, 'cos you and me da look the picture of health. In fact, yer look younger every time I see yer.'

'Oh, it's fine we are, me darlin', thanks to the Good Lord and Rosie. And it's happy we are to see our daughter has brought her husband with her tonight. Sure it's not often we have that pleasure.'

'Yer know I don't like leaving Ruthie in the house on her own, Ma, that's why Jack doesn't come very often. But she's having Bella over for a few hours tonight for a game of Ludo, so I don't mind when there's the two of them, they're both quite sensible, but I've promised Mary Watson I won't keep Bella out too late.' Molly craned her neck to look into the kitchen. 'Where's Rosie?'

Just then there came a clatter of feet on the stairs and Tommy's bride of three weeks entered the room. 'I was combing me hair, Auntie Molly, so I was. Sure, I couldn't have me mother and father-in-law see me looking dowdy. They'd wonder what my dearly beloved husband had let himself in for.' Rosie, with her black hair and blue eyes, was a true Irish beauty, and her rosy apple cheeks were always creased in a smile. When she walked into a room, it was as though the lights had been switched on. Now she kissed Molly's cheek before moving on to Jack. 'It's

41

lovely to see yer, so it is. And, sure, every time I see yer, Uncle Jack, I can see what me darling husband is going to look like when he grows older. A fine, handsome figure of a man.'

Molly looked from Rosie to her own dear mother, and thought, this was indeed history repeating itself. Her ma had come over from Ireland as a young girl to seek work, not knowing a soul in England. She'd managed to find lodgings for the week she sought employment, but had never made any friends. The only work she could find was as a junior pantry maid in a large house in Princes Drive, owned by a wealthy shipping merchant. She never settled down, though, and was homesick for her family and the lush green fields of County Wicklow. That was until the day she met Bob Jackson, who retrieved her hat when it blew off at the Pier Head where she'd gone to feed the pigeons. It had been love at first sight for both of them, and they'd married within two years. The love they'd felt on that first day had never wavered since. They loved each other now nearly fifty years later more than ever, and showed it in every glance and every touch of their hands.

Rosie O'Grady had been more fortunate than Bridie because a distant cousin had written to ask the Jacksons if they would take in a fifteen-year-old girl until she could find work and somewhere to live. The Jacksons fell in love with the young Irish beauty whose lovely lilting brogue was like sweet music to Bridie's ears. Indeed, everyone fell under the spell of Rosie O'Grady, with her beauty, her marvellous sense of humour, and her kind, caring nature. The only one she didn't attract at first was Tommy who at fifteen was at the awkward age where girls are a nuisance and to be avoided at all costs. Especially when she said, in front of all the family, that she was looking for a boyfriend, and wasn't he a fine figure of a man? Molly remembered that night as though it was yesterday. Tommy had run up the stairs, his face the colour of beetroot. Little did he dream then that in a couple of years' time he'd fall head over heels in love with Rosie, and that a few years later they would wed.

When Tommy touched his mother's knee, Molly shook her head to chase away her thoughts. 'Mam, yer've been miles away for the last ten minutes! Yer haven't heard a word anyone's said to yer.'

Molly had been listening to the Irish accent since the day she was born, and when she chose she was quite good at it. 'Well, now, me darlin's, wasn't it meself that was going back over the years in me mind, to when Rosie first came. And wasn't I thinking how her life mirrored that of me own dear mother? Both came to England as young girls to find work. Both of them suffered homesickness for a long time, and both married the first Englishman they exchanged words with. And didn't they both have the sense to pick the best two Englishmen in the land, with the exception of my Jack? Oh, and Steve and Phil, of course. But, sure, doesn't that go without saying, me darlin's?'

'Auntie Molly,' Rosie's long black hair swung on her shoulders, 'isn't it meself that lies in bed every night thinking the very same thing? Sure, God's been good to every one of us, so He has, and it's meself that thanks Him every night in me prayers.'

Bridie reached for her husband's hand. 'It's the truth I'm telling yer when I say me and Bob often sit and talk about how lucky we are, with our family and with our friends. Sure, no one can have been more well blessed than we are.'

Jack nodded. 'When yer think of all our friends, like the McDonoughs, the Corkhills and the likes of Maisie and Alec . . . they're the salt of the earth.'

Molly nodded in agreement. 'Yeah, where would we have been without Corker to help out with food for the two weddings? Not to mention all the parties we've had. And Maisie and Alec have been a godsend through the war, with their extra slices of corned beef, and tea and sugar. Without them we'd never have set eyes on luxuries like biscuits all through the war.'

As soon as she mentioned the word biscuit, Molly's mind went to Nellie. 'Would yer like to hear a little tale about Helen Theresa McDonough and her way with biscuits?'

Tommy was sitting at the table next to Rosie. He slipped his arm around her waist as he smiled and said, 'Go on, Mam, what's me Auntie Nellie been up to now?'

'There isn't minute of the day goes by that yer Auntie Nellie isn't up to something, sunshine, but I'd be here all night if I repeated everything she gets up to. Going to the shops with her every day is like a pantomime. I don't know how she thinks all these things up, because every day is different.' Molly shook her head and tutted. 'We took Victoria to the shops with us today, Ma, just to give her a breath of fresh air. And, honest to God, I didn't know where to put me face at times, 'cos yer know how prim and proper she is. I've never heard her use a swear word in all the years I've known her but, by golly, she's heard plenty from that mate of mine. And when we were in the butcher's – well, I won't go into details, I'll just say I'll not be going to the butcher's with Nellie next time I want breast of lamb for our dinner!'

'Oh, I think Victoria will have enjoyed herself, me darlin', 'cos she's always saying how funny you and Nellie are when yer get together. Sure, she enjoys a joke as well as the next woman, so she does.'

Molly grinned. 'Yeah, I know that, Ma, 'cos I could hear her chuckling when I put me hand over Nellie's mouth to shut her up.'

Tommy was picturing his Auntie Nellie, and tried to guess what her reaction would be to that. 'Did she bite yer hand off, Mam?'

'No, did she heckerslike! I only kept me hand there until we were far enough away from the butcher and his breasts of lamb.

Yer've no idea what she's like, doesn't care what she comes out with or who's in the shops to hear her. If I think she's going too far and could upset some customers with her choice of words, I usually drag her out by the scruff of her neck.'

'Oh, Nellie doesn't upset people, lass, she brings a smile to their faces and a little happiness into their lives,' Bob said. 'She's brightened up my life many times over the years.'

'I know that, Da, and I know how dull my life would be without her. And I could eat her when she looks so innocent and asks me why it's wrong to talk about her voluptuous body when I can see with me own eyes that all the men find her desirable. Then I'm called all the narrow-minded, miserable sods going, and told the only reason I object is because I'm dead jealous 'cos, comparing my body to hers, I'm not in the meg specks.'

'That's all in fun, Mam,' Tommy said, after laughing his head off with the others. 'I bet she wishes she had a figure like yours.'

'She could have, sunshine, if she didn't eat all of the things that make her fat. And that brings me right back to the tale I was going to tell yer about my mate and her craving for sweets and biscuits.'

Molly was determined to make a good job of her impersonation, and gave attention to every little detail. Sitting back in the chair, she folded her arms and pretended her normal-sized bosom was as big as her friend's. Narrowing her eyes, a habit of Nellie's, she said, 'I don't care as long as the tea's wet and warm, girl. And I know yer've got a couple of custard creams in the pantry 'cos I've seen them.'

Taking first the part of her friend, then of herself, Molly put her heart into her performance, and enjoyed every minute. With the guffaws and chuckles coming from her audience to egg her on, she surpassed anything she'd ever done before. She ended with Doreen saying she'd heard on the wireless that sweets were now off rationing, and Nellie punching the air for joy. 'And this is what she said to me: "I'm going to stop at the corner shop on our way out, and I'm buying meself the biggest slab of Cadbury's that Maisie's got in. And I'm not giving yer any, I'm going to eat it all meself. So there!" '

Wiping away the tears, Rosie asked, 'And did she do that, Auntie Molly?'

'No, sunshine, I had the last laugh after all. Yer see, everyone else in the neighbourhood had already heard it on the wireless and within half an hour Maisie had sold every sweet and bar of chocolate in the shop.'

Jack couldn't mention Nellie's name without grinning. 'And was yer mate upset?'

'I don't think upset is the word I'd use to describe her reaction.' Molly pushed her chair back. 'I'll have to stand up to do this justice.'

Rosie's lovely face was agog with anticipation, and as Tommy's knee was the best seat in the house from which to watch a performance, she moved across to him and put an arm around his neck. 'Sure, it's a lucky girl I am, me darlin', marrying such a foine figure of a man as yerself, and getting a wonderful family into the bargain.'

Molly stood in the centre of the room and squared her shoulders. Then she folded her arms, narrowed her eyes and flared her nostrils. Every action exactly like Nellie's. Pretending the sideboard was the counter of the corner shop, she snarled, 'Yer've what, Maisie Porter? Well, I'll be buggered! Yer've sold all yer sweets and chocolates to every Tom, Dick and Harry what came in, and yer have the cheek to say yer never gave a thought to me and Molly, what are yer two best customers.' The eyes became narrower, the lips pursed, and the head began to shake slowly. 'And you, Alec Porter, it's no use making excuses, saying yer were rushed off yer flaming feet. That's the poorest bloody excuse I've ever heard. Ye're never too rushed off yer feet to take our money, are yer? Oh, no, never too busy for that. Well, I'll be going to the sweet shop for me slab of Cadbury's, and in future I'll be getting all me sweets from there. And d'yer know what yer can do with yours? Yer can stick them where Paddy stuck his nuts!'

Molly turned around. 'This is Maisie now. "It's no good going to the sweet shop, Nellie, because they're all sold out as well. I mean, we've been caught on the hop. None of us expected them to take sweets off rationing so quickly, and without giving any notice. We only had the same amount as we've been getting all through the war. But as soon as we get a delivery, Nellie, I'll be sure to put some aside for yer." '

Once again Molly turned to change character. ' "Yer needn't bother yerself, Maisie Porter, I've told yer what to do with yer chocolate, yer can stick it where Paddy stuck his nuts." '

Now Rosie had known many men back in Ireland named Paddy, but she'd never heard of them sticking nuts anywhere. And what would it have to do with Nellie not getting her chocolate? 'I'm sorry to interrupt, Auntie Molly, but it's meself that would like to be knowing why this Paddy didn't eat the nuts instead of sticking them somewhere?'

Molly was laughing so much she had to sit down. 'Oh, sunshine, don't ever ask yer Auntie Nellie about Paddy and his nuts, because she'd tell yer.'

'Well, if I asked her then I'd be expecting her to tell me. But can yer not tell me yerself?'

When Molly looked to her mother for guidance, Bridie's eyes told her she'd got herself into this mess, she could get herself out. 'That would be a bit difficult, sunshine, 'cos it's just a saying that's been around for as long as I can remember.'

But the Irish girl was intrigued and wouldn't let go. 'So, you and Auntie Nellie don't know this Paddy personally? Somebody else told yer about him and where he stuck his nuts?'

Tommy was chuckling inside. When he was younger, he'd asked the same question as his wife had just asked. His Auntie Nellie had used the expression in front of him, and being young and inquisitive, he'd wanted to know where the nuts were stuck. And if his mam hadn't been there to keep his Auntie Nellie in check, she would have told him without seeing any harm in it. As it was, his mam gave her friend daggers, and answered the question herself. To get her off the hook now, he repeated what he'd been told all those years ago. 'Rosie, the man wouldn't tell anyone where he'd put the nuts, except to say it was somewhere where the sun don't shine.'

Rosie's brow furrowed as she gave this matter some thought. 'Sure, the sun doesn't shine in a lot of places, so Paddy was a clever man, so he was.'

Bridie and Bob tried very hard to keep their faces straight, but Bob couldn't resist saying, 'He was a man who must have been able to stand a lot of pain, too.'

This left Rosie totally confused. 'Sure, it must be meself that's not very clever, 'cos I can't see why Paddy should be in pain just because he was hiding his nuts.'

Tommy pulled her close and whispered in her ear. 'I'll tell yer about it when we're in bed tonight, my dearly beloved wife. But for now, don't yer think it would be good manners to make me mam and dad a cup of tea?'

Rosie jumped to her feet, her hand covering her mouth. 'Oh, it's forgetting meself I am. But I'll not be taking all the blame, and that's the truth of it. If Auntie Molly hadn't been so entertaining then yer'd all be sitting with a nice cup of tea in front of yer now.'

'That's right, blame me, sunshine,' Molly said. 'Me shoulders are broad enough.'

Tommy followed his wife to the kitchen. 'I'll give yer a hand with the cups.'

'That's a good excuse, son,' Bridie said. 'But don't think we're too soft not to know it's a few stolen kisses ye're after.'

Bob's hand covered hers. 'Everyone knows their own tricks best, sweetheart. And I still remember that after we got married there was many a night the dinner got cold because we preferred a kiss to a plate of stew. And, if it comes to that, we still do.'

Molly looked over to where her husband sat and jerked her head. 'Are yer listening to this, Jack Bennett? I'm beginning to feel left out, unloved and unwanted. Have yer nothing to say about how we used to sneak kisses in the kitchen?'

The look in her husband's deep brown eyes sent a thrill down Molly's spine because it held all the love he felt for her. 'We didn't need to sneak kisses when we first got married, love, because we had the house to ourselves. But having three children in three years didn't leave us much time or privacy for romance after that. During those three years I don't think we had a full night's sleep without one of the babies crying to be fed. But yer don't need a kiss from me to tell yer how much I love yer, do yer?'

'No, I don't, sunshine. I got a good one when I got you, and I know when I'm well off. And it's not only our children that hampered our romantic inclinations, or have yer forgotten my mate Nellie? She's always come the back way at night, so she could peek through the curtains and see what we were up to. In fact, it's not that long since she last did it.'

'Oh, she's no right to do that, sweetheart,' Bridie said. 'Sure, I'd have something to say if a neighbour of mine came spying.'

'I had something to say all right, Ma, but it's like water off a duck's back. Jack was there, he'll tell yer. Yer can call her all the names under the sun but she doesn't turn a hair. The other week, me and Jack nearly jumped out of our skin when we saw her peeping through the window. And when I asked her what the hell she was playing at, and why she didn't come to the front door like other people, she calmly said she'd come to see what me and Jack were up to, and if she'd knocked on the front door, we'd have stopped doing it and she'd have wasted her time.'

Tommy had been keeping an ear cocked in the kitchen. Now he put a finger over Rosie's lips. 'Shush, my love, and listen. We've got plenty of time for kisses when we're in bed. Listen to how me Auntie Nellie plays Peeping Tom.'

So the two youngsters listened as Bridie said, 'Sure, and what did she think she'd catch yer doing in yer own house?'

Molly glanced towards the kitchen before saying, softly, 'She said she thought she'd catch us half-naked, making mad, passionate love. And yer know how easily she can put an act on. Well, she pretended to have a right cob on because Jack was only reading the paper and I was darning a hole in one of his socks.'

'I told her I was sorry to disappoint her,' Jack said, 'and if I'd known she was coming I'd have tried to oblige. But all I got in reply to that was insults. Apparently I'm too ruddy slow to catch cold, and she's glad she married a man with red blood in his veins who's crazy about her voluptuous body.'

The whistling of the kettle had Molly signalling to remind her husband the youngsters were in the kitchen and that sort of conversation was not fitting for their ears. Not that Rosie was bashful, far from it. When she first came over from Ireland she'd had Bridie's heart in her mouth every time she spoke. After being brought up in the country, with horses, pigs and sheep all around her, she thought nothing of seeing animals mating, and was bewildered when Bridie said it wasn't the done thing to talk about it in company. Especially if there were ladies or children present.

Tommy came through with the tray, followed by Rosie with the teapot. And as they were pouring out the tea and handing the cups around, Bridie asked, 'Did yer see Jill tonight, me darlin'?'

'Yeah, she never misses a night, Ma. I look forward to her coming, then not long after she leaves, Tommy arrives. And I see Doreen and the baby every day, so I'm lucky with me family in that respect.'

'Jill never forgets her grandma and granda, does she, Bob? She comes to see us a few times a week with Steve. They call in on their way down to Nellie's. And Jill looks so bonny, prettier than ever.'

'I'm not making fish of one and flesh of the other, I love all my grandchildren.' Bob smiled at Molly, the only child he and Bridie had. They would have liked more, but it wasn't to be. 'But Jill has always been the gentle, caring one of the family. She would never hurt anyone if she could help it, not even a fly. She'll make a marvellous mother.'

'I'll agree with yer to a certain extent, Da,' Molly said. 'Jill was the perfect child. Good-natured, quiet, never cheeky. And this was more noticeable because Doreen was just the opposite. Noisy, hard-faced, cheeky, and always had to be in the right. She'd have her own way if it killed her. But I've got to say there has been a big change in her since Phil came on the scene. Now they're married, she adores him, and Victoria. She's a cracking little housewife, keeps the house beautiful, waits on Victoria hand and foot, and is the perfect, loving mother. She has certainly surprised me and Jack, and we're very proud of her.'

Tommy nodded. 'I agree with yer, Mam, our Doreen's a different person altogether. She used to be a real tomboy, battering me and Ginger if we wouldn't let her play footie with us. She was bossy, cheeky, and never stopped talking. I never ever thought the day would come when I'd be lifting me hat off to her. But I do now, 'cos she's turned out to be a smasher. And it's all down to Phil Bradley.'

'Did they never hear any more about having their name changed to Phil's real dad's name?' Bridie asked. 'It seems ages since it was mentioned.'

'Funnily enough, Ma, there was a letter from the solicitor this morning, asking Phil to make an appointment to call into his office. The letter arrived after he had left for work, but Doreen said she couldn't bear the strain of waiting to know what was in it, so she opened it. And it rather looks as if it'll be finalized very soon, and Phil will have what he's always wanted – to have his real dad's name. He's always hated the name Bradley, and yer can't blame him considering what the family were.'

'It's his mother I just can't understand.' There was sadness on Bridie's face as she slowly shook her head. 'A lovely boy like that and she never sees him. Sure, it would break my heart, and that's the truth of it.'

'I spend a lot of time thinking about her, and wondering what sort of a mother she is. No matter what the circumstances, I couldn't have done what she did.' Molly heaved a deep sigh. 'It's over twenty years ago now, and in them days, having a baby out of wedlock was something that didn't happen to nice girls. But when she found out she was pregnant after the man she was to marry was killed in an accident, she would have been better trying to fend for herself than marrying a rotter like Tom Bradley. I'm sure her family would have rallied around once they got over the shock. And it can't have taken her long to realize the man she'd married was a burglar and a thief. He never did an honest day's work, just lived by robbing and selling the goods on at any market. If Fanny, had had any pride, or love for her son, she would have got away from there quick, instead of having another three children to the villain and letting Phil be pushed into the background all the time.'

Jack was nodding. 'It was a rum do altogether. Phil doesn't talk about it now, but he told me once that he used to get hammered by his step-father, and his half-sisters and brother, because he wouldn't go out robbing or breaking into houses with them. And his mother used to stand by and do nothing. It was as if she was obsessed with Tom Bradley, and anything he did was all right with her – even her own son being beaten and made a laughing stock of because he didn't want to be like them. Phil must have a strong will because as soon as he left school he got himself a job and is as honest as the day is long. But there must be times when he thinks of his mother, and it must hurt to know she didn't care enough about him to protect him from the rotter who was his step-father.'

Rosie knew little about Phil's early years because it was something the family didn't talk about, for his sake. But Tommy still had one memory fresh in his mind. 'It's funny how things work out, though, isn't it? I remember the night Phil caught his brother trying to break into Miss Clegg's house, and how he beat him up. All the neighbours were out because of the noise, and I can clearly remember our Doreen calling Phil's name, then running home crying. We weren't to know he was the lad she'd met at Barlow's Lane dance hall, the one she never stopped talking about. And she didn't know he was one of the Bradleys until she saw him in the entry that night. It must have been a terrible shock to her.'

'A lot of lives were changed that night,' Molly said. 'And it was mostly down to Corker. He knew it wouldn't be safe for Phil to go home after stopping his step-brother Brian from breaking into Miss Clegg's. Phil had beaten him up and Corker was wise enough to know that wouldn't go unrevenged. So that was the night Corker became Phil's guardian, and the night Miss Clegg took the lad into her home. And apart from the time he was in the army, he's been there ever since.'

Rosie's eyes were like saucers as she listened. All that she was hearing was new to her, she didn't have an inkling. 'Tommy Bennett, yer've never told me about this! Sure, I never knew Phil was beaten by that horrible man, and that his mother used to stand by and watch. It's terrible people they are, to be sure. And wasn't it good that Uncle Corker was there when he was needed, and Aunt Vicky, the little love, taking Phil in? And he had Doreen, of course, who was crazy about him.'

'Ah, well, Phil wasn't so lucky with regard to Doreen, sunshine, she wouldn't look at him for weeks. In the mornings she'd open our front door about the same time as he came out to go to work, and wouldn't even look across the road at him. It must have been a shock to her to find out he was a Bradley because they had a terrible reputation for robbing from their neighbours, causing fights in the street and using foul language. She just knew him as Phil, and he'd never told her where he lived, so she had no idea. She'd fallen for him hook, line and sinker, and had even asked if she could bring him home to meet me and her dad. So finding out in such a way who he was must have broken her heart and dented her pride.'

'But it all came out right in the end, Auntie Molly, and sure, like me and my beloved, they're very much in love. And because of you and Auntie Nellie finding Phil's real dad's family, he's got everything in life he could wish for.'

'You're right, sunshine, he's a contented and happy man. And I'd be grateful if what we've talked about tonight isn't repeated to him. Why remind him of the mother who practically disowned him, and whom he hasn't seen for years?

'I'll not be saying anything, Auntie Molly, yer can depend on that. Sure, it's one big happy family we are now, and I'll not be the one to put a spoke in the wheel.' Rosie's infectious giggle brought a smile to every face. 'Seeing as not one of us have got a bicycle, I should have said I'll not upset the apple-cart.'

Tommy pulled her close, eyes full of the love he felt for this beautiful Irish girl. 'None of us has an apple-cart either, my love.'

'Now didn't I think of that as the words were leaving me mouth, so I did. But, sure, wasn't it too late to take them back? So I'll not say I won't put a spoke in it, I'll say I won't upset the apple-cart.'

'But we haven't got an apple-cart to upset, sweetheart.' Tommy's laughing eyes twinkled. 'So what about that?'

'Ah, yes, but wasn't it meself that thought we stand more chance of getting an apple than we do a spoke. And don't yer think that's very clever of yer dearly beloved wife?'

He chucked her under the chin. 'The most clever thing yer did in yer life, Rosie, was to marry a fine, upstanding, handsome man like meself.'

'And what about me?' Molly asked. 'Wasn't I the clever one who brought this fine, upstanding, handsome lad into the world? Without me, none of this would have come about.'

Bridie squeezed Bob's hand before saying, 'It's meself that's sitting here wondering where any of yer would have been without me and Bob? So I think we should have some of the credit for all the handsome and pretty members of the Bennett family. Not only did we give yer the gift of life, we also passed our good looks on to yer.'

Both Molly and Rosie had the same desire to kiss the man and woman they adored. In the rush, they collided with each other. But Rosie remembered one of her mammy's sayings, that the young should always give way to anyone older than themselves, and stood back. 'After you, Auntie Molly.'

With a smile and a wink, Molly said, 'I'm glad yer didn't say age before beauty, sunshine, 'cos that would have spoilt my day.' She hugged her mother and kissed her on both cheeks before moving on to her father. 'That's for being the best ma and da in the world, and also for being responsible for each member of the family having the looks of a film star.'

Jack decided he wasn't going to be left out. 'Seeing as our Tommy is the spitting image of me, I don't know why ye're all congratulating each other. Praise where praise is due, that's what I always say.'

'Ah, yer poor thing!' Molly nearly choked him when she put an arm around his neck. 'We forgot all about yer, sunshine, and I know how yer hate being left out. And how could I have missed the obvious when Tommy is sitting facing me, looking exactly the same as you did at his age? Isn't that why I fell for yer in the first place, because yer looked good enough to eat?'

'Don't be trying to work yer way into my good books, Molly Bennett, 'cos I'm wise to yer now. And talking about being wise, I think we should be making tracks for home.'

'Ah, are yer not staying for a game of cards?' Bridie looked disappointed. 'Just the one game, sure, it'll only take an hour.'

'We'd love to, Ma, but Jack promised Mary he'd have Bella home early, and yer know what a worry she is over her daughter. She's always wrapped the girl in cotton wool, and had to know where she is all the time. Except when she's at school, of course, and even then Mary is standing at the front door half-an-hour before the kids are due home.' Molly straightened her back and flexed her arm muscles. 'I don't know what she'll do when Bella starts work or finds a boyfriend. That should be interesting.'

'None of us can help they way we're made, sweetheart. Some people take everything in their stride, others worry where there's no need to. But as I say, it's the way we're made and there's little we can do about it.'

Molly glanced at the clock. 'I think Mary will be at the hand-wringing stage now. In five minutes she'll be standing at the window, and in fifteen she'll be at the police station to report a missing child.'

'Then off yer go, sweetheart, 'cos it's no use worrying the woman needlessly. Tell Doreen that me and Grandpa will be calling tomorrow afternoon to see how Bobby is, and pay our respects to Victoria.'

'If yer get there about two o'clock, Ma, Bobby will have been fed, so yer'll be able to sit and nurse him for a while. You and Victoria can take turns.' After kissing her parents, Molly grinned when she saw Rosie and Tommy lining up by the door for their goodnight kiss. On the day Rosie had arrived from Ireland, looking so lost in this strange land and with tears of homesickness waiting to brim over, everyone had wanted to show her she was welcome and there'd been lots of hugs and kisses. And ever since that day she had been treated like one of the family in the Bennett household and the McDonoughs'. Bridie and Bob had given the young Irish beauty their love and their home.

'Goodnight and God bless, Auntie Molly, and you, Uncle Jack.'

'Goodnight and God bless, sunshine, and you keep on looking after this young son of mine. I'm not as fussy as Mary Watson, but underneath I worry just as much.'

'Have no fear, mother dear,' Tommy said. 'She waits on me hand and foot, and takes good care of Grandma and Grandpa. Like me dad, I got a good one.'

Chapter Four

There was a spring in Elsie Flanaghan's step as she neared the corner shop. She was feeling very happy with herself because her washing had been done and was at that moment wafting in the breeze. With a bit of luck it would be ready for ironing in a few hours. But in the meantime she was in the mood for a good chin-wag and gossip. And what better place for that than the corner shop? She had a rare piece of gossip to share this morning, the best she'd had in ages. The women would be hanging on to her every word, even those who usually gave her the cold shoulder.

When Elsie pushed open the door of the shop, however, her spirits fell. There were only four people in the shop, two she only knew by sight, and two who had made it plain several times that they had more to do than listen to someone pulling other people to pieces. Still, what she had to tell them would have them rooted to the spot. Or so she thought. For each one she approached said they were in a hurry to get the washing out, and in a matter of minutes Elsie was left alone in the shop with Maisie standing behind the counter waiting to serve her.

There weren't many customers Maisie didn't like, most of them were ordinary hard-working folk who were cheerful and enjoyed a joke. But Elsie Flanaghan was someone she couldn't stand. The woman was evil, thrived on the misfortunes of others and was always on the lookout for malicious gossip. 'What can I get for yer, Elsie?' she said.

Elsie didn't really want anything, she only came for a jangle, but she could hardly tell the shopkeeper she'd be going down to the main road for her shopping because it was coppers cheaper down there. 'I'll have a quarter of red cheese, please, Maisie.' She looked towards the door leading to the stockroom. 'Alec busy, is he?'

'Alec is always busy, we both are.' As Maisie pulled the length of cutting wire through the cheese, she was reminded of the film she'd seen where French people were sent to the guillotine. What a pity they didn't have it in this country, to put a stop to troublemakers like Elsie. Then as she put the cheese on the scales she told herself that was a bit extreme. Having their tongue cut out was nearly as bad, so perhaps they could just sew their mouths up to stop them from spreading rumours. 'Sixpence, please, Elsie.'

Elsie could have given her the right money, because she had a sixpence in her purse, but that would have meant she had no excuse to hang around. So she handed a shilling over the counter. And as the shopkeeper walked towards the till, said in a matter-of-fact voice, 'I see yer friend's daughter is expecting.'

'Oh, aye, and what friend is that, Elsie?' Maisie asked as she put the change down on the counter so her fingers wouldn't have to come into contact with the hand of the woman she could see was dying to pass on the latest gossip. 'Me and Alec have a lot of friends among our customers. Not all of them, as yer'll under-stand. There are some we just can't stand the sight of.'

Anyone else would have been put off by the shopkeeper's words and the look on her face. But not Elsie, she was as hard as nails. The only person she minded her manners with, and who she would be afraid to upset, was her husband Edward. He was a quiet bloke, not given to making friends easily, and ruled his wife with a rod of iron. 'I'm talking about Molly Bennett's daughter, Jill. Her what lives with Lizzie Corkhill. She looks about four or five months pregnant to me.'

'I wouldn't know,' Maisie said, grinding her teeth together. 'Even if I did, I wouldn't tell yer, 'cos it's none of our business.'

Even this didn't put Elsie off. 'It's Lizzie I feel sorry for. She's too old for all this, and yer'd think the families would put a stop to it.'

'I'm going into the stockroom to give Alec a hand and have a hard-earned cup of tea. Close the door behind yer, Elsie, if yer don't mind.'

Elsie's jaw dropped. But as she was now alone in the shop, she had little option but to turn on her heel and walk out. 'Oh, I'll shut the door all right,' she muttered, putting all her anger into pulling it so hard she nearly yarned it off its hinges. 'The stuck-up flamer! She needs taking down a peg or two.' Almost foaming at the mouth, she stood on the pavement vowing to get her own back on the woman who had just insulted her. Such was her temper, if there'd been a brick handy, she'd have hurled it through the window. Here she was with the juiciest piece of gossip she'd ever had, and no one to tell it to. Then she suddenly remembered there was one woman who'd be glad to see her: Fanny Maddox. Now she was nosy and delighted in bits of gossip about her neighbours.

Her mind made up, and feeling slightly less angry, Elsie turned left at the corner to go to her own street. But as she turned, out of the corner of her eye she saw a woman halfway down the street, on her knees scrubbing the front step. She recognised that woman as Molly Bennett and thought she'd just stroll down as though she was on her way to the shops, and have a few words with Mrs High and Mighty Bennett.

Molly wiped the step over with a clean floorcloth and was about to throw it into the bucket when she saw who was approaching.

She groaned inwardly. Her first instinct was to pick up the bucket and get indoors smartish. But that would look as though she was afraid of the woman, and Molly wasn't going to give her that satisfaction.

Unknown to both women was the fact that Nellie McDonough just happened to be looking through her own window when Elsie went past. And because the gossip was a particular enemy of Nellie's, and didn't live in their street anyway, the little woman lifted her curtain out of curiosity.

'Good morning, Molly. Busy, I see?'

'No more than usual.' Molly pushed herself to her feet and lifted the bucket. 'I'm going to get meself ready now for the shops 'cos me mate will be waiting.' She wasn't to know her mate had her ear to the window and could hear every word.

'Oh, before yer go in, I see yer other daughter is expecting. She must be four or five months now.'

'So, what about it? Is it unusual for a married couple to have a baby? And why are you taking such an interest? It really hasn't anything to do with you.'

Elsie had an unfortunate habit of curling her top lip, which made her look as though she was sneering. That was how she looked when she said, 'I just wondered what Lizzie Corkhill thinks about it. She's a bit old to be expected to have a baby in the house. I mean, it was very good of her to take in yer daughter and Steve McDonough, 'cos she must have a lot extra to pay out with two more to feed. But expecting her to keep a baby as well, that's disgusting. I think they should be ashamed of themselves and I'm surprised yer haven't done something about it.'

Molly was facing up the street, still holding the bucket in her hand, so she saw her mate's door open and Nellie step down. Unfortunately for Elsie, she was facing the opposite direction and saw nothing. Now Molly was in a dilemma. Should she warn Elsie Flanaghan or not? But she didn't deserve such consideration, not after what she'd just said, and needed someone to sort her out. So Molly stayed silent, and Elsie was totally unprepared for what happened next.

Nellie's huge stomach was like a battering ram. She lurched forward now, all her weight behind the shove which had Elsie flat out the pavement. And, horror of horrors, her false teeth had fallen out, and because her hands were under her body, she couldn't reach them. For anyone to see her without her teeth, well, that was the worst thing that could happen to her. At least she thought it was but there was a further indignity to come. 'You stupid bitch, I'll have yer for this! I'll have the police on to you, you just see if I don't,' she mumbled.

From a window opposite, Doreen and Victoria watched open-mouthed. 'I suppose I should go out and see what's going on,' Doreen said. 'But I can't stand that Mrs Flanaghan, she's a horror. I bet she's said something to upset me mam and Auntie Nellie heard her.'

'Oh, I'd stay where you are, sweetheart, because I don't think Nellie is finished yet.'

And Victoria was right. For while the hapless Elsie was trying to struggle to her feet, Nellie took the bucket from Molly.

'Yer needn't bother, sunshine, I can carry it,' Molly said, thinking her friend was being thoughtful and taking the weight off her. 'It's not heavy.'

'That's all right, girl, it'll be a lot lighter now.' And with that the whole bucketful of dirty water was thrown over the woman who had come to cause trouble, but found herself on the receiving end instead. 'I heard what yer said to Molly about my Steve and Jill scrounging off Lizzie Corkhill, you bad-minded bitch, and ye're lucky to be getting off so lightly.'

Molly gasped when she saw Elsie Flanaghan stagger to her feet, drenched through to the skin and clutching her set of false teeth in her hand. Nellie would never have got the bucket off her if she'd known what she intended doing with it. But perhaps it would teach the other woman a lesson and stop her spreading rumours. What she'd said about Steve and Jill cadging off Lizzie Corkhill was sheer, wicked bad-mindedness. And the frightening thing was, she'd probably told the whole neighbourhood. Jill would be really upset if she knew and Steve would go mad, for the young couple more than paid their way and Lizzie was much better off financially with them living there. So Elsie Flanaghan needed to get her facts straight, as well as being taught a lesson.

With water dripping off the end of her nose, her hair hanging limp, and feeling a right fool, Elsie put a hand to her mouth and pretended to cough while she put her top set of teeth in. At least she would look more dignified with them in, especially when she began to call Nellie all the names under the sun. 'You fat cow! I'll make yer pay for what yer've done, just you wait and see.' Without further warning Elsie swung her arm back then brought it round with all her strength and anger behind it, to hit Nellie in the face with her handbag. It happened so quickly no one could have stopped it. And after the initial shock, Molly stood with her mouth open, wondering what she should do.

Still watching through the window, Victoria and Doreen stood with their hands covering their mouths. Then Doreen said in a hushed voice, 'Oh, me Auntie Nellie won't stand for that, she'll belt her one back.'

By this time several of the neighbours had come out to see what the commotion was, and stood quietly looking on with their arms folded. No one asked what was happening or if their help was needed because they all knew Nellie could hold her own with anyone and Molly was the peacemaker. Besides which, Elsie Flanaghan had caused trouble in many a home with her wicked tongue, and was thoroughly disliked in the neighbourhood. It would be a pleasure to see her get her comeuppance.

Which, from her bedraggled appearance, was what she was getting.

Molly, who was rooted to the spot, saw them and shrugged her shoulders, as if to say she didn't know what to do to stop it.

But Nellie knew what to do. Her cheek still stinging from the blow from Elsie's handbag, she began to roll up her sleeves, and with a grim expression on her chubby face, lunged towards the other woman. But the action brought Molly to her senses and she quickly put herself between the two of them. 'That's enough now, yer've got the whole street out and ye're making an exhibition of yerselves.'

'Let me get at her, girl,' Nellie said, trying to push Molly's arm out of the way. 'She's not belting me and getting away with it. And I'll teach her not to tell lies with that manisus tongue of hers.'

Even in the midst of this commotion, Molly found herself wanting to smile. But now wasn't the time to tell Nellie that the word she wanted was malicious.

'Leave it for now, sunshine, she's not worth soiling yer hands on. I'll put a stop to her spreading rumours about Jill and Steve, but I'll do it in me own way, without the whole street looking on, and without bawling like a fishwife.' Molly glared at Elsie. 'I'd advise yer to leave now, while ye're still in one piece. But I haven't finished with you, not by a long chalk. Now go, while the going's good.'

Aggie, who lived two doors away, waited until Elsie was out of earshot, then asked, 'Has that she-devil been talking about your Jill?'

All the Bennett children and the McDonoughs were well liked by the neighbours. They were never cheeky and always willing to run a message if asked. The other women moved nearer to hear what Molly had to say. Nellie was still seething, and though well aware that her mate knew what she was doing, couldn't stop herself from saying, 'Jill and our Steve! The bitch said they were taking advantage of Lizzie Corkhill. Said they lived off her and didn't pay for nothing. I'd have given her a good hiding but Molly stopped me. And I know what our Steve would do if he found out what she was saying. Elsie's a two-faced bitch, and that's putting it mild. If I said what I really feel, me mate would go mad 'cos she doesn't like me swearing.'

'She's bad 'un and no mistake,' Aggie said. 'A real trouble-maker.'

Florrie, another neighbour, nodded her head knowingly. 'She makes all these stories up, and then tells everyone they're true. I've had more than one set-to with her, but it doesn't do no good, 'cos she's just wicked and won't change. She'll go too far one of these days and end up in hospital or in the ruddy cemetery.'

Doreen came hurrying across the cobbles. 'What was all that in aid of, Mam? I'm surprised Auntie Nellie didn't marmalize her.'

Molly didn't want to go into too much detail, not with so many women listening in, so she told her daughter briefly what the row was about. Doreen was furious. 'Oh, Mam, what a horrible woman she is! Fancy saying that about our Jill and Steve, when they're so good to Mrs Corkhill and she loves having them.'

'I did think of putting her wise, then I thought, no, I'm not explaining my daughter's business to you, why should I? And I wasn't going to sink to her level by arguing in the street. But I haven't finished with Elsie Flanaghan, sunshine, I'll definitely be putting a halt to her gallop. What's really got to me is that she came down this street with the intention of telling me to me face what she's probably told half the neighbourhood already. How she had the nerve to stand there and look me in the eye and say that I should be ashamed of meself for letting me daughter put on Lizzie Corkhill, well, I'll never know. But the story doesn't end there, sunshine. I'll sort Elsie Flanaghan out in me own way.' Molly glanced across the street. 'Where have yer left Bobby?'

'He's on the couch, Mam, as safe as houses. I'll get back over there, though, because Aunt Vicky will be dying with curiosity. But before I go, tell me, are yer going to mention this to me dad? I think yer should.'

'We'll see, sunshine, we'll see. Right now I'm going in to make meself a cup of tea and have a sitdown for a while until me heart stops pounding and me nerves sort themselves out. I know I shouldn't let someone like Elsie Flanaghan get to me, everyone knows what she's like and I should have just ignored her, gone in the house and put her out of me mind. But I was so mad, it took me all me time to keep me hands off her.' Molly wiped the back of a hand across her brow. 'Anyway, I'll see yer later, sunshine, I'm going in now for a cuppa.'

'Yer letting me come in with yer, aren't yer, girl?' Nellie asked. 'I could do with a sit down and a cuppa, 'cos me nerves are shattered and I could spit blood.'

'Of course yer can come in. Yer come in every morning, don't yer? This morning has been a bit out of the ordinary, but I'm not going to let it upset our routine.' Molly picked up the scrubbing brush and floorcloth which had dropped out of the bucket when Nellie emptied it over Elsie Flanaghan. 'When I've settled down, I'm going to have a good laugh over this. Because the sight of you emptying the dirty water over her, well, it was like something out of a Buster Keaton short comedy.' She threw the brush and cloth into the bucket and bent her arm. 'Put yer leg in, sunshine, and we'll go in and make a cuppa. Yer never know, I might just find a couple of custard creams. We could do with something to cheer us up.' Nodding at her neighbours, she said, 'Ta-ra, ladies, I'll let yer know what transpires in the next day or two.'

'We would have helped yer if yer'd wanted, Molly,' Aggie said. 'We wouldn't have stood by if she'd got stroppy with yer.'

'I know that, Aggie, I've got the best neighbours I could ask for.' Molly gave Nellie a dig to get her moving. 'Up yer go, sunshine, we're both ready for a bit of quiet.'

While Nellie's mouth was going fifteen to the dozen about how she would have pulverized Elsie Flanaghan if she'd had her way, crumbs from the custard cream she was eating were flying everywhere. 'Yer shouldn't have stopped me, yer know, girl, 'cos she was asking for a good hiding.'

'Don't speak with yer mouth full, sunshine, ye're making a mess of me chenille cloth.' Molly flicked the crumbs on to the floor. It was easier to wipe the lino over than it would be to take the cloth off and shake it in the yard. 'There's one bright spot in all this, and it's the thought of her having to walk home looking as though she'd fallen in the canal. She'd have a hard job explaining that to her neighbours.'

Nellie's grin took her chubby cheeks upwards until they almost covered her eyes. 'Yeah, I bet she felt a right nit. She couldn't put on airs and graces, or try to be lah-di-dah, when she looked like a drowned rat.' Her eyes kept going to the plate where a solitary custard cream sat. 'Shall I break it in half, girl, and we'll share?'

'Nellie McDonough, ye're not half a cheeky article! Yer can't look at a biscuit without yer tummy urging yer to eat it. Your mouth is an ever-open door.' Molly clicked her tongue on the roof of her mouth before giving in. 'Oh, go on, I hate to see a grown woman crying like a baby.'

Nellie made a grab for the biscuit and it was between her teeth when she asked, 'Are yer sure, girl, 'cos yer can have half if yer like?'

Once again Molly clicked her tongue. 'That's very kind of yer, seeing as yer've already eaten half the ruddy thing.'

'Well, ye're not quick enough, yer see, girl, that's your trouble. Yer get nothing in this life if ye're slow on the uptake.' Nellie popped the last of the biscuit in her mouth and crunched it before asking, 'What are we going to do about the Flanaghan woman? We can't let her get away with it, she's got to be stopped. I could go round right now, and after five minutes alone with her, she'd never mention any of our family again. But yer won't let me, will yer, 'cos ye're frightened of what the neighbours would say.'

'I am not frightened of my neighbours, sunshine, I always treat them with respect because that is the way they treat me. You never see them out in the street bawling and shouting, or exchanging blows, do yer?'

Swinging her short legs under the chair, Nellie looked up at the ceiling. 'What about that time Minnie Hughes knocked Sally Mac arse over elbow? They had a real set-to, it was a right ding-dong.'

Molly looked at her with disbelief. 'Nellie, that was well before the war! Ye're going back over ten years!'

'Yeah, well, yer see, I'm like an elephant, girl, I never forget. I remember laughing meself sick when Sally ended up with her legs in the air. It was the funniest thing I'd seen. Mind you, she didn't see the funny side of it. She asked me afterwards if I didn't have anything better to do with me time than watch people getting battered.'

Molly shook her head. 'My God, whenever yer borrow money off me, saying yer'll pay me back the next day, and I ask yer for it, yer can't remember borrowing it. Yer can forget that in one day, yet yer can remember something that happened ten years ago! I'd say yer've got a very convenient memory, sunshine, and I wish I had one too.'

'I don't 'cos then where would I be if yer started pulling the same stunts as I do? I'd have to take money with me every time I go to the shops! Oh, no, girl, I really couldn't be arsed doing that. So you just stay as yer are and I'll know where I'm working.'

'Oh, yeah, I'll carry on being the soft one just to please you. What yer'd do if I wasn't here, well, God only knows.'

'I'd be lost without yer, girl, and I know that better than anyone. My harbour in a storm, that's what you are. And God will pay yer back for that.'

Molly's brow furrowed. 'Why should God pay me back for being good to you? Why can't yer pay me back yerself?'

'Because yer know I always forget me purse, and I've never got any money on me. Yer always get it back in the end, though.'

'Nellie, I've got to drag it off yer, it's like trying to get blood out of a stone.'

'Oh, don't be exaggerating, girl, it's not that bad.' Nellie bit on her bottom lip, and the first part of her body to shake was her tummy, causing the table to bounce up and down. 'I've got a confession to make, Molly, and I'll tell yer if yer cross yer heart and hope to die, then promise me yer won't fall out with me?'

'Before I make any promises, sunshine, let me ask yer something. This confession wouldn't have anything to do with yer purse, would it? With yer always having it with yer when we go to the shops, but telling me yer've left it at home so I'll pay up like a sucker and wait until yer feel like paying me back? And it's a little game yer've had going for the last twenty years 'cos yer like to see me getting all worked up?'

Nellie's legs ceased to swing and her bosom left the table as she sat back in the chair with a look of disbelief on her face. 'How did yer know that? I never put the purse in me basket, so how did yer know?'

Molly smiled across the table. 'Nellie, one of yer pockets is always weighed down with the purse and the money in it.

69

I'd have to be tuppence short of a shilling not to have noticed that, seeing as we go to the shops every day. And I'm not blind. Yer purse is big enough, God knows. Yer've ruined a few coats over the years through it, even though yer've always pretended to be surprised when the lining falls to pieces. Oh, some of yer best acting has come about with yer trying to pull the wool over my eyes, but yer seemed to enjoy yer little game so I went along with it to humour yer. They say small things amuse small minds, and who am I to spoil someone else's fun?'

Nellie gave this some serious thought before giving Molly the benefit of her decision. 'That's as bad as telling lies, that is, Molly Bennett. Pretending yer didn't know when yer did all the time . . . that's like telling fibs. I'm surprised at yer for being so sneaky. Yer should go to confession and tell Father Kelly how underhand yer've been. I bet he'd give yer three Hail Marys and three Our Fathers for penance.'

Molly let her head drop back and roared with laughter. 'Yer don't half have a cock-eyed way of looking at things, sunshine! It wasn't me telling lies, it was you! I saw the purse in yer pocket, yeah, but I didn't say anything so I wasn't lying. But every day you looked me square in the eyes and said yer didn't have any money on yer and would I lend yer some. It's you what wants to go to confession, not me. Never a day goes by that yer don't tell at least three lies over something or other, so when you do decide to clear yer conscience and go to church, take some sandwiches with yer 'cos yer'll be there a long time. Father Kelly will give yer a real ticking off.'

'No, I've made a New Year resolution, girl, and I'm sticking to it. No more lies.'

'A New Year resolution! Nellie, it's September!'

The little woman feigned surprise. 'It isn't, is it? Well, that's flown over, it seems like only yesterday we were eating our

Christmas turkey.' Her face still registering surprise, she said, 'Well, I'll be buggered!'

'Listen, sunshine, will yer do me a favour?'

Nellie sat up straight. 'Yer know I will, girl, what is it?'

'When yer go to confession and yer telling Father Kelly about all the lies, don't forget to mention yer bad language, will yer?'

'If I have to go through all the wrong things I do, girl, I'd be there for hours. So I think I'll tell God instead. I'll add forgiveness for all me sins to me prayers tonight and get it over with. I mean, it's always best to go straight to the top man, don't yer think?'

Molly threw out her hands. 'I give up, Helen Theresa McDonough, ye're past redemption. I don't think there's any hope for yer.'

'Don't worry about me, I'll make it all up on the last lap, you'll see. I'll be right next to yer at the pearly gates 'cos ye're not going anywhere without me. And now, girl, before yer say it's time to go to the shops, have yer made up yer mind what we're going to do about Elsie Flanaghan? The news will have spread around the streets by now, about me drowning her and her belting me with her handbag. So what do we say if we get stopped?'

'We'll say as little as possible because heaven knows what tale Elsie's told them. We'll take things as they come, but I doubt if anyone will have much to say because she's not very well-liked. As for settling scores with her, which I fully intend to do, I'll have a word with Jack and see what he thinks. But you keep it to yerself, Nellie, for now, 'cos I don't want it to get back to Jill or Steve. And just look at the time, that article has put us right behind with our shopping. That's another thing against her.'

'Well, I'll nip home and get me coat and basket, then, sunshine.' Nellie put her hands flat on the table and pushed herself to her feet. 'And what shall I do with me purse?'

'Oh, do what yer always do, Nellie, don't change the habit of a lifetime. I'm so used to yer borrowing off me, I'd get all confused if Tony in the butcher's said, "That'll be two and thru'pence, Nellie," and yer paid him. I'd feel funny, like we weren't mates any more.'

'We can't have yer thinking that, girl, can we? I wouldn't want yer to think we weren't mates any more, not when ye're me very bestest mate.'

'That's what I mean, sunshine, so let's do what we always do. I'll pay for your shopping, then in the morning, as usual, I'll fight for me money back. How's that?'

Nellie waddled towards the front door. 'Just the job, girl, just the job.'

Chapter Five

Molly could feel herself getting more impatient by the minute.
She was on pins waiting to tell Jack about the events of the day
but didn't want to do it with Ruthie around listening in. She'd be
bound to tell her best friend Bella. They'd been about ten years
of age when Molly had overheard them making a pact that they
would always best friends and would never keep a secret from
each other. It wouldn't be right to ask her daughter to break that
promise. But the one night Molly wanted her out of the way
appeared to be the one night the girl wasn't gulping her meal
down so she could be off over the road.

'Aren't yer going to Bella's tonight, sunshine?' Molly kept
her tone casual so as not to arouse suspicion. 'Ye're usually out
by this time.'

'Yeah, I'm going over.' The girl was pushing a solitary potato
around the plate as she tried to make up her mind whether there
was enough room in her tummy for it. Her mam didn't like to see
food thrown in the bin, and as she was after a favour Ruthie
quickly stabbed the potato and popped it into her mouth. 'There's
no hurry, we're only going to have a game of Ludo.' She put on
a coaxing, pleading expression. 'Can yer spare a penny for me to
buy some sweets from the corner shop? I would share them with
Bella.'

'Oh, all right, bugger-lugs, but make sure yer share them
because Bella gives you half of everything she's got. I'm sure

Mary must think she's got two daughters 'cos ye're always over there.' Molly was pushing her chair back to get her purse from the sideboard when Jack flagged her down. 'I'll treat her tonight.' He reached into his trouser pocket and brought out a threepenny piece. 'Here yer are, love, ask Maisie to put the sweets into two bags for yer.'

This brought a huge smile to Ruthie's face. 'Thanks, Dad! Wait until I start work. I'll mug yer to five Woodbines every week then. But not for the first few weeks, though, 'cos I'll need all me pocket money to buy some grown-up things for meself.' Her eyes became dreamy as she visualized herself in four months' time. 'Like long stockings with seams up the back, and lipstick in cherry red.'

Molly nearly fell off the chair. 'Lipstick? Young girls of fourteen don't wear lipstick! The trouble with you, me lady, is that yer can't wait to grow up and ye're wishing yer life away. And mark my words, sunshine, when yer get to thirty yer'll wish yer were back to being fourteen with the best years of yer life in front of yer.'

Ruthie's mouth dropped open in horror. 'Thirty! I'll be an old woman then!'

Jack chuckled. 'I've been wondering why I'm slowing down, I never thought to blame it on me being an old man.'

'Ye're not an old man, Dad!' Ruthie could have kicked herself. 'You and me mam are the nicest-looking parents in the street and yer don't look anything like yer age.'

'If I were you, sunshine, I'd quit while ye're ahead. Any more back-handed compliments and me and yer dad will be going out buying ourselves walking sticks. So poppy off and don't forget to share the sweets with Bella.'

Her face set, Ruthie picked up the threepenny piece and walked towards the door. Before opening it, she chuckled softly and called, 'I won't stay out late, Mam, 'cos I know you and me dad need to go to bed early at your age.'

'Hop it while yer've got the chance.' Molly waited until she heard the door slam, then puckered her lips and blew out her breath. 'I thought she'd never go! I've been waiting to tell yer about the terrible day me and Nellie have had and didn't want to in front of Ruthie 'cos yer know what she is for repeating everything to Bella.'

Jack took his packet of Woodbines down from the mantelpiece and eased himself into his fireside chair. After lighting up, he asked, 'What was so terrible about today?'

Molly started from where she'd seen Elsie Flanaghan walking towards her, and her husband listened intently as she gave him the details, word for word and action for action. At one point, when he heard what the gossip had said about Jill and Steve, anger showed in his face and he would have vented this anger on the chair arm if Molly hadn't waved him to silence. But when it came to what Nellie had done with the bucket of dirty water, Jack was nodding his head. 'She did the right thing, I'd have done the same meself.'

'Hang on, yer haven't heard the best yet.' Doing all the actions, Molly showed how Nellie had been hit with the handbag. 'Yer should have seen her face! She was rolling her sleeves up and was making a dive for Elsie, saying she was going to kill her, when I stepped between them before they did each other an injury. Nellie was hopping mad, trying to push past me, but there was no way I was going to let two women knock spots off each other outside my house.'

'Did any of the neighbours see all this?'

'A few came out and stood watching. They didn't hear all that she'd said about our Jill and Steve, but they knew the row concerned them. Elsie Flanaghan isn't liked, as yer know, and Aggie and Florrie told me they'd have interfered if things got really nasty. And of course our Doreen and Victoria had the best seats in the house. They saw everything from their window.'

Jack lit another Woodbine to help him think. 'What she said about Jill and Steve not paying their way, that was a wicked thing to say. And although yer say no one likes the Flanaghan woman, yer only need one to say there must be some truth in it. Then another one to say there's no smoke without fire.'

'I know that, love, that's what I'm afraid of – and why I don't want Nellie knocking seven bells out of her. But Elsie's got to be stopped, Jack, because if our Jill found out she wouldn't stay at Lizzie's, she'd look for somewhere miles away, and that would break Lizzie's heart and mine. The problem is, how do we sort this out?'

Jack looked pensive. 'Is Elsie's husband's name Ted?'

'I couldn't tell yer, love, I wouldn't know him from Adam. I know she hasn't got a family, but that's about all.' Molly clicked her tongue. 'It's a pity she hasn't any children, it would give her something to do instead of making other people's lives a misery.' She glanced sideways at Jack. 'What made yer mention her husband? Yer don't know him, do yer?'

'No, but I think I know someone who does. And if I'm right he's the ideal person to sort this whole thing out.'

'Who are yer talking about?'

'One of your favourite people, our next-door neighbour Corker. I might be mistaken, 'cos I don't go to the pub often and don't know the regulars, but if Elsie Flanaghan's husband is called Ted, then he's the feller Corker introduced me to one night. A quiet bloke, sits in the corner of the snug on his own and doesn't bother with anyone. But he always lets on to Corker.'

Molly tapped her chin. 'I wonder now? It would be marvellous if Corker knows him well enough to have a word with him. Because I have heard that while Elsie likes to act the boss outside, she certainly isn't the boss inside.'

'Nip next door and ask, love. After all, Mrs Corkhill's name is being bandied about, so I'm sure Corker would want to know.'

Molly glanced at the clock. 'It's a bit early yet, the children won't have gone out. I'll leave it until I see Phoebe and Paul pass the window, 'cos they're usually the last to go. Meanwhile I'll clear the table and wash up.' She collected the three dirty plates and cutlery, took them out to the kitchen, then came straight back to give her husband a kiss. 'That's for being a clever boy and telling me about Mr Flanaghan.'

'Ooh, don't rely on it being gospel, love, 'cos I might have got it wrong.'

'In that case, I'll have me kiss back.'

Jack grabbed Molly's hand as she went to walk away. 'What if I'm right, love? Wouldn't yer say that deserved more than a kiss?'

Molly cupped her chin with her free hand and pretended to give the matter some thought. 'I believe you're right, Mr Bennett, because it would be a very valuable piece of information. So after I've had a word with Corker, and all being well, you and I will discuss what your reward should be.'

'Oh, I don't think the discussion will take up much time, love. Just as much time as it takes me to get you up the stairs.'

'D'yer know, you should have married Nellie, yer'd have made an ideal couple. Both of yer are sex mad.' But as Molly walked back to the kitchen the smile on her face showed she wasn't displeased.

Ellen's face registered surprise and pleasure. 'Hello, Molly, I thought yer were one of the kids come back for something they'd forgotten.' She held the door wide. 'Come in, there's only me and Corker.'

Molly stepped up into the hall. 'Thanks, Ellen, it was yer husband I came to see.'

She laughed as she closed the door and pushed Molly into the living room. 'I've always known yer had a soft spot for my husband, so I'll not be leaving yer alone in the room with him.'

Corker, a mountain of a man, jumped to his feet as he always did when a woman entered a room. 'Molly, me darlin', this is an unexpected pleasure. And seeing as my wife doesn't trust us to be alone together, I'll put the kettle on for a cuppa.'

'Go 'way with yer, yer daft beggar,' Ellen laughed, 'I'll see to a pot of tea. I can always keep me eye on yer through the crack in the door.'

Molly waved her hand. 'I've just had a cup so don't be bothering about me, sunshine. Sit yerself down and listen to this. There was some bother in the street today with that trouble-maker Elsie Flanaghan, and I was hoping for a bit of advice from Corker on what I should do, and how to go about it.'

'Sit yerself down, me darlin', and tell me exactly what's upsetting yer. If I can help yer at all, yer know I'll be only too pleased to do so.' Corker ran his fingers through his thick mop of hair. 'Is Nellie involved in this?'

'I'll say she is! Just wait until yer hear what I've got to tell yer.' Molly sank down on to the couch and for the second time in two hours related all that had happened, leaving nothing out. She ended by saying, 'It's not the first time Elsie Flanaghan's had a go at our Jill and Steve. She stopped me a few months ago, just after they'd moved in with yer mother, and said practically the same as today. Except now her eagle eyes have noticed Jill is pregnant and it's given her more ammunition to fire. Last time I just told her to mind her own business. Although I thought she had a bloody cheek then, it didn't upset me as much as this has.'

Corker had been stroking his beard the whole time he was listening, his face impassive. Molly was the one person he would trust to tell the truth and not add bits to make it sound more exciting. 'She's a nasty piece of work is Elsie Flanaghan, she's been noted for causing trouble for as long as I can remember. Me ma has always steered clear of her, wouldn't let her over the

78

threshold the few times she knocked hoping to pick up snippets of gossip. But she's gone too far this time, bringing trouble to my family and friends. And I'll not have her hurting Jill, my little princess, not in her condition.'

He reached for his packet of Capstan Full Strength and struck a match. He watched the smoke as it rose and spiralled towards the ceiling before speaking again. 'It's no good you getting yerself upset and worrying about it, Molly, and it certainly wouldn't do any good for you to confront her and tell her to stop spreading rumours because she's as hard as nails and it wouldn't have any effect. But I think I know a way of putting a stop to it without any fuss. So leave it with me, me darlin', and I'll see ye're not bothered by Elsie Flanaghan ever again. Nor will any of the other poor neighbours who've had to put up with her because she's put the fear of God into them and they're terrified of her.'

Ellen, her thin arms folded over her chest, raised her brows. 'How can you do anything, love. Yer don't even know the woman well enough to talk to.'

Corker tapped the side of his nose. 'I know what I'm doing, love, and I'll tell yer when the deed is done. Give me a few days and we'll see if the air is cleared.'

'He's a man of mystery is my husband, but he usually comes up trumps,' Ellen said. 'I'm sure yer can rely on him, Molly.'

'Oh, yer don't need to tell me that, sunshine, I'd trust him with me life.'

'Ay, I would have loved to have been there when Nellie poured that water over Elsie. Dirty water at that! Wait until I tell Tony, he'll be over the moon because he can't stand the woman.' Ellen grinned as a picture came into her mind's eye. 'You were in the shop that day Elsie fell flat on her face, weren't yer, Molly? Well, that made Tony's day. He said it couldn't have happened to a better person.'

'She didn't fall, Ellen, she was tripped up by Nellie. It was the day after Elsie first hinted Jill and Steve were living off yer ma, Corker, and when I told me mate she was all for going round to the Flanaghans' house and altering the shape of Elsie's face. I wouldn't let her, and gave her a good lecture on how nice ladies don't fight in the street. I thought that was the end of it but when she saw the queer one in front of us at the butcher's, well, the temptation must have been too much for her. Cross my heart I didn't know what she was going to do, and yer've known Nellie long enough to agree with me when I say she can look angelic when it suits her. So when Elsie fell flat on her face, I was as surprised as she was, except I looked more decent 'cos I was standing up and not showing all me knickers.'

The laughter rumbled in Corker's tummy before it filled the room. 'She's a real caution is Nellie, and yer've got to laugh at her. She may be only four foot ten or something like that, but by God she's got more go in her than most people. I've always said she's funnier than Buster Keaton or Charlie Chase any day. And she doesn't get paid for amusing people, she does it 'cos she enjoys seeing her friends happy and laughing. Can yer imagine a party without Nellie there to entertain us?'

Molly was feeling better now Corker had taken the worry off her shoulders and she sat back and relaxed. 'When Elsie Flanaghan was walking home today, saturated through to the skin and dirty water dripping from her nose and hair, I don't think she'd find that very entertaining. But still, I can't feel sorry for her, she asked for it.'

'Yes, she did.' Corker looked across at his wife. 'Seeing as yer've got someone to talk to, love, would yer mind if I went for a pint?'

'Now have I ever minded? Anyone would think I was a real nagger to hear you talk. Me and Molly will have a nice cuppa and a chat, so yer can go for a pint with a clear conscience.'

It was months since Corker had given up the sea for a land job but Molly still found it strange to see him without his peaked sailor's cap set at a jaunty angle and his seaman's bag slung over his shoulder. He was one hell of a man was Corker, looked as though he could easily handle himself in a fight. But he was a gentle giant who turned heads wherever he went because of his size and good looks, not a fierce reputation. He was almost as handsome as her Jack.

These thoughts reminded Molly that her husband would be sitting patiently waiting for her to come home. 'Don't make a night of it, Corker, I won't be staying very long. I told Jack I'd only be half an hour because if I'm not there when Ruthie gets in from Bella's, she'll play him up something woeful. He has a terrible time trying to get her to go bed. At least that's what he tells me, but I'm inclined to think he's too soft with her. She can wind him round her little finger if she wants anything.'

'I'll not be more than an hour, so my darling wife won't be on her own for too long. And I'll see yer tomorrow, Molly. Goodnight and God bless.' Corker waved as he bent his head to step through the front door. They didn't make doors to fit men of six foot four inches, there wasn't much call for them.

Molly tilted her head at Ellen. 'Yer've got a good one there, sunshine.'

'And don't I know it, Molly?'

It was ten o'clock the next morning when Molly heard the knock. She was on her knees cleaning the fireplace, and sighed and rolled her eyes to the ceiling. 'I'll kill that Nellie, she's half an hour early and I'm not finished me work.'

Ready to read the riot act to her mate, Molly opened her mouth at the same time as she opened the door. But the words died on her lips when she found herself looking into the face of Elsie Flanaghan. The sight of the woman had Molly's temper rising for two reasons. First because the trouble-maker had the nerve to come knocking on her door, and secondly because she felt at a disadvantage. For while she still had her pinny on, and hadn't even combed her hair yet, Elsie was looking very tidy and smart. 'What do you want?' The words came through Molly's clenched teeth. 'If yer've come to cause more trouble then I'll tell yer straight that although I've never hit a woman in me life, there's a first time for everything and I'm just in the mood. So before yer say anything, I'd advise yer to get out of my sight right now and don't ever come knocking on my door again.'

Molly was closing the door when Elsie said, 'I haven't come to cause trouble.' Her voice was so subdued, so different from her usual strident tones that could be heard from one end of the street to the other, that Molly opened the door wide. 'I've come to say I'm sorry for the things I said about yer daughter and Steve McDonough. I was thinking it over in bed last night and I know now it was very wrong of me to say what I did.'

'Oh, aye, and what's brought this on? It's a far cry from the way yer spoke yesterday, and the wicked things yer said then. What happened to change yer?'

Elsie lowered her eyes. 'Nothing's happened, it's just as I said. I lay in bed and it came to me that I'd been very wrong in the things I said, so I've come to apologize and say I'm sorry.'

Molly studied the woman's face for several seconds and could see she wasn't here from choice. Right away she knew that Corker had somehow brought this about. How exactly she'd maybe never find out because the big man wasn't one for telling tales. He would help anyone but never brag about it. 'I think Mrs McDonough should hear this because it was her son yer involved in this and she has every right to be given an apology too.'

This didn't suit Elsie who was beginning to look very uncomfortable. 'Couldn't you just tell her I said I'm sorry and will never mention her son's name again?'

'Oh, no, Elsie, that would be very cowardly of yer. I know you and Nellie have come to fisticuffs several times, but only when you started something. She's as much entitled to an apology as I am.' Molly stepped down on to the pavement. 'I'll give her a knock, she'll only be a matter of seconds.'

'She won't take off on me, will she? After all, I have come and said I'm sorry and she should accept my apologies because I came in good faith.'

'I'll see she doesn't take off on yer, Elsie, and it's better to get it all over with and put behind us. It'll all be done in five minutes.'

Nellie's face lit up when she saw her mate. 'Yer'll have to wait for me, girl, 'cos I'm not ready yet.'

Molly stepped up into the hall. 'Nellie, as yer can see, I'm not ready meself yet. But I've just had a big surprise. Elsie Flanaghan has called to apologize for all the things she's ever said about Jill and Steve. And she means it, Nellie, so I said she should apologize to you as well and then we can put it all behind us.'

'And yer believe her, girl? I wouldn't trust a word that comes out of her mouth, the lying cow! There's no way I'm going to forget what she said and she needn't think I will. I've a good mind to break her bleedin' neck for her.'

'Nellie, will yer watch yer language, please? And I want yer to come and listen to what she has to say and accept her apologies like a lady. She's had the guts to come around and say she's sorry, so can't you have the decency to meet her halfway?' Molly put her arm across her mate's shoulders. 'She looks terrified, sunshine, and I think she'd rather be anywhere right now but outside my front door waiting for you. She'll expect yer to have a go at her, but just for once prove her wrong. Act like a lady and yer'll be treated like a lady, that's what my ma always says.'

Nellie was slowly weakening. 'Yer wasting yer time trying to make a lady out of me, girl, but I'll come and see Elsie and I'll try and keep me hands off her.'

Elsie kept moving her handbag from one hand to the other, her nerves shattered. Nellie McDonough was the one woman she knew she'd never beat in a fight. So when the little woman waddled towards her, she stepped back a little. Her lips bone dry, she coughed before saying, 'I've come to say I'm sorry, Nellie, and I'll never say another wrong word about Jill or Steve again. I was in the wrong and I'm sorry.'

Nellie folded her arms and hitched up her bosom. Chin jutting out and eyes narrowed, she said, 'It's all very well for you to stand there and think everything will be forgotten if yer just say ye're sorry, but how do we know yer mean it and won't start yer shenanigans again when the mood takes yer?'

'Yer can believe me, Nellie,' Elsie said, thinking of the warning she'd had from her husband the night before. 'I swear I'll never again speak ill of you or Molly, or yer families. So I'd be grateful if yer would both accept my apologies.'

Molly could see Nellie wasn't in a forgiving mood and any acceptance of the apology would be begrudged. But better a begrudged one than none at all. 'I'll accept yer apology in the spirit it was given, Elsie, and I'm sure Nellie will too, because she's not the type to bear grudges, are yer, sunshine?'

Nellie's expression was not one of forgiveness. 'I'll go along with Molly because she's me best mate and we stick together. But if it wasn't for her, I'd tell yer where to go with yer false apologies. To be truthful, I wouldn't pass yer the time of day if I could avoid it. But I'll do as me mate says, to please her. If she nods to yer in the street, I'll do the same. But I'm not as soft-hearted as her, so don't ever look sideways at me or, so help me, I'll batter yer.'

With that the little woman turned and walked the few yards to her house with as much dignity as she could muster. She'd done as Molly asked, but she didn't trust Elsie Flanaghan and would be keeping her eyes and ears open.

Molly shrugged her shoulders. 'That's as much as yer'll get, Elsie, and I've got to say I think ye're lucky Nellie even spoke to yer after the trouble yer've caused. But if you stay out of our way in future, I promise we'll stay out of yours. And now I'll have to get back to my work, which is only half done. So, ta-ra for now, Elsie.'

Molly put the handle of the basket in the crook of her left arm so it hung between her and Nellie. She was hoping it would protect her from the bumping of her friend's wide hips as they swayed from side to side. But halfway down the street she reached the conclusion that the basket was causing her more bruises than ever Nellie's hips could. 'Hang on a minute, sunshine, while I swap me basket over. I'd rather be pushed to the wall by your hips than the ruddy basket. But I'd be eternally grateful to yer if yer'd try and walk in a straight line so I don't end up getting squashed.'

'Ye're always saying that, girl, but I do walk in a straight line. I know I do, 'cos I always fix me eyes on one spot at the bottom of the street so I'll walk straight and won't have yer moaning at me.'

'And what spot, pray, have yer got yer eyes fixed on now?' Molly was dying to laugh at the hurt expression Nellie had put on her face. 'We started off walking in the middle of the pavement, we are now against the wall. All I can say, sunshine, is that yer must be cockeyed.'

'I am not cockeyed!' Nellie sounded quite put out. 'I'll have yer know there's nothing wrong with my eyesight, it's perfect.'

'Well, tell me what spot yer had yer eyes on?'

'On the sweetshop, smart arse. The one on the other side of the main road.'

Molly looked down the street. 'And you reckon that by keeping yer eyes fixed on Simpson's, yer were walking in a straight line?'

'Well, it stands to reason, girl, that if yer keep yer eyes fixed on something as ye're walking, yer must walk right up to it.'

'It might make sense to you, but I'm blowed if it does to me. You reckon if we carry on walking as we were, we'd end up opposite the sweetshop?'

'Of course we would.' Nellie looked up at the sky. 'After all the fuss, Lord, she's finally seen the light.'

'I may have seen the light,' Molly told her, 'but I haven't seen the sweetshop. Point it out to me, sunshine, 'cos I'm blowed if I can see it.'

Nellie screwed up her eyes, scratched her head, lifted her left arm and then pointed a finger. And while Molly laughed inwardly, Nellie's arm began to move slowly to the left until her finger was pointing at the houses lower down the street on the opposite side.

'What are yer doing, sunshine?'

'Playing silly buggers, what d'yer think? If ye're watching properly, yer'll know what I'm doing. Showing yer how I know I was walking in a straight line and couldn't be pushing yer like ye're always saying I am.'

'Nellie, by no stretch of the imagination is the sweetshop on the main road facing us. If we crossed over to the other side of the street we might just see the side wall of it.'

Nellie the actress put on a fine performance. Her brows raised in surprise, she said, 'I didn't say the sweetshop, did I, girl? Well, aren't I the stupid one! I meant to say the wool shop but I must have got mixed up. Silly old me, eh, girl?'

'I would never say yer were silly, sunshine, not by a long chalk. But I would say yer were a crafty so-and-so who acted daft when it suited her. We've wasted ten minutes arguing over something when yer knew all along yer were in the wrong. So would yer mind if we started walking again before Tony sells out of meat and Hanley's sell out of bread?'

'There's no need to be sarky, girl, anyone can make a mistake. I mean, none of us are perfect, even you. You've just forgotten something, but nothing is said when you make a mistake.'

'And what have I forgotten, for heaven's sake?'

'Well, yer said Tony might have sold out of meat, and the bread shop out of bread. But yer never mentioned the greengrocer, did yer? For all we know Mike might have sold out of spuds.'

'Seeing as that's not likely to have happened, let's not spend any more time considering the consequences.' Molly bent her arm. 'Stick yer leg in, sunshine, and let's be on our way.'

Nellie was chuckling as she linked arms. 'Ay, girl, can yer just imagine me lifting me leg to put under your arm? That would be a sight to see, wouldn't it? We could sell tickets for it and make a few bob.'

They were crossing the main road when Nellie asked, 'What are yer getting for the dinner?'

'I'm not telling yer,' Molly said, 'in case Tony only has one and I'm not taking a chance on you getting in before me.'

Nellie was quiet as they neared the shop, then without warning she took to her heels to get there before Molly. There was only one customer in there being served by Tony, and he looked surprised to see Nellie on her own. But before he had time to open his mouth, she'd nudged the customer to one side.

With one eye on the door for Molly, she said, 'I'll have one.'

'One what, Nellie?'

'I don't know until me mate tells yer what she wants. But remember, if yer've only got one of what she does ask for, then I was here first and it's mine.'

The customer gave her daggers. 'D'yer mind? Tony was serving me when yer so rudely interrupted. And I object to being pushed aside by anyone.'

Nellie's hands went to her hips, and it was on the tip of her tongue to ask the woman who she thought she was talking to. But she had second thoughts when she saw Molly inspecting the meat in the window. Her mate wouldn't take kindly to her starting a fight in the butcher's shop, so her arms dropped to her sides and as sweet as honey she said, 'I'm very sorry, my dear, I don't know what possessed me. My mind must have been miles away. Please forgive me.'

Ellen, who was working in the back room, recognized Nellie's voice and was listening with a smile on her face. But the last few words had her poking her head into the shop. For Nellie to apologize to anyone was something unheard of. 'Are yer all right this morning, Nellie?'

'Yeah, I'm fine, girl, never felt better! I'm waiting for me mate to come in, but she's taking her time eyeing the meat in the window. Anyone would think she was buying the lot.'

'I'll serve yer if yer like, I'm only cleaning up out here.'

'Thanks, girl, but I'll wait for me mate to come in so I can make up me mind what I want.'

Molly sauntered into the shop. She knew Nellie was up to something and had deliberately taken her time looking in the window. 'Morning, Tony, and you, Ellen. I hope ye're both feeling well. I'm surprised yer haven't served me mate yet, though, I thought she'd be well attended to by this time.'

Before Tony could give the game away, Nellie said, 'I told them I'd wait for you, girl, 'cos yer always like to get served first.'

'I'm in no hurry, sunshine, so you go right ahead and get what yer want.'

Nellie's lips set in a straight line. 'I've been stood here patiently waiting for yer to finish gawping in the window, so yer could be served first. And as I haven't made up me mind what we're having to eat anyway, you may as well go first.'

Molly nodded to Tony as his other customer left the shop. 'A ham shank, Tony, please, nice and lean with plenty of meat on.'

Nellie had a smirk on her face. 'Ah, ye're too late, girl! I've already told Tony that's what I want, and as he's only got one I'm afraid yer've had it.'

Tony's eyebrows almost touched his hairline. 'I never said I only had one ham shank, Nellie, so what are yer on about? Yer never even asked for one, yer said yer hadn't made up yer mind what yer wanted.'

Molly decided to pull a fast one on her mate. 'It's all right, Tony, let her have the ham shank, I'd changed me mind anyway. I'll take three-quarters of stew, instead.'

Tony and Ellen were beginning to see the light now, and wondered how Nellie would get herself out of the situation she'd got herself into. There was no doubt in their minds that she would talk herself out of it, but it should be interesting.

'Oh, go on, I'll have three-quarters of stew as well.' Nellie's wink was so broad it had her chins holding their breath as they wondered whether she would shake her head or nod. 'It's no good changing the habit of a bleedin' lifetime.'

'Are yer sure, sunshine?' Molly asked. 'I'd hate to think yer were doing it just to please me.'

'No, I'm quite happy, girl, 'cos yer can't beat a pan of stew, can yer? It's a favourite with all the family.'

'In that case, as long as ye're sure and are happy about it,' Molly said, 'I'll take that ham shank, Tony, 'cos that's my family's favourite.'

The butcher was beginning to enjoy himself and joined in the spirit of the game. 'Ellen, get Molly one of those ham shanks. It's a pity Nellie changed her mind because they're all a nice size with plenty of lean meat on them.'

They all thought Nellie had talked herself into a corner she couldn't get out of, but they really should have known better.

The little woman screwed up her face. 'Nah, save Tony getting the tray of stew out of the window, yer may as well make that two ham shanks, Ellen. Just make sure they're exactly the same size and as alike as twins.'

'Will yer be able to tell by looking at them whether they're twins or not, Nellie?' Tony asked. 'Or would yer like me to give yer a certificate saying they come from the same pig?'

Nellie pretended to take a fit of coughing to give her time to get her thoughts together. Tony was being sarky and she was thinking of a way to get her own back. Making her face straight, and adding a touch of innocence for good measure, she said, 'Pig! Yer must think I came over on the banana boat, Tony Reynolds. I know ham shanks don't come from pigs, so don't come that with me. Huh! The very idea!'

Molly studied her friend's face to see if she was having them on, but although she thought she knew Nellie inside out, she could read nothing this time. 'What makes yer think ham doesn't come from pigs, sunshine?'

'Yer'll not be catching me out, girl, so don't be trying. Pork comes from pigs, not ham.'

Coming through from the cold room with two ham shanks, Ellen hadn't heard what Nellie said. 'There yer are, plenty of meat on them and so alike they could be sisters. I'd say they were both back legs of the same poor pig.'

When Nellie went to open her mouth, she found Molly's hand covering it. 'That's enough larking about for one day, sunshine, so not another word on the origins of those shanks. Be a good girl and behave yerself.'

Nellie stood to attention, her bust thrust forward and head held high. 'Yes, miss. Three bags full, miss.' And turning her head she could be heard muttering, 'My mate can be a bleedin' misery at times. I don't know how I've put up with her for all these years. A saint, that's what I am.'

'Are you calling me for everything, Nellie McDonough? If yer are, have the decency to say it to me face.'

'I wasn't saying nothing about you, girl! Ye're me very best mate, aren't yer? No, I was just going to tell Tony and Ellen that they'll never guess who came knocking on my door this morning and got down on her knees to apologize.'

Molly's jaw dropped. 'No one knocked at your door, it was mine they came to.'

Nellie acted as though she hadn't heard. 'Ellen, that Elsie Flanaghan came and said she was sorry for everything she'd said about Jill and Steve, and she begged me and Molly to accept her apologies. How about that, eh?'

It was the turn of Ellen's jaw to drop, she was so surprised. And like Molly had, she quickly thought Corker must have had a hand in this. It was too much of a coincidence after they'd been discussing it only last night. 'She didn't, did she? Molly, is Nellie telling the truth?'

Molly was standing behind her mate, and shook her head at Ellen to let her know she didn't want to say too much. 'Well, it's not all as Nellie says, but that's neither here nor there. Elsie did come round and she offered her apologies which we both accepted.'

'Ay, girl, to hear you talking anyone would think we'd shaken hands and become the best of friends! But I told Elsie Flanaghan straight that if she looked sideways at me I'd batter her, and I meant it. One wrong word or glance and she's had it.'

'We both agreed to meet her halfway, sunshine, even though you weren't very keen. If she keeps out of our way in future, we'll keep out of hers. And if yer don't mind, Tony and Ellen, I don't want this spread around. She humbled herself by coming and I don't want to rub salt in the wound. Just let bygones be bygones and let's get on with our lives.' Molly put an arm across Nellie's shoulder. 'Me mate's bark is sometimes worse than her

91

bite, but I have to say she acted like a little lady this morning.'

Praise from her best friend was always enough to lift Nellie's spirits. 'Ay, Tony, are yer going to wrap those bleedin' ham shanks up or not? They'll be walking out of the door on their own soon, and trotting back to the farm where they came from. They're probably missing their mummy pig, the poor buggers. But I won't tell the family I'm sorry for them 'cos it'll put them off their meal.'

'Tony, will yer tell us what we owe yer, or the day will be over before we know it. I like to steep a shank in cold water for an hour or so to get some of the salt out before I boil it.'

'Oh, that's an idea, girl, yer can put mine in to steep with yours. That big pan of yours will take two of them.'

Molly raised her brows. 'Sod off, Nellie! The next thing yer'll be asking me to boil it for yer as well!'

'Well, the thought had crossed me mind, girl, but I can see by the gob on yer that if I did yer'd get a right cob on and tell me to sling me hook. So I won't ask yer.'

Chapter Six

Nellie came through from the kitchen as George was closing the front door after letting Archie in. She grinned at her daughter's boyfriend. 'Hello, son, we timed that well, didn't we? Like in that film, *Brief Encounter*, where the lovers face each other across the room.'

George dropped into his fireside chair and picked up the evening paper he'd put aside when he went to open the door. 'Nellie, that couple met in a cafe at a railway station.' He chuckled at what he was about to say. 'And you don't look a bit like Celia Johnson.'

'Oh, I don't know.' Archie tilted his head and studied the woman he hoped would be his mother-in-law in the near future. 'There is a slight resemblance.'

Nellie jerked her head back, waking up her chins. They thought they'd finished work for the day and were taken by surprise. 'Anyone listening, who had never seen my feller, would think he looked like John Wayne, or Robert Taylor. They'd get a big shock, though, when they found he was more a Buster Keaton or Charlie Chase.' She smiled across at her husband and blew him a kiss. 'Never mind, George, I'd still love yer no matter what yer looked like. I mean, yer can't go on looks alone, can yer? For all we know John Wayne could be a right bad-tempered sod to live with.'

'I don't think you'd keep me waiting like yer daughter does, would yer, Mrs Mac?' Archie asked. 'She's never ready on time, I always have to wait.'

The newspaper rustled as George turned a page. 'It's a woman's prerogative to be late, lad, yer should know that by now.'

'It's a woman's what?' Nellie asked. 'Don't you start coming out with these big words, I've enough trouble with Molly over that. Some of the words she comes out with I can't say, spell or understand. I'm sure she does it deliberate, but most times I just nod and try to look intelligent as though I know what she's talking about.' She waved Archie to a chair. 'Sit yerself down, son, yer make the room look untidy. And yer may as well take the weight off yer feet 'cos Tilly Mint could be another half-hour titivating herself up.'

Lily came running down the stairs. 'I heard that, Mam! And for your information I am not late, it's Archie who's early.' She smiled at her boyfriend, her eyes telling him she was very happy to see him. 'Where are we going, anyway?'

'There's a comedy on at the Astoria with Cary Grant and Myrna Loy, called *Bachelor Knight*. You like Cary Grant, don't yer?'

'Yeah, I think he's handsome and very funny.' Lily stood in front of the mirror over the fireplace fiddling with hair that was already perfect. 'We'll go there, then.'

Nellie shook her head and tutted. 'It's a wonder yer've got any hair left the way ye're always messing with it. It's a pity yer haven't got a head of hair like mine, I only have to comb it once a day and it stays put.'

Eyeing her over the top of the paper, George said, 'You used to have hair like that, but yer never bother to look after it now.'

Lily said, 'Mam, your hair stays put because it's frightened not to.'

And Archie said, 'Mrs Mac, I love yer just the way yer are.'

'Ah, that's nice of yer, son. At least somebody loves me.'

'Ooh, I know that tone,' Lily said, taking Archie's arm. 'We'd better go because she's starting to feel sorry for herself.'

'Isn't Paul in to hold yer hand, Mrs Mac?'

'Nah, he's off somewhere with Phoebe. Anyway, son, the only time our Paul holds my hand is when he wants money.'

'Now then, Nellie,' George growled, 'yer know that's not true.'

'Everyone knows it's not true, yer miserable bugger! I'm wasting me time with you 'cos yer can't take a joke.'

Lily and Archie were going out of the front door when they heard Nellie add, 'And don't say I can't take a joke, 'cos I married you, didn't I?'

'Does yer dad ever get the better of her?' Archie asked, his hand covering Lily's slipped into the crook of his arm. 'She's always got an answer for everything.'

'That's only when there's someone else there, so don't be fooled. When they're on their own, she's putty in his hands. The pair of them adore each other but yer need to be there all the time for that to sink in.'

'I will be there a lot more when we're married, won't I?' The very thought had Archie walking taller. He'd fallen for Lily the first night they'd met at a party in the Bennetts' house. She was with a lad she'd been courting for a year or so, who wasn't very popular with her family and friends, and they were proved right in their judgement because in the end he turned out to be a rotter. It took Lily a long time to trust anyone else. But Archie had been patient, and finally he'd won her hand and her heart. 'I hope we manage to find a house around here, near your family and friends.'

'Don't worry, I've no intention of moving far away from me mam, I'd miss her too much. Jill and Doreen Bennett were lucky to stay in the street, so let's hope we'll be as lucky.'

'I'll think meself the luckiest bloke alive the day we get married, and the happiest. The time can't come quick enough for me. Next summer seems a long way off.'

As they turned into the entrance of the Astoria, Lily said, 'The time will fly over, it'll be here before yer know it.'

Archie walked to the ticket kiosk and handed over half a crown. 'Two back stalls, please.' His mind was elsewhere when the girl handed him the tickets. Lily had said the time would fly over but it seemed to be dragging painfully slowly to him.

Sitting on the back row with Archie's arm about her shoulders, Lily was thoroughly enjoying the film. Cary Grant and Myrna Loy were hilarious and there was lots of laughter from the audience. She turned her head to say something to Archie and found his eyes weren't on the screen but on her. 'Aren't yer enjoying the picture?'

'I've got other things on me mind, love, and I can't concentrate. I know it's a good film, but I'm enjoying my thoughts better.'

'Oh, aye, and what thoughts might they be?'

'I was thinking I would like to bring our wedding forward a couple of months. I think that's long enough for yer to keep me waiting.'

The longing in his deep brown eyes made Lily's heart flip. 'We can't do that, love, it takes ages to arrange everything for a wedding.'

'I don't see why it can't be done. I've got enough money saved up to cover everything. So what else is there?'

'There's lots of things need doing that a man wouldn't think about. I know because of when our Steve got married. If me Auntie Molly hadn't seen to everything the wedding would have been a flop because me mam hasn't a clue.' Lily could hear people near them tutting and turning around to glare at the couple who were spoiling the film for them. She was only whispering, but it was enough to irritate those sitting near them. 'Come on, let's go, we can't talk in here.'

'No, we'll stay and see the film if you're enjoying it. We can talk later.'

But looking into his dear face, Lily could feel herself warming to the idea. 'No, I've lost the plot now, let's go.'

There was a pub right by the picture house, and Archie nodded towards it. 'Let's have a drink and sit and talk it over. We'll go in the snug, it'll be quieter there.'

With a pint of bitter in front of Archie, and a glass of port in front of Lily, the couple gazed across the table at each other. 'You started it, Archie Higgins, and seeing as yer spoilt the film for me I think yer should explain what yer've got in mind.'

He took a mouthful of beer to give him courage. 'I want us to get married as soon as is possible because I want to be with yer every day. I want to wake up every morning and see yer face on the pillow next to mine, and I want yer to be there every night when I get home from work.'

'I would like the same things, Archie, because I do love you. But what you're asking for is a miracle. And miracles don't happen often in our neck of the woods. I know we said we'd get married in early summer, May or June, but haven't yet set a proper date. I believe we could bring it forward a few months because the church won't be booked up every Saturday so early in the year. But there is still a huge obstacle in the way. Where would we live? We couldn't stay in our house because Paul is there. You live in a two-up-two-down, so yer know the back bedrooms aren't very big to start with. Ours has been partitioned down the middle so I could have some privacy from the boys, and yer can't swing a cat round.'

'We could live in ours,' Archie said, 'there's only me and me mam.'

'I get on well with yer mam, Archie, I think she's lovely. But it's so far away from my family it means I wouldn't see them as often as I'd like.'

'And that's the only thing standing in the way of us getting married earlier? Say March or April?' Archie would move mountains to make Lily his wife soon. 'Yer could be an Easter bride.'

'That would be nice.' She was as eager as he was, but didn't want to build up his hopes and then have them dashed. They had to be practical. 'I would marry yer tomorrow, Archie, if everything was organized and plans were in place. In fact, everything can be organized in time, I'm sure it can, except for the big question of where we'll live!'

'Yer could ask yer man to have a word with the rent man to see if there's anything going in a street near you. I know it's no good asking for one in yours, because me mam's got her name down for the first house that comes empty. She's had it down for ages now.'

Lily could feel herself getting excited. 'It's not up to the rent man who gets the tenancies, it's up to the owner, Mr Henry. And I know the very two people who have known Mr Henry for years and get on well with him. Not that they see him often, but he would certainly do what he could if they asked him.'

'And who are these two people?'

'Auntie Molly and Uncle Corker. I don't think they'd mind if I asked them to do us a favour, I've known them all me life.'

'I'll come with yer tomorrow night and we'll ask them together.' Archie reached across the table and covered her hand with his. Most of the men in the snug were past the romantic stage, their pleasures in life were a pint every night when money allowed, and enough tobacco to fill their briar pipes. 'Let's go home now and tell yer mam and dad. My heart will burst if I don't tell someone soon. And the first to know should be yer parents.'

'We can't tell them tonight, they'll either be in bed or getting ready for it.'

'I've got a feeling yer mam would be very happy to be woken with such good news. It would please her no end.'

Lily emptied her glass and picked up her handbag. 'If they're in bed, there's no way I'm going to wake them up. You can if yer like, but on yer own head be it.'

Outside the pub Archie took her in his arms and held her tight. 'Mmm, I do love yer, Lily McDonough, and I will until the day I die.'

'Good heavens, Archie, ye're telling me yer love me and asking me to get married in a matter of five or six months, and in the same breath yer talk about dying! If my mam heard yer saying that, she'd ask, "Make up yer bleeding mind, son, is it a wedding we're having or a ruddy funeral? I'm only asking, like, so I'll know whether to buy a black hat or not." '

He chuckled and held her tight. 'Ye're a chip off the old block, love, another Mrs Mac in the making. And I couldn't be happier.' He stepped back and took her hand. 'Let's run for it and see if we can get home before they go to bed. I'm so excited I'd never be able to sleep tonight if I don't tell someone.'

Nellie was sitting with her feet in a bucket of warm water, a look of bliss on her face. 'Ooh, yer can't beat this, it takes the tiredness out of yer feet.'

George grinned across at her. 'Well, if it makes yer happy, love, yer should do it every night, it doesn't cost nothing.'

'If we had hot running water I would do them every night, but it's having to boil a kettle that gets me down. It's about time the Corporation did something about it.'

'I don't know whether they're responsible for the likes of that, or the landlord. After all it's his house and I think yer'll find the Corporation aren't going to spend money on modernizing private property.'

It was then the knock came on the door and Nellie came out with a mouthful. 'Bloody hell, who can be knocking at this time of night! It's a quarter-past ten! And look at the state of me, I look a right mess.' She lifted her feet out of the bucket and put them on a towel she had ready on the floor. 'Whoever it is will get the length of me tongue, calling this time of night.'

George pushed himself out of his chair. 'Keep yer hair on, Nellie, it's probably one of the neighbours after change for the gas meter. And if it's one of our friends there's no need to panic, yer can have the bucket and towel back in the kitchen before I open the door and no one will be any the wiser.'

Nellie became flustered. Fancy anyone knocking this time of night, had they no ruddy consideration? She put the towel over her arm and lifted the heavy bucket. 'Don't be too quick opening the door, George, give me time.' She put the bucket down on the floor in the kitchen and tried to dry her feet on the towel, but she couldn't bend because her tummy got in the way. Then she heard George's voice.

'You two are back early, aren't yer? Yer frightened the life out of yer mam, she was sitting with her feet in the bucket.'

'Who is it, George?'

'It's Lily and Archie, love. The picture must have been no good and they didn't wait to see the end.'

'No, the picture was good, Dad,' Lily said, still hanging on to Archie's hand. 'Cary Grant has never been in a bad picture.'

Nellie waddled in looking quite put out. 'Why the hell didn't yer stay until the end then, instead of having me dash out with a bucketful of water? I was enjoying steeping me feet, me corns were in heaven, and you two silly buggers have to spoil me fun.'

Then she narrowed her eyes. 'Why are yer looking so happy, Lily? And you, Archie. Yer look like a pair of Cheshire cats what are sharing the cream off the top of someone's milk.'

'Sit down, Mam, we want to talk to yer.' Lily pulled two chairs out from under the table before tugging on Archie's hand to sit him in the seat beside her. 'We wanted to catch yer before yer went to bed.'

'Couldn't yer have told us before yer went out?' George asked. 'Or wouldn't it have kept until tomorrow? Then yer could have stayed and seen the end of the picture.'

'Yer can blame me, Mr Mac,' Archie said. 'Lily would have waited until tomorrow but I couldn't. I wouldn't have got a wink's sleep if it wasn't sorted out.'

After reaching the conclusion that the pair looked too happy for it to be bad news, Nellie sat back in her fireside chair. 'Go on then, out with it! And whatever it is had better put a smile on me face 'cos me feet aren't very pleased with me for taking them out of the bucket so abruptly, and they'll make me pay for it. Me corns are the troublemakers, they'll talk me toes into coming out on strike. Which means I'll be hobbling to the shops tomorrow in absolute agony.'

'Nellie, are yer going to listen to what they have to say?' George asked in his quiet voice. 'I'm sure they're dying to get a word in, if it's humanly possible.'

His wife folded her arms over her bosom, found it too uncomfortable and slid them under the warm, soft flesh. 'I'm all ears.' Then she chuckled. 'Well, I'm not all ears, really. Compared to the rest of me they're only fiddling little things. Important, though, 'cos I'd miss a lot in life if I couldn't hear nothing.'

George leaned forward in his chair. 'Nellie!'

'Right, I'll be as good as gold. Off yer go, Lily.'

'Me and Archie would like to bring the wedding forward a few months, and we wondered how you felt about it?'

101

Nellie jumped up from her chair and punched the air. 'Oh, girl, that would be the gear!' She rounded the table to get to her daughter, forgot she was in her bare feet and banged her little toe on the table leg. It put a halt to her gallop for a few seconds while she called the table leg and her little toe fit to burn. 'Yer'll get no sympathy from me, yer miserable buggers, so don't pretend it hurts!' After giving the table leg daggers, she reached her daughter and crushed her in her arms. While being smothered, Lily smiled at a memory of long ago, when she was little and had hurt herself, and how she'd always found comfort in the warm, soft body of the woman she adored.

Nellie finally stepped back. 'Me and yer dad will be happy to go along with whatever yer want to do, won't we, George?'

Her husband's face was one big smile. Archie was a firm favourite with him, and George knew his daughter would be in safe hands. She would be well looked after and cherished, of that he had no doubt. 'If that's what yer want, me and yer mam will fit in with any plans yer make. And yer'll be a very welcome addition to the family, son.'

Archie tapped Nellie on the shoulder. 'Don't I get a kiss, Mrs Mac? You know, a kiss to welcome yer future son-in-law?'

When Nellie turned to face him, tears were running down her chubby cheeks. She wiped them away with the back of a hand, sniffed up, then held her arms wide. 'Come here, yer daft ha'porth. But don't think because ye're a future son-in-law that it entitles yer to take liberties with me. George has got his eye on us, so behave yerself.'

After a fresh pot of tea was made, they sat around the table and discussed the dates they would like. Lily and Archie would visit the priest the following night and see if it was possible to book the wedding in for Easter Saturday, the date they would really like. Particularly Lily, who imagined an Easter wedding would be like a fairy tale. Once they'd got a definite date, they could concentrate on the reception, bridesmaids, best man and guests.

'That's about it for tonight, we can't do any more until we have a firm date.' Lily was absolutely glowing and Archie couldn't keep his eyes off her. 'We can make a list tomorrow night of everything we need to do.'

Nellie pushed herself up from the chair. 'I'd better get going then, if I can get me ruddy shoes on.'

'Going where, Mam? It's turned eleven o'clock.'

'I'm going to slip down to me mate's and let her know what's going on.'

'My God, woman, but you'll do no such thing!' George sighed and raised his eyes to the ceiling. 'Have yer lost the run of yer senses? Molly and Jack will be in bed now, and they'd chase yer if yer knocked at this time of night, so forget it. Time enough to tell her in the morning.'

'She wouldn't chase me, she'd be interested 'cos she's me best mate.'

'I said, forget it, woman, so let's hear no more about it.'

'Your husband is right, Mrs Mac, it is very late to call on anyone.' Archie smiled. 'It's way past my bedtime so I'll be making tracks now before I miss the last tram.' She looked so crestfallen he felt sorry for her. 'Just think, yer'll have lots to tell Mrs B over yer morning cup of tea and custard cream.'

'That's right, Mam, you and Auntie Molly will have loads to talk about for the next four and a half months.' Lily added a little hint. 'She'll be able to help yer with things, seeing as she's had three of her children married off.'

Nellie looked happier. 'Yeah, we'll have plenty to talk about tomorrow.'

Molly was scrubbing the draining board down after washing the breakfast dishes and jumped when a loud knock came on the living-room window. It sounded like one of Nellie's but it couldn't be her, it was only half-past nine.

Wiping her hands on the kitchen towel, Molly walked through the living room to the front door. 'In the name of God, Nellie, what time d'yer call this?'

The little woman passed her without a by-your-leave, and when Molly turned back after closing the door it was to see her friend carrying the carver chair to the table. 'I come bearing good news, girl, so put the kettle on.'

Molly shook her head from side to side, her lips set. 'Oh, no, yer don't, Nellie, yer can just sod off. At half-past nine in the morning I don't care whether yer good news is that a long-lost relative yer didn't know existed has died and left yer a thousand pounds. Yer can get yer backside off that chair and come back at the usual time of ten-thirty. By that time I will have done what needs doing and will sit and listen to yer with a free mind.'

But Nellie had no intention of budging. 'I haven't got no rich relative what has died and left me a thousand pound, girl, so I don't blame yer for not being interested. But I thought yer might be interested in our Lily and Archie getting married.'

'I know they're getting married, sunshine, 'cos they're engaged. And that's not enough to come knocking on me door, or I should say me window, at this hour.'

'Ah, but yer don't know they've set a date.' Nellie liked to add a bit of spice to everything, even if it wasn't quite true. 'And it's not that far off.'

Molly began to take an interest, but first she had to satisfy herself that Nellie was telling the truth and this was not just an excuse for a cup of tea and a natter. 'Oh, aye, and what date have they chosen?'

'Easter Saturday, girl, isn't that the gear?'

'I thought they were getting married around June?' Molly

wasn't yet persuaded all this wasn't a figment of her mate's imagination. 'Why the change of mind?'

'Our Lily and Archie came back from the pictures last night and said they were bringing the wedding forward. It was Archie's idea, he said he can't wait to make her his wife.'

'Before I put the kettle on, put yer hand on where yer think yer heart is and swear that what ye're telling me is the truth.'

Nellie looked down at her bosom. 'It's somewhere behind this one, girl, but I'll never find it so yer'll have to take my word for it. But Lily and Archie are calling tonight, after they've been to see Father Kelly, so they'll tell yer themselves.'

'I'd better put the kettle on, then, 'cos I know nothing will shift yer off that chair until yer've got it all out. But yer've only got half an hour because I've got stacks of work to do. And just remember this is not an extra cup of tea, it's the one yer would have been having at half-ten. I can't afford to be taking breaks every time you've got something to tell me that yer think won't keep for an hour.'

Nellie, settled comfortably in the carver chair with her elbows resting on the arms and her legs swinging, wagged her head, and her chins, from side to side. 'Ye're wasting time telling me yer haven't got any time! The kettle could have been boiled by now if yer didn't talk so much.'

A few minutes later Molly was putting the two cups on the table and pulling out a chair for herself. 'While I was waiting for the water to boil, I did some thinking. If Lily does get married at Easter, it's only about four and a half months away. Ye're going to be mad busy getting everything arranged in time, particularly with Christmas coming up in about six weeks.'

'After they've seen Father Kelly tonight, Lily said we'll sit down and make a list of everything that we need to attend to. Like bridesmaids, best man, cars, flowers and reception.' Nellie was holding the cup between her two hands because her fingers were too chubby to go through the handle. She was feeling very important, seeing as she was the mother of the bride, but she knew her limitations. 'I know I should really do everything, like booking the reception, but you've been through it, girl, and know how to go about everything. So if they do get a definite date tonight, will yer see Edna Hanley for us to book the reception? I know yer will, being me best mate, but I thought I'd better ask.'

Molly also knew her mate's limitations, and it went without saying that she'd do all she could to help. 'Of course I will, sunshine, I'll enjoy getting a bit involved. Just don't expect me to take over from yer, that's all.'

'It'll be good, won't it, girl? I can't wait to wear me posh hat again.'

Molly gasped. 'Over my dead body, sunshine, will yer wear that ruddy hat again! Yer've worn it for all the weddings! No, Nellie, don't even think of it.'

'But it's me posh hat, I paid three guineas for it. For that money I've got to get me wear out of it.'

'Nellie, I don't care if it cost the thousand pound that the long-lost relative would have left yer if yer'd had one.' Molly clicked her tongue in exasperation. 'Listen, sunshine, we had those hats for the other weddings, but we'll not be wearing them at Lily's if I've got anything to do with it. She's yer only daughter, for heaven's sake, and yer've got to do her proud. As mother of the bride you will have to look really special. I'll be making the effort because I've known Lily since the day she was born and she's like one of me own. So I'm going to make sure that she's proud of her mam and her Auntie Molly. You and me will outshine everyone, you mark my words.'

Nellie was so pleased she was lost for words. She knew herself she'd be out of her depth over the finer details because she wasn't as fussy as her friend, but with Molly helping it would be one of the best weddings the neighbourhood had ever seen. And the idea of a brand new hat was beginning to sound very attractive. George couldn't complain no matter how much she paid for it, seeing as it was their daughter's big day. Mind you, he didn't complain about her paying three guineas for the other one because she didn't tell him until six months after the wedding, and then it just slipped out.

'What colour dress d'yer think I should get, girl? I rather fancy something in a nice pale blue or pink.'

Molly was of the opinion that her friend wouldn't suit either of the colours because of her size, but she wasn't going to say anything that would take away that look of happiness. 'Let's leave it until we know for sure, sunshine. Then I'll ask our Doreen if she'll make our dresses. She makes them just as good as the ones in the shop and at only a third of the price.'

'Ooh, I'd be over the moon if she made me one like she did last time, girl, 'cos it fitted me a treat. I would have a hell of a job trying to buy a really nice one, they don't make anything glamorous for someone with a figure like mine. And as yer said, I've got to look special.'

Molly gazed fondly at her friend. When they'd first moved into the street as newly weds, Nellie had only been half the size she was now. But after Steve was born the pounds piled on, and even more after Lily and Paul came along. She was quite content with herself, though, and Molly couldn't imagine her any different. She loved the bones of her as she was, for what she was.

'I'll have a word with Doreen, sunshine, and tell her we'll mind the baby while she's doing the sewing. We can't expect her to see to Bobby, Victoria, the house *and* be at the sewing machine for hours at a time. It would be far too much for her.'

'That would be the gear, girl, and we could try TJ's for the material, they have a good selection. We could go down on Saturday.'

'First things first, sunshine, let's wait until we hear what happens tonight when they go to see Father Kelly. And don't forget we've got Christmas not far off, that's another load on our mind.'

Nellie's legs were swinging faster with excitement. 'I'm dead chuffed, girl, and I promise yer I'll definitely get a new hat. I'll even let yer choose it for me.'

'Thank God for that!' Molly said. 'And now the half hour is well up and my work awaits me. So off yer go, sunshine, and I'll see yer later.'

Nellie was reluctant to move, but she could see the determination on Molly's face and knew she had no choice. Why her friend had to be so houseproud was a mystery to her. The dust she shifted today would be back again tomorrow and so the whole rigmarole would start all over again. It didn't make sense to Nellie. Still, it wouldn't do for everyone to be the same, it would be a dull old world.

Chapter Seven

They were walking through the church gates when Archie felt Lily's shiver of apprehension. 'Ye're not nervous, are yer? Father Kelly won't eat yer, I won't let him.'

'I am just a bit nervous. I don't know what he'll say when we give him the date we want. I was awake most of last night thinking how lovely it would be to look back in future years and say we were married on Easter Saturday. And I couldn't concentrate in work, me mind was miles away.'

'Don't meet trouble halfway, pet. I bet in half an hour we'll be walking back through these gates and yer'll be wondering what yer were worried about. If we can't have Easter Saturday it's not the end of the world. The week before or after would be just as good. And I'll have yer a bet that yer'll come out of here with a smile on yer face.'

And Archie's words came true. For when they came back through the gates Lily was walking on air. 'I feel on top of the world, Archie, I can't remember ever feeling so happy. When Father Kelly said he had two weddings booked for Easter Saturday, my heart stopped because I thought that was it. And when he said he could fit us in at one o'clock, I don't know how I stopped meself from kissing him.'

Archie pulled her to a halt 'I really don't think it's the done thing to kiss a priest, love, but it's very much the done thing to kiss your husband-to-be.' He pulled her close and claimed her lips, much to the amusement of a couple passing by. 'Mmm, I did enjoy that, it was worth waiting all day for. And now it's home to tell yer parents and the rest of the gang our news.'

It was when they were nearing her home that Lily said, 'Archie, I'm going to pull me mam's leg, so don't be surprised by anything I say.'

'The only thing that would surprise me, love, would be for her to let yer get away with it. My money would be on Mrs Mac to pull a fast one on you.'

They were outside her house now, and Lily whispered, 'I've lived with her a long time, Archie, and know her inside out. I'll tell the truth after a few minutes, but let's try and play a joke on her. Heaven knows she plays enough on us, and she will see the joke, I promise.'

The front door opened then, and Nellie appeared on the top step. 'Where the blazes have yer been? I've been back and forward to the window since half-past seven.'

'Mam, I didn't leave here to go and meet Archie until a quarter-past seven, so how could I have met him, been to see the priest and walked home by half-past? It would have been impossible.'

'Well, don't stand there arguing the toss with me, get inside and tell us how yer got on. I've been on pins.'

Lily straightened her face before joining her mother in the living room. 'Father Kelly wouldn't be able to marry us on an Easter Saturday for about two years. He's fully booked up.'

'Two years! Bloody hell, yer could have had a family in that time! I'm going to see him tomorrow, he's not getting away with that.' Nellie began to pace the floor, her hands on her hips and her head bent. 'I'll take Molly with me, for a bit of support, like, and I bet he'll change his mind with two of us there. I know one thing, I won't leave that church until he's agreed to marry yer on Easter Sunday.' Then, to no one in particular, she mumbled,

'He's not making a laughing stock out of me, not when I've told the whole ruddy neighbourhood.'

Lily rolled her eyes at Archie, saying she wasn't expecting that. But his eyes told her he did warn her she wouldn't win with her mother, so why didn't she just give in now? 'Mam, yer had no right to do that, why couldn't yer have waited to find out for sure?'

Nellie stopped pacing and lifted her head. 'While yer were in church, did yer go to confession?'

'No, we didn't go in the church, we went to the priest's house. Anyway, I don't need to go to confession.'

'That's what you think, girl, but I think different. It's a sin to tell lies, and ye're standing there lying yer ruddy head off!'

Lily lifted her hands in surrender. 'I must make a lousy liar, Mam, if yer can see through me. How did yer guess?'

'Because I'm a mind-reader, that's why. I always know when someone is telling an untruth because I was born with this gift.'

'The only gift you were born with, Nellie,' George said, 'was the art of lip-reading and being able to hear through brickwork and wood.' He grinned at his daughter. 'She saw yer coming up the street and had her ear to the door when yer were standing outside. No matter how low yer whisper, she can hear yer. I should know because I've never been able to sneak in after being out for a bevvy without her hearing me, even when I think I haven't made a sound. I stop breathing but it doesn't do no good, she's got ears like a hawk.'

Nellie pretended to glare at him. 'Oh, aye, ye're there, are yer? It wouldn't be a show without Punch. He was just as eager for yer to come home as I was, but he'd never tell yer that. Anyway, for his sins, he can put the kettle on while we sit down and hear how yer got on.'

'I thought Paul would be here,' Lily said. 'He told me he was going to wait in but it looks as though he's changed his mind.'

'No, he hasn't.' George gave his wife a knowing look. 'He's only in Phoebe's, and yer mam promised to give him a knock when yer came in. So while I see to the kettle, she can go for Paul and Phoebe.'

'I'll go,' Archie offered. 'Save yer going out in the cold, Mrs Mac.'

Nellie touched his arm. 'Hang on a minute, I want to ask Lily if she minds Molly coming? I'll need her to help me out with organizing 'cos she's got more sense than me, and better taste.'

'Yeah, I'd like her to be here.' Lily was relieved. She loved her mother dearly, but wouldn't dream of giving her a free hand with planning the wedding. It would end up like one of the Keystone Cops films. A good laugh for everyone, except the bride and groom who wanted the day to be perfect. 'We can ask her to see Mrs Hanley for us and book the room over the shop for the reception. The Hanleys did a very good job with the other two weddings, and everything ran like clockwork.' Lily suddenly remembered she wasn't the only person involved. 'That's if it suits Archie, of course?'

'Anything you say, love, because yer couldn't fault those receptions, or the parties in the evening. There was everything yer could ask for. Plenty of food and music to dance to.' He opened the front door. 'I'll knock at the Corkhills' for Paul and Phoebe, and then for Mrs B.'

Half an hour later it would have been difficult to say who was the happiest, Lily or Nellie. Lily was delighted because everyone was so excited now things had definitely been decided and she had a date for the wedding. And with Archie sitting next to her, with his arm around her waist and looking at her with eyes that said he absolutely adored her, she was in her seventh heaven. Nellie was happy because her house was the centre of attention, and she was the mother of the bride-to-be. Molly was right, she'd have to look the part on the day.

'Ye're lucky beggars getting the day yer want,' Paul said, his handsome face happy for his sister. 'I didn't think yer stood a chance with leaving it so late.' He was holding his girlfriend's hand and lifted it to his lips. 'Me and Phoebe will be the next.'

'Ay, son, leave it for a year or two, will yer?' Nellie asked. 'It'll take me that long to get over this one.'

Phoebe, always the gentle and quiet one, surprised them all by saying, 'Oh, we can't leave it a couple of years, Mrs Mac, 'cos I don't want to take a chance on Paul finding another girlfriend. I'm going to grab him as soon as we've got enough money saved.'

George smiled at the young girl who never put a foot wrong or said a word out of place. A young girl he'd grown very fond of and whom he thought was just the one to tame his son. 'I don't think yer've got any worries on that score, love, our Paul's not that soft. He knows when he's got one of the best.'

'Can we get on with it, please?' Lily asked. 'We want to go and tell Archie's mother, she'll be wondering how we got on.'

'Why didn't yer tell yer mam to come here, lad, so she could have joined the gang?' When Archie had started courting Lily, he had brought his widowed mother to meet the family. And much to everyone's surprise and pleasure, it turned out that Nellie had gone to school with her where they'd been best friends, sharing the same desk. 'We can't leave Ida out, she should be involved in everything, seeing as her son is the groom.' Nellie looked towards Molly with a grin on her face and the devil lurking in her eyes. 'Ay, girl, does the mother of the groom have to dress up as posh as the mother of the bride? Are we in competition, like?'

'I'm sure Ida is quite capable of sorting herself out, sunshine. It's you I'm going to keep me eye on to make sure that ruddy hat, with its ruddy feather, doesn't put in an appearance.'

There was laughter around the table. Nellie and the feather in her hat had been a source of much amusement at the last two weddings. 'I don't know, Mrs B,' Archie said, 'I think that three guinea hat was well worth the money. I don't think there was a person in the church who wasn't tickled by that feather at some time.'

'Yer were only jealous,' Nellie said, although she could see the joke as much as anyone, 'because not one of yer had a hat to come up to it.'

George's chuckle came up from his tummy. 'Yer've never spoken a truer word, Nellie, there wasn't a hat there that stood out like yours.'

Lily looked to Molly for help. 'Can we start, Auntie Molly, or this lot will sit gabbing all night and we'll get nowhere. Would yer let me and Archie pick yer brains?'

'That's what I'm here for, sunshine, and although I think you and Archie have probably got more brains than I have, I'll give yer any help I can.'

Archie appealed to Lily. 'Can I ask Mrs B a few questions, love, then make tracks to tell me mam? She'll be sitting there on tenterhooks.' He gave her a quick peck on the cheek before turning his attention to Molly. 'I know there's some things we'll need to do right away, can yer help us out with them?'

'Well, there are certain things that don't have to be done right away, like flowers or clothes, but you do need to see to the reception, cars and photographer. If yer don't book those soon, yer may find yerselves left in the lurch because Easter will be a busy time. So I'd advise yer not to leave it too long to get them sorted out, then yer can take it easy over everything else.'

'Isn't there a certain etiquette over who pays for what? I mean, what exactly am I responsible for?' Then Archie was blushing. That had sounded as though he only intended to pay for what he strictly had to, and no more, which wasn't what he'd meant at all. 'I didn't mean it to come out like that, but seeing as I've never been married before I don't want to put me foot in it, miss something out and have yer all thinking I'm a skinflint.'

'No one would think that of yer, sunshine, we know yer too well for that. But the bride's family pay for the reception, the flowers and the bridesmaid's dresses. The groom is responsible for the cars, photographer, presents for the bridesmaids, drink for the toasts at the reception, and also for the party in the evening, if yer're having one.'

'Of course we're having a knees-up at night.' Nellie sat up straight to lend emphasis to her words. 'Who ever heard of a wedding with no party at night! We'd be the talk of the bleeding wash-house!'

Lily gave Archie a dig. 'Look at the time, love, I feel awful about yer mam.'

'Just another two minutes, love, then we'll go.' He looked from Molly to Nellie. 'Can I ask you ladies to see Mrs Hanley tomorrow, and if possible book the room above the shop for Easter Saturday? I'll ask for an hour off in the afternoon and get the cars and photographer sorted out.'

'If the room's not already spoken for, I'll tell Edna to book it for you. She'll need to know the number of guests at the reception, and how many for the buffet in the evening. But I'll tell her we'll let her know in a few days.'

'Won't she need a deposit?'

Molly nodded. 'Yes, she will ask for one, but yer can sort that out tomorrow night, Edna knows we're not going to run away.'

'Thanks, Mrs B, we're beholden to yer.'

115

When Lily and Archie reached for their coats, which they'd thrown on the couch, Nellie was so disappointed her chins nearly hit the table. 'Ay, what about bridesmaids and things like that? I thought we were going to sort all that out tonight.'

It was Molly who answered her friend. 'Yer know what date they're getting married on, don't yer, sunshine? And yer know the reception, cars and photographer are all in hand? So don't yer think Ida has as much right to know as you do? She's sitting at home waiting for news of her son's wedding while you know all about it! Doesn't seem fair, does it?'

Nellie screwed up her face and shook her head, giving her chins the first chance of the night to stretch themselves. 'No, ye're right, girl, as usual. Dead bleeding selfish, that's what I am. And it makes it worse when yer think me and Ida were best of friends all through our school days. Many's the time she got the cane for doing something naughty, when all the time it was me what did it. And never once did she snitch on me.'

'Did yer never think of doing the honourable thing and owning up?' Paul asked. 'Yer'll never get into heaven when yer die, Mam, that's for sure. The next time Mrs Higgins comes, yer should tell her how sorry yer are and ask her to forgive yer.'

Nellie looked at him as though he'd gone soft. 'Is there something wrong with you, son? What about the time you and yer mates were playing footie in the street and yer knocked young Joan Simpson off her bike? I don't remember yer getting down on yer knees and saying yer were sorry then. Oh, no, yer were too busy saying it wasn't you what done it.'

By this time Lily had had enough. She grabbed Archie's hand, and with all her might pulled him towards the front door she'd opened five minutes ago. Taken off balance, he was tottering sideways as he called, 'Goodnight, all, I'll see yer tomorrow.'

Nellie looked disgusted. 'Wouldn't yer think Archie would have asked Ida to come here tonight, then they wouldn't have had to go rushing off like that. I was expecting all the lists to be done tonight.' She turned a glum face to Molly. 'You know, girl, like we did over the other weddings.'

Molly leaned across and pinched one of those chubby cheeks. 'It's a smile yer should have on yer face, sunshine, and a song in yer heart. Lily and Archie have been lucky enough to have a dream come true and are being married on the day they wanted. That should make you very happy for them. Yer can't plan a wedding in an hour. I should know, I've been through it. So put a smile on yer face and think of the fun we'll have, starting tomorrow when we see Edna Hanley.'

'Auntie Molly's right, Mam,' Paul said, his dimples deepening when he smiled. 'Think of going around the shops looking for a posh outfit. Not forgetting the really important thing that will be on top of yer shopping list, and that's the most eye-catching hat in the city of Liverpool!'

That did the trick and Nellie's smile reappeared. 'Yeah, me and me mate are going to have a great time choosing our clothes and hats.'

George, his face deadpan and his voice sounding serious, said, 'I want to see the receipt for any hat yer buy, Nellie. Yer'll not fool me again by saying it was thirty bob when all the time yer were spending three guineas of my money on the ruddy thing. It wasn't worth anywhere near that. If yer took the feather off, there'd be nothing there.'

Nellie's smile turned into a full-blown hearty laugh, sending her bosom bouncing up and down, and the table with it. 'What the eye don't see, George, then the heart don't grieve over. Yer were quite content with the hat when yer thought it was thirty bob, and yer never would have known any different if I hadn't let it slip when I wasn't in control of me mouth.'

'Aye, well, I've had a chuckle over it meself, I've got to admit. But this time ye're not going to be allowed to make any slips because I'll be in charge of the money. It's our daughter's wedding and I intend it to be a day she'll never forget. She'll have nothing but the best, like Jill and Doreen had. So as there isn't a lot of time to save up, and we've a lot to fork out for, we'll have to tighten our belts. I don't mean we've got to go short on anything, but there'll be no luxuries for the time being.' George lit up a cigarette before adding, 'I've never kept yer short, Nellie, but yer haven't a clue where money is concerned. So I'm making sure yer don't go overboard and spend any unnecessarily.'

She opened her mouth to argue, but before she had a chance to utter a word, Molly spoke. 'George is right, Nellie, he's being sensible. Me and Jack had to cut down for the girls' weddings, and for Tommy's. It doesn't mean yer have to starve, just be careful.' She grinned at the expression on her mate's face. 'Remember when I told yer I couldn't afford cakes, and this, that and the other? And yer moaned and told me I was being miserable because I cut down on things I didn't think were necessary? Yer must remember, sunshine, 'cos it's not that long ago. Well, now it's your turn to be thrifty. Cakes, biscuits and chocolates are off the menu from now on. But I don't think yer'll mind, not when it's for the biggest day of yer daughter's life.'

'I'm not going to have much choice, am I, with you keeping yer eye on me all the time and misery guts over there keeping me short of money?' The actress in Nellie was never far away. Resting her elbows on the table, she dropped her head into her hands and in a voice full of melodrama, cried, 'Oh, woe is me. I'm to be thrown out on to the street because I can't pay the rent. Oh, what is to become of me? Can yer not take pity on a poor woman who hasn't eaten in four days, and who is to be cruelly thrown out into the snow without a penny to me name?'

Phoebe's eyes were like saucers. She never ceased to be amazed at the way Mrs Mac could change character. If she hadn't known her all her life, there were times when she would have been taken in by her boyfriend's mother. Oh, Phoebe knew that what was happening now was an act, but she wasn't sure whether Mr Mac was putting his foot down in earnest, or whether he was pulling his wife's leg. It would be fun to be married into this family, because apart from the fact that she'd grown very fond of all of them, she knew life here would never be dull.

'Very good, sunshine, but not yer best performance. I have seen yer do better.'

Nellie lifted her head. 'Oh, aye, girl, when was that?'

'When yer did the Ethel Barrymore one, that was a cracker.'

'I don't know, Mrs B,' Paul said. 'I think me mam was very good just then.'

'But yer've never seen her do Ethel Barrymore, have yer? I'd say without a doubt that that is her finest performance.'

'There's one way of finding out, son, I'll do it for yer if yer like?'

'That would be great, Mam, me and Phoebe would love to see it.'

That was all Nellie needed. She pushed her chair back, ignoring its creaks and groans, and made for the couch. George had thrown his *Echo* there earlier, and now she threw it back on to his lap. 'Give the performer some space, lad, like what she deserves.'

George crossed his legs and sat back. The smile of affection on his face told those present that he may well put his foot down over money, but he wouldn't put it down hard.

Nellie stood in front of the couch, gearing herself up for the performance. One hand rested lightly on her bosom while the other hand was covering her mouth as she coughed politely the way she swore posh people did. Then she fell full-length on to the couch with the back of one hand across her brow. 'My life is meaningless now, I have nothing to live for.' Pretending there was a maid or footman standing by offering help, she waved them away. 'Leave me alone, please, nothing you can say will help me in my sorrow.' Then, with a straight-from-the-heart sigh, she sobbed, 'Oh, how can I live without my beloved? My only true love is dead and I wish death would take me so I can be with him again. Until then, I will never leave this room because this is where we spent our happiest moments. I can feel his presence here still, and while I'm here I know he will be with me in spirit.' Again a sigh and a sob, then Nellie lifted her hand and pretended to pull down a curtain. 'End of the first act, ladies and gentlemen.'

There was a ripple of applause as she stood up, and like a true professional took bow after bow. Then Ethel Barrymore was forgotten and Nellie McDonough was back in style. 'I dunno, not even one ruddy flower. I bust a gut, and not a flower, even a dead one. If I'd been on at the Empire, I'd have been loaded down with bouquets and the stage would have been covered in roses.'

'Ah, yes, Mam, and rightly so. But when people go to the theatre they know what they are in for and go prepared.' Paul thought his mother was brilliant, no matter what she did or said. He was very proud of her and her ability to make people have fun and be happy. 'We weren't prepared for such a magnificent impromptu performance, or we would have brought a bunch of dandelions with us. And they'd have been richly deserved.'

'That was great, sunshine, yer've got more talent in yer little finger than any of us has in our whole body.' Molly smiled as she winked at her mate. 'But much as I'd like to stop for the second act, I'm afraid I can't. Yer see, I have a husband at home who likes me to sit and talk to him about what we've both been up to during the day. Just the two of us, until Ruthie comes in. It's nice and quiet, I'd almost say romantic.'

Nellie opened her mouth to ask why they didn't go to bed where it would be more comfortable and definitely more romantic, but caught a warning light in her husband's eyes as he glanced from her to Phoebe. The young girl would be very embarrassed and wouldn't think the remark a bit funny. So Nellie was put in her place for once. No use getting a lecture off Molly and George, so she answered her friend in words that no one could get upset over. But she couldn't help a little sarcasm creeping in. 'Of course, my dear, how silly of me to forget you had a husband hat home waiting for you. Do forgive my hignorance, won't you, my dear? And tell Jack I was hasking after him, the darling man.' Nellie thought she was looking down her nose and being haughty, but her nose was too small and chubby for that. 'Hi'll see you tomorrow then, Mrs Bennett, hand accompany you to the confectioner's to book the reception room for my daughter's marriage to Mr Harchibald Higgins.'

Nellie's contorted face as she fought to sound dignified had them all crying with laughter. When she tried to act posh, she really was a scream. 'Sunshine, yer'd brighten up the darkest day, you would.' Molly got to her feet and leaned across to ruffle her mate's hair. Not that it looked any worse after she'd done it because Nellie wasn't one for standing looking in mirrors or titivating herself. She combed her hair every morning and as far as she was concerned that suited her and to hell with what anyone else thought. 'I'll expect yer at half-ten, Nellie, and not a minute before.'

Paul made a move then. 'Me and Phoebe will come with yer.' He held out his hand and helped his girlfriend to her feet. 'Save opening the door twice and letting the cold in.'

'Why are you two going?' Nellie asked. 'It's too late for yer to go to the pictures or a dance, so what are yer rushing off for?'

Phoebe blushed, but Paul was more bold-faced, like his mother. 'We're going to sit in Phoebe's until everyone goes to bed. Then we can have the couch to ourselves, to sit and cuddle and whisper sweet nothings in each other's ear.'

Nellie grinned. 'What it is to be young and in love, eh, girl?'

Molly raised her brows. 'I might not be in the first flush of youth, sunshine, but I'm still as much in love with my Jack as I was when I married him.'

'I hope ye're listening to this, George.' Nellie jerked her head at her husband. 'When they've gone, shall *we* cuddle up on the couch and whisper sweet nothings in each other's ear?'

He chuckled. 'If yer like, love. But don't forget I've got to be up early in the morning to go out and do a day's work.'

Nellie tutted. 'How about that for being romantic, eh?'

'Well, it depends upon what yer whisper in his ear, sunshine. Men like to be cuddled and petted, and if yer do it right he might just forget about work.'

'Aye, and pigs might fly, girl.'

'Yer'll have to sort yer own love life out, sunshine, 'cos I'm definitely going now or Jack will have a cob on. Whenever I come here I always forget to say I'm leaving half an hour before I need to. That's how long it takes to get from the chair to the front door. But I'm taking a firm stand now, and I'm on me way before yer think of something to stop me. Are yer coming, Paul and Phoebe?'

George looked at the clock. 'I'd say it was far too early for Ellen and Corker to be going to bed. So why don't yer steal a few kisses in the side entry, son? That's what yer mam and I used to do. And I've always found that stolen kisses taste much sweeter.'

'We'll give that a try, Dad, and let yer know tomorrow whether we prefer the entry to the Corkhills' couch.'

'Goodnight, George,' Molly said, 'and Nellie, this time I mean it. I don't want to see yer at half-nine in the morning, or even ten o'clock. I won't open the door before half-ten.'

'If I'm a few minutes early, girl, can I sit on yer step while I'm waiting for yer to let me in? I'll bring a little mat with me so I don't dirty it.'

'Yer can do what yer like, sunshine, yer can even bring yer bed and plonk it outside me house. But it won't make no difference, I still won't let yer in.'

'Ay, Mam, that wouldn't half give the neighbours something to talk about,' Paul chortled. 'You in bed on the pavement outside Auntie Molly's! Now that is a sight yer could make a few bob on, flogging tickets.'

George's guffaw was loud. 'Yer've never seen yer mam in bed in the morning, son. It is not a pretty sight to behold, I can assure yer. Particularly now the weather is cold, she's a picture no artist could paint. She puts an old pair of my socks on, my pyjama jacket under an old cardigan I would have thrown out years ago, and she's got pipe cleaners in her hair which make her look like Topsy.'

Nellie was laughing as she turned her head towards him and squinted. 'Yer can laugh all yer want, lad, but just tell me who's the warmest in bed? Whose back do yer put yer feet on to warm them up?'

Molly put a hand to her forehead. 'D'yer know, every time I come here I feel as though I've got a piece of elastic tied to me waist. Because whenever I get near the front door, I'm pulled back!'

'Ooh, eh, girl, that's just reminded me of something. We used to live near a man who did that with a ten-bob note. He asked for what he wanted in a shop, or the pub, and when he'd been served he would hand the ten-bob note over and wait until the shop-keeper got near the till before pulling on the elastic. Then he'd hop it hell for leather and disappear down the jiggers.'

'That does it,' Molly said. 'I'm off. Paul, you and Phoebe can please yerselves.'

'No, we'll come with yer, Auntie Molly, or the night will be over and I won't even have had a kiss or a cuddle. And one of Phoebe's kisses is worth more than a yard of elastic any day.'

Chapter Eight

It was ten-past ten when Molly ran a comb through her hair as she stood in front of the mirror over the mantelpiece. She was feeling pleased with herself because she'd finished all her work and would be able to slip across the road before Nellie came, to ask Doreen if she wanted anything from the shops. After throwing the comb in a sideboard drawer she opened her purse to make sure she had the front-door key, then slipped her arms into her coat. The lining was cold, and she rubbed her arms vigorously before closing the door behind her.

'Ye're a bit early this morning, Mam.' Doreen lifted her face for a kiss. 'Ooh, yer cheeks are like ice.'

'I'm not surprised, sunshine, 'cos it's freezing out there, the wind cuts right through yer.' Molly warmed her hands in front of the roaring fire for a few seconds before giving Victoria her morning kiss. 'I don't light the fire in the mornings, not till I get back from the shops. The room is still warm from the night before when Jack and Ruthie are getting ready, otherwise I would light it 'cos I wouldn't want them going out cold. But it seems such a waste of coal when there's only me there. Ye're in the right place here, Victoria, because it's a real cold November day. I haven't even bothered putting me bit of washing on the line 'cos there's no dry out. I've hung the clothes on the ceiling rack in the kitchen.'

'The trouble with that, Molly,' Victoria said, 'is the

condensation it causes. The house will be full of it and it gets on yer chest.'

'It won't be so bad, I've left the kitchen window open a bit. And I can put the clothes around the grate tonight when we go to bed so they'll be dry enough for ironing in the morning.' Molly turned to her daughter. 'Where's the baby?'

'I've just changed him and he's laying in the middle of the bed. He doesn't half enjoy it, Mam, he loves kicking his legs out and waving his arms about.'

'Aye, well, yer won't be able to leave him like that much longer. Another few weeks and he'll be able to roll about and could end up on the floor.'

Victoria laughed softly. 'There's not much danger of that happening, Molly, because Doreen has pillows all around him.'

'Oh, I know my daughter's not soft, Victoria, she's taken to being a mother like a duck takes to water. Anyway, I came to see if yer want anything from the shops, sunshine?'

'No, thanks, Mam, I'm going to take Bobby out in his pram for a bit of fresh air. And before yer say anything, I'll make sure he's well wrapped up and the hood will keep the wind off him. But we both need an outing, it's not healthy to be cooped up in a warm house every day. And Aunt Vicky says she'll be fine on her own for an hour or so, she'll rock herself to sleep in her chair.'

'I might meet yer down at the shops, then, sunshine.'

'I don't think so, Mam, 'cos I won't be going for an hour or so. Bobby's had his bath in front of the fire and he's got all clean clothes on, but he's due for a feed and any minute now he'll be yelling to remind me he's hungry.' Doreen was facing the window, Molly had her back to it. 'Ay, Mam, whoever built these houses did a good job on them. How old are they anyway?'

'Oh, I couldn't tell yer that, sunshine, I haven't got a clue. Me and yer dad moved in about twenty-three years ago, but some of the neighbours, like Victoria, have been here for fifty years or more. But why the interest all of a sudden?'

'It's just that your window frame has put up with many a hammering over the years, and it's stood up to it.' Doreen kept a smile from showing. 'Perhaps I should have touched wood when I said that, because the hammering it's taking off Auntie Nellie right now could possibly be the last straw.'

Molly spun around. 'Oh, my God, yer can hear it rattling from here!' And she was out of the door like a shot, calling over her shoulder that she'd see them later.

Nellie was like a raging bull, stamping her feet, and Molly swore afterwards that fire was coming from her nostrils. 'Yer've been and gone and told her, haven't yer?'

'Calm down, sunshine, I don't want yer having a heart attack outside my front door 'cos there's no one to help me lift yer. Apart from the fact it would make me late getting me shopping in. Anyway, who have I told what to?'

'Yer know very well what, Molly Bennett, so don't come the innocent with me. Yer've told them about our Lily instead of letting me tell them.'

'As a matter of fact I never mentioned it, Nellie McDonough, so there! It's not my business to be telling anyone what goes on in your house. If yer want them to know, yer can tell them yerself. And don't be so flaming bad-minded in future, get yer facts right before yer start another ruddy war.'

Nellie had now turned from raging bull to meek lamb. 'Don't be shouting at me, girl, yer'll have all the neighbours out. And I was only kidding, but perhaps it's too early in the morning for yer to see the joke.'

'Oh, I'll see the joke when I'm choking yer, sunshine, believe me! How would you like me to accuse you of something yer hadn't done?'

126

Nellie shrugged her shoulders. 'If yer were accusing me, girl, then chances are I would have done it, I'd be guilty. I'm not as good as you are, yer see. And anyway, seeing as I was only having yer on, can't yer forget about it and let's go in yours for a cuppa?'

'No, yer can't come in mine for a cuppa. And I'm not childish enough to be punishing yer for being naughty, so yer needn't think so. I promised Lily and Archie we'd see the Hanleys today about hiring the room over their shop for the reception. And it could just happen that if we were to waste half an hour over a cuppa here, someone could use that time to walk in the shop and book the hall for their own party.'

'I'd break their neck if they did, girl. Doing our Lily out of the place she's set her heart on for the reception! Why, they must be terrible people and I'd tell them so.'

'But yer wouldn't know who they were, would yer, sunshine? And why wouldn't yer know who they were? Because yer'd be too busy guzzling tea to see them. So be a good girl now and let's get to Hanley's.'

'Yeah, we better had, girl, before that other crowd get there before us. The cheeky beggars, trying to push us out.'

Molly looked at her mate for a trace of sarcasm, but all she could see was an innocent, chubby face smiling sweetly. 'All right, sunshine, put yer arm in and let's get to the cake shop before we go anywhere else. No stopping until we've got the reception hall booked and off our minds.'

'No, we won't stop nowhere, for no one.' The words were still coming out of Nellie's mouth when a woman stepped down on to the pavement from a house four doors away. Nellie dropped Molly's arm and ran forward. 'Mabel! Hey, Mabel, wait until I tell yer me good news.' Mabel Bristow waited for Nellie to reach her. 'What news is that, then, Nellie?'

'Our Lily's getting married on Easter Saturday.' Molly caught up with her friend and Nellie said, 'Isn't that right, girl?'

'I'm very pleased for yer, Nellie,' Mabel said, 'she's a nice girl is your Lily. And her young man seems a good bloke.'

'Are yer going up the street or down, Mabel?' Molly asked, wanting to be on their way. 'We're going down to the main road.'

'Oh, I'm going the opposite way.' Mabel seemed very pleased indeed that she was going in the other direction. She liked Nellie McDonough, nearly everyone in the street did, but once she got talking to you it was hopeless trying to get away. 'Tell Lily I'm glad for her, Nellie, and I'll be seeing yer. Ta-ra!'

Nellie watched her retreating back. 'She didn't have much to say for herself, did she? Mind you, she's probably a bit jealous. Their Irene is the same age as Lily and she's not even courting yet.'

'Of course she's not jealous, Nellie, that's a terrible thing to say. Irene is a lovely-looking girl, and I'm sure she has plenty of lads after her. Perhaps she doesn't want to settle down until she's a bit older.'

Two early-bird shoppers were coming up on the opposite side of the street, their baskets over their arms and deep in conversation. Without a by-your-leave to Molly, Nellie ran across the cobbles. Once again she conveyed her news. This time the women seemed interested and pleased for Nellie's daughter as they nodded and smiled, making her feel happy and important. When Nellie at last rejoined her mate, she was in a good frame of mind.

'I'll do a deal with yer, sunshine,' Molly said, feeling irritated. 'If you don't stop again before we get to Hanley's, when we've completed our business there, which I'm hoping we will successfully, I'll get on with me shopping on me own and leave you free to tell the world and his friend about the coming wedding.'

'Yer mean, yer'd leave me and get yer shopping in without me? That's being a bit selfish, girl, and not a bit like you.' Nellie looked sideways at her friend. 'Are yer not feeling well, girl, is that it? Are yer feeling a bit off colour?'

'Not off colour at the moment, sunshine, but I've got a feeling in me bones that I'm going to be browned off very quickly if you and I don't part company for a while. I haven't got the patience to stop every few minutes and stand quietly by while you tell everyone about the wedding. They'll find out soon enough without that. I wouldn't mind if it was relations or close friends, I could understand that, but not people yer barely know. Yer didn't hear me broadcasting my daughters' weddings, or Tommy's, did yer?'

'Yer didn't have to, girl, 'cos I did it for yer.'

While Molly gazed down into her friend's face she asked herself how she could fall out with someone who came out with a remark like that? Nellie definitely couldn't see the harm in discussing her friend's business with everyone from Scotland Road to the Pier Head. On the contrary, she believed she was doing Molly a favour. 'Yes, sunshine, yer did. The whole of the neighbourhood knew before Jack did.'

'Well, I promise I won't stop and tell anyone else,' Nellie said, nodding her head and chins to confirm what she'd said. 'Let's march on to Hanley's and I won't turn me head either way, then I won't see no one.'

And Nellie stuck to her word until they were almost at the cake shop when she recognized a familiar figure walking in front of them. Then her promise was forgotten. 'There's Elsie Flanaghan.' She rushed forward, hand raised, shouting, 'Elsie, hang on a minute!'

Molly took off after Nellie, thinking her mate was going to cause trouble with the woman, and at the same time Elsie Flanaghan turned around. She gave one look out of eyes as wide as saucers, saw Nellie shaking a fist at her, as she thought, and took off like a bat out of hell. You couldn't see her feet touch the ground, she moved so fast. Knowing she could never catch up with the sprightly woman, Nellie stopped and put her hands on her hips. 'What's wrong with her, the silly cow?'

Molly couldn't speak for laughing. It was the funniest thing she'd seen for ages. Nellie was full of good will, but Elsie wasn't to know that. She wouldn't know there was a first time for everything, and this was the one occasion she didn't have to worry she'd end up flat on the pavement. Oh, dear, oh, dear, Molly thought. What a performance that was. She'd never forget the look on Elsie's face when she saw Nellie running after her.

Nellie screwed up her eyes. 'What are yer laughing at, girl? I don't think it's funny, and I'll clock Elsie Flanaghan when I see her.'

'That's what she thought yer were going to do to her, sunshine, and she wasn't going to hang around to let you.'

Nellie looked surprised. 'But I was only going to tell her about the wedding, the stupid cow!'

'You know that, and I know that now, but how was Elsie to know? Last time yer spoke to her yer told her if she looked sideways at yer, yer'd batter her.' Molly began to shake with laughter. 'Oh, that was hilarious, sunshine, it's really bucked me up.'

'Oh, well, that's good, isn't it, girl? At least yer haven't got a cob on no more, and yer won't make me go shopping on me own, will yer? Not when yer've been really bucked up?'

'What happens now is up to you. If we get to Hanley's without any further obstacles being put in the way by your good self, then I'll reconsider the shopping arrangements.'

Nellie walked on with her head down. Why couldn't her mate use plain English like what she did, so she'd know where she was up to? Obstacles and reconsider . . . what did she use words like that for when they were only going to Tony's for a pound of mince? They'd been doing that for years now and never once before had Molly said she'd have to reconsider. But Nellie wasn't going to show her ignorance by mentioning the fact. 'Whatever you say, girl, is all right by me. I won't talk to no one, and if anyone tries to stop me, I'll walk over them.'

'That's a bit drastic, sunshine, but I think yer've got the gist of it. So let's go. And if we do happen to meet Elsie by chance, keep yer arms by yer side and she might not run away.'

'She was daft doing that, though, wasn't she girl? Because she doesn't know me good news now.'

'Oh, I think yer'll find some way of letting her know, sunshine, I can't see her being the only one to escape yer net. But let's get Hanley's sorted out, then we can relax when we know whether it's good news for Lily and Archie.'

Edna Hanley was passing a customer's change over the counter when Molly and Nellie walked into the shop. 'Good morning, ladies, I hope we find yer in good form today?'

'Yeah, we're fine, thanks, Edna. Nellie has something she wants to ask yer, so can yer see to her first before we get our bread?' Then, to give herself a laugh, Molly added, 'Can yer come to the end of the counter, 'cos Nellie doesn't want anyone to know.'

'Oh, er, I hope it's interesting, Nellie, because I could do with livening up.' Edna gave her daughter a pat on the shoulder as she was passing her. 'You serve this customer, Emily, there's a good girl. If it starts getting busy I'll be right back.'

'You tell her, girl, ye're better at it than I am, I get meself all flummoxed,' Nellie muttered to her friend.

'Oh, no, yer don't, sunshine, ye're not getting away with that. Ye're quick enough to tell the likes of Mabel Bristow but can't find the words to tell Edna! At least, not tell her, ask her.'

Nellie lifted her bosom and laid it on the counter with her arms circling it. 'Well, it's like this, Edna. Our Lily and her boyfriend went to see the priest last night and he's going to marry them on Easter Saturday. And they were hoping, like, that they could have their reception here. They both said what a good job yer'd done for Molly, with everything just right, and they're praying yer'll do the same for them.'

Because Nellie was always pulling someone's leg, Edna thought she'd play her at her own game. So looking as sad as she could, she said, 'Ooh, Nellie, did yer say Easter Saturday? Yer've left it very late because Easter Saturday is a popular day for couples getting married and everyone gets their name down very early.'

Nellie's jaw dropped as she turned her head to Molly. 'It's those people yer were talking about, they've got here before us.'

Molly, who knew everything was going to be all right because Edna had given her a sly wink, managed to put an element of surprise in her voice. 'What people are they, sunshine? Remind me.'

'Yer know very well who I'm talking about, girl, so don't come that with me. Yer said if we stopped and had a cuppa, that someone could just come in and book the room. Well, they bloody well have, and they cheated because we didn't have no cuppa!'

Edna was looking from one to the other. 'Would someone tell me what's going on, 'cos yer've lost me.'

'It's very simple, really,' Molly told her. 'Nellie has been asked to book your reception room for Lily and Archie's wedding on Easter Saturday, if ye're not already booked.'

The shopkeeper bent down and brought a ledger from under the counter. 'What day did yer say, Nellie?'

'Easter Saturday, girl, and yer've no need to pretend because I saw yer giving me mate a wink. I'm not soft, yer know, or blind.'

'Nellie, not for one second would I think yer were daft or blind. Far from it. Wily is the word that springs to mind to describe you.'

Nellie stood up straight. 'Ay, Edna, did yer go to the same school as me mate by any chance? I'm only asking because yer both like to use foreign words. I mean, what does wily mean when it's out? Are yer complimenting me or insulting me?'

Molly chuckled. 'Think carefully before yer answer that, Edna, because Elsie Flanaghan took one look at Nellie before and then took to her heels and scarpered hell for leather.'

The shopkeeper nodded. 'Of course, Mrs McDonough, you'll be treated with the greatest respect, I can assure you.'

'Will yer stop fiddling around, for crying out loud!' Nellie banged on the counter with her fist, and Molly and Edna and the customers held their breath as the glass display cases rattled. Even Nellie herself got a fright because she'd only done it in fun The trouble was, she didn't know her own strength. 'Sorry about that, Edna, and if I've been responsible for any of the cakes being squashed, I think it only fair to buy them off yer for half price.'

'How soft you are!' Molly said. 'If any cakes are squashed it's your fault and yer should buy them all at full price.'

'Oh, I can't do that, girl, much as I'd like to. And if Edna objects then you'll have to explain to her about the lectures I keep getting about going careful with me money. Especially now with the wedding coming soon.'

Emily, the daughter of the house, who was in between serving two customers, said, 'No harm done, Mrs Mac, all cakes intact.' Nellie was a firm favourite with the young girl and had there been any cakes squashed, she would have patted them back into shape before her mother saw them. 'Ye're off the hook.'

'Off the hook and in the book,' Edna said. 'I've booked the reception, Nellie, but I'll have to know how many to cater for, and what your daughter wants in the way of food. And I'll also need a deposit.'

'That's all right, Edna, I'll get that sorted out.' Nellie nodded. 'It'll be a roast dinner with the weather being cold.'

'It's cold today, sunshine, 'cos it's winter. But it might not be so cold when they get married so I wouldn't start suggesting anything yet.' Molly didn't want to interfere, but she knew of old that her friend was hopeless when it came to organizing anything, she really couldn't be depended on. 'The numbers will be sorted out as soon as possible, Edna, I imagine they'll be around the same number we had. And Lily did mention a buffet in the evening, but that's another thing they've got to sort out yet. Yer see, it's all happened so quickly, they only found out last night that the church could fit them in on Easter Saturday.'

Molly waited to see if Nellie would speak up, but her friend was standing there with a pleased expression on her face. 'I'll ask Lily to call in and see yer on Saturday, Edna, and the two of yer can go over all the details, like numbers and catering for the reception. How many will be coming in the evening, and if she wants yer to make the wedding cake. And when she comes she can pay yer the deposit.' She put her arm around Nellie's shoulders. 'Is that all right with you, sunshine, or is there anything yer'd like to add or any questions you need to ask?'

'No, girl, yer've said all that can be said so far.' Nellie's eyes narrowed. 'How much deposit will yer be asking for, Edna, so Lily isn't caught on the hop? Me and George are paying for the reception as a wedding present, so he will give her the money for the deposit if yer'll tell me what it is?'

'Just twenty pound as a deposit off the room, queen, and I can wait for that until Saturday. But ask Lily to come late-afternoon if yer will, 'cos we're rushed off our feet during the day and I wouldn't have time to sit and go through things with her earlier. Say about four o'clock, then I'll have time to spare and won't be rushing her. When she tells me what she wants serving at the reception, and the buffet, and for how many, then me and Tom can work out the prices and give Lily the grand total in a couple of days. How does that suit yer, Nellie?'

'Sound as a pound, girl, sound as a pound.' Nellie straightened herself up. 'We'll get our bread now, eh, Molly? And don't you go tempting me with any fresh cream cakes, Edna Hanley, 'cos me mate said I've got to tighten me belt. The wedding will be a big expense what with having to buy a new outfit and a posh hat.' Her eyes brightened. 'Eh, yer didn't see the posh hat I had for the other weddings, did yer? Well, yer missed something 'cos that's a real humdinger.'

'I saw it, Nellie, 'cos yer wore it for both receptions and for the buffets at night. Everyone could see how much yer loved the hat because yer wouldn't be parted from it. I remember asking if yer'd let me try it on but yer told me to bugger off.'

'That sounds like my mate,' Molly said. 'She doesn't mince her words, always short and to the point.'

'You lying hound!' Nellie pretended to get on her high horse. 'I never told yer to bugger off, Edna Hanley, and you know it. Lots of people tried me hat on, even the men. And I've got to say it looked better on Corker than it did on me.'

Molly was chuckling at the memory. 'Yeah, he didn't half suit the feather. It made him look like one of those knights of old, with their fancy hats with huge ostrich feathers in.'

Nellie rubbed her chin. 'I won't be wearing it no more 'cos me mate said I can't let Lily down by wearing the same hat and spoiling the wedding for her. So I'm just wondering if Corker would like to buy it off me? What d'yer think, girl?'

'Personally I think yer'd be wasting yer time, sunshine, because he wouldn't have much cause to use it unless he joined the amateur dramatic group in Walton.'

'He could use it to tickle his fancy,' Edna laughed. 'I can't think of any other use.'

Emily was trying to catch her mother's eye as there were four customers waiting to be served. In the end, she called, 'I need a hand, Mam.'

Edna quickly put the ledger under the counter and went to help her daughter. 'Sorry, sweetheart, but yer know what it's like when Nellie comes in.'

One of the customers said, 'We all know what it's like getting away from Nellie McDonough. Many's the time I've burnt the backside out of a pan because she's kept me talking. And the dinner's been ruined as well.'

Nellie's face brightened up. 'Hello, Lizzie, I didn't see yer for the minute. Ay, yer'll never guess, but our Lily's getting married on Easter Saturday. I've just been booking the room upstairs for the reception.'

'That's nice for yer, queen, and I hope everything goes off well for yer.' Lizzie's hand took her change while her feet took her towards the door and freedom. 'But I'll see yer before then, Nellie, ta-ra for now.'

The little woman's face was aglow as she turned to Molly. 'There yer are, girl, yer see how pleased Lizzie was for me?'

Molly bit on the inside of her bottom lip to stop herself from laughing. 'Yes, I noticed that, sunshine. And I noticed how eager she was to get home, so she must have her dinner cooking on the stove.'

'I can serve you two ladies now,' Edna said, as the shop emptied apart from an old lady being served by Emily. 'Is it just bread yer want today?'

'Yes, please, Edna, and I'd be glad if yer could slice it for me. Jack says when I cut the bread his sandwiches are like doorsteps and he can't get his mouth around them.'

The loaf was placed on the slicing machine and Edna was adjusting the setting. 'So yer want it thinly sliced, do yer, Molly?'

'Please, but not wafer thin or I'll get complaints about that.'

Nellie wasn't going to be left out. Whatever her mate had, she had to have. 'Yer can do mine the same, Edna, while ye're at it.'

'Oh, why is that, sunshine? Has your feller been complaining about thick slices as well?'

'No, but it stands to reason that if they won't fit into Jack's mouth, they won't fit into George's.' Nellie got into her fighting stance, feet apart and clenched fist raised. 'Or are yer implying that my George has a bigger mouth than your Jack?'

The little old lady had been served and had put her bread into her basket. But she was only going home to an empty house and wouldn't see another soul until she came to the shops the next day. So she quickly decided that watching Nellie McDonough act the goat was a much better way to make the time go over.

And Edna was beginning to enjoy herself. This beat running after customers all day and listening to complaints. So rolling her shoulders as she'd seen boxers do before a fight, she said, 'Right, everybody out of the ring, please. Give the boxers room. Mrs Burton, come behind the counter if yer will.'

Mrs Burton was in her eighties and quite frail but she managed to do her own housework, shopping and cooking. She was very popular with everyone because she never moaned and always had a smile on her face. Now, as she moved behind the counter, she was really delighted she'd stayed in the shop to see the fun. And what fun it was!

Nellie had both fists clenched now and her shoulders rounded. She circled Molly, who was standing in the middle of the shop floor with her arms folded. Nellie's right fist came out with some force and hit the air. 'Take that, you bugger!' Then around she'd go again before her left fist shot out. 'That'll teach yer to say my feller's got a big mouth!'

Two regular customers who had a loaf ordered each day walked up to the shop only to be waved back by Emily who was leaning forward into the window. She put a finger to her lips to ask them to be quiet then, mouthing the words, asked them to stand by the door. The two women couldn't make her out at first, until they saw Nellie dancing around, as light on her feet as a ballerina. One customer, a woman called Nancy, gave her friend Freda a dig in the ribs and whispered, 'Will yer just look at the state of Nellie.'

Molly still stood with her arms folded and didn't even blink when Nellie's fist came within inches of her face. This wasn't the first time she'd been the boxer who didn't fight back. But then she knew her mate's aim was perfect, otherwise she wouldn't be standing in the middle of the shop with her arms folded looking like a stupid nit. Anyway, by now there were about six people crowded into the doorway and she didn't want to spoil their fun.

Nellie was still dancing about punching the air. 'I'll teach yer a lesson yer'll never forget, you swine! Take that, and that.' A few more jabs near Molly's nose, and lots of tittering from the onlookers. 'Yer'll not forget this in a hurry, that's two of yer front teeth on the floor. And if yer don't take that grin off yer face, I'll be giving yer a cauliflower ear.' Then she gave one more sharp jab, looked down to the floor and lifted both hands above her head. 'It's a knock-out, folks. Helen Theresa McDonough wins in the third round. And a well-deserved win it is too, her opponent didn't even land a punch.'

There was a round of applause and Nellie was walking the floor with her arms in the air when Tom Hanley came through from the back, wiping his hands on the white apron he was wearing. 'What's going on here? I'm working away in the back, sweat pouring off me as I clean the ovens and trays, and you lot are standing here enjoying yerselves. I could hear yer laughter from the bakery.'

'Yer missed a treat, Dad,' Emily told him. 'Mrs Mac had just been showing us how to box, and it was really funny.'

'She was acting daft, as usual, Tom, shadow boxing,' Molly said. 'She'll show yer sometime, but right now we have to get to the butcher's.'

Nellie wasn't going to miss an opportunity when it was handed to her on a plate. There were five customers here now, and she wasn't one to miss a trick. 'Yeah, Tom, we're going along to tell Tony and Ellen about our Lily and her boyfriend getting married on Easter Saturday. We're all very excited about it.'

'I'm sure yer are. But next time yer put a show on, Nellie, don't start without me. I miss all the fun being stuck out there.'

'Ah, yer poor thing,' Edna said. 'Look, he's pouting.'

'Now, if you and Tom are going to start a fight, I'll be on me way.' Molly passed one shilling and sixpence over. 'That's for Nellie's bread as well, she can pay me back later. And I'll take her with me, out of yer way. Unless yer'd like her to teach yer a few left hooks, Edna? She's pretty good at that.'

'Nah, me and Tom don't fight, we've never got the energy after a day's work. I'll see yer both tomorrow, ta-ra for now.'

Nellie didn't arrive on the pavement until a few minutes after Molly because some of the women stopped her to say how pleased they were for her daughter. She was smiling when she joined Molly. 'I haven't half enjoyed meself, girl, it's been the gear.'

'I'm glad about that, sunshine, and I hate to spoil yer fun, but d'yer think we could make the effort to be home by half-twelve? I want to get the mince on, then go round and see me ma and da for an hour.'

'I'll come with yer, girl!'

'Not on your life yer won't, sunshine, 'cos I've had a bellyful of talk about the wedding. I'll be in a better mood tomorrow, I promise. I don't want to be a spoilsport, but yer can only take so much of a good thing, Nellie, and I've really had enough. While I'm at me ma's, you could do the rounds on yer own. In fact, if yer hadn't frightened Elsie Flanaghan off, yer wouldn't have to bother telling anyone, she'd have done it for yer. The whole neighbourhood would know by now 'cos she doesn't waste any time. I sometimes think she has a list of possible suckers that she knows will listen to her. Anyway, it's not worth talking about, so let's get to the butcher's.' The friends linked arms. 'Our Doreen was coming out with the baby for a bit of fresh air, and I thought we might see her in one of the shops. Perhaps she'll be in Tony's.'

'She doesn't know about the wedding yet, does she, girl?'

'No, she doesn't, sunshine. I'm going to leave it to you to tell her.'

Chapter Nine

'I don't know how we've come to miss our Doreen and the baby,' Molly said as she walked home with Nellie. 'Tony said she was in about twenty minutes before us, bought some chops and said she was going on to Irwin's. It's a mystery how she passed us without her seeing us or us seeing her.'

'We were in the cake shop a long time, girl, and she could easily have passed the window when we had our backs to it. If it was fresh air she wanted, as yer said, then perhaps she's gone as far as the park.'

'That's probably what's happened, sunshine. I'll watch out for her while the mince is cooking, then if I haven't managed to catch her, I'll call over before I go to me ma's.'

'I don't know what ye're fretting for, she's a big girl is Doreen, and nothing is going to happen to her or the baby.'

'I know all that, Nellie, and when you're a grandmother I'll remind yer of it when I see ye're worried about yer grandchild. It's human nature, sunshine, as yer'll find out.' They turned into their street and Molly noticed a woman knocking on a door halfway up. 'Is that woman knocking on my door, sunshine, or am I seeing things?'

'No, ye're not seeing things, girl, it is your house and it's Beryl Mowbray knocking. I wonder what she's calling at yours for. It's not as though ye're that friendly with her.'

Molly quickened her pace. 'There's only one way to find out,

141

and that's to ask. Anyway, I'm not unfriendly with Beryl, we're civil with each other. Anyone listening to you would think we were enemies!'

Beryl saw them coming and leaned against the wall until they came abreast. 'I've knocked a few times 'cos I was a bit concerned. Oh, it might be nothing, Molly, just me being bad-minded, but I've told meself it's better to be sure than sorry. So I'm telling yer anyway, 'cos I think yer should be told so yer can be on yer guard.'

'Whatever is it, Beryl? And don't worry if yer think ye're making a mountain out of a molehill, 'cos as yer say, better to be sure than sorry. So what's on yer mind, sunshine?'

Beryl let out a sigh. 'I was cleaning me front bedroom windows and I saw your Doreen getting the pram down the step and then walking down the street. I watched for a few seconds, yer know how daft women are over babies, and I was just about to turn away when I saw a movement in that side entry opposite. There was a man there, and it was his actions that caused me to stay and see what he was up to. He was a really shifty-looking character. Kept popping his head out into the street, and he was watching your Doreen walking down it with the pram.'

'What did this man look like, Beryl?' Molly asked, fear in her heart. 'Young, old, tall, small, blond or dark hair?'

'Oh, he wasn't young, queen, I'd say he was about the same age as we are, in his forties. Medium height, very thin, with dark hair going grey at the temples. I thought he looked an unsavoury character, up to no good. That's why I watched him for a while.'

'And what happened next, sunshine? Did he move on then?'

Beryl shook her head. 'He watched until Doreen turned the corner into the main road, and all the time his eyes were darting everywhere. He didn't see me because I hid behind the curtain. I knew he was there for a purpose, 'cos I've never seen a man looking so shifty before. Anyway, after a while he came out of the entry, his eyes everywhere, keeping close to the wall. He stopped outside Miss Clegg's, and me heart was in me mouth because after making sure he wasn't being watched, he put his eyes to the window to try and see inside. He didn't stay there long, probably afraid of being seen, but he definitely tried to see into the room.'

'Yer know who that is, don't yer, girl?' Nellie was nodding her head knowingly. 'If I get me hands on him, I'll choke the bugger.'

'Oh, yer know the man, do yer?' Beryl looked surprised. 'He didn't look your type, and I'd swear he was up to no good.'

Molly gave her friend daggers. Why couldn't she think before she opened her mouth? If the man was Tom Bradley, and the description certainly fitted, then it wasn't something she wanted broadcasting. And the less the neighbours knew the better. 'He sounds like someone who lived at the top end of the street, ooh, it must be five years ago. He was a rotter and would steal the eyes out of yer head. The neighbours forced him and his family out of the street because he'd robbed from every one of them. It might not be the same bloke, but he does fit the description.'

Nellie realized she'd put her foot in it and was cursing herself. Me and my big mouth, she thought, why can't I be like Molly and think first? 'He was a bad 'un, the feller we think it might be, but I can't help wondering what he's come back here for.'

'We'll have to keep our eyes open,' Molly said. 'If yer see him again, Beryl, will yer let me know? But come round the back instead of the front, and I might be able to catch him unawares and ask what he's doing round here.'

'Beryl could give me a knock on the wall, girl, and I could come and tell yer. Then the two of us could catch him. He couldn't get away from two of us, not like he could if yer were by yerself.'

143

'Oh, I'll keep me eye open for him, yer can rely on that. If I see him this side of the street I'll chase him, we don't want no one robbing our houses. Especially with Christmas nearly on us and most women with things put away for the kids.' Beryl had only just thought of this. 'That's probably what he had in mind 'cos he wasn't half fishy-looking. It would be a good idea to warn people to be on the lookout for him. Forewarned is forearmed.'

'I wouldn't start frightening people, Beryl,' Molly said quickly. 'It might not be the bloke we think it is, and it wouldn't be right to worry people unnecessarily. If he turns up again, then that's the time to warn our neighbours.'

'Yes, ye're right, queen, I'm letting me imagination run away with me. Perhaps I shouldn't have told yer 'cos there might be nothing in it, but I still say, no matter who he is, he was up to no good.'

'I'm glad yer did tell us, Beryl, it was the neighbourly thing to do. We can keep our eyes peeled in the future. And it was clever of yer to think about the extra toys and other things that people will have in for Christmas. Any burglar would get a good haul now.'

'They wouldn't get much from my house, girl, 'cos I haven't got nothing in for Christmas yet. And neither have you, come to that.'

'I'm starting this weekend.' Molly took the front-door key from her pocket. 'I'd better get in and prepare the dinner. But do us a favour, Beryl, and don't mention what yer've told us to anyone else. It would frighten the life out of our Doreen if she thought a man had his eye on the house. She'd be terrified to leave Victoria in on her own. So, not a word, eh?'

'My lips are sealed,' Beryl said, 'and I'm going to see to me own dinner now I've got it off me chest. Ta-ra for now.'

'Ta-ra, Beryl, and thanks again.' Molly opened the front door and jerked her head at Nellie. 'I think yer'd better come in, sunshine, we need to talk.'

That suited her down to the ground and she hopped up the step like a two-year-old. 'Yes, girl, I think ye're right.'

Molly slipped her coat off and hung it up. 'I'll put the kettle on. I need a cuppa to calm me down, me nerves are shot to pieces.'

'Don't you be worrying about it, girl, 'cos we'll sort it out, you and me. McDonough and Bennett, Private Detectives,' Nellie called through to the kitchen as she moved one of the dining chairs out of the way so she could put the carver chair in its place. She could be here quite a while so she may as well make herself at home. She could think better when she was comfortable. 'From the description, I'd lay odds on it being the queer feller. But what the hell would he be doing around here? He knows half the street would be after him if they set eyes on him.'

'Me head's aching already, trying to think. The only thing that springs to mind is that he's after money off Phil.' Molly carried two steaming cups through. 'Oh, and by the way, me mind might be full but I heard what yer said, and it's Bennett and McDonough, Private Detective Agency. I'm not having you pull rank on me.'

Nellie was rubbing her hands at the thought of something exciting. She loved it when she and Molly played detectives. They were good at it, too, 'cos they always got their man, like the Canadian Mounties.

'I don't know what to do for the best,' Molly said, her hands circling the cup. 'I don't think I'll tell Doreen or Phil because they'd be worried sick in case Tom Bradley started coming round again, demanding money. Doreen would be terrified for the baby and Victoria if we told her the man looked in the window.' She gave a deep sigh. 'I think my best bet is to say nothing unless he shows his face again. It's no good worrying the life out of Doreen and Phil when they're so happy now. It would only remind Phil of the terrible time he had with Tom Bradley as his step-father.'

'Yer wouldn't know what to do for the best, girl, I'll grant yer that. But I think yer'll be seeing him again because Beryl's description was spot on.'

'I agree with yer, sunshine. And the more I think about it, the more sick with worry I feel. If it was him, and I'm becoming more convinced by the minute, he knows Doreen's got a baby now and that will give him a hold over them. Yer know how he used to threaten Phil before when he was after money.'

'If I was you, girl, I wouldn't wait for him to come back again, I'd see him and put the fear of God into him. We could do that, you and me.'

'That's if we knew where to find him.'

'We found him once before, girl, when we were told he had a scrap yard where he used to sell his ill-gotten gains. Don't yer remember us knocking on the door of that woman's house, and her telling us all about him? I can't remember her name, but she was really nice and invited us into her house and made us a cup of tea.'

'I doubt very much if he'll still be in the same place. From what we were told, the Bradleys never stayed anywhere long because of the life they lived. Stealing and breaking into houses, they couldn't afford to stay long in the one place.'

'Yer may be right, girl, but I bet we could find him if we set out to do it. We found Phil's family for him, didn't we?'

Molly nodded. 'We did, sunshine, but that was a different kettle of fish. We were lucky finding the Mitchells because they hadn't moved out of Bootle and we did get a few leads. We wouldn't be so lucky finding the queer feller and his family.'

'I wonder if Phil's mother ever thinks of him, girl? She wouldn't be normal if she didn't. And if she finds out she's a grandma, well, chances are she'd try and make contact to see the baby. No matter how hard she is, she'd want to see her own grandchild.'

Molly leaned her elbow on the table and cupped her chin. 'That's given me more food for thought, sunshine. I wonder if she has found out about Bobby, and that's what Tom Bradley was hanging around for?'

'Ay, if we find out it was him, d'yer know the best person to tell, girl?' Nellie's arms left the support of the carver chair and she moved forward quickly, eager to share her thoughts with her mate. But in the process she banged her bosom on the table and grimaced with pain. 'Oh, blimey, that hurt, that did! And it's your ruddy table what did it.'

'Don't be blaming my table, Nellie McDonough. It's not my fault yer've got breasts as big as barrage balloons. Yer've had them long enough, yer should know by now that they're there and treat them with more care.'

'I know, it's me own fault, I'm too quick-headed. I was thinking of the time the Bradley kids stole that boy's bike from the top of the street, and how Corker got it back for him. He's very clever at sorting things out, is Corker, and if anything turns up that yer need help with, then he's the very man to ask.'

Molly too was remembering. 'Yeah, and it was Corker who calmed things down on the night Phil caught his brother trying to break into Victoria's house. Our Doreen wouldn't be married to Phil now if it wasn't for Corker. He always thought Phil was a good lad, and often says he feels like a father to him. So ye're right, sunshine, he would be the one to go to in trouble. Just the sight of him would have Tom Bradley running hell for leather in the opposite direction.' But it was only a matter of days since she'd last gone to Corker for help; she couldn't keep running to him every time something went wrong. No, if there was any truth in what Beryl had told them, then she'd sort it out herself, with Nellie's help, if it were possible. Only as a last resort would she go to Corker.

'So, have yer made up yer mind what ye're going to do about it, girl? I'll always go with yer if yer want to try and find him.'

'I'm not going to do anything until I've calmed down enough to think straight. My best bet would be to have a good talk to Jack tonight and see what his feelings are.'

'Well, yer know where I am if yer want me, girl. And before yer say it, no, I will not tell a living soul.' Nellie pushed the chair back and lifted it to take it back to its usual place next to the sideboard. 'I'll make tracks now and get me dinner on the go. And it won't only be the spuds I peel, I'll also have me eyes peeled in case the queer feller decides to come back and pay Doreen a visit.'

'I've got it in me head that now he knows she takes the baby out in the pram, he'll be watching for the next time she goes out, then he'll knock on the door and hope Victoria invites him in. He's a crafty bugger, as we all know, and could easily spin her a sob story to get money off her.' Molly put a hand to her head and grimaced. 'The more I think of it, the worse I feel. Victoria said she was going to take a nap in her chair while Doreen was out, and I can only hope to God she did. Just imagine the fright she'd get if she saw a man peering in the window. At her age, the shock would be enough to bring on a stroke or a heart attack.'

'She wouldn't know who he was would she?' Nellie asked. 'It was years ago now he was last here, and I don't think she ever saw him close up. If she saw him at all, it would only have been from a distance so she wouldn't recognize him.'

'I hope not, sunshine, 'cos it would upset Doreen and Phil, and worry them to death.'

Nellie was on her way to the door when she spotted Doreen through the window. 'There's Doreen and the baby now, girl, so I'll nip over and give her a hand up with the pram. These small halls are so narrow it's a bugger trying to get a pram through.' She opened the front door and called across, 'Hang on, girl, I'll give yer a hand up with the pram.'

Molly waved to her daughter and watched as Nellie lifted the back wheels of the pram and waited for Doreen to give her a sign to push. The pram was a big heavy one, a beautiful Silver Cross, fit for a princess. It was too big for the small house, but as far as Phil was concerned nothing was too good for his son who had to have the best. But getting it in and out of the house was a labour of love.

'Okay, Auntie Nellie,' Doreen shouted, 'will yer push it in, please?'

Nellie was holding the pram as though it was as light as a feather, and if Molly hadn't had her head filled with other things, the sight would have brought a smile to her face. 'Okay, Doreen girl.' Nellie never spoke quietly, she always shouted. 'I'll be seeing yer! Ta-ra!'

Molly waved to her as she crossed the cobbled street, and then to her daughter. But when the other two doors closed, Molly didn't go back into her house. She stood on the step for a while with bated breath. If Victoria had seen anything amiss, she would tell Doreen right away. But as the seconds ticked by and there was no sound or sign of activity from the house opposite, Molly backed into the hallway and closed the front door. She leaned back against it and let out a long sigh. Surely Tom Bradley wasn't going to come back into Phil's life and spoil it for him again? Things were so good now for all her family, and if she had anything to do with it they would stay that way. She wouldn't allow anyone to spoil what they had. Especially a rotter like Tom Bradley.

Another sigh escaped her lips, then Molly pulled herself together and walked through to the kitchen to put the minced meat on. While it was cooking, she would keep her eyes on the house and side entry opposite. She couldn't see down the entry from her window, it was a little higher up. Nellie and Beryl would have a better view because it was directly facing their windows, and Molly knew she could rely on her mate to keep a close watch. In fact, there was nothing Nellie liked better than a scrap, and woe betide Tom Bradley if her friend got her hands on him. He would stand a better chance with Corker, who would rather reason than use his fists, while Nellie would act first and reason afterwards.

Jack put a match to his Woodbine and puffed at it until it was lit. Then he threw the match in the fire and turned his attention to Molly. 'If yer want my view, love, I'd leave things be for now. Ye're going on a short description Mrs Mowbray gave yer, and that description could fit nearly half the male population hereabouts. I mean, she's never actually seen Tom Bradley, so the man she saw could be anybody.'

'I hope ye're right, sunshine, but I think we've got to look at it from both sides and then consider what to do if it was him. I don't want to tell Doreen or Phil because it would upset their lives. They look the picture of happiness when yer see them together, and they adore Bobby and Victoria. The very mention of the name Bradley would shatter all that.'

'But their name isn't Bradley now, it's Mitchell. Apart from Fanny Bradley being his mother, the rest of the family have no claim on Phil. He's turned twenty-one and can do as he wishes. I say leave well alone. If Bradley does turn up again, then I agree with you that something will have to be done. What, I don't know. But I'll think of some way to stop him from ruining my daughter's life.'

'If he's seen in the neighbourhood again, me and Nellie will find him and I'll put the fear of God into him. In fact, although I shouldn't say it, I bet Nellie is hoping he shows his face in the street so she can have a go at him. Not that I'd let her, 'cos think of the humiliation and embarrassment it would cause Phil. No, if we get him it will be near his home, not around here. As Nellie said, we found him once, we can find him again.'

Jack sat forward in his chair. 'I don't want you getting involved, love, in case yer get hurt. He's a devious swine is Tom Bradley, and I wouldn't put anything past him. Better for a man to deal with him than a woman. So promise me yer'll do nothing without first telling me?'

'I'm sorry, sunshine, but I can't do that! Suppose you're at work and he comes knocking on Doreen's door? I can't stand by and do nothing, or ask him to sit and have a cup of tea while we wait for you to come home to sort him out.'

'If I could be here waiting for him to show his face, I would be, love, but I have to go to work. I can't alter that. But I want yer to promise not to get yerself into a situation yer can't get yerself out of. And just remember, yer can't trust that rotter as far as yer could throw him. Don't fall for any sob story he gives yer.' Jack shook his head. 'What am I going on about it for when it may never happen! Mrs Mowbray saw a man acting suspiciously and brought all this on. The man could have had a perfectly good reason to be there. He could have been a bookie's runner for all we know. So don't be getting yerself all upset and meeting worry halfway. Put it out of yer mind and think of something nice, like Christmas, and what ye're buying for yer grandson.'

Molly nodded. 'I'll do what yer say, love, I'll forget about it.' But she only spoke those words to stop her husband from worrying. She had no intention of forgetting it. How could she when someone in her family might be hurt?

Molly opened the door to Nellie the next morning with an apology on her lips. 'I'm sorry I didn't come last night, sunshine, but I had to wait until Ruthie went to bed to tell Jack about the mystery man Beryl saw.'

Nellie walked in rubbing her arms. 'It's not often I feel the cold, me fat usually keeps me warm, but it's bitter out today.' She made for the fire which Molly had stoked up for her friend's arrival. 'Don't worry about last night, I told Lily yer had something on.' She turned from the fire with a grin on her face. 'They got through a lot last night, girl. The guest list is done, but Archie said to allow for another couple just in case. And he's going to see Edna on Saturday with Lily. They want Hanley's to make the wedding cake with three tiers, girl, like they did for Doreen's and Jill's reception.'

Seeing her friend's happy face cheered Molly up. 'I knew they'd get everything sorted, Archie is a very organized man who always seems to have things under control. Have they made up their minds on bridesmaids and best man?'

Nellie waddled over to get her carver chair. And while she always felt posh sitting in that chair, today she felt powerful as well as posh. 'They have, girl, but they warned me not to say anything. They want to ask everyone themselves first.' She set the chair down before looking up at her mate. 'It's no good looking at me like that, girl, it's not my fault. And anyway, yer can understand why Archie wants to ask the bloke he wants as best man before the feller hears the news from someone else. It would spoil the surprise. The same with the bridesmaids. Lily wants to ask them herself, and discuss material and colours and what not.'

'The kettle's been boiled, it won't take me long to make a cuppa. And I can even manage a fig biscuit each.' Molly walked through to the kitchen where she allowed herself a very quiet titter. Nellie would be full of good intentions about keeping her promise to Lily, and she'd have crossed her heart and sworn to her daughter that she'd die before giving the game away. But that was last night, and this was another day. There was no way she could keep it all bottled up for a whole twenty-four hours. So although Molly was nosy enough to want to know everything right now, if she kept her patience she knew she'd find out soon enough.

'Here yer are, sunshine, tea up.' Molly had brought the tray in with a plate of biscuits on it. 'I've emptied the biscuit tin on to the plate, but that doesn't mean you and me are going to eat them all. I want to save a few because Jack and Ruthie love fig biscuits.'

'Okay, girl, I'll make sure I leave them one each.'

'Oh, don't starve yerself, Nellie, whatever yer do.'

Nellie didn't hear that bit of sarcasm, she was too busy filling her mouth with half a fig biscuit and sighing with bliss. 'Ay, what did Jack have to say about Tom Bradley turning up again after all this time?'

'He said we don't know for sure it was him, and he's right, Nellie! As he said, it could have been a bookie's runner, or someone like that. And he doesn't want me to do anything unless I know for sure what's going on. So I'll keep me eyes open from now on, and I'll be keeping a watch on our Doreen's house and peeping down all the entries.'

'I'll be doing the same, girl, and so will Beryl. If he shows his face around here one of us is bound to see him.'

'Yer didn't tell yer family, did yer, sunshine? Not after me asking yer not to.'

'No, I didn't tell them, girl, and I'll tell yer straight I'm getting fed up with being told to keep me mouth shut. If it keeps up I'll be terrified to speak to a soul. I'll have to pretend I'm dumb if someone asks me anything. You've told me not to say a word about Tom Bradley, and our Lily and Archie have sworn me to silence over Archie asking your Tommy to be his best man.'

Molly didn't know whether to laugh, pretend she hadn't heard or show surprise. In the end she decided on the latter. 'Ooh, is he?'

'Is he what, girl?'

'Is Archie going to ask our Tommy to be best man?'

'I couldn't tell yer that, girl! Whoever told yer that knows more than I do. But they want to try keeping their mouth shut in future.'

'All right, sunshine, I won't ask yer anything else. I must have misheard what yer said, so we'll forget about it, eh?'

'The best thing all round, girl, then no one can get the blame.' Nellie put her cup back in the saucer. 'Yer didn't get to yer ma's last night, then?'

Molly shook her head. 'Our Ruthie brought Bella over for a game of Snakes and Ladders, and it was nine before she went home. I shouldn't complain because our Ruthie is over in the Watsons' every night. But the one time I wanted to talk to Jack privately had to be the night she brought Bella over to ours. Still, I'll go to me ma's tonight.'

'You do that, girl, 'cos I've got a feeling yer might hear something to cheer yer up.'

'Do I look as though I need cheering up?'

'Well, all I can say, girl, is that when yer opened the door to me before, I said to meself, I hope she's up-to-date with her insurance policy.'

'Oh, come on now, Nellie, I don't look that bad.'

'Have yer looked at yerself in the mirror this morning? Yer look at though yer've been awake all night.'

'Half the night, sunshine, and what sleep I did get wasn't restful, I kept tossing and turning. It's a wonder I didn't wake Jack up, but he slept like a baby. I couldn't get Tom Bradley out of me mind and it's left me with a splitting headache. If it was anyone else I wouldn't worry, I'd tell them to get lost and that

154

would be the end of it. But I kept thinking of all the bad things his family did in the short time they lived here. The way those two young daughters of his stole from Lizzie Corkhill and frightened her into giving them food. It's hard to get yer own back on someone who has no scruples and no feelings.'

'I can tell yer how we can get rid of yer headache, girl, and cheer yer up. Shall I tell yer?'

'If I said I didn't want to know, yer'd still tell me, sunshine, so go ahead.'

'Instead of going to the shops, we'll skip them today and go to Paddy's Market. We could have a look for some Christmas presents for the family. It's not long off now, girl, and we've got nothing in yet.'

'I've got to go to the shops, Nellie, I've nothing in for the dinner. And I need bread, I used the last of the loaf for breakfast.'

'Oh, sod the shops for one day, girl! Let's enjoy ourselves and live dangerously. We've both got enough spuds in to make chips, and we could buy half a dozen eggs and a tin of peas on Great Homer Street. We could get our bread there, too! The family won't mind for once, and even if they do it's too bloody bad, they can sod off.'

Molly was warming to the idea. The bustle of the market and the humour of the stallholders would take her mind off things. 'I don't think Jack or Ruthie would mind because they both love egg and chips.'

Nellie was happy inside because she didn't like to see her friend upset and worried. 'That's settled then. And when we get to Paddy's Market we could go and see Mary Ann and Sadie, see how they're getting on. Sadie was getting engaged last time we were there, remember?'

Molly made a quick decision. 'We'll do as yer say, sunshine, and to hell with Tom Bradley and everything else. I'd love to see Mary Ann and Sadie, they always cheer me up. And I've got a few pounds put away for Christmas presents, so we could make a start.'

Nellie put her two hands flat on the table and pushed herself up. 'That's my girl! I'll go and put something decent on, this coat has seen better days. In fact there's probably better coats on the second-hand stalls than this one, I might just mug meself. I only want one to go to the shops in, I don't have to look like a mannequin.' She got as far as the door before looking over her shoulder. 'I wouldn't mind a cup of tea before we go out, girl, to warm us up. Yer wouldn't want yer best mate to be cold, would yer?'

'Ay, I want to get meself changed, yer know, I don't want to go out looking like a scruff. So it will be just a quick cup, sunshine, and yer can drink it standing up. Once you put yer backside on that chair, it's hard to get yer off.'

'I don't mind standing up to drink me tea, girl.' Nellie opened the front door with a smile on her face. 'I'll even stand up to eat another fig biscuit as well.'

The cushion Molly threw at her missed her by inches and she chuckled all the way home. Her mate was looking more cheerful than she had before, and that made Nellie happy.

Chapter Ten

'It's not as busy here as I thought it would be, girl. Remember last time we came we nearly got trampled underfoot?'

'There's not much money around on a weekday, sunshine. It's on a Saturday, after the men get their wages, that this place gets mad busy. Wait until next week when the tontines are paid out. Yer won't be able to move here, it'll be packed.'

'We should join a tontine, yer know, girl, because it comes in handy at Christmas. There's a woman lives a couple of streets from us who runs one, and all the women are in it. A shilling a week they pay, and at Christmas they get two pound ten shillings. And we wouldn't miss a shilling a week.'

'It was a shilling a week before the war, Nellie, and two pound ten shillings was a lot of money then. But prices have shot up since and the money from a tontine wouldn't get yer very much now.'

'It's better than a kick in the teeth, girl!'

Molly shook her head. 'No, I'll stick to paying into the shop clubs. I know where I'm working then. At least I don't have to worry about the turkey, or the potatoes, veg and fruit. And the sweetshop club comes in very handy.'

'Yer forgot to mention the corner shop, girl, and we've both got a few pound in there.'

'Yes, I know, and I'm quite proud of meself. After all the money me and Jack spent on Tommy's wedding, I thought

Christmas was going to be a poor do this year with no money for presents. But it shows what yer can do when yer put yer mind to it. We haven't gone hungry, but I did pinch and scrape over everything and I'm really glad I did because I'm reaping the reward now. I'm not loaded by any means, but everyone will get a present.'

Nellie gave her a nudge. 'Hey, look, girl, that stall looks as though it sells stuff worth looking at. Yer said yer wanted long stockings for Ruthie, well, I can see some on the stall.'

The stallholder was coaxing passersby to stop and see what good value his goods were. 'I'm not only the cheapest in the market, ladies, not only the cheapest in the whole of Liverpool even. No, you can go anywhere in England and if yer find such quality goods cheaper than mine, then I'll give yer the difference in the money back.'

When he saw Molly and Nellie showing interest in his wares, he said, 'I'm telling yer, I'm the cheapest in the market so why waste yer shoe leather looking elsewhere?'

Nellie was ready for a bit of fun. 'How much are those long stockings, lad?'

'Elevenpence ha'penny, queen, and yer'll not get them cheaper anywhere.'

'Yeah, I heard yer saying yer'd refund the money if someone found them any cheaper in another market. Well, lad, I'm sorry to tell yer, but last week I saw them a penny cheaper in another market. Which means that unless ye're all talk, yer've got to sell yours for the same price. That's tenpence ha'penny.'

The stallholder scratched his head. 'Anyone that sold them for that price would be losing money on them. And I've got a family to keep, I can't afford to give stuff away.'

'Then yer shouldn't tell lies to people, should yer, lad? I can understand yer having a family to keep, 'cos I've got three kids meself, but that doesn't give yer the right to mislead yer customers.'

There were a few women at the stall now, all showing interest in the conversation going on between Nellie and the by now red-faced stallholder. And they all seemed to be on Nellie's side because they were nodding their heads in agreement with her words. Trying to keep his voice even because he knew he could lose custom here, he spread out his hands. 'If yer can prove yer've seen those stockings cheaper elsewhere, then I'll do what I said I would. But I need proof in the form of a receipt.'

Molly's eyes were wide. She hadn't got a clue what her mate was up to because never once had the price of stockings been mentioned. And as she was always with Nellie at the shops, she'd know if she'd bought stockings. But like the rest of the women now listening in, she'd have to wait and see what came next.

'Oh, I haven't got no receipt, lad, I threw it out of the train window.'

'What are yer on about, missus, which train window?'

'The train I was sitting on with the stockings in a bag on me knee.'

'Yer've lost me now, missus.' The man knew he couldn't afford to lose his temper. Even though his patience was wearing thin he controlled his words and voice. 'What has the train got to do with the price of my stockings?'

'Nothing really, lad. I was just telling yer, I was sitting on a train. Yer see, I bought the stockings in a market in Glasgow and was on me way home, on the Glasgow to Liverpool train.'

The man saw Molly put a hand over her mouth to keep the laughter back, and heard the tittering of the other women. And because he wouldn't have lasted a week on the market, never mind ten years, if he hadn't a sense of humour, he threw his head back and roared. 'Oh, dear, oh, dear, yer really had me going then, missus. I didn't know whether to ask yer politely to move on, or strangle yer. And now I don't know whether to ask yer to marry me, or offer yer a job.'

'Oh, I've already got one feller, lad, and as I'm very fond of him I wouldn't want to swap him for a younger model. And I'm not after a job, either, but the offer was a nice thought and I thank yer. What I would accept is an offer to sell me those long stockings for tenpence ha'penny a pair.'

'No can do, missus, 'cos I can't stand the sight of me kids crying with hunger. What I will do, because yer've been a good sport and livened up me day, I'll split me loss with yer and yer can have the stockings for elevenpence. How's that?'

Nellie's grin stretched from ear to ear. It didn't take her long to count how many girls there were she could give stockings to for Christmas. And she didn't forget her mate, either. There was Jill, Doreen, Rosie, Lily, Phoebe and Ruthie. And the same again for Molly. 'Seeing as ye're being so kind, I'll take twelve pairs of stockings off yer hands for elevenpence a pair. What d'yer say, is that a deal?'

It certainly was, but the stallholder wasn't going to show his pleasure. If the women knew he was making threepence profit on each pair, they'd hang him. Selling them for elevenpence dropped his profit to tuppence ha'penny, but twelve pairs at once more than evened things up. 'Go on, yer twisted me arm.'

Four of the six women at the stall said they'd have a pair each, seeing as they were such a bargain. So all in all, the man was more than happy and even began to take a liking to Nellie. If he had someone like her working on his stall they'd do a roaring trade. 'I'll put them in a bag for yer, missus.'

'We're not in a hurry, lad, we want to see what else yer've got. See to the others first while me and me mate decide what we want.'

The two women walked along side the stall. 'Who are the stockings for, Nellie?' Molly asked. 'I need some too, yer know.'

She began to tick them off on her fingers. 'I want to give Jill, Doreen, Lily, Rosie and Phoebe a pair. That's five. And as you want the same, only with two pair for Ruthie, then that's about right.'

'What about you and me, sunshine? Aren't we going to have a decent pair of stockings for Christmas? I'm fed up walking round with ladders all the time.'

'I'll ask him for an extra two pair, girl, then we'll be sorted.' Nellie's eyes were moving over the goods on display. 'Ay, there's something your Ruthie would like.'

Molly picked up one of the small comb cases her mate was pointing to. When she opened it up, she chuckled. 'It's got a comb and mirror in. Our Ruthie would be over the moon with one of these 'cos she's not half vain. She spends a lot of time looking at herself in the mirror. She's a lot more forward than Jill and Doreen were at that age, and older in the head. If she got one of these she'd be made up and spend half her life looking into the mirror and combing her hair. In a month it would be worn out.'

'Have they got a price on, girl?'

'A shilling, which isn't bad. And I can get the money off Jack so he can give it to her as her present.'

'What are yer getting for the other two? Yer usually buy underskirts.'

'I know, but there's not much use this year because Jill is getting quite big, it would be tight across her tummy, and Doreen's making her own. Plus she's making two for Ruthie, which is a big help. So I'm stuck as to what to buy the older girls. Ruthie will need a blouse and skirt, maybe a jumper, because hopefully she'll get a job after Christmas.'

Nellie was fingering a scarf which was on top of a pile she was leaning her elbow on. 'Feel this, girl, how nice and soft it is. I bet the girls would appreciate one of these to keep them warm through the winter. And he's got them in all different colours.'

Molly rubbed the soft fleecy material between two fingers.

'Oh, yeah, sunshine, ye're right, they do feel nice and soft, and they'd be warm. How much are they?'

'Two and six it says on the card. And that's not bad considering the quality.'

'No, it isn't. I think I'll take a maroon one and the other in dark blue. And I can get them a box of chocolates to go with them.' She put her hand to her mouth. 'I nearly forgot about Rosie, what's the matter with me! Put a dark beige one with the other two, Nellie, while I reckon up how much it will all come to. I'm cutting the stockings down to four pair because if I'm giving the girls scarves and chocolates, I don't need to give them stockings as well. So, two pair for Ruthie and two pair for me. I'm going all reckless with me money because I'd hate to get a ladder in me stockings on Christmas morning and not have a pair to change into. The man won't mind me cutting down on the stockings, not when I'm buying the comb case and three scarves as well.'

Nellie contorted her face. 'I've been thinking . . . I could get a scarf for Lily and one for Phoebe. They're nice presents and I'll give them stockings as well. When the bloke comes over I'll ask him how much I owe.'

'Well, I want four pairs at elevenpence each, a shilling for the comb set and three scarves at half a crown.' Molly was deep in concentration as she mentally added up how much she would be paying out, her lips moving as she murmured to herself.

Nellie watched the concentration on her friend's face as she was adding up the prices in her head. Nellie couldn't count up in her head like that, she'd have to use her fingers and toes. And as she was getting five pairs of stockings at elevenpence each, she didn't have enough fingers and toes to go round, so she'd wait until the man worked it out and asked for his money. She wouldn't be overcharged because her mate would be watching and counting.

'I get that to twelve and tuppence, sunshine, so that's not bad at all. I'll get a pair of those socks for Jack, plus a packet of hankies, and I'll get him cigarettes off me sweet club.'

There had been a little rush as customers buying always brought more people to a stall. So the stallholder was a happy man when he made his way over to the two women. 'I'm sorry to have kept yer. I had quite a little spurt there, I'm glad to say. But I'm all yours now, so what was it yer wanted – twelve pair of stockings?'

'Oh, ye're too late now, lad, we've changed our mind.' Nellie saw the man's face drop and, telling herself he was only trying to make a living like her own husband, she quickly put his mind at rest. 'It's all right, lad, I think yer'll be pleased about our change of mind 'cos it's more business for yer.'

He grinned and rubbed his hands together. 'Suits me, queen. What are yer after now?'

'Serve me mate first, so we don't get mixed up with the money. I'll wait until she's given yer her order.'

Molly smiled at the man who had been very patient with Nellie when she was rambling on. Not many people would have seen the joke. 'I'll have four pair of the stockings, please. And those three scarves me friend's got in her hand, plus this comb and mirror set. I got that lot to twelve and tuppence before, and I want to add a packet of men's hankies and a pair of black socks. So what will the damage be for all of it?'

The stallholder added up as he gathered her goods together. 'That's thirteen and six, queen, and I don't think yer'll find I've cheated yer when yer look at the prices on other stalls.' He put Molly's purchases in a big brown paper bag and took the pound note she was holding out to him. 'If those hankies and socks are for yer husband, wouldn't yer think of treating him to a shirt as well?'

'Ay, I'm not made of money, yer know. And he'll be getting cigarettes to go with those, so he won't be doing too badly.'

'That's a shame because I've got a new stock of shirts in and they are really pukka quality. Best I've ever had at the money, and I'm not spinning yer a yarn either. But if ye're not interested then not to worry.' The man turned to Nellie. 'What's your order, queen?'

'Four pair of stockings, lad, and these two scarves. And yer can show me one of those shirts yer were trying to flog me friend. My feller takes a sixteen and he likes white.'

The stallholder reached across to the other side of the stall and picked up a white shirt from the top of a pile. 'There yer are, missus, just look at the quality of that. Good cotton that will wash and wash until the cows come home. Not like the cheap muck yer buy that looks like a rag after the first wash. That's only a size fifteen, but I've got one in sixteen if ye're interested.'

Molly was peering over her friend's shoulder. 'Ay, that is good cotton, yer can tell by just looking at it. But how much are they?'

'Four and eleven, queen, and I couldn't knock anything off that 'cos I'm selling them at rock-bottom price as it is.'

Molly looked at the change in her hand. There were two half crowns there, and Jack really did deserve to have something decent to wear over Christmas. God knows he worked hard enough. Never a day off. Even if he was dying of cold he still turned out for work because he knew they'd be hard pushed for money if he was a day short in his wages.

'I'll have a white one, lad,' Nellie said. 'Only it's got to be a size sixteen collar.'

Molly took the plunge. 'I'll have one as well, sunshine, a blue one in size fifteen and a half collar. Yer can put it in the bag with me other things. And when I've paid yer for it, do me a favour and chase me. Otherwise I'll go on spending and won't even have enough left to pay me tram fare home.'

'I'll pay yer tram fare, girl, if that's all ye're worried about. I'd be a poor mate if I sat on a tram and waved to yer through the window as yer walked home.'

'I wouldn't mind walking, the fresh air would do me good. I wouldn't even mind yer waving to me through the window as yer passed me by, sunshine. But I wouldn't appreciate yer blowing me a kiss because that would really look as though yer were rubbing me nose in it.'

The stallholder grinned as he collected Nellie's purchases. He could tell the two women were best of friends because they seemed to get on so well together and had the same sense of humour. But in looks they were as different as chalk from cheese. He'd heard the tall one referred to as Molly, and the short one as Nellie. Molly was quite a pretty woman with a neat figure, blonde hair and clear blue eyes. It was easy to see she'd been a cracker when she was younger. The small one, Nellie, was about seven inches shorter than her friend and at a guess she was about eighteen stone. It was amusing to see her squinting up at her friend with her face doing contortions, as though acting out what she was saying. He imagined she'd be a cuddly bunch of fun, who enjoyed playing tricks on people. Another guess told the stallholder that Molly was the sensible one who kept her friend in check and stopped her from taking her jokes too far.

'D'yer live near each other?' he asked. 'Neighbours?'

'Neighbours and friends for over twenty years, lad,' Nellie told him proudly. 'Yer could say we're practically sisters.' She winked up at Molly before adding. 'Even blood relations, eh, girl?'

Oh, lord, Molly thought, she's going to tell him the tale about cutting our arms and joining them together like the Indians did. 'I wouldn't go as far as blood relations, sunshine, but we're definitely best mates. Always have been and always will be. And as there are a few potential customers at the stall, I suggest we go on our way and leave the man to earn his living.'

'Any time ye're in the market, ladies, don't walk on by. Stop and pass the time of day with me, and I promise not to try and flog yer anything.'

If it was possible for Nellie's breasts to become larger, then they did at that moment. She thought it was a compliment to be asked to stop and talk to the man, as though he was a friend. She'd bet he didn't say that to many of his customers. When she linked Molly's arm and looked up at her, she said, 'That's nice of him, isn't it, girl? And we will do, next time we're in the market. Ta-ra, lad, I hope yer have a good day and yer takings are up.' Then, because there were a few customers listening in, she put on her poshest voice and swanked like no one's business. 'We're going to see one of our friends now. She has a stall the other end of the market. Well, two friends, really, Mary Ann and Sadie.'

'Oh, yer know Mary Ann, do yer?' The stallholder laughed. 'Tell her about the ticket yer threw out of the train window. And tell her Mick said she'd enjoy the joke.'

'Yer know her and Sadie, do you?' Molly asked.

'There's no one who doesn't know Mary Ann, queen, she's been here for donkey's years, and her mother before her. And as for Sadie, every red-blooded bloke on the market was after her when she first started working here. She's a real beauty, and a nice girl as well.'

'Fancy that now!' Nellie's chins were glad when she started to nod her head because being shaken would warm them up. 'It's a small world, isn't it, lad? Well, we'll tell them yer were asking after them. Ta-ra for now.'

As they walked away, she said, 'Yer wouldn't believe it, would yer, girl? Yer don't know who ye're talking to half the time. Yer could be pulling someone to pieces, calling them all the names under the sun, and it could be their sister yer were talking to.'

'I've told yer that dozens of times, sunshine, but yer don't take no notice. Many's the time I've had to shut yer up when the person yer were calling fit to burn was walking behind us. And I have warned yer that yer won't always get away with it. Besides which, I'd probably be the one to get the blame and would end up with me nose broken. They wouldn't go for you 'cos yer nose would be too low down for them.'

Nellie was quiet for a few seconds, her eyes cast down to the ground. Then she looked up and said, 'I'm trying to figure out whether ye're being neighbourly and giving me good advice, or whether yer telling me in a nice way that I'm a midget.'

'A midget! Who said yer were a midget, sunshine, 'cos I'll knock their block off! No, ye're just nice and cuddly.'

Nellie grinned. 'Ay, girl, can yer hear Mary Ann? She can't half shout, can't she? They'll be able to hear her down at the Pier Head.'

'Good for business. Just look at the people round her stall. I'd say it's the only one in the market doing good business. Mind you, it's a lot bigger than any of the others, and I suppose that's because she's been here so long. She did tell us once that the stall used to be her mother's, and her grandmother's before that.'

'Let's go to the end of this trestle table, girl, then we won't be in anyone's way and can have a word with Sadie when she has time. She's bound to come over when she sees us.'

It wasn't long before they were spotted by the beautiful Sadie, whose blonde hair shone like gold-dust and whose bright blue eyes reminded you of the sky on a summer's day. 'Mary Ann was only saying the other day that we hadn't seen yer for a while. We thought yer'd fallen out with us.' When Sadie smiled the sun seemed to come out and shine on those around her. 'How are yer both?'

Molly had taken this girl to her heart from the moment she first set eyes on her. Mary Ann had told her on the quiet that the girl had come from a dreadful home and family. The eldest child, she'd left home because she could no longer stand the abuse and filth. In the few years she'd worked for Mary Ann, she had managed to get two of her sisters and a brother away from the clouts, the foul language and hunger they'd suffered since birth. From the drunken father who would rather spend his money on horses and beer than put clothes on his children's backs, shoes on their feet and food in their belly. A father who had abused her from the age of three, and when she was old enough to stop him, had turned to her younger sisters. A father who would lash out with his hands and feet if any of the children dared to complain about being hungry or going barefoot in the depth of winter.

Molly dragged herself from thoughts of what she would like to do to the parents of this girl who would make any normal person very proud. 'We're fine, sunshine, and I don't have to ask how you are 'cos yer look the picture of health. Still crazy about that boyfriend of yours, are yer?'

'More than ever! And I'll let yer into a little secret. Me and Harry are getting married next year when we've saved up enough money. We're both saving like mad, but it seems to be taking forever. Mind you, yer know me two younger sisters are courting, don't yer? Well, they're helping with the housekeeping money, and me kid brother Jimmy started work a couple of months ago, so that helps as well.'

Mary Ann had spotted them and to the customer she was helping to look through one of the piles of second-hand clothes for a jumper, said, 'You keep rooting through there, Florrie, while I go and see a man about a dog.' She started to shake her head and tut when Florrie pulled out a bright yellow jumper and held it up. 'Put it down, queen, yer'd look like a ruddy canary in that! Besides which, yer'd need a bleeding shoe horn to get into it. Just hang on till I get back and I'll have yer fixed up in no time.'

Lifting her long black skirt, Mary Ann did a jig as she crossed over to Molly and Nellie. 'Strangers in the camp, eh? Where have yer been putting yerselves?' Her sharp eyes never missed a trick and they fastened on a customer nearby who was holding a blue jumper up, inspecting it for holes and also stretching it to see if it would fit her ample figure.

'Elsie, that jumper was a medium size when yer picked it up, and if it's now large with yer pulling it all ways, then ye're buying it whether yer like it or not. Yer've got the ruddy thing pulled out of shape so yer either buy it or stand there and try and sell it to someone else. The price is sixpence, but if yer can sell it for more then I won't mind yer making a profit as long as I get me tanner.'

The woman threw the jumper back on the pile. 'Ye're all heart, aren't yer, Mary Ann? Yer don't mind me selling it and making a profit as long as yer get your money. Well, yer can sod off, that's what yer can do. The flaming thing isn't worth a tanner.'

Molly had seen Mary Ann and Sadie in action before with awkward customers, and thought they were fantastic at smoothing things over with a laugh and a joke. She wondered if their technique would work for her. There was only one way to find out. She called across to the woman, 'Don't worry, sunshine, I'll buy the jumper off Mary Ann. I was watching yer with it 'cos it's me very favourite colour and it would fit me. I had me fingers crossed that yer'd put it down and I could have it. Yer've done me a favour, sunshine, and I'm delighted. Will yer throw it over here, please?'

This got Elsie's back up. 'Well, you cheeky cow! Who the hell do yer think you are, telling me to throw the jumper over to you? Yer can sod off, lady, 'cos I saw it first and I'm the one what's going to buy it. If you want a jumper, then look for one yerself like I had to do.' She opened her purse and took out a silver sixpence which she held out to Sadie. 'Here yer are, girl, pass it to Mary Ann right away so she can't charge me a day's interest on the money.'

Mary Ann had bright red hair tied up in a bun on top of her head, and she had a very loud laugh. Hair and laugh went very well together. Molly's first piece of negotiating had tickled her fancy. 'Oh, that was brilliant, queen, I couldn't have done better meself. Don't yer think she was good, Elsie?'

The customer was pushing the blue jumper into a large bag and didn't know whether to laugh or cry. She had been hoping to get a penny knocked off the price, and probably would have done if that nosy cow had minded her own business. But she wasn't going to let anyone know she was discommoded. And anyway, the jumper was well worth sixpence and would look good on her on Christmas Day. 'I'll see yer at the weekend when my feller gets paid, Mary Ann, 'cos I need a skirt to go with the jumper. Will yer keep yer eye open for one for us?' Elsie's mouth did a good impression of a sneer as she glanced at Molly. 'After all, I am one of yer best customers. Not like some I could mention.'

'Of course yer are, Elsie. If it weren't for the likes of you my kids wouldn't be getting best butter on their bread, it would be back to dripping. The backbone of my trade, that's what you and me other regular customers are, Elsie, as yer keep reminding me. And I'll have a skirt for yer when yer come on Saturday. Whether it's the colour yer want, or whether it'll fit yer or not is another thing, but I will have a skirt for yer.'

Sadie tapped the stallholder on the arm. In a voice thick with laughter, she said, 'Mary Ann, will yer just look at Florrie? She's trying to get that yellow jumper on over her coat and she's got herself in a hell of a state. She can't get it on, and she can't get it off, and she's struggling like mad which is making things worse. Yer can't see her head or arms.'

'Oh, my God, will yer look at the state of her!' Her voice as loud as a foghorn, Mary Ann started to shout at the same time as she lifted her long skirt and made for the unfortunate woman.

'Stop struggling, Florrie, yer stupid cow, d'yer want to give yerself a heart attack? I mean, if that's what ye're trying to do, well that's your business. But I'd be grateful if yer would spare a thought for my trade if yer did. The nearest hospital is miles away so I'd just have to leave yer to get on with it. Except I'd be beholden to yer if yer could manage to fall backwards because these trestle tables are only light and they'd never stand yer weight if yer fell on them.'

A muffled voice came from within the yellow jumper. 'Thanks for yer consideration, Mary Ann, I knew I could rely on yer for sympathy and support. And if yer could see yer way to helping me out of me predicament then I'll do as yer ask and fall backwards. I'll have me heart attack on the shoe stall opposite, there's more room there.'

The crowd that had gathered watched as Mary Ann stood with arms folded and her head tilted to give the matter some thought. 'How the hell yer got in that state, Florrie, is a mystery to me. After me telling yer the jumper was too small for yer, what do yer go and do as soon as me back's turned? You not only try it on, like the stupid cow yer are, yer try it on over yer ruddy coat, that's all! Now tell me where yer head is, Florrie?'

'Attached to me bloody neck, where d'yer think! Of all the bloody stupid questions to be asking when I can't even get me breath . . .'

'The best way to help yerself, Florrie, is to stop struggling as ye're making things ten times worse. Just stay calm and me and Sadie will have that off yer in no time.'

Sadie came hurrying across, concern on her face now. She was very fond of all the regular customers, especially the elderly ones who had always treated her with respect and friendliness. 'How on earth did she get like that?'

'Silly bugger put her arms in first, then when she realised it wasn't such a good idea it was too late and she couldn't get them out again to pull the ruddy thing off her face. If you get one side, sweetheart, and I get the other, we can try and ease it off her. She must be gasping for breath in there.'

It was a slow process because Florrie had got herself all worked up by this time and insisted on struggling inside the jumper. 'If yer don't keep still, queen, I'm either going to knock yer out or send for the fire brigade. It's up to you.'

The struggling stopped and the poor woman stood like a statue, or as a woman standing nearby said: 'She looks like one of them mummy things what yer see in horror films, only they're covered in bandages from head to foot.'

Mary Ann nodded to Sadie. 'Come on, sweetheart, let's get going. We'll inch it up each side a bit at a time.'

It took them ten minutes to get the jumper off, and by that time it had been stretched enough to fit King Kong. Florrie was bright red in the face and was bending over the trestle table taking deep breaths. She looked in such a sad state Mary Ann felt sorry for her. 'Take it easy for a while, Florrie, until yer heart calms down and yer breathing is steady.' She put an arm around the older woman and smiled into her face. 'There's one good thing has come out of it, queen. The jumper didn't fit yer before because it was too small, wasn't it? Well, now you and your feller can both get in it and keep each other warm.'

'Ah, ye're not going to make me buy it, are yer, Mary Ann?'

'No, queen, I'm going to let yer have it for a Christmas present. If yer wash it in warm water and dry it flat, it will probably go back into shape. I still think yer'd look like a canary in it, but yer seem to have taken a liking to it and yer were very good not to have had a heart attack at my stall. That was very thoughtful of yer. But if yer take my advice, yer'll go home now and rest for a while to settle yerself down.'

Sadie rounded the stall to give the woman a hug. 'You take care of yerself, Florrie, 'cos ye're one of me favourite customers.'

That cheered Florrie up no end, and after pushing the jumper into her large handbag, she turned in the direction of her home. 'I'll see yer tomorrow, love, ta-ra. And you, Mary Ann, I'm sorry I made a nuisance of meself, I'll take heed of what yer say in future. Ta-ra.'

As they watched her walk away, Mary Ann put her arm around Sadie's waist and sighed. 'I'll probably be able to laugh about this later, but she had me worried there for a while. She must have got frightened when she found she couldn't get the ruddy thing off, and although I made fun of her having a heart attack, it could very well have happened.' Another deep sigh. 'Anyway, all's well that ends well.'

'I'll get back to Molly and Nellie,' Sadie said. 'I was telling them the superior quality clothing isn't on the stall now, we have two racks for the clothes in good condition. And when I told them we had some very good stuff in, they were interested. I was about to show them when I saw that all wasn't well with Florrie. But if you can manage on yer own for a while, I'll take them now.'

'We're not exactly run off our feet, are we, sweetheart? I can manage. If I get a rush on, I'll give yer a call. And when Molly and Nellie do buy anything, they usually spend a few bob, not just sixpence for a jumper with no holes in, or fourpence for a jumper with. I'll see them before they leave to have a laugh and a joke with them. Unless, of course, a miracle happens and we have a sudden rush of customers.' Mary Ann grinned. 'Whoever heard of a miracle at Paddy's Market?'

On impulse, Sadie leaned forward and kissed the woman who had been like a mother to her. 'I do love you, Mary Ann. And the day I first came to this market and met you, well, that was surely a miracle.'

Chapter Eleven

Molly and Nellie came away from Paddy's Market laden down with bags and bundles of every shape and size. But both wore a pleased expression at three hours well spent in both time and money.

'It's no use thinking of getting the eggs and bread down here,' Molly said. 'It's taking me all me time to carry this lot. I'll have to get what I want from the corner shop when I get home.'

'Yeah, me too, girl, I feel as though me arms are being pulled out of their sockets.' Nellie was so pleased with herself she would have been walking on air if it weren't for being so weighed down. 'But we did very well, girl, and I feel dead chuffed with me little self.'

Molly turned her head when she heard the sound of a tram trundling towards them on its journey from the Pier Head to the terminus at Fazakerley, in the distance. 'There's a tram coming, sunshine, d'yer think yer'll be able to cross the road with that load in time to catch it?'

'I'll try, girl, but I couldn't run with this lot for the life of me. I'll try and walk quick, but I'm not promising I won't fall flat on me face in the middle of the road.'

'Here, give me that big bag to carry, that should lighten yer load. I'll run across and keep the tram until yer get there. But for God's sake, sunshine, keep yer eye on the traffic 'cos it's a busy road.'

174

Molly looked both ways, then made a dive for the other side of the wide road. She just made it to the pavement when the tram stopped. 'Hang on a minute, please, until me mate gets here. She's crossing the road now.'

The driver looked out of his side window. 'Oh, blimey, look who it is! Mrs Trouble herself! I've a good mind to go without her.'

Out of breath, Nellie threw her parcels on to the platform. 'I heard that, and if I wasn't so out of breath I'd clock yer one. And I'm surprised yer waited for me 'cos ye're a miserable bugger.'

While this exchange was going on, Molly had placed all the parcels in the space under the stairs so she and Nellie could sit comfortably on the short journey home. Now she turned to where her mate was standing. 'Come on, sunshine, let me give yer a hand up.'

With one hand on the rail of the tram, and the other tight in Molly's hand, Nellie hoisted herself on board. 'Thanks, girl, ye're a real lady.' She narrowed her eyes and glared at the driver. 'That's more than what can be said for you, misery guts.'

'I should ruddy well hope so, missus, 'cos I'm not a lady!'

'Oh, aren't yer! Well, I never would have guessed. So, lad, that means ye're not anything really. You say ye're not a lady, and I can believe that 'cos ye're too ugly. And ye're certainly no gentleman, or not in my eyes anyway. If yer were yer'd know how to treat a lady.'

The driver could hear tutting and clicking of tongues from the other passengers because they should be at the next stop by now. But he wasn't going to let Nellie have the last word. 'Oh, I do know how to treat a lady, missus, when I meet one.'

The man was joking, Nellie knew he was joking, but Molly wasn't taking any chances. With a firm grip on her friend's arm, she pulled her down the aisle. 'Get in that seat by the window where yer can't get up to any mischief.'

'Ah, girl, yer know I can't sit by the window, me backside takes up all the room and there's no space for you. Let me sit on the outside and I promise I won't open me mouth. And, anyway, the driver was only acting daft, he does it every time I get on his tram.'

'I know that, sunshine, but we haven't seen the conductor yet, have we? If he's one of yer sparring partners we could be in for a rough ride and I want you where yer can't get up to any of yer shenanigans.'

So Nellie lifted her bosom with one hand and pressed her tummy in with the other while she struggled into the seat, and grumbled all the time the exercise was taking place. 'Whoever made these seats wants his ruddy bumps feeling. He must think everyone is as thin as a brush handle. Doesn't he know there are woman like me with voluptuous figures who need a bit more space if they're to look ladylike and not show everyone their fleecy-lined drawers?'

'All right, sunshine, ye're in now without any mishaps, so stop yer moaning.'

'I might be in, girl, but you're not! I bet one cheek of yer backside is sitting on fresh air, like mine does when I'm on the outside. And we pay for our seats, so we should be able to get all of our body on them. Next time I'm stuck on the end I'm only going to pay half-price for me ticket 'cos only half of me is on the seat.'

'Well, yer've got a full seat today, sunshine, so we don't need to go through that with the conductor when he comes. Besides, I don't wear fleecy-lined drawers so there'll be no peep show for anyone.'

Nellie gave her friend a dig in the ribs and nearly sent her flying. Just in time Molly grabbed the rail of the seat in front, otherwise she'd have ended up sprawled on the floor showing more than her knickers. 'For heaven's sake, Nellie, what did yer do that for? Yer nearly pushed me off the seat!'

'I didn't mean to, girl, it's just that I don't know me own strength sometimes. Anyway yer haven't fallen off so don't be crying before ye're hurt. I only wanted to tell yer how made up I am over all the things we got today. I think everything we bought was a bargain, don't you? Some of the stuff Mary Ann had on those rails was like new. No one would ever dream that they were second-hand.'

Molly saw the woman in the seat in front of them prick up her ears, and although she wasn't ashamed of buying second-hand clothes, Molly didn't think it was anyone else's business and didn't want it advertised. So it was her turn to dig her friend in the ribs. 'We'll talk about it when we get home, sunshine, and we'll take them out of the bags and have another look at them over a nice hot cup of tea. Then mine are going away in the wardrobe until I get some Christmas paper to wrap them in.'

'Oh, I'll be wearing my coat tomorrow, girl, I'm not waiting for Christmas. It's not as though it's . . .' Nellie was stopped in mid-sentence by a sharp kick on her shin bone. 'What was that in aid of? That didn't half hurt.'

Molly nodded her head to the lady sitting in front and put a finger to her lips. 'Little pigs have big ears, sunshine.' She spoke in a low voice. 'I don't want the whole world to know my business.'

Nellie and her chins nodded knowingly. 'I get yer, girl, some people are too bloody nosy for their own good.'

The trouble was, Nellie didn't believe in whispering and the woman in the seat in front turned around and glared. 'Are you insinuating that I've nothing better to do than listen to what people like you get up to? I've more to do with me time, Mrs Whoever Yer Are.'

'That's a contradiction in terms, Mrs Whatever-yer-name-is,' Nellie replied. 'If yer weren't listening to me and me mate, how did yer know what we were taking about?'

The woman flushed. 'Because you have a voice like a foghorn and it would be difficult not to hear you.'

'I think that's enough, if yer don't mind,' Molly interrupted. 'Ye're behaving like children. Why don't yer both grow up?'

'Excuse me,' said Mrs Hoity-Toity in front, her back now as stiff as a ramrod, 'it wasn't me that started this off, it was your friend.'

'Yeah, and I'll ruddy well finish it off if yer don't shut that mouth of yours.' Nellie was in fighting mood, with her jaw jutting out. 'And I don't know why ye're trying to speak as if yer've got a plum in yer mouth 'cos anyone can tell ye're as common as muck.'

'Well, I declare! How dare you call me common!' The woman was bristling with indignation. 'I'll have you know I live in a six-roomed house in a very respectable street. I wasn't brought up in the gutter.'

All heads turned in the direction of the feuding couple. The passengers were making up their minds who they thought would win if it came to blows. If the truth be told, most of them would have put their money on Nellie. The other woman seemed a snob, and she hadn't made herself any friends by bragging about her six-roomed house. So when Molly tried to bring the argument to an end they were disappointed and mentally labelled her a spoilsport.

'That's enough from both of yer!' She said in a very determined voice. 'Ye're acting like two-year-olds.' She turned her head. 'Nellie, not another word out of yer or I'll get off the tram and leave yer to make yer own way home with all yer baggage.' Then she tapped the shoulder of the woman in front. 'If I were you, missus, I'd keep me remarks to meself until I got back to me six-roomed house in the very respectable street ye're fond of bragging about.'

The conductor had come down the stairs after collecting the fares from the passengers on the top deck, just as the confrontation started. Being a wise man, he decided not to collect the fares until the situation had been sorted out. Now, as peace seemed to have been restored, he clicked his ticket machine. 'Fares, please.'

Molly had the fourpence ready in the palm of her hand. 'I'll pay while you look out of the window at the scenery, sunshine.' She winked at the conductor as she handed the money over. 'Pretend the gas lamps are big green trees and the pavements are strewn with flowers. That will cheer yer up.'

The conductor was grinning as he turned the handle on his ticket machine and handed over the two tickets. 'D'yer know, I think I'll try that meself, missus. A bit of greenery and flowers would certainly cheer me up. I'll have to get me imagination working, 'cos I don't think we pass one tree or bit of greenery from the Pier Head to the cemetery in Longmoor Lane, Fazakerley.'

Nellie turned, about to tell him he must be blind because there were odd trees here and there, but the look on her mate's face told her if wouldn't be wise. So she did as she was told and stared out of the window of the moving tram. But no matter how hard she tried, for the life of her she couldn't see any resemblance between a lamp post and a ruddy tree.

The passenger in front got off the tram at the stop before the friends were due to alight, and as soon as she was out of earshot Nellie growled, 'Stuck-up cow! I could willingly have clocked her one. I wonder who she thinks she is? She was looking down her nose at us, girl, didn't yer notice?'

'Of course I noticed, sunshine, but it didn't get up my nose like it did yours. I feel sorry for people like her. She's so busy trying to be something she isn't, she must lead a very miserable life.' Molly leaned towards her friend and chuckled. 'She wouldn't know a joke if it jumped up and bit her on the nose. I bet she doesn't laugh a lot or enjoy life as we do, so I wouldn't waste me breath talking to her. And now, sunshine, it's time for us to make our way to the platform so I can get all the bags together before the tram stops. I'll get off first with them, then I'll give yer a hand to get down.'

But Molly's hand wasn't needed because the conductor came to their assistance and put all the bags on the pavement. Then he helped Nellie down and raised his peaked hat to them before pressing the bell to let the driver know it was safe to be on their way.

'Now let's get organized, sunshine, and make life easier for ourselves.' Molly moved the bags and bundles into two piles, and said, 'I'll take the biggest, you take that one. We'll manage okay because they're more awkward than heavy really, and we haven't got far to go. When we get to the bottom of our street we can take a breather if we need to.'

'Whatever yer say, girl, is fine by me.' Nellie lifted both arms while her friend put a package under each, then she put as many as she could in each hand and the last one she put under her chin. 'I won't be able to talk, girl, so don't be worrying, thinking I'm sick.'

'If you didn't speak for two minutes, sunshine, then I would think yer were sick. But let's press on and get home as quick as we can. I could just murder a cup of tea.'

Forgetting she had a bag under her chin, Nellie nodded and the bag fell to the ground. 'I'm sorry, girl, I forgot. And I can't pick it up, either, or I'll drop the ruddy lot.'

After retrieving the parcel, Molly put it back under Nellie's layers of chins, and said, 'Don't move yer mouth to answer this, sunshine, but when we get home I'd like yer to remind me never to go shopping with yer again. It's an experience that doesn't do me heart or me temper any good.' Setting forth, she encouraged her friend, 'Come on, Nellie, just think of the nice cup of tea yer can have as soon as we get home. And if our Ruthie didn't pinch them before she went to school, yer can have two custard creams and two ginger nuts.'

That was the wrong thing to say because it pleased Nellie so much she smiled and nodded her head, letting the parcel fall again. 'I couldn't help it, girl, so don't be giving me daggers. If yer don't want me to talk, then don't speak to me.'

Molly picked the parcel up, pushed it against Nellie's neck and pulled her head down to anchor it safely. 'Not another word out of either of us, d'yer hear? Oh, and don't answer that, Nellie, for both our sakes.'

Feeling refreshed after a hot cup of tea and some biscuits, the two friends started to open the packages. 'I'll do this big one first, girl, 'cos it's me coat and I can't wait to try it on properly. It seemed to fit me all right in the market, but with no mirrors it was hard to tell what I looked like in it.' Nellie lifted the navy blue coat from its wrapping, shook it out, then slipped her arms into the sleeves. 'There yer are, girl, what d'yer think? It's a good fit, but that's not much good if it looks terrible on me.'

'It doesn't look terrible at all, sunshine, it looks a treat on yer. It fits well, the colour suits yer, and what a bargain it was at seven and sixpence! If you put that in to be dry cleaned, it would come back looking like a brand new coat. No one would believe where yer got it from and how much yer paid for it.'

'I don't care what people think, girl, they don't put the bread on the table. I'll tell me family, but I ain't telling no one else.' Nellie stood back on tiptoe so she could see as much of herself in the mirror over the mantelpiece as possible. Then, nodding her head, she said, 'Even though I say it and shouldn't, I've got to admit it does something for me. Don't yer think it makes me look thinner and younger, girl?'

Molly nodded. 'George will fall for yer all over again when he sees yer in it. And what about the blouse yer bought? Get it out and let's see what it looks like on yer.'

'What about you, girl? You've bought stuff as well. Don't yer want to have a look at the things yer've got for yerself?'

'This room isn't big enough for both of us to be trying things on, so I'll wait until we've seen everything of yours.'

Nellie draped the coat over the arm of the couch before taking off her jumper and trying on the cream-coloured blouse. It had long sleeves, fastened at the wrists with pearl buttons which matched the ones down the front, and a tailored collar. And there was plenty of material in it, which was what Nellie needed, for it wasn't tight on her breasts and tummy like most of the clothes she wore. 'Ooh, ay, I don't half feel like a toff in this. It feels lovely and soft on me arms, and there's plenty of room for me to move around in it.' She made a dive for the rest of the parcels. 'Which one is the skirt in, I wonder?'

'Have patience, sunshine, and open each parcel until yer come to it.'

The navy blue skirt Nellie unearthed wasn't in such good condition as the blouse or coat, but it fitted her well and the colours blended with each other. 'I think yer got bargains there, sunshine, they all fit and look really good,' Molly told her. 'On the whole it's been a good day for Helen Theresa McDonough, private investigator and now fashion model.'

Nellie's face screwed up when she smiled. 'It won't make no difference to me, yer know, girl. I'm not like that snooty cow on the tram what lives in a six-roomed house. Oh, no. No matter how high I go in society, I'll still be yer mate.'

'Gee, thanks, sunshine, I'll be able to sleep soundly tonight, knowing that.' Molly pushed her chair back. 'Now you've seen everything yer bought, yer can wrap it all up again so I can have a dekko at mine. I want to put all the presents away upstairs before our Ruthie gets home otherwise she'll want to wear the blouse and skirt I bought her to show off in school tomorrow. She's not seeing them until Christmas morning, when they'll look better because they'll be washed and pressed by then.'

'Can I leave the presents I bought here, girl? 'Cos yer know what I'm like, I can't keep anything to meself.'

'Of course yer can, sunshine, they can go on top of the wardrobe with mine.' Molly shook her head as she watched her friend trying to fold the second-hand coat, blouse and skirt to get them back in the bag Sadie had put them in. But Nellie wasn't used to being as neat as Sadie, she was always in too much of a hurry, and she was making a right mess of the procedure. 'I'll do it, Nellie, or they'll look like rags by the time yer've finished with them.'

Nellie wasn't going to argue with that! So she stepped aside, knowing Molly would take as much care of the clothes as she would if they'd come from the most expensive shop in the city of Liverpool. The teapot caught her eye as she sat down and she automatically put her hand out towards it. 'Ay, girl, this tea's still warm. If we put a drop of boiling water to it we could have another cuppa.'

'Blimey, I thought I was a tea tank, sunshine, but ye're worse than me! Put a drop of water in the kettle and put a light under the gas ring then, but don't fill the ruddy kettle – just enough for a couple of cups. Yer'll eat and drink me out of house and home, you will.'

While Nellie went out to the kitchen, Molly found the skirt and blouse she'd bought off Sadie's superior quality rail. The blouse was maroon, in a crêpe material, with a frilled neck and long sleeves. It fitted Molly to perfection, as did the light grey skirt which was shaped to the hip then fell in soft folds. There were a few marks on it, but what could you expect for half a crown? And they'd come off with a bit of attention.

Nellie stood in the doorway. 'Ay, girl, yer don't half look nice. That colour really suits yer.'

Molly inspected herself in the mirror. 'Well, I should look presentable on Christmas Day if nothing else.'

'Oh, yer've got to look yer best on Christmas Day, with you being the hostess.'

'Hostess?'

'At yer party, of course, soft girl.'

'Oh, I'm having a party, am I? Well, that's the first I've heard of it, sunshine. Or is it supposed to be a surprise?'

Nellie pretended to lose patience. 'How can it be a surprise when it's in your house? Yer'd have to know about it to see to the eats and everything. But since I'm deputy hostess, I'll help yer like I always do.'

'Nellie, do I have any say in this party which you seem to think is a foregone conclusion?'

'Of course yer do, girl! But I don't know why yer make such a song and dance about it every Christmas because yer always give in in the end. Corker and Alec are seeing to the drinks as usual, and the women are going to club together for the food. They'll all do their share of making cakes and sandwiches. So what more can yer ask for?'

'I think yer've got a ruddy cheek, Nellie McDonough. It's all signed, sealed and delivered as far as you're concerned, and to hell with what I want.'

'Ye're an ungrateful bugger, Molly Bennett, that's what yer are. All yer friends are rallying around to help, and all ye're doing is moaning.'

The two friends faced each other across the table and burst out laughing. They both enjoyed this yearly ritual even though they knew in advance how it was going to end. Molly loved having the party in her house, she wouldn't have it any other way. She would have liked to be able to afford the food and drinks, but that was impossible on Jack's wages. Even if he was on twice as much money they couldn't afford the food and drink for about twenty people.

'Yer've done the rounds, have yer, sunshine?' The kettle began to whistle and Molly hastened to the kitchen. 'Hang on, Nellie, I won't be long. And don't be shouting things out to me, I hate it when I can't see yer face.'

Nellie waited patiently until Molly came through with two steaming cups. 'What did yer mean, girl, by saying yer hated it when yer couldn't see me face?'

After putting the cups down, Molly said, 'Well, it's like this, yer see. Your face is a dead give-away. I can always tell if ye're telling the truth or having me on.'

'Well, that's nice I must say! Anyone would think I was the biggest liar on God's earth! And I never tell no lies to you, girl. Or if I do they're only little white ones.'

'Who said anything about lies? I never mentioned the word, which goes to show what a bad mind yer've got, Nellie McDonough. I said when yer were having me on, and there's a world of difference between that and telling lies.'

Her friend opened a hand and slapped herself across the face. 'Take that for being bad-minded, Nellie, and watch out or the next slap will be harder.'

Molly shook her head and grinned. 'Ye're as thick as two short planks, d'yer know that? Or as they say, ye're two sheets to the wind.'

'Yer could also say I was tuppence short of a shilling, girl, 'cos I've heard someone saying that. It wasn't to me, like, or I'd have clocked her one, but I remember hearing it.'

'I could also call meself daft for putting up with it, I suppose, so that makes us even. And now we've agreed that we're both a bit batty, can we go back to what we were talking about? Have yer been doing the usual rounds?'

Nellie lifted a stiffened finger. 'If we're going to talk business, girl, I'm getting me posh chair. I can think better sitting in that with me elbows on the arms, and I'm sure it makes me a bit more intelligent.'

Molly nodded. 'Oh, right, girl, whatever makes yer happy.' She watched as her friend moved the wooden dining chair to the end of the table before carrying over the carver. Then once her friend's elbows were on the arms of the chair, and her little legs were swinging backwards and forwards, Molly repeated, 'Have yer been doing yer usual rounds? Yer see, it's just over a week off and I'd like to be kept up-to-date about the arrangements for my party. It's not too much to ask, is it?'

Nellie's bosom swelled with the importance of what she was about to say. 'Corker, George and Alec are seeing to all the drink, even for the youngsters who are having their party next door in the Corkhills'. And Maisie, Ellen and meself are going to make the cakes and provide the fillings for the sandwiches.'

'Did I hear yer say you were making some cakes, or were my ears deceiving me?'

'There's nothing wrong with yer hearing, girl, even I know that.'

'But yer can't make cakes, Nellie! Even yer fairy cakes turn out like rocks! Have yer told Ellen and Maisie yer can't bake?'

Her friend had the grace to lower her head in shame. 'No, I haven't, girl. I thought I'd buy a dozen from Hanley's and they wouldn't know the difference.' She looked up with a ferocious expression on her face. 'Unless you told them, like a clat-tale, and I wouldn't never speak to yer again if yer did that.'

'So yer wouldn't come to the Christmas party? Wouldn't be my deputy hostess?'

'Well, if yer put it like that, girl, I could always leave it until after Christmas to fall out with yer.' Then the little woman had a thought. 'Better still, I'd leave it until after the New Year 'cos I don't want to miss that party either.' The carver chair was slightly lower than the wooden dining chairs and Nellie kept forgetting that while her bosom fitted nicely on top of the table from a dining chair, it wasn't so with her posh chair. And when she leaned forward quickly, she always banged herself. 'Yer wouldn't believe it but I've done it again.' She rubbed a tender spot. 'D'yer know, girl, I'm black and blue all over. My feller is beginning to think I've got a fancy man on the quiet.'

'What d'yer want me to do, sunshine, put a sign up saying, "Beware"?'

'Nah! It'll do George good to think he's got a rival. If he beats it out of me, I'll have to say it's your Jack, or Tony from the butcher's.'

'Yer can leave my Jack out of it, he's quite happy with the woman he's got. And I think it's time to wrap it up for the day, I want everything put away before Ruthie comes in. I'll give yer a hand with your stuff as far as yer front door.'

'Yer can be real hard-hearted when yer want, girl,' Nellie sighed as she pushed her chair back.' I was going to say yer haven't got a heart, yer've got a swinging brick, but I won't say that, I'll stick to a heart of stone.'

'Oh, aye? What's a brick made of, Nellie?'

'How the hell do I know, girl? They didn't teach me nothing like that at school. What good would it have done me anyway? A girl can't get a job as a brickie.'

'So yer don't know that a stone is the same as a brick, then?'

'I've never given it much thought, really, but whatever you say I'll take your word for it. Although it's not something that's going to improve me education and change me whole lifestyle, is it? Like I'm never going to learn all those big words you use sometimes, just 'cos yer know I haven't got a clue what they mean.'

'That's yer own fault, sunshine, because how many times have I told yer to buy a dictionary?'

'And how many times have I told yer that yer have to know how to spell a word before yer can look it up in the bleeding dictionary? I mean, if yer wanted to make it yer life's work, well, that's a different matter, but meself, I couldn't be arsed.' Nellie picked up one of the bags, and a sly look came over her face. 'I'll get yer one of these fine days, though, girl, and it'll be with a word yer've never in yer life heard of, so there!'

Molly heaved up the heaviest bag. 'You go through that dictionary tonight, sunshine, and get George to help yer find a word with about twelve or thirteen letters in it. And I'll bet yer a tanner I can tell yer what it means.'

Nellie grinned. 'Have yer tanner ready tomorrow, girl, 'cos my George is good at words and I bet he'll come up with one that'll have yer stumped.'

Molly chuckled. 'It's a bet, sunshine. But you have yer tanner with yer when yer come in the morning, ready to hand over when yer lose.' She pushed her friend towards the door. 'That's it, now on yer way, Nellie, and no more excuses to keep yer here. I'll be behind yer with this bag and I'll drop it in the hall for yer.'

Molly just managed to get all her shopping upstairs and into the wardrobe when she heard the door knocker. Ruthie didn't have a key to let herself in so Molly tripped down the stairs. Because she was happy to have bought so many presents, she was smiling when she opened the door. 'Hello, sunshine.' She noticed her daughter was out of breath and asked, 'Have yer been running? Ye're puffing like a steam train.'

'Oh, Mam, yer'll never guess.' The girl had a hand pressed to her chest which was painful after running so fast and so far. 'I'm going after a job tomorrow, Miss Harrison has given me and Bella cards to take with us. And guess where it is?'

'I couldn't guess, sunshine, There's so many places we could be here all day and I still wouldn't guess right. Come on, don't keep me in suspense, tell me.'

Ruthie took a deep breath. 'Johnson's Dye Works.'

Her mother's mouth opened wide in surprise. 'Go 'way! Where our Doreen started when she left school? Well, fancy that now! Wait until she knows, she'll be made up. That's where she met Maureen, when they both went for an interview, and they loved it there. Oh, Ruthie, sunshine, I hope yer get the job because they're a good family firm.'

'Mam, can I ask yer a favour?' There was pleading in the girl's bright blue eyes. 'I don't want to go in me gymslip, so d'yer think Doreen will lend me one of her skirts and a blouse or jumper? The skirt will be a bit big around the waist but I could put a pin in it.'

'What about Bella, sunshine, will she be wearing her gymslip? She wouldn't like it if she went in her school uniform and you went all dressed up.' Molly was trying to remember what Doreen wore for her interview, but couldn't think because it was over six years ago now. 'Does Bella know ye're going to ask this?'

Ruthie nodded. 'She's hoping her mam will let her wear a skirt and jumper she's got her for Christmas. And I'd look daft in me long black stockings and gymslip. Go on, Mam, say I can go and ask Doreen? I bet she'd lend me something to wear.'

It was on the tip of Molly's tongue to tell her daughter about the clothes she'd just hidden away upstairs, but common sense told her they weren't fit to wear as they were, they'd need to be washed and pressed and there wasn't time for that. 'Go on, sunshine, I'm sure Doreen will help yer out. She'll give yer a few tips on what to say at the interview as well.' When Ruthie turned to go back through the door, her heart beating fast with excitement, Molly said, 'Don't stay too long, sunshine, 'cos I'll need yer to go to the chippy later. I haven't cooked a dinner today, I thought we'd like something from the chippy for a change.'

'There's plenty of time, Mam, me dad doesn't get in from work until a quarter to six.' Ruthie threw her arms around her mother's waist and pressed her head close. 'I feel a bit sick with excitement, and worrying that I'll do all right at the interview.'

Molly stroked her long blonde hair. 'I think if yer ask Doreen yer'll find she felt exactly the same as you do. In fact, everyone does when they go for an interview. I remember being scared stiff, and could hardly answer the questions I was being asked. But I got the job, and I bet you will too. So go and have a word with yer sister and she'll give yer a few tips and put yer mind at rest.' She stood on the front step until the door opposite opened and she waved to Doreen. 'Wait until yer hear what yer sister has to tell yer. I'll see yer later, ta-ra.'

It felt strange to Molly having no dinner to see to. And she'd done her housework this morning before she went out, so there was nothing to do, only put a few cobs of coal on the fire so the house was warm for Jack to come home to. The fireside chair looked tempting and Molly told herself there was no point in looking for work, she may as well as take the weight off her feet while she had the chance. But old habits die hard, and after fifteen minutes she became restless. Usually she'd be bustling about in the kitchen, keeping her eye on the potatoes and veg and whatever meat they were having. Hanging around like this didn't suit her at all.

And as though in answer to her needs, through the window she saw her two daughters hurrying across the cobbled street. She had the door open before they had a chance to knock.

'What about that for coincidence, Mam?' Doreen looked as pleased as Punch. 'Fancy her getting an interview at Johnson's of all places! I've told her to tell whoever interviews her that I worked there until I was called up for war work. And she's not to forget to say how much I enjoyed working there, and how the sewing and cutting out I learned has really come in useful. It might not do any good, but it certainly won't do any harm.'

Ruthie pulled on Molly's skirt. 'Look, Mam, Doreen said I can wear this skirt and jumper tomorrow, and she's lending me a pair of long stockings.'

'Oh, I'll lend her a pair of stockings in case she ladders them,' Molly said. 'You take those back, Doreen, I'll find her a pair.'

'No, Mam, I've made a deal with Ruthie. If she gets the job she can keep all of the clothes. They're not in bad condition so she'd get plenty of wear out of them.'

'If a woman interviews me, I'll tell her she's got to give me the job or I won't have a stitch of clothing to me name. And I'm sure she wouldn't like to be the cause of me walking the streets without a coat to me back.'

Molly smiled. This youngest daughter of hers had so much confidence she'd talk herself into the job. 'And what happens if it's a man who interviews yer, sunshine? Ye're not allowed to pick and choose, yer know.'

'Oh, if it's a man I won't say nothing. I wouldn't be able to, yer see, I'd be struck dumb, scared out of me wits.'

'You, scared out of yer wits? You, who can talk anyone under the table? That is something I'll believe when I see it for meself, sunshine.'

Doreen chuckled. 'I think yer got yerself mixed up there, Mam. Yer don't talk someone under the table, yer talk to them until the cows come home. It's drunks that can drink yer under the table. And that little piece of information I won't charge yer for because ye're me mam and I love the bones of yer.'

Molly put an arm around each of her daughters. 'And I love the bones of you two. And the rest of me family. I reckon I'm the luckiest mother in Liverpool to have the family I've got. And that includes me two sons-in-law and me daughter-in-law. Also me ma and da, Victoria, and all me friends.'

Doreen tapped her on the shoulder. 'Mam, that's what they mean by talking till the cows come home. Because if yer had to mention each of yer friends by name we'd be here all day. And that just tells yer how lucky yer are.'

Chapter Twelve

Molly bit on a piece of toast as she watched her youngest daughter getting ready for an interview for her first job. Already it seemed the baby of the family had turned into a young woman. Out of the gymslip and into a nice blue skirt, blue jumper and long stockings. 'Are yer nervous, sunshine?'

'Terrified, Mam! But Doreen said when she went for the interview there were about six other girls there and they were all nervous too. She said she was glad when Maureen came to sit next to her and started talking because it took her mind off what was to come, and made the time go quicker.'

'Your sister made a life-long friend that day. Her and Maureen are good friends, both loyal to each other and always there when needed.' Molly smiled at her daughter's reflection in the mirror. If she combed her hair much more she'd have a sore scalp. 'I could come on the tram with you and Bella if it would make yer feel better. I don't mean go into the building with yer, just see yer got there safely.'

Ruthie rolled her eyes. 'Don't you start, Mam, it was bad enough yesterday when Mrs Watson said the same thing. I was glad when Bella said no and stuck to her guns. We're quite capable of finding our own way there. Doreen told me to get off the tram the stop after the park and we can't miss the building, it's so big.'

'Here's Bella now, sunshine, yer'd better open the door for her.'

But Bella wasn't alone, she had a very anxious mother in tow. What a worrier Mary Watson was where her only child was concerned. She hated the girl to be out of her sight and had to know where she was at all times. Except for school, of course, and even then if she was five minutes late getting home Mary would stand at the front door wringing her hands. Molly had been telling her for years that she wasn't doing her daughter any favours by wrapping her in cotton wool, but Mary couldn't help the way she was made.

'Molly, I want to go with them, just to make sure they get there safely, I don't like the idea of them getting on the tram on their own. But Bella won't hear of it, she's being very stubborn.'

'We're fourteen now, Mam, not babies!' Bella's face bore the look of someone who had made up their mind and nothing on God's earth would change it. 'We don't need to be mollycoddled. If the girls in our class found out my mother had come along to the interview to hold my hand, I'd be a laughing stock.'

'They'll be all right, Mary, our Ruthie's been on the tram dozens of times on her own.' Molly wouldn't be in the least surprised if Mary didn't follow the girls no matter what anyone said, so she sought to nip it in the bud. 'Mary, yer've got to let go of the apron strings sometime, and what better time than the day Bella goes for her first interview? Let her learn to make her own way in life. In moderation, I mean, not all at once. She can't come to any harm today. Both her and Ruthie have got their heads screwed on the right way. I never went with Jill or Doreen for their first interview, they'd have been horrified if I'd even suggested it. They managed all right, and got the jobs they were after.'

When Mary still didn't look convinced, Molly went on. 'Yer'd really embarrass Bella if yer went, Mary, and she'd be a nervous wreck going in for her interview. Yer don't want that for yer daughter, do yer?'

Ruthie sucked in her breath through clenched teeth. She was getting very impatient with all the talking. If they were old enough to get a job, they were old enough to be trusted to go out on their own. What would Mrs Watson do if Bella got the job? Would she want to take her to work every morning? 'Mam, it says on the card we have to present ourselves for the interview at nine-thirty, and if we don't put a move on we'll never make it on time. If we miss the interview through lateness, Miss Harrison wouldn't be very pleased with us.'

'Go on then, sunshine, and the best of luck. Give us a kiss before yer go. And you give yer mam a kiss, too, Bella. We won't go to the door with yer, but you hurry home and let's know how yer get on. I'm going to make a fresh pot of tea for me and Mary.'

Ruthie winked as she kissed her mother's face. 'Thanks, Mam.'

'I'll be all right, Mam,' Bella told the mother she loved dearly but whom she wished would allow her some breathing space. 'We've got to go to school to let Miss Harrison know how we got on, but she'll let us come home early.'

Both girls, friends since they were toddlers, turned back when they reached the front door. 'Keep yer fingers crossed. Ta-ra!'

Molly nodded her head towards a chair. 'Mary, for heaven's sake will yer sit down, stop rubbing yer hands together and keep those tears away. Yer'll have me a nervous wreck if yer keep that up. I'll make us a nice fresh pot of tea and yer'll feel a bit better.'

'I won't feel settled until she's home. And I can't help the way I'm made, Molly, no more than anyone else can.'

'That is something I can understand and sympathize with, sunshine. Your daughter can't help the way ye're made either, but she shouldn't have to suffer for it. This day is a milestone in her life, one she should look back on with pleasure. Today her and Ruthie are feeling grown-up, going after their first job, so don't let's spoil it for them. And whether they get the job or not, let us be happy for them.' Molly made her way to put the kettle on. 'Sit down and make yerself at home, sunshine, I don't charge.'

Nellie was looking very smug when Molly opened the door to her at dead on half-past ten. 'Have yer got yer tanner ready, girl?'

'Have you got yer word ready, sunshine? That's more to the point. And don't forget it'll have to be a good one for yer to win a tanner off me.'

'Oh, it's a good one, girl, don't worry yerself about that. Me and George spent an hour last night going through the dictionary. It's got thirteen letters in it . . . or is it fourteen? I forget now, but it's a real tongue-twister.' Rubbing her hands together in front of the fire, Nellie had never felt so cocksure as she did now. 'And I don't want yer to give me the sixpence in ha'pennies and pennies, either, 'cos that looks as though it's begrudged.'

'Listen, sunshine, if I lost a tanner on a bet with you, then believe me it would be begrudged.' Molly was dying to laugh at the devilment in her mate's eyes and wondered if she should give in to her for once and let her think she'd won. But that thought didn't linger with her for long because she knew she'd have cause to regret it. Nellie would brag to everyone she knew, and even people she didn't know. 'D'yer want me to make our tea first, or do yer want to know the result of the bet?'

'Let's have our cuppa first, I could just do with one.' Nellie showed scant respect for the old wooden dining-chair as she pushed it away before carrying the carver chair over. 'Ay, I saw Mary coming over with Bella earlier, what did she want?'

Molly popped her head around the kitchen door. 'Do you spend all yer time at the window, Nellie? Yer must do 'cos yer never miss a thing.' She went back to put a light under the kettle. 'Mary didn't want anything, it was just because it's a big day for the girls, going on their first interview for a job. She came over so we could see them off and wish them well.'

'They'll get the jobs, girl, I can feel it in me bones.' While she was speaking Nellie was also hoping there'd be biscuits with the cup of tea. 'And I'm not usually wrong. With your Doreen working there for a few years, that should stand your Ruthie in good stead.'

'Don't say any more, sunshine, or yer'll have me counting me chickens before they're hatched. I hope they do, though, because it would be nice for them to work together after being friends all through their school years. And besides, it's a good firm to work for.'

Nellie happened to glance through the back window and saw washing on the clothes line. 'Have yer washed the clothes we got at the market? You've been bloody quick off the mark, haven't yer?'

Molly came through with the cups of tea. 'I've only washed the skirts and blouses I bought off Sadie for me and Ruthie. I know they won't dry out because it's too cold, but there's a stiff wind, so with a bit of luck most of the wet will be blown away. Then I can put them over the maiden before we go to bed and they'll be dry enough to iron by morning. I've just got to be careful Ruthie doesn't see them, I want them to be a surprise on Christmas morning.'

When Molly sat down, Nellie's heart sank. 'What, no biscuit? Not even a miserly one?'

'Sorry, sunshine, but I've only got an ordinary biscuit tin, not a magic one that keeps filling itself up. But I'll tell yer what, to take that scowl off yer face, I'll buy us two cream cakes out of the tanner I'm going to win off yer.'

'Then all I can say, girl, is that we'll be waiting a long time for the cakes, 'cos there's no way that ye're going to win. My George has seen to that.'

'Then why can't you have the decency to say that if you win, you'll buy the two cream cakes? I did, so why can't you?'

Nellie cupped a hand and rested her chin on it. She gave the matter some considerable thought. Her mouth was watering already in anticipation of her teeth sinking into the fresh cream that would ooze out of the cake and which her tongue would lap up. She had to have a cake no matter how she came by it. 'If it makes yer feel any better, girl, then I'll agree to your terms, but don't come crying when yer lose 'cos I can't abide people what are bad losers.'

'Until yer tell me what the word is, sunshine, we'll never find out who the winner is. So come on, out with it.'

But Nellie wasn't ready yet. 'It's bad enough not getting a biscuit with me cup of tea, but yer haven't said a word about me coat yet.'

'It looks really smart on yer, Nellie. But yer knew that because I told yer yesterday when yer tried it on in here. It looks a real treat on yer. And what did yer family have to say, did they think yer got a bargain?'

'I'll say! George said at twenty-seven and six it was a real snip, and he wished he could get a bargain like that for himself.'

Molly looked shocked. 'Nellie, yer only paid seven and six for it! Don't tell me yer added a pound to it so yer could diddle George?'

'How did I diddle him, girl? He asked me how much it was and when I told him he gave me the twenty-seven and six and said he'd mug me to it.'

'You lied to him, and yer diddled him! I don't know how yer can do that to yer husband when yer know he's trying to save for Lily's wedding. You'll definitely never get into heaven, Nellie

McDonough, and I'd say yer didn't deserve to. Not after pulling a trick like that on yer own husband.'

'No, I'm only pulling yer leg, girl, so yer've no need to worry about St Peter not letting me into heaven. Yer see, what really happened was, our Lily and Paul were there and they gave ten bob each towards it, so my feller only had to put the seven and six to it and that won't leave him skint.'

'It gets worse by the minute, Nellie! Yer've not only lied to yer husband, yer've also lied to yer daughter and yer son! I don't know how yer can do that and sleep soundly at night.'

Nellie began to shake with laughter, her tummy lifting the table inches off the floor. 'Don't be worrying yerself about my George, girl, because he'll get more than his seven and six worth in bed tonight.'

Molly was getting annoyed with herself for seeing the funny side, but it was hard not to let a chuckle out when her mate's laughter was so infectious. 'Let's leave your bedroom behind, sunshine, and concentrate on the matter in hand. Will yer tell me what word you and George came up with?'

Nellie wiped her eyes with the back of a hand. 'I've got two words, girl. Just in case yer get the first one I've got another for yer. And even you are not that bleeding clever yer'll know what these two mean.'

'Ye're moving the goal posts, Nellie, and that's not fair. It's bad enough George helping yer to find a word, but when it comes to two words, that is definitely not playing the game.'

There was a crafty look in Nellie's eyes. 'Are yer backing out, girl?'

'No, I'm not backing out, but I'm going to put the goal posts back in place so I'm in with a chance. If I get one of the two words right, then I've won and you buy the cream cakes.'

Nellie was so certain Molly would be baffled by the two words George had written down on the piece of paper in her bag, she nodded in agreement. 'Okay, girl, just to show there's no ill-feeling, I'll be generous.'

'Well, give me the word, Nellie, unless yer expect me to guess what it is?'

Reaching down for her handbag which was propped up by the table leg, Nellie shook her head and tutted. 'Now, now, girl, there's no need to be sarky. I don't mind yer getting peeved when yer lose yer tanner, but I object to sarcasm before we even start.' Taking her time, she unfolded the piece of paper and held it in front of her eyes. 'I'll have to read this one out slowly 'cos I can't understand George's handwriting. Here we go. Supp-er-flow-sley.' Proud of herself, she looked at her friend. 'Now, let's see yer get yer tongue around that and tell us what it means.'

'I've never even heard of it, Nellie! Now let's see if I heard right. Did yer say supperflowsley?'

With victory in sight, Nellie nodded. 'That's what's written down here, but I think George said it a bit different than I did. He would, though, wouldn't he, having a man's voice? Anyway, don't be trying to get out of it, girl, and tell us what it means?'

'I can't tell yer what it means 'cos I've never heard of it! And don't be saying George would say it different because he's a man. Whether man or woman, the pronunciation of any word should be the same. The best thing is for yer to let me see it written down and I'll tell yer whether I've ever heard of it or not. The thing is, Nellie Mac, I don't trust yer, so give us that piece of paper.'

Nellie pulled her hand back and held the paper to her chest. 'Yer can't see it 'cos it's got the other word on it as well. So give in and say yer don't know what the word I've just told yer means.'

'I most certainly will not! Until I've seen it written down, I'm not saying anything! Why can't yer tear the piece of paper in two and keep hold of the other piece?'

'Oh, I wouldn't have thought of that, girl, silly woman that I am.' Nellie looked at the piece of paper again. 'Turn yer head away while I tear it. If you don't trust me then I'm not going to trust you.'

'In the name of God, sunshine, we could have been to the shops and back by now! Put a move on, will yer, or it'll be dark before we get out!'

But Nellie sat there and wouldn't budge until Molly turned her head away. And then the little woman, her tongue peeping out of the side of her mouth, tore the paper in half. 'There yer are, girl, that's the first word.'

Molly glanced at the paper, then at her friend. 'The word is superfluously, sunshine, not supperflowsley like you said. And for your information it means too much, or more than yer need and yer've got some over. So give us the tanner.'

'Ay, not so quick, Molly smart arse! What about this other word what George and me found in the dictionary? This one's got fifteen letters and I'll bet yer a pound to a pinch of snuff that yer'll never get it in a month of Sundays.'

'Nellie, I've already won the bet, what more d'yer want? If I get the next one right, what's to say yer won't come up with another, then another?'

Nellie crossed the place she thought her heart was. 'Cross my heart and hope to die, girl. If yer get this right, then yer deserve to win 'cos George said it's a word he's never used in his life and never heard anyone else use it.'

'But I've still won whether I get it right or not, eh? That was the deal and I'll make sure yer stick to it.'

Nellie put the other piece of paper in front of her. 'I wouldn't even attempt to say this, I'd never get me tongue around it. So I'm going to have to trust yer to be honest.'

'You've got some cheek, Nellie McDonough, talking about me being honest when you are so dishonest yerself.' Molly took the piece of paper and glanced down at it. 'Mmm, that is most certainly a long one. Fifteen letters, did yer say? Well, I think I can say it properly, and tell yer what it means, so the cakes are on you tomorrow as well as today.' She pretended to mumble behind her hand before smiling at her mate. 'It's pronounced inconsequential, and it means it doesn't matter, it's of no importance.'

Nellie's mouth gaped. 'Well, I'll be buggered! You've cheated, Molly Bennett, and yer can't say yer haven't. Either yer saw George on his way to work this morning and wheedled it out of him, or yer stayed up all night going through the bleeding dictionary.'

Molly chuckled. 'D'yer remember us going to see Robert Donat in *The Thirty-nine Steps*? There was a memory man in it who could remember everything. I think his name was Leslie something-or-other. Well, he's the only one I can think of who could read a dictionary and remember every word in it.'

'All I can say, Molly Bennett, is that ye're too ruddy clever for yer own good, or yer've cheated somehow.' But although Nellie sounded put out, she wasn't really worried because the way things had worked out she could have a fresh cream cake today and another one tomorrow without getting a lecture off her mate. But it would spoil things if she gave in too easily. Molly would smell a rat. 'The more I think of it, though, yer definitely couldn't have won unless yer cheated. And I'll figure out how before the day's over.'

'Ye're only saying that to try and get out of buying the cakes. Ye're a terrible bad sport, sunshine, but I've got yer taped.' Molly could be as crafty as Nellie if she wanted to be. And this was one time she wanted to see how her best mate was going to wriggle out of the trap she had in mind for her. 'But it wouldn't worry me if I didn't get a cake, I'm not as fussy on them as you are. So to save any more argument, let's not bother, eh? It'll not do us any harm to do without. We won't bother going to Hanley's for our bread, we'll get it at Irwin's instead.'

Nellie thought, Huh, not on your blinking life we won't. But aloud she said, 'No, I never break a promise, girl, even though it was to a cheat. So I'll buy yer a cake like I said I would, and again tomorrow. You might be a cheat, but my conscience will be clear.'

Molly was aching inside from the need to let her laughter out. If only Nellie could see her own face now, and the scheming glint in her eyes. Anyone who knew her well would be able to read her like a book. 'No, sunshine, if you think I cheated then I wouldn't want yer to spend yer money on me. And I couldn't eat a cake you bought me if I tried, it would choke me.'

Nellie stood up so quickly her chair went toppling backwards. Her beloved carver chair which made her feel posh and important, and she didn't even give it a glance because all she could think about was the fresh cream cake she now had a craving for. Making fists of her chubby hands, she leaned across the table and with nostrils flared and sparks coming from her eyes, she snarled, 'Listen to me, girl, and listen good. You and me are going to Hanley's where I will purchase two cream slices. Ones what I will make sure are not squashed. And if I have to ram one down yer ruddy throat, then I will. We've mentioned cream cakes about fifty times since I came in. Now I've reached the point where if I don't have one soon I'm liable to commit harry-carry.'

Molly frowned. 'What's harry-carry?'

'Blimey!' Nellie tutted. 'All those long bleeding words yer come out with and yer don't know the meaning of harry-carry?'

'No, sunshine, so enlighten me?'

'It means when yer kill yerself, like suicide.'

'Oh, fancy that now! I tell yer, sunshine, yer learn something new every day. I've heard of kamikaze, but never harry-carry. So yer've taught me something today, Nellie, and I'll have to remember it when things are looking bad.'

'Things will be looking bad for yer sooner than yer think, girl, if yer don't hurry and get yer coat on. And if Hanley's have sold out of cakes when we get there, I'd advise yer to take to yer heels as though the devil was after yer, 'cos I won't be responsible for me actions.'

Molly had her head turned sideways talking to her friend when they rounded the corner into their street. But Nellie was looking straight ahead and suddenly she stopped in her tracks, gave a cry, disengaged her arm from her friend's and began to sprint up the street. 'There's a man at your Doreen's door, girl, and if it's not that swine Tom Bradley, I'll eat me bleeding hat.'

The women were hindered by their shopping baskets and before they were halfway up the street they saw the man turn away then disappear down the side entry. Nellie dropped her basket and kept on running. 'See to that for us, girl, and I'll try to catch him.'

'Yer'll never catch him, sunshine, he's like a ruddy whippet! Come back before yer give yerself a heart attack. Doreen will tell us what's been going on and what the queer feller was after. That's if it was him, of course, we might have been mistaken. In which case we both need to wear glasses.'

'Of course it was him, girl, I'd know him a mile away.'

'Then it'll be money he's after, but he's got a ruddy cheek showing his face around here again after all the trouble he caused. And if he's upset our Doreen, or Victoria, then I personally will wring his neck.'

Doreen was about to close the door when she heard them and popped her head out. 'Oh, yer don't know what yer've missed, Mam!'

'Yes, we do, sunshine, Nellie spotted him as we turned into the street. We were hoping to catch up with him but there was no chance. What was the rotter after?'

'Come in and I'll tell yer, I don't want the whole street to know.' Doreen waited until both women were in before closing the door. Her first thought was for Victoria. 'It's all right, Aunt Vicky, I chased him off. And if he knows what's good for him he won't be knocking on this door again.'

Molly put her basket down and went to the couch where the baby was lying fast asleep. 'Every time I see him he looks bigger and more like his dad.' She smiled at Victoria, and keeping her concern out of her voice, said, 'Beryl Mowbray told me and Nellie a few days ago that a man had been hanging round the side entry and she thought he was up to no good. She said she saw him standing watching you walking down the street with the pram, and it warned her. By the description she gave, me and Nellie guessed it would be Bradley but I didn't say anything in case I was worrying yer for nothing. After all, it could have been anyone.'

Molly could see Nellie was all for telling them that Beryl also said the man had peered in to their window, but just in time she caught the warning glint in Molly's eyes. There was no point in putting the fear of God into Victoria, it was something she could well do without at her age.

'Mam, I am so proud of meself! I'm a nervous wreck now, but I was so cool at the door, I can't believe it. As calm as yer like I asked him what he wanted, and he said he was wanting to talk to his son. I said that no son of his lived here, he must have the wrong house. He tried to get tough with me then. "Don't be giving me that, I know me son lives here with you and an old lady. And I've a right to speak to me own son." I asked him what his name was then, and for a second I thought he was going to clout me. "Yer know very well his name's Phil Bradley so don't start getting funny with me or yer'll be sorry." I told him there was no one lived here called Phil Bradley, and started to close the door. But he stuck his foot out, and if looks could kill I'd be dead by now. But d'yer know what, Mam, I wasn't the least bit frightened of him. I thought of the terrible life Phil had had with him, and I got more angry than frightened. I told him to take his foot away before I called for the neighbours, and that the name of my husband and myself was Mitchell and not Bradley.'

Molly gave her a big hug. 'I'm very proud of yer, sunshine, yer were very clever to have thought of that, and very brave. Let's hope that's the last yer ever see of him.'

'I think I surprised him, Mam, because he looked puzzled when I said me name was Mitchell, but I don't think I frightened him off. I think you and Auntie Nellie did that. I saw him glance down the street and the next minute he'd legged it down the entry. I think he'll be back at a time when he thinks Phil will be in, 'cos he's definitely on the cadge for money. I hope not, though, 'cos we're so happy now, and it would upset Phil if they tried to get back into his life for what they could get off him.'

Molly was looking at Nellie when she told her daughter, 'Perhaps it might be better if yer didn't mention it to Phil right now. It would spoil Christmas for him and that would be a shame with it being Bobby's first Christmas. If Tom Bradley does turn up then there's little yer can do about it except leave it to Phil. But I don't think yer should put that worry on his shoulders when nothing might come of it. Leave things as they are, sunshine, 'cos perhaps with yer saying yer name was Mitchell, that might have put him off.'

'Yer mam's right, girl, I'd forget about it for now.' Nellie's chins danced in agreement with her nodding head. 'Never trouble trouble, until trouble troubles you. That's what my old ma used to say. Isn't that right, Victoria?'

'That's right, Nellie, it does no good to worry.' Victoria didn't know why she thought so, but she had a strong feeling that these two friends were either up to something regarding Tom Bradley, or they soon would be. Molly was like a mother hen where her children were concerned, it was woe betide anyone who hurt them. 'I wouldn't tell Phil, Doreen, not unless the blighter comes back again and yer have no choice. But I heard yer at the door and I think yer were marvellous the way yer stood up to him. He might very well be thinking there's nothing to be gained by coming back.' But the old lady didn't believe that for one second because she'd heard what Doreen hadn't told her mother and that was the threatening tone in Bradley's voice when he'd told the girl: 'Yer stupid cow! Yer can't stop me from seeing me step-son and I'll be back. Oh, yeah, I'll be back, yer can count on that.'

Victoria sighed inwardly. If Doreen didn't want to tell her mother the whole story then she'd keep it to herself. But she couldn't help feeling apprehensive. What if he called when Doreen was at the shops and she was in the house on her own? She wouldn't let him in, she decided, and if he banged the door down the neighbours would be there like a shot.

'Well, as long as ye're all right, sunshine, me and Nellie will be off home with our shopping. But if yer feel the least bit on edge, I'll come back and stay with yer until Phil gets in from work.'

'No, there's no need for that, Mam, I'll take the poker to the door with me if he calls again, and I wouldn't hesitate to use it if he put a foot over the threshold.'

'Listen, girl, yer don't have to go that far,' Nellie said. 'All yer need to do is yell yer head off and yer wouldn't see his heels for dust. He robbed a lot of people in this street and if they saw him they'd lynch him.'

Molly shook her head. 'It won't come to that, sunshine, because although Tom Bradley is a rotter, a liar, and a thief who'd steal from a blind man, what he is not is stupid. And he would have to be stupid to start trouble in this street. And another thing – don't be worrying yer pretty head about him spoiling things for yer. Yer've got Christmas to look forward to and don't let a swine like him take the enjoyment away from yer.'

Doreen gave her a hug. 'I won't, Mam, and you mustn't either. Ruthie might come home as happy as can be if she gets the job, and we'll all have to show her how pleased we are. And if she's not successful, then we'll have to cheer her up and let her know it's not the end of the world.'

'I won't say I'll let yer know as soon as she gets in,' Molly chuckled, 'because the whole street will know by then. Your kid sister is not one to keep things to herself. But I do hope both her and Bella get taken on, because if only one is picked it'll be heartbreak for the other.'

Nellie picked up her basket, eager to get into Molly's house so they could open up the McDonough and Bennett Private Detective Agency and decide what to do about Tom Bradley. If they left it too late, Ruthie would be home with Bella and their day's experiences would be the topic of conversation. Everything else would be forgotten. This was understandable, of course, but something had to be done about Tom Bradley before he wrecked the lives of people she loved, and whom she considered part of her own family. She didn't intend to let a rat like him upset them. 'Come on, girl, we've got work to do.'

Chapter Thirteen

Nellie followed Molly into the living room and put her shopping on the couch. 'I'll put these cakes on a plate, shall I, girl?'

'Yeah, okay, sunshine, and I'll stick the kettle on. Ruthie might be in any minute because she did say they had to go back to school after the interview but Miss Harrison would probably let them come home early. So whatever we've got to say, we'd better get it over with as soon as possible.'

In record time they were sitting at the table, their cakes quickly eaten and their tea cool enough to drink when the conversation allowed. 'I've been thinking, Nellie, and d'yer remember last time we went looking for Tom Bradley and found the scrapyard he had?'

'Of course I remember it, girl, 'cos wasn't I the one who pointed it out when we went past it in the tram? It's a good job I happened to be looking out of the window at the time.'

Molly wasn't going to remind her that the sole reason they were on that tram was because they'd heard Tom Bradley had a scrapyard somewhere in the Westminster Road or Scotland Road area, and they were both on the lookout from the tram windows, their heads turning from left to right. But her mate would argue until the cows came home that she was the one who saw the yard first, and as they were pushed for time it was easier to give in to her. 'Well, can yer remember which street we went down, and which house we knocked at to ask if they knew the Bradleys? I can recall the woman's face as clear as day, but I can't for the life of me think of her name or the number of her house.'

'I'd find the street again, girl, with no trouble, and I remember the house was halfway down on the left, but that's about all. Oh, I remember she was very friendly and asked us in. She even made us a cup of tea.'

Molly nodded. 'She also told us a lot about the Bradleys. In fact, she said the whole neighbourhood had cause to know them because so many people had been robbed by them.'

'We could find the woman again, girl, all we've got to do is knock on a few doors. And when we were leaving she did say to call in any time we were in the area, that we'd always be welcome.'

Molly closed her eyes, encouraging her mind to go back to that day and what the woman had told them. She was frowning in concentration when her eyes suddenly opened. 'Nellie, didn't she say that one of her neighbours was having a baby to Tom Bradley? Or she'd had it, one or the other?'

'Oh, yeah!' Nellie's bosom was heaved on to the table. 'She said the woman had no shame and was telling everyone the baby was Bradley's.' It was all coming back to her now. 'She said the brazen hussy was always round at the scrapyard, and her and the queer feller spent a lot of time in a brokendown hut he had.' There was nothing Nellie liked better than a bit of gossip. 'Ay, I wonder how that went down with Phil's mother, Fanny Bradley? When they were living at the top of the street here, the neighbours said she was besotted with him and did everything he told her to. He cracked the whip and she jumped. But surely she wouldn't put up with him getting another woman in the family way?'

'God only knows, sunshine, they were a such a funny family yer wouldn't know what they'd get up to. Any mother that would encourage her two young daughters to steal from an old lady, like they did with Lizzie Corkhill, well, yer couldn't trust them as far as yer could throw them. But I've got to say the more I think about it, the more confused I get. Didn't Phil's grandma say, the day we found her and told her she had a grandson, how she was surprised that Frances had turned out like that. She said she was a lovely girl and all the family liked her. So perhaps she was so grateful to Tom Bradley for marrying her when she was expecting another man's baby that she just went along with the life he led. And frankly, sunshine, I wouldn't care what they did, or how they lived, if they'd only keep away from Phil and Doreen. But while there is a danger of them turning up again, I'll do everything in my power to stop them.'

'In that case, girl, let's make up our minds to go out tomorrow and try and find them. We could try that woman first. She might know where they are because Tom Bradley might still have the scrapyard. If she can't help, then we'll seek high and low until we do find them.'

'Okay, sunshine, we'll do that. But don't be surprised if they've done a runner because from what we know of the family, they never stay long in one place. As soon as people find out what they're like, they move on to pastures new, where there are richer pickings.'

'That's not the attitude to take and I'm surprised at yer. Be determined and stick to yer guns. When we go out of this front door tomorrow morning, go out with the intention of finding what we're looking for. If I call for yer in the morning and yer look like a wet rag, then I'll tell yer to get on with it yer bleeding self.'

Molly grinned. 'Then I'd better look like the joys of spring, hadn't I? Face powder on, lipstick on me lips and a smile on me face. Will that suit yer?'

Nellie grinned back. 'Well, I'll give yer the benefit of the doubt, girl, 'cos I've never in all me life seen a wet cloth with powder and lipstick on.' Suddenly the little woman put a hand to her mouth. 'Ay, girl, those clothes are still on yer washing line and yer said yer didn't want Ruthie to see them! Had yer forgotten them?'

Molly's chair was scraped back. 'Thank goodness yer noticed them, sunshine, 'cos I'd clean forgot. I'd better get them in quick because she should be here any minute.'

Nellie raised her brows and put on a posh accent. 'There har some people hi know what have said hi ham a nosy bugger. But they har glad hi ham nosy when hit suits them.'

Molly was chuckling as she took the pegs off the line and put the clothes over her arm. They weren't dry, but at least the wet was out. With a bit of luck they'd dry over the maiden tonight and she could hide them in the wardrobe and iron them when her daughter wasn't around. It wouldn't be tomorrow because she had a feeling it was going to take a long time to find the whereabouts of the Bradley family. She and Nellie might be walking up the street with long faces after a day spent searching and ending up with nothing. But it was best she did as her friend said and go out feeling positive and not looking like a wet rag.

Molly was on the top stair when she heard the knock. 'Open the door, sunshine,' she shouted down, 'I'll only be a minute.' The clothes were too damp to put in the wardrobe, so she folded them and put them on the floor where they couldn't be seen. 'Talk about being saved by the bell isn't in it,' she told the empty room. 'But I'll be positive about that as well, and say how lucky I am.'

As she was going down the stairs, Molly could hear her daughter saying, 'I'm not telling yer, Auntie Nellie, until me mam comes down.'

'I'm here now, sunshine, and dying to know how yer got on. Yer've been on me mind all day and I did say a few prayers.'

Ruthie's heart was beating so fast and thudding so hard, she thought it was going to break out of her body. How proud she was to say, 'We got taken on, Mam, both me and Bella.' She had to wait until her mother had hugged and kissed her, and then Auntie Nellie had, before she could go on. 'I was nervous when we were sitting in the corridor waiting for our names to be called out, but Bella was a lot worse than me. Her hands were shaking and she kept biting her bottom lip.' Ruthie's cheeks had a rosy glow whipped up by the wind, her eyes were like saucers and the words poured from her mouth like a rushing waterfall. 'When a woman came out and called my name I nearly fell off the chair, and me legs were wobbling as I followed her into an office. There was this woman sitting behind a desk and I saw she had the card I'd handed in as soon as we got there, and I could see the envelope Miss Harrison had given me with my school report in.'

When her daughter stopped to take a deep breath, Molly said gently, 'Whoa, slow down, sunshine, and take yer time. There's no hurry, and me and Auntie Nellie don't want yer to miss anything out.'

'The woman was very nice and when she smiled at me I felt better. She said her name was Miss Jones, and d'yer know what she told me, Mam? That looking at me took her back several years to when she interviewed my sister Doreen. She said she'd noted the name and address on the card and wondered if there was any connection, but when she saw me she had no need to ask because I was so like Doreen it was uncanny.'

'Oh, fancy that, sunshine! Yer wouldn't think she'd remember Doreen after all these years. I mean, she must interview a lot of girls.'

'I'm sorry to interrupt, girl, but yer know how pig ignorant I am. What did the woman say it was that Ruthie was so like her sister?'

'Uncanny, sunshine, which means strange or extraordinary.'

Nellie's eyes rolled to the ceiling. 'I understood strange, girl, so yer had no need to baffle me with science by using a word the length of our street.'

Ruthie had so much to say and was so full of her own importance, yet she could still appreciate her auntie's humour. 'Not quite as long as the street, Auntie Nellie, just about as long as from our house to yours.'

'Oh, blimey, we've got another clever so-and-so in the family. It's a good job they took yer on, girl, so I don't have you and yer mam throwing big words at me.'

'Nellie, will yer keep quiet and let Ruthie get on with it?' Molly turned from her mate's rolling eyes to her daughter. 'As I said, sunshine, I'm surprised she remembered Doreen after all these years.'

'She remembered her all right, and she even mentioned Maureen. And she asked me to remember her to them! So I told her Doreen was married now to a very nice boy and that she had a new baby. And I thought I might as well tell her that Maureen was getting married very soon.'

Molly was amazed. How times had changed from when she was fourteen. Then you wouldn't have dreamed of talking to an adult as an equal. It was the war that had caused a lot of the changes because with the air raids you never knew whether the next bomb might have your name on it. Children were given a lot more freedom and a lot less discipline as a result. 'Tell me something, sunshine, who did the interviewing, you or Miss Jones?'

Nellie's throaty chuckle behind her brought a smile to Ruthie's face. 'The lady did, of course, and I was very polite. But I had to answer her questions, didn't I, or she'd have thought I had no manners.'

'At what stage was it mentioned that you were there because yer'd applied for a job?'

214

'Oh, she asked me a lot of questions about school, and said the report from Miss Harrison was very good. Then she asked if I had my heart set on any particular type of work, because it was important to like the job yer were doing. That's when I told her that Doreen had always enjoyed working at Johnson's, and that she had learned a lot from it. She seemed very pleased when I told her me sister made all her own clothes, and asked if I would follow in Doreen's footsteps and learn things that would stand me in good stead in the future. Of course I said I would, and I got the job!'

'I'd say she gave yer the job to shut yer up, girl,' Nellie said. 'If all the applicants talked as much as you, she wouldn't get through many in a day.'

'I wasn't in there that long, Auntie Nellie, and if she hadn't mentioned our Doreen I wouldn't have talked so much. But it paid off in the end, so I must have done something right. Me and Bella start on the day after Boxing Day, at eight o'clock.'

'I bet Bella is over the moon, is she? It'll do her good to mix with people, bring her out of her shell. And as for you, well, you've got a workmate before yer even start work.'

'Mam, can I go over and tell Doreen? I bet she's dying to know how I got on, and to be honest with yer, I think it was her being me sister that got me taken on.'

'Of course yer can go over, but don't knock too hard in case the baby is asleep. And when we've had our dinner and washed up, I'll walk round with yer to me ma's so yer can tell yer grandma and granda that in a couple of years yer should be a managing director of Johnson's, or at the very least a supervisor.'

'I like the sound of managing director better, Mam, it has a bit of class, don't yer think? So I'm going to think big and aim for the top.' After giving her mother and auntie a quick kiss, Ruthie was out of the door like a shot, eager to give her sister all the news.

When she'd gone, Molly pulled a face. 'They grow up quick these days, don't they, sunshine? It doesn't seem so long since I was pushing her in a pram.'

'She seems to have sprung up quicker than the others.' Nellie began to ease herself off the chair. 'And I'll tell yer this much: she'll get on in life 'cos she's got her head screwed on the right way and there's nothing shy about her. If she thinks something is right, no one on God's earth will make her change her mind. She takes after you, there, girl, 'cos you can be as stubborn as a bleeding mule when the mood takes yer. What yer should have bought for Ruthie to put in her stocking on Christmas Eve was a dictionary. Teach her some of those fifteen-letter words that yer come out with, and she'll be managing director by the time she's eighteen, and probably own the ruddy place by the time she's twenty-one.' Nellie gave a sly grin because she knew Molly would bite her head off when she heard what was coming next. 'That, of course, is if she isn't married by that time. She's got an eye for the boys has your Ruthie, but yer don't need me to tell yer that. She's just turned fourteen and already she's got her eye on three likely lads.'

'Oh, don't be exaggerating Nellie McDonough! The girl's still a schoolgirl until the end of the week, far too young to be thinking of boys.'

'I know that, girl, you know that, and probably the mothers of the three lads know it. The trouble is Ruthie doesn't agree with what we think, and as I say, she's very stubborn.'

'If Jack heard yer saying that he'd go mad! You'd cause trouble in an empty house, you would, Nellie, with yer cock-eyed ideas.' Molly did try hard, but in the end curiosity got the better of her. 'Anyway, what three lads are yer talking about?'

Nellie's tummy and bosom were moving up and down with her laughter. 'Well, girl, since yer ask, I'd say that way out in front is Gordon Corkhill, and I'd put him down as even money.

Coming up on the rails is Jeffrey Mowbray, the bookies have him at three to one. But the rank outsider who started at twenty to one is coming up on the outside and closing the gap. It wouldn't surprise me if he didn't romp home the winner.'

Molly clicked her tongue. 'Really, sunshine, there are times when I think yer imagination will be the end of yer.' Molly knew she should leave it at that, but once again her curiosity told her she wouldn't sleep if she didn't ask. 'And who is this third lad yer have in mind?'

'A rank outsider like I said, girl, but he has as much chance as the other two.'

'I'm as crazy as you are for even bothering to ask, but just to get things straight in me mind, what is this lad's name?'

'Johnny Stewart from the next street. Whenever your Ruthie is about yer can bet yer bottom dollar he's not far away. He's a nice lad, always well-dressed, good parents and he's working with his dad. He left school last year.'

'What colour socks does he wear, sunshine?'

'How the hell should I know?'

'I thought yer'd know that as yer seem to know everything else about the lad. And for your information I do know him and I know his parents. But that's about it as far as I'm concerned. He might be friendly with Ruthie, but that's where it ends. So don't you be putting ideas into her head 'cos she's growing up quick enough as it is.'

Nellie spread out her palms. 'Now why would I be putting ideas into her head? Me what has a heart as pure as the driven snow.'

'Well, you and yer heart what's as pure as the driven snow can make yer way home now so I can see to me family's dinner. And I think we should start off at ten o'clock tomorrow, if yer can manage to be half an hour earlier than usual?'

'I'll be on the dot, girl, right on the dot.'

* * *

Ruthie had told half of the street by the time Jack and Tommy came in from work, but she'd lost none of her exuberance. Both men showed they were suitably impressed. Tommy lifted his kid sister until her head was nearly touching the ceiling. 'I am proud of yer, our kid, yer've done well. In fact all the Bennetts did well when it came to getting work. We all got the first job we went after.'

'Let me down, yer silly nit, ye're pulling me skirt up and showing me underskirt.' When she was standing on her two feet, Ruthie straightened her clothes before pointing a stiffened finger. 'Don't you tell me grandma and granda, our Tommy, 'cos I want to tell them meself. Or Rosie, even though she is yer beloved wife and yer shouldn't keep secrets from her.'

'I'll not say a word, I promise. But remember when I started work, what was the first thing yer said to me? Yer said I should give yer a penny a week pocket money, and I'm wondering now will the same rules apply when you get your first wage packet? Will I be a penny a week better off, or not?'

'Oh, I think you'll be out of luck, son,' Jack said with his arm across his daughter's shoulders and a smile of pride on his face. 'She's already promised to buy me five Woodbines every week, and yer mam a tuppenny slab of Cadbury's.'

'In that case I'll let yer off, our kid, and I think it's very generous of yer to remember yer mam and dad.' Tommy ruffled her hair. 'Grow up like yer two sisters and yer won't go wrong.'

'I'll walk round to me ma's tonight with her.' Molly had made up her mind not to tell Jack or her son about Tom Bradley until she knew if she and Nellie could find out anything else tomorrow. 'I don't want her walking round there on her own in the dark. But we'll give yer time to get yer dinner over first, we won't catch yer on the hop.'

Tommy's head fell back and he roared with laughter. 'Mam,

never in a month of Sundays would yer catch me nan or Rosie on the hop. When I come in from work me nan has the place spotless, not a thing out of place. And after our meal, Rosie makes sure it's back to being spotless again. Not a crumb to be seen anywhere.'

How Molly loved the bones of this tall, handsome, thoughtful son of hers. 'Then I promise yer me and Ruthie will wipe our feet on the mat before we enter the living room.'

'There's no need for that, Mam, I'll give yer a piggy back.'

'Get on home, yer big daft ha'porth, yer wife will think yer've run off with another woman.' Molly pushed him towards the door. 'We'll see yer later, but don't forget ye're carrying a very important secret.'

Molly was sitting next to her ma on the couch as Ruthie went over all the details of the interview for about the twentieth time that day, her excitement in no way dimmed. 'She's done well for herself, hasn't she, Ma?'

'Wonderful, so she has! And it's no more than she deserves, otherwise if they'd thought she wasn't good enough she wouldn't have got the job, and that's the top and bottom of it.'

Bob, content to be sitting by his wife's side, said, 'I'll tell yer something, sweetheart, me and yer grandma were very lucky when God blessed us with yer mam for our daughter. It's because of her we have such a wonderful, loving family now. Where would we have been without every one of yer to help fill our lives?' He smiled gently at his youngest grandchild who seemed to have grown up so quickly. 'Not only with beauty, but love and laughter.'

Rosie looked surprised when the knock on the door came. 'I wasn't expecting visitors, were you, Tommy?'

'No, I wasn't, my beloved, but there is a really good way of finding out who it is, and that is to open the front door.'

'Is that a fact now?' Rosie looked at Molly. 'Did yer not teach yer son any manners, Mrs Bennett? There's a big six-foot man expecting a little thing like me to open the door while he stays put! Not on your life, Tommy Bennett, yer can open the door yerself. I'll not be a servant to yer, that I'll not.'

Tommy's grin would melt any heart. 'Sure, I didn't marry yer to be a servant to me, Rosie O'Grady. I married yer because yer were beautiful and yer promised to love, honour and obey me. Love and honour me yer have, that's for sure, but I can't get yer to understand what the word obey means.'

'Ah, well, yer see, my beloved, on the day we got married, when the priest came to the word obey, I had me fingers crossed which told the Good Lord that it was the one word I wasn't too sure about.'

'I hate to interrupt a lovers' argument,' Molly said, 'but whoever it was knocked on the door will be blocks of ice by now.'

It took just three strides of Tommy's long legs to reach the door, and his pleasure at seeing who was standing there could be heard in his voice. 'Lily! Archie! Oh, it's good to see yer, come on in and get warm. Me darling wife insisted on finishing an argument before she'd let me open the door.'

'May God forgive yer, Tommy Bennett.' Rosie rushed to kiss Lily and take her coat to hang up. 'It's a pleasant surprise, so it is.'

And Ruthie couldn't have been happier. Another audience to hear her tale which was delivered again with as much enthusiasm as if it was the first time of telling.

After congratulating her, Lily said, 'We have some more news for yer that we think yer might like. But I'll let Archie get on with his first.'

Bride started to push herself to the edge of the couch. 'I'll put the kettle on for a pot of tea to warm yer up. Sure, I can feel the cold air coming from yer.'

'News and requests first, Mrs Jackson,' Archie said, holding Lily's hand firmly in his. 'Sit down, it won't take a minute and then we'll welcome a cup of tea.' He was feeling so happy he had to get the words out quickly. 'Me and Lily have brought the wedding forward to Easter, which means it's only three months away. But it was what we both wanted, to be married on Easter Saturday.' He faced Tommy, his comrade in the army and best friend in civvies. 'We've come to ask if yer would be me best man?'

It took two seconds for it to sink in, then Tommy was slapping his hero on the back and shaking his hand off. 'I'd be honoured, Archie and I can say with all honesty that there is no one I would rather be best man to than you.'

And Rosie's beautiful face was aglow with happiness. Anything that made her beloved husband happy, made her happy. After kissing Lily and Archie, she said, 'Sure, yer'd never find a more handsome best man if yer searched the four corners of the earth, and that's the truth of it.'

Bridie and Bob smiled at Rosie's straightforward way of speaking. If the Irish beauty thought it, she spoke it. 'Then Archie will indeed be a very lucky man,' Bridie said. 'With a beautiful bride on his arm, and the most handsome man in the world at his side.'

'I can't ask Doreen or Jill to be bridesmaids or maids of honour.' Ruthie was listening with eyes wide, so Lily had to think her words over carefully before adding, 'Not with Doreen having a young baby and Jill being indisposed.'

None of this was any surprise to Molly who had known for days what was coming. But she was looking forward to her youngest daughter's reaction. This was going to be a day to remember for the girl who would always be her baby. 'Have yer made up yer mind who yer'd like to have for bridesmaids then, Lily?'

'Yes, we know who we'd like.' Lily could see Ruthie watching her mouth, waiting for the words that she wanted to hear to come out. 'There's Phoebe and Dorothy Corkhill, and of course our first choice was Ruthie. That's if she would like to be, of course?'

This was too much happiness to take as a matter of course. Ruthie couldn't prevent a tear from trickling down each cheek. Her mother was the first one she ran to. 'Oh, Mam, aren't I a very lucky girl? I bet there's no one in the whole of Liverpool who's been as lucky as I have today. Just wait until I tell Bella, she won't believe it.'

'How would yer like Bella to be a bridesmaid as well?' This had been in Lily's mind for days, and Archie was in agreement, but she pretended it was something that had just come into her mind. 'Would yer like me to ask her? Or I believe it should be her mother I ask first. It would be ideal, with you and Bella being the same height, and hardly any difference between Phoebe and Dorothy.'

Now this was news to Molly, and she was delighted. With having no brothers or sisters, Bella had led a more sheltered life than Ruthie, and had never been a bridesmaid. And there was no prospect she ever would be but for this invitation. 'Oh, wouldn't that be wonderful, sunshine? You and yer best mate being asked to be bridesmaids on the same day yer both get taken on at Johnson's? This certainly is your lucky day.'

'We'll go and see Mary Watson after Mrs Jackson has kindly made us a cup of tea.' Lily held out her hand and Ruthie ran to her. 'Your best mate doesn't go to bed very early, does she?'

'No. When we had our fourteenth birthdays the other week, we were told we could stay up until ten o'clock. And if there's a play on the wireless, me mam lets me stay up a bit longer to listen to the end of it.'

'Then we'll have a nice warm cuppa, and if it's all right with Archie, we'll go and see Bella and her mam afterwards.'

Her boyfriend didn't hear, he was too busy telling Tommy how far he'd got with the arrangements for the wedding. The fact that it couldn't come quickly enough was very obvious from his tone and his every movement. 'Me mam's been a big help. What with me going to work every day, she's seen to most of the ordering. And of course your mam and Mrs Mac organized the reception and evening buffet. I can't wait, I'm counting the days.'

'I know how yer feel,' Tommy told him. 'And I've got to say that yer can't beat married life. My head's still in the clouds, and me and Rosie are like a courting couple. This is one marriage that will never go stale.'

'Not if I have anything to do with it.' Rosie wasn't bashful about listening to other people's conversation, especially when it involved her dearly beloved husband. 'We are going to be like yer grandma and granda – as much in love after fifty years of marriage as they were on the day they wed. And as me mammy would say, "Sure, and that's a marriage made in heaven, so it is."'

'Then, Rosie, sunshine, yer mammy can say that about the Jackson marriage, and the many branches that came from it.' Molly felt her mother pressing her curled fists into the seat of the couch to push herself forward, again, and she put out a restraining arm. 'You stay where you are, Ma, me and me daughter-in-law are quite capable of making a pot of tea. You and Da enjoy a natter with your guests.'

Ruthie followed them into the kitchen. 'Isn't it exciting, Mam? I'll never forget this day, it'll be the best of me life.'

'Sure, that's a big statement from a fourteen-year-old girl,' Rosie said. 'What about the day yer meet a boy and fall in love? Or the day yer marry the man of yer dreams? There'll be a lot of days to come, Ruthie, when yer'll be saying those very words. And aren't I the very one that should be saying this, when so many of my own dreams have come true?'

With her tongue peeping out of the side of her mouth, Ruthie gave this some considerable thought. 'Well, I'll just say that this is the happiest day of me life so far, eh? And that I'm hoping for many more.'

'Can I suggest yer forget everything for now and make yerself useful?' Molly pointed to the wooden tray on the draining board. 'Set the cups out on there, sunshine, with the sugar basin, milk jug and teaspoons. I don't want us to take too long over tea, I'd hate to be knocking yer dad up at midnight.'

Molly pulled on the bannister when she was climbing the stairs, with Jack just a few treads behind her. 'It's been a hectic day and I'll be away in dreamland as soon as my head hits the pillow.'

'Yes, it's late for us, love, we're usually in bed before this.' Jack pinched her bottom. 'I'll have no trouble dropping off.'

And he was true to his word. He was soon snoring gently while Molly lay by his side wide awake. She'd tried her left side, then her right, but still couldn't drop off. The trouble was, so much had happened during the day, her mind was too active and she couldn't relax. Her youngest daughter had got a job and was to be a bridesmaid to Lily and Archie, but the most significant and worrying thing was Tom Bradley's visit to Doreen and his threat to return. She must do all in her power to stop him from ruining the lives of the young family across the street. And so her thoughts raced on, starting off a splitting headache.

Then suddenly a scene entered her mind, and it was like watching a film at the picture house. It was so real she sat up in bed gasping, and Jack turned his head on the pillow and grunted, 'What's up, love?'

'Nothing, sunshine, just some cramp in me leg. You go back to sleep.'

Within seconds she was back inside a sweetshop with Nellie, and there was a little girl in there crying her eyes out because her older brother had run off and left her. He'd bought some sweets with the penny given to him by their mother, and he was supposed to take his little sister home and share the Dolly Mixtures with her. But as soon as the boy had the sweets in his hand he'd scarpered and left the three-year-old crying. The shop assistant was doing her best to calm the child, but to no avail. As she explained to the two women, she would take the girl home herself, but couldn't leave the shop unattended. And that's when Molly had asked how far it was to the girl's home.

'That's how it was!' The words were out of Molly's mouth before she realized she was talking aloud. She glanced at Jack but he was still purring like a pussy cat. 'So we didn't go knocking on doors, we didn't have to! The shop assistant gave us her address, we took the girl home, and from the time we knocked on her door, it happened how me and Nellie said it did this morning.' The child's mother had been very thankful and welcoming, and told them all she knew about Bradley. So all they had to do tomorrow was ask the woman in the sweetshop for the address of that little girl.

Molly sighed as she fell back on to the pillow. Thank goodness for that, she knew where they were up to now. No day wasted knocking on doors, just the one where, if she remembered rightly, there lived a very nice lady about whom she had a strong feeling. This woman would help them, she knew it instinctively.

Chapter Fourteen

Molly was standing by the window just before ten o'clock the next morning. She had a woollen scarf around her neck because she could tell by the cold draught coming in under the front and back doors that it was bitterly cold out, and she had an old pair of woolly gloves in her hand which were years old with holes in the fingers, but they were better than nothing.

Nellie passed the window and Molly had the door open before her mate could knock. 'Come in a minute, sunshine, there's something I want to talk to yer about.'

'Can't yer tell me on the tram, girl? I thought yer wanted to get away early?'

'I did, and I know! But it'll only take me a few minutes to say what's been on me mind all night.' Molly started to pull the tattered woollen gloves on. 'I think you and me must be getting forgetful in our old age, sunshine, 'cos we were miles out when we were talking about what happened the last time we went looking for Tom Bradley.'

'Old age! Ay, girl, if you want to grow old that's your business, but don't be taking me along with yer. I'm forty-three, but as they say ye're as young as yer feel, then I'm only eighteen. So don't you be putting years on me.'

'Then how come yer didn't remember us going into a sweetshop to buy a pennyworth of Mint Imperials, hoping we could worm some information from the shopkeeper? And what

226

about the little girl what was crying because her brother had scarpered with her sweets and she was too young to go home on her own? And who was the kind, generous woman who offered to walk the child home if the assistant would give us her address?'

You could almost see the light dawn in Nellie's eyes. 'Oh, yeah, girl, ye're right! Ooh, ay, fancy us forgetting that! What made yer think of it now, and not the other day when we were trying to remember whose house it was where we had a cup of tea?'

'It just came to me in bed last night. I couldn't drop off to sleep even though I was dead beat 'cos me mind was too full. And suddenly I saw us in that sweetshop with that little girl. I can see the assistant, as plain as day, telling us where the child lived, and me saying we'd see she got home safely.'

Nellie knew this wasn't a time for laughter, and her friend wouldn't appreciate it, but she couldn't help the cheeky grin that appeared on her face. 'It came to yer in bed last night, did it, girl? Well, I had something come to me, as well, so yer weren't the only one.'

'Don't tell me yer had the same dream as me, sunshine?'

'I didn't say I had no dream, now, girl, I said something came to me. Well, it was my feller came to me, and while you were sitting up in bed worrying, I was having the time of me life.'

'Tut-tut, Nellie, will yer ever grow up?'

'While I'm having so much fun I've no intention of growing up, girl, I'm not that soft. Make hay while the sun shines, that's what I always say.'

'That's what yer always say! Nellie McDonough, that's the first time I've ever heard yer say it in all the years I've known yer.'

'Because every time I open me mouth about what goes on in me bedroom, yer always shut me up quick. So it's yer own fault if yer've never heard me say it.'

'Well, can we get back to the matter in hand, please? Would you know the sweetshop again if yer saw it?'

'Of course I would! It was right on the corner of the street where we got off the tram. We couldn't miss it if we tried.'

'Right, then let's be on our way.' Molly put the handle of her handbag in the crook of her arm then pushed her friend towards the front door. 'I've banked the fire up with slack, so I'm hoping it'll last until we get home. We should only be a couple of hours because the woman in the sweetshop will tell us where that little girl lives. And if her mother's in, it'll save us knocking on any doors.'

'Ye're asking for a lot, girl, and I hope ye're not disappointed.' Nellie linked her friend's arm and swayed her way down the street. 'The woman who worked in the sweetshop might not be there any more, or the little girl's family could have moved to another area. So don't expect things to go like clockwork, then yer won't be disappointed.'

'Enjoyed yerself in bed last night, did yer, sunshine? Happy with yer little self?'

Nellie smelled a rat and her eyes narrowed. 'What made yer ask that, girl, 'cos ye're not usually interested in me bedroom antics.'

'Ye're right, I'm not interested. But I just wanted to tell yer that as you had a bit of good luck last night, it's my turn to have some today.'

Nellie's whole eighteen-stone body shook from head to toe. It was the first time her chins had had cause to move that day, and they were a little bit slow in their effort to keep up with a body that could bounce like a rubber ball. 'If yer want the same sort of luck and thrill that I had last night, girl, yer'll not get it down a side street off Scotland Road. Yer'd be better off staying on the tram and making yer way down to Lime Street. I believe there's a good pitch outside of the railway station, but yer'd have to take those ruddy gloves off and show a bit of leg to attract attention.'

'I get enough of that sort of attention off me husband, sunshine, I don't go short in that department. But that's between me and Jack, and that's the way it will stay. So put yer mind on the matter in hand and if yer concentrate enough, we might get somewhere. And here's a tram coming so get yer skates on, it's too cold to stand around waiting for the next one.'

'You run ahead, girl, and keep it for me. I won't be far behind yer.' As Molly sprinted ahead, Nellie shouted after her, 'Tell the driver I had a very busy night last night and it's taken it out of me. He'll understand what I mean, even if you don't.'

Needless to say she didn't get an answer to that, and by the time she reached the tram she was too out of breath to tell the driver herself. Pity that, it might have given him a laugh. Unless he was a goody-goody like her mate, then he wouldn't see the joke and she'd be wasting her time. As she pulled herself aboard with Molly's help, she was thinking some people didn't half miss out in life. Mind you, she had heard that some women weren't the least bit interested in bedroom antics, and lay like logs counting the flowers on the wallpaper. One woman actually admitted they had fifteen cracks in their bedroom ceiling. Now how the hell would she know that unless she spent time on her back counting them?

'The next stop is ours, girl, so let's get up. It takes me ages walking down the aisle when the tram's swaying from side to side.'

'Are yer sure this is our stop?' Molly asked. 'It's too cold to be wandering around trying to find the sweetshop. There's probably dozens of them on this road.'

'Not as many as there are pubs, girl, there's one of them on every corner. But I'm sure this is where we get off.' Holding on to the back of one of the seats for support, Nellie bent down in front of the passenger who had the misfortune to be sitting in the seat and gave the poor woman the benefit of having a mountainous, soft bosom thrust in her face. The woman would have objected had she been able to. Unfortunately her breath had been cut off and she couldn't speak. Nellie didn't hear the gasps coming from the region of the valley between her breasts, she was too busy pointing a stiffened finger out of the window. 'Look, girl, that's the corner where Tom Bradley had his scrapyard. It's just waste ground now with nothing on it.'

'Doesn't look familiar to me,' Molly said as she waited for the tram to stop so she could hop off and help her mate down. 'I hope it's not going to be a wasted journey, I'll spit if it is.'

Now Nellie hated getting on and off trams because the step down from the platform to the pavement was steep and she couldn't manage it without losing her dignity. No matter which leg she used to step down, it couldn't be done without her showing a few inches of her blue fleecy-lined bloomers. So as Molly stood looking up, her hand outstretched in readiness, Nellie turned to the driver. 'Keep yer eyes on the road, lad, ye're not getting a peep-show off me.'

'I've got me eyes on the road, missus, and me hand on the wheel ready to start moving when you finally decide to get off and let the other passengers go about their business. Besides, yer've got nothing that my wife hasn't got – except you've got a hell of a lot more.'

Nellie made the drop, falling into Molly's arms. But she wasn't prepared to let the man have the last word. She shook a curled fist at him as the tram began to move away. 'I feel sorry for the woman what's married to you! I bet she knows how many cracks you've got on yer bedroom ceiling.'

Molly pulled her away. 'Yer've had the last word so come on, let's do the job we set out to do. I hope it's not one of those days where ye're looking to pick a fight with someone just to put a bit of excitement into yer life.' Molly looked around. 'Which way is it to this sweetshop yer said yer'd recognize?'

With one podgy finger tapping her cheek, Nellie asked, 'Now, which way do yer feel like turning, girl? Left or right?'

'Don't play games, sunshine, I'm not in the mood. Where is this sweetshop, or have yer been pulling me leg and haven't got a clue?'

Nellie lifted an arm to let her handbag drop into the crook, then she put a hand on each of Molly's shoulders and turned her around. 'There yer are, misery guts, if it was any closer yer would have bumped into it.'

Molly's jaw dropped. Her friend was right, she remembered the shop clearly now. And finding it so easily augured well for a successful day. Mind you, it was unlucky to take things for granted, she mustn't expect success all the way along the line. 'Shall we go in and ask the assistant for the name and address we're after?'

'No need to, girl, I'll know the house when I see it. And I've got a sneaking feeling that the woman's name is Monica. So I don't think there's any need to ask in the shop 'cos yer only filling people's mouths. We'll manage without any help, you'll see. And with a bit of luck we'll soon have a hot cup of tea in our hands to warm us up.'

'Forever the optimist.' Molly bent her arm for Nellie to link. 'I hope yer don't give out any hints about being cold or thirsty, sunshine, or I'll shrivel up with embarrassment. I'd welcome a hot cup of tea, but it would be cheeky to ask for one.'

They were halfway down the next side street when Nellie pulled her friend to a halt. 'That's the house, girl, I'm positive,' And before Molly could object, the iron gate was opened and they were standing on the path. 'I'll knock 'cos me luck seems to be in today.'

As they waited, Molly said, softly, 'I feel like an intruder. I hope she doesn't think we've got a ruddy cheek.'

When the door opened, the woman looked at them as though they were strangers and was about to ask what they wanted when recognition dawned. 'Well, I'll be blowed! I've often thought about you two, but I never expected to see you again.' She opened the door wide with a welcoming smile. 'Come on in, I could just do with a bit of a natter and a good laugh. I think we had plenty of both last time yer were here.' As the two friends were passing her to walk into the hall, she said, 'If my memory serves me right, it's Molly and Nellie, isn't it?'

Nellie beamed, as proud as a peacock that she'd been remembered after all this time. And there was nothing she liked to see more than someone with a friendly face and an ear for a joke. 'Yer've got a good memory, girl, 'cos it was quite a while back.'

'I had my husband in stitches when he came in from work that night, telling him about you two and the tricks yer got up to. He said if yer called again I was to ask yer to move into this street, preferably in the house next door. He enjoys a laugh, does my feller, and he'd appreciate you two.'

'Where are the children? Yer had a little girl and boy, didn't yer?' Molly felt awful not remembering the woman's name when she was so friendly with them. So she took a chance on her friend being right. 'The little girl was the image of you, Monica.'

'Their grandma has taken them both into town to see Father Christmas at TJ's grotto. Oh, yer should have seen how excited they were when they went out. They're still young enough to believe in Father Christmas, thank God. These days most kids are old before their time. Anyway, I'm glad they're out for the morning so we can have a nice chat. I'll put the kettle on and then yer can tell me what ye're doing down this neck of the woods.'

'I'm ashamed to tell yer 'cos yer'll think we've got a ruddy cheek making use of yer. I'm just hoping yer don't throw us out.' Molly waved a hand frantically at Nellie who was sitting on the couch with her legs wide spread and showing everything she'd got. 'Close yer legs, sunshine, I can see what yer had for breakfast.'

'What are yer worrying about, girl? I've got clean knickers on.'

'I know yer've got nice clean, blue fleecy-lined knickers on, sunshine, and the driver of the tram knows it too! But ye're a guest here, so behave yerself.'

Monica poked her head around the kitchen door, not wanting to miss anything, and she burst out laughing when she saw Nellie. 'My ma used to wear fleecy-lined bloomers, just like that. But aren't yer a bit young for them, Nellie? Surely they're only for older women.'

'It's Hobson's choice, girl, I'm afraid. The knickers that Molly wears, and I suppose you do, well, yer see, they won't go near me. I have to buy big ones 'cos look at the size of me bottom, it's twice the size of yours. And anyway, I've got the laugh on you thin ones today, 'cos these fleecy-lined don't half keep me nice and warm. I could feel Molly shivering as we walked down this street, but all my personal belongings are being kept in good condition for me husband.'

'The tram driver saw her bloomers as she was getting off the tram,' Molly said. 'But he wouldn't have thought anything of it if Tilly Mint hadn't told him to keep his eyes on the road. Honest, there are times when I don't know where to put meself, I'm that embarrassed.'

Nellie's eyes rolled. 'She's only jealous, Monica, 'cos I've got twice as much of everything as she has. Me voluptuous figure has all the men looking at me, and yer'd think, being me best mate, that Molly would be pleased and proud for me! But, oh, no, she goes mad and flies off the handle.' Her legs still wide apart, Nellie started her chins dancing when she nodded her head. 'I've told her it's not my fault that all the fellers fancy me, but she's like a child and gets a cob on.'

The kettle began to whistle and Monica lifted a hand. 'I'll have the tea here in two minutes, don't say another word until then.' She reached the kitchen and they could hear her say, 'Oh, what I wouldn't give to have a camera right now.'

When Monica came back from the kitchen carrying a tray, she became one of Nellie's favourite people. For with the cups and sugar basin, there was a plate containing a mixture of custard creams, ginger snaps and arrowroot biscuits. And when their hostess put their cups down in front of them, she said, 'Help yerselves to sugar and biscuits.'

Nellie was ready to pounce until she felt Molly's eyes on her. It made her keep a tight rein on herself for the next ten seconds, then her arm shot out and a chubby hand reached for the plate of biscuits.

Monica pulled a chair out and sat down. 'While I was seeing to the tea, I found meself thinking back to the last time yer were here. Didn't yer tell me yer were calling yerselves the Bennett and McDonough Private Detective Agency?'

'No, girl, yer've got it the wrong way round. It's the McDonough and Bennett Private Detective Agency.'

'Nellie, how many times do I have to tell yer that as I am the senior partner, Bennett comes before McDonough?' Molly was chuckling inside. 'When I'm old and grey, sunshine, and past it, then you'll be the senior partner and have yer name first.'

Shooting biscuit crumbs in all directions, Nellie spluttered, 'When you're old and grey, girl, I'll probably be pushing the daisies up! Ye're not soft, are yer?'

'I'll pack in after the Christmas holiday if yer want to be boss, sunshine, then yer can start throwing yer weight about.'

'Nah,' Nellie said, her eye on the last custard cream. 'If you're sitting on yer backside all day, I'm not going slogging me guts out.' She couldn't resist and the custard cream was in her hand before she went on, 'Besides, it doesn't sound the same without the Bennett, I'd never get any business.'

'In that case I'll retire early and leave the agency in your very capable hands.' Molly grinned at the thought of the chaos her friend could cause if they were talking about a real-life situation. 'How does that sound?'

'As I've said, girl, if you intend sitting on yer backside all day doing nowt, then yer can count me in. Whatever you do, wherever you go, then yours truly will be right beside yer.'

Monica was in her element looking from one to the other. This was a much better way of spending her day than trying to keep two young children from wrecking the place. Her mother couldn't have picked a better day to take them to the grotto. 'Do yer get much work in this detective agency?'

'Ooh, yeah!' Nellie deliberately avoided Molly's eyes. In fact it's the agency's business what brings us here, isn't it, girl?'

Molly nodded. 'It sounds terrible to say we came here today for help again, like we did last time. But yer were so good telling us what yer did about the Bradleys, me and Nellie thought yer wouldn't mind. I'll quite understand if yer want to send us packing, sunshine, but I'm keeping me fingers crossed that yer won't.'

'Didn't yer sort him out the last time? I thought yer were going to see him when yer left here? At least that was my understanding.'

'Thanks to you he was sorted out, and kept away from my family for a while.' Molly let out a sigh. 'But he's turned up again now and I'm sure he's going to cause trouble for me daughter and her husband. I've had a hectic time since I saw yer last, with two of me daughters married and me only son. I've only got the one girl at home now, and she leaves school at the weekend. She's got herself a job to go to after Christmas, and I'm dead chuffed for her. But Tom Bradley knocked on me daughter's door, asking for Phil, his step-son. Phil is a lovely lad and him and our Doreen are very happy. Oh, and I'm a grandma now, to their baby, Bobby. They changed their name by deed poll to Phil's real dad's name, because he hated the Bradley family so much. When the queer feller called at me daughter's yesterday, she told him there was no one of that name lived there and sent him packing. But apparently he threatened that he'd be back, and she could depend on it.'

Nellie could see her mate was getting upset talking about it, so she stepped in. 'He's a bad bugger, that Tom Bradley, I wouldn't trust him as far as I could throw him. We could get plenty of big strong men to sort him out, but Molly doesn't want that. She hasn't told anyone about him calling, and she made Doreen promise she wouldn't tell Phil because it would upset him something terrible. He had a bad life with them, even his own mother didn't stick up for him. But he's put it all behind him and made a good life for himself and his little family.'

'And no one will alter that, not if I've got anything to do with it,' Molly said with real determination. 'I'm going to do my best to put a stop to him coming back once and for all. And if I can't do it, then I'll get the men to put the fear of God into him.'

'He hasn't got the scrapyard now, yer know,' Monica said. 'That went over a year ago. Did I tell yer last time that there was a woman having a baby to him and she was bragging about it to anyone who would listen? She was a hard-faced cow, she was. But anyway, from what I've heard Mrs Bradley found out, and although no one knows the true story of what really happened, the next we knew the woman had done a moonlight flit and left the area, and the scrapyard was closed down.'

This was right up Nellie's street and her face had been doing contortions as Monica told them the tale. 'Did this woman, the one what had his baby, have a husband and a family of her own?'

Monica nodded. 'Oh, yeah, she's got a husband and two young children. I think she'd kidded her husband into believing the baby was his, but the neighbours were so fed up with her bragging about it and parading around as though she'd done something to be proud of, they all got together and put him wise. She was sporting a black eye for a couple of days, so she didn't get off scot-free, and then the next we knew, the whole family had disappeared into thin air. Didn't tell a soul, not even the landlord.'

'And the Bradleys have left the area, then, have they?' As Molly asked, she had her fingers crossed. 'Is that why the scrapyard closed?'

'Oh, no, they're still around. They live less than a five-minute walk away from here. Tom and his son go out with a cart every day, taking in old clothes. There's two daughters and they go to school, but they're hard-faced articles. Yer've only got to look at them and they give yer a mouthful of abuse.'

'What about Fanny Bradley?' Molly asked. 'Is she still as loud and foul-mouthed as she's always been?'

'That I couldn't tell yer, Molly, because I never hear anything about her. I never see her at the shops, and I can only think she's keeping out of everyone's way after the scandal about the baby.'

'Well, I can't say I blame her, 'cos it's a pretty kettle of fish, isn't it? In her place I'd be too ashamed to show me face.' These were just words, though, for Molly wasn't feeling any pity for Fanny Bradley, not after the terrible life she'd put Phil through. 'Perhaps she's getting paid back for her sins.'

'That's what it is, girl!' Nellie was so much in agreement the table rocked along with her tummy, bosom and chins. 'Ye're always saying that people who sin have to pay back for it in the end.'

Molly looked into her friend's chubby face, creased up now as though the very thought of sin disgusted her. She was a little love, was Nellie, and Molly loved the bones of her. But an angel she certainly wasn't. 'Haven't yer ever wondered why I keep saying that to yer, sunshine? Yer never hear me saying it to anyone else, do yer?'

Monica recognized the implication right away, and was trying to file away in her mind everything this wonderfully funny couple said. She often had one of the neighbours in for a cup of tea, and she enjoyed it, but their conversations were never this interesting or amusing.

Nellie's face became more creased as she tried to figure that one out. Her eyes disappeared as chubby cheeks, as red as polished apples, covered them. There was complete silence for a while, then after very careful consideration she glared at Molly. 'My sins are only little ones what God wouldn't even bother taking notice of. I don't go round having babies to men what I'm not married to.'

She looked surprised as Molly and Monica burst out laughing. What had she said that was so funny? 'Would the pair of yer kindly let me into the joke, please? I can't see nothing funny in yer best mate calling yer a bleeding liar!'

Molly used the back of her hand to wipe away the tears. 'Oh, sunshine, what would I do without yer? My life would be as dull as ditchwater. If yer could only see yer face now, with yer lips clamped together and yer nostrils flared. All yer need to do is breathe out flames and yer'd make the perfect dragon.'

The little woman was slightly mollified, but only slightly. She'd made them laugh, which was good, but were they laughing with her or at her? That was the question. 'I'm glad ye're both enjoying yerselves at my expense, but before I join yer, Molly

Bennett, yer'd better take back what yer said about me being a liar.'

'But yer are a liar, Nellie!'

'Yeah, I know, but only a little white lie one.'

'Okay, we'll call it quits on that. You agree that ye're a liar, and I'll agree that ye're just a little white lie one.'

Monica was fascinated when Nellie's head nodded and all her chins began to do the quickstep. Or was it a slow foxtrot? Whatever it was they all kept in time and were very graceful.

'I'll tell yer something, girl, I'll never again mention it when I diddle my feller out of a few bob. I never hear the end of it 'cos yer won't let me. So in future I'll keep it to meself and yer won't know whether I'm a liar or a saint.'

'Nellie, ye're made up with yerself when yer diddle George, and 'cos yer think it's clever there's no way yer could keep that to yerself.'

'Yer don't really diddle yer husband, do yer, Nellie?' Monica thought it was hilarious that you could call your friend a liar to her face and she'd agree with you. 'I'm sure yer wouldn't do a thing like that.'

If Molly hadn't been there, Nellie wouldn't have hesitated to say that of course she wouldn't lie to her husband. But with her mate's eyes on her, she could hardly tell a lie by saying she never lied. This was a fine how's yer father, this was. She was damned if she did and damned if she didn't. 'The way I look at it, Monica, is that if I tell my feller I paid ten bob for something that I only paid seven and six for, and he believes me, then I'd be daft not to take it and make a bit of profit. Yer see, I earn the difference in the price by using me brains. Not in the butcher's or the likes of Irwin's 'cos they won't let yer haggle. But in the other shops, or the market, I always get them to knock something off the price. So the way I see it, my George is only paying what I was asked for in the first place. And Molly will bear me out on this 'cos she never tells lies, white, blue or black. Isn't that right, girl?'

She's a crafty little beggar, Molly was thinking, she'd worm her way out of anything. 'Well, I suppose roughly speaking it's right. The only thing I would say on George's behalf, seeing as he's not here, is that he never, ever gets a bargain. *You* get them all.'

'He's never there to get them, is he, girl?' Nellie spread her hands. 'That's not my fault. No, It's me what gets the bargains. Me with the voluptuous figure, hair like Maureen O'Sullivan and a face like Norma Shearer.'

'And legs like the ones on my dining-room table,' Molly told her, spluttering with laughter. 'D'yer know, for years I've wondered where I'd seen a table with legs like mine, and all the while it was you what they reminded me of. I see yer every day and yet it only came to me now, when yer were saying how much like those film stars yer are.'

But Nellie was ready for her. 'That's a compliment, that is, girl, 'cos your table has fine legs. A damned sight more shapely than yours are.'

Monica was pressing a hand to her side to ease the pain caused by laughter. 'Do you two ever fall out, or come to blows?'

'Good gracious, no! We argue like cat and dog sometimes, but haven't fallen out in nearly twenty years.' Molly smiled across at her friend. 'We had one good set-to when your Steve was about two and Jill was a baby sitting up in the pram. Some kid had made her cry and I thought it was Steve because he was the one standing near the pram rocking it. We could easily have come to blows that day, and been enemies for life. But we didn't, did we, sunshine? We realized how stupid it was to fight over kids, started to laugh, and have been friends ever since. And we've never stopped laughing since either.'

'That's marvellous, that is,' Monica said. 'I've got plenty of friends in the street, but not one I can say is me best mate, like you two can. I hope yer both appreciate how lucky yer are.'

'We certainly do, in more ways than one, sunshine!' Molly winked at her mate. 'We're lucky with our families and friends, they're the best in the world. Am I right, Nellie?'

'I'll say yer are, girl, they're the truest words yer ever spoke. Molly's family are mine, and mine are hers. What was it yer called it? Yer know what I'm like for remembering big words.'

'We've got an extended family, which consists of the Bennetts, the McDonoughs and the Corkhills. Friends for over twenty years, we've always been there for each other when we needed help, and always shared things when times were hard. Mind you, all those years ago it wasn't as big as it is now.' Molly did some quick adding up. 'I reckon our extended family stands at twenty-four now.'

Nellie looked as proud and as pleased as Punch. 'And d'yer know what, Monica? My mate will have them all in her house for a real knees-up party on Christmas Day. Every year, she never fails, except now she has to bring her dining table up to our house and scrape the wallpaper off her walls to make room for them all.' And this time her smile was so wide it stretched from ear to ear. 'And I'm assistant hostess, I help me mate looking after the guests and making sure they have a good time. I don't stand no nonsense, either. No drunks or loose women allowed.'

There was fondness in Molly's smile. 'I don't know what I'd do without yer, sunshine, and that's a fact. But I think we've taken up enough of Monica's time now, so I suggest we make a move.'

'Oh, yer've no need to hurry away on my account.' Monica liked them so much she would have been happy for them to take up residence. 'I've got an easy day today.'

'No, we really should be on our way, but thank you for having us, yer've been an angel. And after Christmas is over, I promise we'll come and tell yer how we got on. That's if yer'll give us the Bradleys' address.'

'I couldn't give yer the address, Molly, 'cos I'm not sure of the number. But I know the house, so I'll slip me coat on and come with yer. I'll point it out to yer, then leave yer to it. And the best of luck.'

Chapter Fifteen

The two friends thanked Monica outside the house opposite the one where she'd said the Bradley family lived. They stood and watched until she reached the end of the street and turned to wave them a final farewell. She went with a firm promise from both that they would visit her again when the festivities were over to tell her how they'd got on.

There were no gates or paths in front of the houses in this street, and like their own two-up-two-downs it was just a step up from the pavement into the living room, although most people had partitioned off a portion of the room near the front door to make a tiny hall and stop the draughts from coming in. It made the living room smaller, of course, but it was worth it to keep the warmth in.

The two friends stood away from the house Monica had pointed out so they could look it over without being seen from the living-room window. It looked rundown and uncared for, as though nobody loved it enough to keep it looking nice. The dark brown paint on the front door had peeled off in several places, and the once shiny brass knocker looked as though it hadn't been polished for years. And the front step, unlike the houses to either side, was filthy. It was a long time since it had seen a donkey stone or a scrubbing brush. The words that sprang to Molly's mind were shabby and neglected. It looked like a house you would find in the slums, while the neighbouring ones were immaculate.

Nellie squeezed her friend's arm. 'It looks an eyesore, doesn't it, girl? I bet the neighbours aren't very happy living next to that 'cos it spoils the look of their houses. If she lived next to me I'd have her life, the dirty beggar.'

Molly sighed. 'At least she's got curtains and nets on the window, which is more than she did when she lived in our street. They're anything but clean, but they're better than nothing. Remember she had newspapers at the windows at one time?'

'I suppose it's an improvement on what she had before, but I still wouldn't want her living next to me. Look at the bleeding state of the step, it's black! I don't care what anyone says, she is one lazy faggot.'

'Yeah, I know, sunshine, but we'd better get it over with or people will wonder why we're just standing here gawping.' Molly felt herself shiver as she wondered what sort of a reception they'd get. 'I'll knock, Nellie, and you leave all the talking to me. That's providing there's someone in and we get an answer.'

'If it's Tom Bradley who opens the door, and he starts getting shirty with yer, girl, then he'll wonder what's hit him 'cos I'll knock him into the middle of next week.'

'I doubt he'll be in,' Molly said, moving forward. 'If he's a rag man, he probably has to go out every day to earn a living. Anyway, here goes.' With that she lifted the knocker and brought it down hard.

When the door opened, the friends looked at the woman before then and then at each other. This wasn't Fanny Bradley, surely? This woman was only half Fanny's size, with a very pale complexion and sunken eyes. Her hair was thin and almost white.

'What do you two want?'

'That voice, though far softer than they had heard it, and the fact that she knew them, brought a low gasp from Molly. What had happened to the Fanny Bradley they remembered? The woman who could out-fight any man and never spoke below a scream. Whose language was that of the gutter, and whose fists were always ready to land a blow if someone said something she didn't like.

'I asked yer what yer wanted, are yer deaf?'

Molly decided this was one time she wasn't going to beat about the bush. 'Your husband called to my daughter's house the other day and threatened her. He was probably after money, as usual, but he'll not get any and I'm here to say he'd better keep away from her or he'll find himself in trouble with my husband. So will yer pass the message on to him that he'll be sorry if he doesn't heed my words?'

The door was opened wider. 'Come in, will yer?' Once again the friends looked at each other for guidance. Then Nellie asked, 'Is yer husband in?'

Fanny shook her head. 'No, I'm alone in the house.'

Molly stepped up into the hall. 'Come on, sunshine, but we can't stay long.' She was first to stand in the middle of the room, and while waiting for Nellie was quick to note that although the room was as scruffy as the outside of the house, there was at least no smell. 'Why have yer asked us in, Mrs Bradley, when I told yer what we'd come for? All I want is for yer to tell yer husband to keep away from me and mine.'

Fanny put her hand on the arm of the couch before lowering herself down on to it. It was the sound of her laboured breathing in the quiet room, and her unhealthy pallor, that started alarm bells ringing in Molly's head. This woman was sick, and it wasn't just with a winter cold either. 'D'yer mind if we sit down, Fanny?'

Nellie looked at her friend as though she'd lost the run of her senses. What was Molly thinking of? They'd come here to cross swords and there was her mate asking if they could sit down! Mind you, she had to admit that Fanny Bradley wasn't half the woman she used to be, she looked really old. And she didn't look as though she had the strength to punch a hole in a paper bag. So Nellie followed Molly's actions and sat down.

It was Molly who started the conversation off. She'd come on the bounce, angry that her daughter's life, and that of her family, had been threatened with trouble. But she hadn't come to argue with a sick woman. 'If yer don't mind me saying so, Fanny, yer don't look very well. Have yer been sick?'

The woman nodded without meeting her eyes. 'Tom called to yer daughter's house because I asked him to. He wasn't after money, he wanted to leave a message for Phil. But yer daughter chased him and said there was no one called Bradley lived there. So Tom got mad and didn't leave the message.'

'Was the message to tell Phil yer weren't well?' Molly's dislike of Phil's mother was falling away. To say Fanny Bradley wasn't well would in fact be a great understatement because this was obviously one very sick woman. And she didn't intend to argue with a sick woman. 'Was that the message?'

Nellie, always wise after the event, was sitting forward in her chair now and telling herself she'd known as soon as she set eyes on her that Fanny Bradley was ill. The more yer looked at her, the more yer could see she had hardly any flesh on her, she was all bones.

Fanny nodded. 'I haven't been well for a year or so now, and the doctors in the hospital say there's not much they can do. As yer can see, there's hardly anything left of me.' The tears could be heard in her voice, and Molly and Nellie couldn't help being affected. 'I often used to stand at the bottom of your street and wait to see Phil coming home from work. He never saw me 'cos I used to hide in a shop doorway. And I knew his wife was expecting a baby 'cos I've seen her a few times. Only twice since the baby was born, though, 'cos I'm not strong enough to get on and off buses or trams now.' The tears had left her voice and were running down her cheeks. 'I know I don't deserve it, and I know what yer think of me. I don't blame yer 'cos I was everything yer thought I was. But I'd give anything to see me son again and tell him how sorry I am for the way I treated him. And I'd give the world to see me grandchild.'

Molly moved quickly to sit beside the heartbroken woman and put an arm across her shoulders. 'Don't be getting yerself upset now, everything will sort itself out, you'll see. We haven't always seen eye to eye, Fanny, but that's all in the past. Let's put it behind us and let bygones be bygones.'

It wasn't often Nellie was emotionally moved, but her friend's words were having a profound effect on her. 'How d'yer manage with the housework, Fanny, and the shopping? D'yer get any help with it?'

'The two girls do the shopping when they get home from school. They do odd jobs around the house, but not much. They're tearaways, been left to run wild, but it's not their fault. It's the way they've been brought up. They do their best so I can't complain. And Tom and me son are very good when they're at home, won't let me lift a finger.' Fanny sighed. 'We had a big upset in the family about two years ago, it wasn't a good time for me. It was sorted out, though, and we're all right now. Tom and the boy are out working every day and they bring in enough money to keep us going.'

Nellie didn't know the meaning of the word tactless. It was on the tip of her tongue to ask if the upset was when another woman had a baby to Tom. But to her own amazement she bit the words back and told herself off for even thinking of being so thoughtless when she could see how ill and upset Fanny was. Why, she asked herself as she heard Molly offering comforting words to the sick woman, can't I be as kind and gentle as my mate? Why can't I find the right words to say, like she does?

'Would yer like me to tell yer how Phil has been since yer last saw him, sunshine, and what he's done with his life?'

Fanny grasped her hand. 'Yes, please, Molly, I'm hungry for news of him. I have been for years, but I didn't have the guts to face him. I know he went into the army.'

'He didn't wait to be called up, yer know, he volunteered.' Molly hesitated, wondering if it would be the right thing to tell her about Phil being injured, or would it be too upsetting? Then she quickly decided to keep nothing back. 'He was invalided out a year before the war ended because he'd been injured when a mine blew up and he got shrapnel in one of his legs.' She felt the hand she was holding begin to shake. 'He got over it, though, and although he's still got a bit of a limp no one would notice. He was in hospital for a while, then when he was able he went back to his old job. He courted Doreen, who idolizes him, and made his home with Miss Clegg who took him in when he had nowhere to go. When him and Doreen got married, Miss Clegg wanted them to live with her and be the family she never had. And now, as yer know, there's a baby come along and their happiness knows no bounds.'

'He's made a good husband and a good father,' Nellie told her. 'And he's loved by our two families and popular with everyone in the street.'

'He certainly is, we all love the bones of him,' Molly agreed. 'And what a handsome lad he is. Yer can be proud of him.'

Fanny shook her head. 'No, I haven't earned the right to be proud of him. Whatever he's done, and however he's turned out to be, is all his own doing. I pulled him down to the gutter and I'm glad he was strong enough to pull himself out of it. Thank you for telling me all the things that have happened in his life, it makes me feel a bit closer to him.'

Molly thought very hard before she said what she had in mind. 'There is more still to tell yer, Fanny, and I hope it doesn't upset yer. But I think it's time to wipe the slate clean, bring everything out into the open and hold nothing back. You see, when Phil came home wounded from the war, me and Nellie felt so sorry for him because he had no one of his own. He had us, and I've always treated him like a son, but no one to call his own, no one of his own flesh and blood.' She saw the woman flinch and just prayed she was doing the right thing. 'He told us about you giving him the photograph of his dad, and telling him what his name was. And I'll never forget the happiness on his face when he showed us that snap. He was so proud that at last he had that information, and the man in the photograph was so like him, it could have been Phil himself.'

'His father was one of the best men yer could ever meet. Handsome, caring, full of fun and laughter. I loved him so much I felt like killing meself when he got killed in an accident. Three weeks before we were to be married and I was carrying his child. I was ashamed and afraid to tell anyone, so when Tom Bradley said he'd marry me I saw it as me only way out. And no matter what he does, or what anyone thinks about him, I'll always be grateful to Tom for that.'

Molly was amazed at the change in Phil's mother. Not just in her appearance but also in the way she spoke. Not one swear word or obscenity had passed her lips since they'd arrived. But for the fickle hand of fate dealing her a bad hand, Molly was convinced she would have made a good wife and mother.

'I've some more to tell yer, Fanny, so I'll get on with it. Me and Nellie managed to track down the Mitchells. We found Phil's grandmother first, Mary. Then through her his aunts, uncles and cousins. They welcomed him with open arms, as I'm sure they would have done if you'd gone to them and told them yer were carrying their son's baby. But it's too late now to turn back the clock, or dwell on what might have been.'

Fanny was sitting as still as a statue, she didn't appear to be blinking or breathing. Becoming concerned, Molly rubbed her hand. 'Are yer all right, sunshine? Perhaps I shouldn't have told yer all this, I might have known it would upset yer.'

Her voice as low as the whisper of a leaf falling, Fanny said, 'I haven't been a good mother to Phil, haven't been a mother at all. But I'm not such a bad person that I begrudge him the happiness others have given him. I'm glad yer made contact with the Mitchells for him, they're good people. And now he's got the family he always deserved.'

In for a penny, in for a pound, were Molly's thoughts. 'He also has their name, sunshine. He changed his name by deed-poll to Mitchell. And they've called their new baby Bobby Mitchell, after the father he never knew.'

The floodgates opened then, and Fanny's body shook with sobs. Holding her close, Molly sobbed with her. 'It's all right, sunshine, you get your crying done now. And, please God, yer'll never have cause to cry for yer son again. It will all come right, I promise yer. Yer'll see yer son very soon, and yer grandson. There'll be no hard feelings, either, 'cos Phil isn't that sort of man. Where you'll meet I can't say now, but I hope yer'll understand if Phil refuses to come to this house. He doesn't have fond memories of Tom Bradley and I for one think he'd have every reason not to want to come into his home. But I'll see Phil tonight and we'll sort something out. Would you have any objections to going to his house?'

'I'd go to the ends of the earth to see me son and grandson, but it's not possible because I hardly have the strength to stand. I'd never make the journey on me own, Molly, not on and off trams.'

'Yer won't need to, sunshine. Me and Nellie would come for yer, wouldn't we, Nellie?'

Happy not to be left out, she nodded her head so vigorously her chins threatened to go on strike. 'Yeah, 'course we will, Fanny! Me and me mate could give yer an arm each and we'd practically carry yer.' How quickly the little woman was learning how to be tactful. For she'd almost said they could manage her 'cos there was nothing of her, and was pleased with herself because she hadn't.

'I'll see what I can sort out tonight when Phil comes home, and me and Nellie will come back tomorrow and let yer know. It'll have to be a time that suits Phil and his work. But no matter what, Fanny, yer'll see us in the morning, about the same time. And now we are going to have to love yer and leave yer, we've got shopping and housework to do.'

Fanny pulled herself up by the arm of the couch. 'I can't thank yer enough, both of yer. You have no idea what this means to me.'

'Oh, I think we do, sunshine. Now we'll see ourselves out, so don't bother coming to the door. We'll see yer tomorrow without fail. Ta-ra for now, Fanny.'

Nellie was linking Molly's arm as they made their way to the tram stop. Now and again she had to give a little hop to keep in step. 'Are yer calling to Doreen's to tell her, girl? I've got a feeling she won't be very happy to hear the Bradleys might come back into their lives.'

Molly shook her head. 'I'll tell her tonight when Phil is there. I'd rather they were all together, Victoria as well, to hear what I've got to say.'

'But I thought yer said yer were going to see yer ma tonight?'

'I was, but I'll have to swap it around. I'll go to me ma's this afternoon instead.'

'Will yer tell her what we found out today?'

'No, I'm not telling a soul, sunshine, and neither are you. We'll keep this to ourselves until we see how Phil reacts. And even then it's up to him if he wants to tell the rest of his family and friends. Perhaps he's not ready to forgive his mam for what she put him through. Then again he might want to see her. I don't intend to pull any punches with him, or Doreen for that matter. I've called Fanny Bradley for everything in the past, for what she did to Phil and the fact that she didn't try to stop her husband and children from robbing right, left and centre, but no one seeing the state she's in now could help but feel sorry for her. She really pulled on my heart strings today, Nellie, and I couldn't stand aside and not help her.'

'She got to me, too, girl! It's not often I cry, but she brought a lump to me throat that was so big I thought it would choke me. I've never seen anyone go down the nick like she has, I couldn't believe me eyes when she opened the door.'

'I thought Monica had made a mistake. It was only when she spoke I knew it was Fanny. But what a change in her! I don't mean in her appearance, it's easy to see the woman is dying, but in the way she speaks. Not one word out of place the whole time we were there.'

Nellie stopped in her tracks. 'I know she's very sick, girl, but she's not going to die, is she?'

'I'm afraid so, sunshine, and the sad thing is she knows it. The doctors have told her there's nothing they can do for her, and I would think that's pretty final.'

'Then I hope Phil doesn't refuse to see her, or let her see the baby. That would be cruel, that would, and I'd tell him so.'

'He won't refuse, Nellie, yer should know him better than that. He'll forget all the bad times and remember that, after all's said and done, she is his mother. I bet Fanny sees her son before the week is out. And the baby, too!'

Molly put her face to the window of a sweetshop to see the time on the wall clock, and she groaned when she saw it was later than she expected. 'It's going to be a mad dash, sunshine, so let's put a move on. I'll get stew for the tea and make a pan of scouse which can be cooking on a low light while I go round to see if me ma and da are all right. So don't try and wangle a cup of tea off me 'cos I really won't have enough time.'

'Does that mean I've got to wait until tomorrow to find out what Phil says? Ah, that's not fair, that's not, girl! How would you like it if yer were in my place? I bet yer'd have plenty to complain about. I go all the way down there with yer to see Fanny, then yer expect me to wait until yer feel yer have the time to tell me what's going on!'

'Don't be getting yer knickers in a twist, sunshine, I haven't said yer'd have to wait until tomorrow. I'll give yer a knock when I'm coming back from our Doreen's and yer can come in ours and listen while I'm telling Jack. That's what yer call killing two birds with one stone.'

There was a spring in Nellie's step then, and she appeared to bounce up and down like a rubber ball. A big one, mind, but a rubber ball nonetheless. 'I'll be ready for yer, girl, I won't keep yer waiting.'

'Right, here's a tram so let's move ourselves.'

Doreen opened the door. 'Hello, Mam, I wasn't expecting yer tonight, yer usually call in during the day. Aunt Vicky was just saying it was unusual for a day to go by without yer calling in.'

Molly stepped up into the hall and gave her daughter a kiss. 'I had somewhere to go, sunshine, that's why I'm late in coming over.'

Phil and Victoria greeted her with a smile, both glad to see her. 'Yer've missed Bobby, Mrs B, he's just been put down in his cot.' There was always a look of love and pride on Phil's handsome face when he spoke of his son. 'I'm not saying he'll go to sleep, but he's got to learn that he won't be picked up every time he cries.'

Doreen held out her hand. 'Give us yer coat, Mam, or yer won't feel the benefit when it's time for yer to go.'

'Ye're right, love, it is nippy out tonight.' Molly rubbed her hands in front of the fire. 'Mind you, it's nearly Christmas so we can't expect nice weather. And although most people are happy when it snows on Christmas Day, I'm not one of them. It's nice to look at through the window, but miserable to walk in when it turns to slush.'

'Would yer like a cup of tea, Mrs B?' Phil hovered by the kitchen door. 'It won't take a minute to boil the kettle.'

'No, thanks, sunshine, I've not long had me dinner and two cups of tea. I've got something quite important to tell yer, so d'yer want to sit down and make yerselves comfortable.'

Doreen looked anxious. 'It's not about Tom Bradley, is it, Mam? I told Phil about him calling and he went mad. Said I had to shut the door in his face if he comes back.'

'No, it's nothing to do with Tom Bradley, it's Phil's mother I've come to see yer about. And no matter what yer think while I'm telling yer, I'd be grateful if you didn't interrupt and kept back what yer have to say until I've finished.'

Phil pulled one of the wooden dining chairs near to where Molly was sitting. 'What about my mother, Mrs B, have yer seen her?'

'It would be much easier for me if yer would let me start at the beginning, sunshine, rather than at the end. Yer'd only get all muddled up if I did that. But I'll be as quick as I can and yer'll soon have as much information as I have.'

Molly fixed her eyes on the flickering flames in the grate as she had no desire to see the expression on their faces. 'Me and Nellie met a woman about eighteen months ago and got pally with her. I won't go into any more detail because it's got nothing to do with what I'm going to tell yer, except in a roundabout way. Anyway, we made a promise to call and see her again, and we did that today. And as she knew where the Bradleys lived, I thought I'd call in and warn them about coming here again making a nuisance of themselves and upsetting my daughter.'

When Molly paused for breath, she could hear various sounds of surprise, but kept her eyes fixed firmly on the leaping flames. 'It just so happens that yer stepdad and his son go out every day with a handcart to earn some money, and the two girls go to school. So there was only yer mother at home, Phil.' God give me strength, Molly prayed, this is going to be harder than I imagined. And she coughed to try and clear her throat before going on. 'Your mother is very ill, we didn't recognize her at first. The flesh has fallen off her and she's not half the woman she was. That flame-coloured mop of hair is now thin and white.

Molly was filling up and had to stop before she burst into tears. Leaning towards her, Phil asked quietly, 'What's wrong with me mam, Mrs B?'

With bad memories of Phil's family fresh in her mind, Doreen said, 'She's probably putting in one, trying to make yer feel sorry for her. It's just the sort of thing she would do.'

Turning to her daughter, Molly asked, 'Do yer think I'm so stupid? The woman is dying, Doreen, so have some compassion, please! She didn't need to put on an act, yer only have to look at the poor soul to see she's very ill. Forget what's happened in the past and have some sympathy for a woman whose only wish now is to see her son and grandson before it's too late. She told me and Nellie that she used to come down often to see Phil coming home from work. She used to hide in a shop doorway so he couldn't see him because she didn't have the guts to face him after the way she'd treated him. And she's seen you a few times, Doreen, and knew yer were pregnant.' There was fire in her voice when she asked, 'Yer don't think I'd make this all up do yer? I'm just sorry Phil has to hear it this way. But he has to, like it or not, because the woman is his mother.'

Phil took hold of her hand. 'Of course you have every right to tell me, it was something I needed to know. As yer say, she is my mother, and I don't think a day has passed that I haven't thought of her and wondered how she was. She wasn't a good mother, it would be a lie to say otherwise, but I've always blamed Tom Bradley for the way she was. Anyway, there's nothing to be gained by bringing that up. Did me mam say what was wrong with her, Mrs B?'

Molly shook her head. 'No, and I didn't like to ask. She just said the hospital said there was nothing they could do for her. She knows she's dying, Phil, that's the saddest part about it! I've never had any love for her, as yer well know, but my heart went out to her when I saw her today and I promised I'd make it my business to see that she got the chance to see you and the baby very soon. Did I do the right thing when I made that promise?'

'Of course yer did, I'll go and see me mam tomorrow. That's if yer'll give me the address 'cos I haven't a clue where she lives.'

'I don't think I could give yer the address, but I could take yer to the house if that's what yer want? I did tell Fanny that I didn't think yer'd want to go to their house, not with the way things are between you and the rest of the family.' Molly suddenly remembered something. 'Oh, by the way, Doreen, Tom Bradley didn't come on the scrounge, he came because Fanny asked him to. He'd come with a message for Phil, to say how ill his mam was, but when yer took off on him he got in a temper and left without telling yer.'

'How was I to know that, Mam! And he could have given me the message, there was nothing to stop him doing that.'

'No, sunshine, yer weren't to know that. And he's a funny bloke is Tom Bradley, I think he got a cob on when yer told him about the change in yer name. But I wouldn't worry about that now, there's more serious things to worry about.' Molly turned to Phil. 'Yer mam isn't strong enough to come all this way on her own, not getting on and off trams, so I did say that if yer were all agreeable, me and Nellie would go for her. She'd be all right with us, we could take an arm each. Besides, if you went there, she wouldn't get to see the baby.'

'I don't want to leave it too long, Mrs B, not if she's as bad as yer say she is. I'd like us to spend some time together before it's too late.'

Victoria had been quiet until now, believing she shouldn't interfere in the family's business. But she'd been very moved by what she'd heard, and said, 'I would like her to come here, if that is possible.'

'Me and Nellie could go for her tomorrow.' Molly said, her eyes on Phil. 'Is that soon enough for yer?'

'That would be marvellous, Mrs B, ye're an angel.' A yearning was starting to grow within Phil, a yearning to see his mother. When he was a young lad all he'd ever wanted was for her to love him. He wanted to be the most important person in her life, but she always took the side of the Bradleys and when they taunted him because he wouldn't go robbing with them, she never took his side. He was happy now, happier than he'd ever thought possible, with a lovely, loving wife, his adopted Aunt Vicky, his new baby, and the love and friendship of the Bennetts, McDonoughs and Corkhills. But although he'd never told a soul, he still longed for the love of his mother. 'If you could pick her up in the morning, I'll take the afternoon off work and it'll give us plenty of time together.'

'And I'll get something nice in for a sandwich,' Doreen said, wishing she hadn't sounded so hard-hearted before. 'Some lean boiled ham or pork.'

'I'll buy cakes for everyone if I'm allowed.' Victoria thought it was very sad that a person half her age should be dying, after missing so many years of her son's life. Although her loss had been Victoria's gain, it was still very sad. 'Cream slices would go down well, I think. Most people seem to like them.'

'Do yer think it would be best if I gave yer the money to bring me mam in a taxi, Mrs B, if she's not strong enough to travel?'

Molly shook her head. 'No, sunshine, me and Nellie will manage her fine. We'll make sure she doesn't over-exert herself. And quite honestly, I think she could do with a bit of fresh air because her skin is a terrible colour and sitting in the house all day will make her feel weak. No, me and Nellie said we'd go for her, and that's what we'll do.'

She looked at her son-in-law and managed a shaky grin. 'Phil, if yer live to be a hundred, yer'll never give anyone a present that will be appreciated as much as the one ye're giving yer mother. She will be so happy, but I imagine it will be very emotional for both of yer. For all of us, if it comes to that, 'cos I've wept buckets today. And Nellie, God love her, thought she was going to choke on the big lump she had in her throat. She is the best mate anyone could have, is Nellie, and I'm leaving yer now to go and tell her what's happening tomorrow. And Jack, of course, will be on tenterhooks until I get home. So I'll love yer and leave yer until tomorrow.'

Molly gave everyone a goodnight kiss and was on the point of opening the front door when Victoria called, 'Will yer tell Mrs Bradley we're all looking forward to seeing her and she'll be made very welcome?'

'Will do, sunshine. Goodnight and God bless.'

Chapter Sixteen

Molly banged the door shut behind her, stepped down on to the pavement, and as she was putting her key in her bag, said to Nellie, 'Wait here a minute, sunshine, I just want to have a word with our Doreen.'

'Ah, why can't I come with yer?'

'There's no point in yer crossing the street then having to come straight back. I won't be going in the house, I'll speak to her at the door.' Molly could see the petulant droop to Nellie's mouth and clicked her tongue. 'Honest to God, ye're worse than a ruddy child. But to satisfy yer curiosity, I'm only going to tell Doreen something I never thought of saying last night. It came to me when I was in bed and it kept me awake for ages. Yer see, I never thought to tell them not to let Fanny see how upset they are when they see her. Phil's in for a real shock, and I'd hate him or Doreen or Victoria to let what they're thinking show on their faces. They should act normal, as though they don't notice any difference in her. I think I'm better to prepare them 'cos I'd hate to see her get upset and break down.'

Nellie immediately felt contrite. Trust her to sound selfish when all her friend was trying to do was stop someone from getting hurt. 'Ye're doing the right thing, girl, 'cos Phil is going to get the shock of his life. Go on, you run across and I'll wait here for yer.'

When Doreen opened the door, Molly lost no time in explaining things. 'Warn Phil, for heaven's sake, sunshine, won't yer? It'll not be so bad for you and Victoria 'cos yer didn't know her well or see much of her.'

'I'll tell him, Mam, don't worry. He didn't show it much last night, but he really was upset. I could feel him tossing and turning in bed and I'd be surprised if he got an hour's sleep. Anyway, he's asking the boss if he can finish work at eleven, so he'll be home by the time you get here. I've been up early and got me work over with, and as soon as I've seen to Bobby I'll nip down to the shops for something to eat. Phil said she might eat a bit of dinner, which would do her more good than sandwiches, so I'll make a steak and kidney pie with Aunt Vicky's help. Left on me own, I'm hopeless with pastry, but Aunt Vicky's melts in yer mouth. And I'll do some roast potatoes with it.'

'Don't expect Phil's mam to tuck into a big dinner, sunshine, and don't be disappointed if yer go to a lot of trouble and she only eats enough to feed a bird. When yer see her yer'll know I'm not exaggerating. And, sunshine, for Phil's sake and the baby's, take her to yer heart.'

Without waiting for an answer because she could feel herself filling up again, Molly crossed over to her friend. 'We're all set now, so let's go.'

Nellie was unusually quiet as they walked down the street, and after a while Molly asked, 'Are yer all right, sunshine? I've never known yer be so quiet.'

'Well, yer weren't the only one thinking in bed last night, girl, 'cos I had plenty on me mind. I was going over all the things you and me have got up to over the years. All the baddies we've confronted to help someone, and all the nice people we've been able to help. We haven't half done a lot, Molly, when yer come to think of it. But what we're doing today, for Phil and his mam, well, I think it's the best thing we've ever done. I feel really good about it.'

'So yer should, sunshine, 'cos yer've been a big help. I wouldn't have been able to do it without you by my side, and I told the family that last night. But, ay, Nellie, who'd have thought the day would ever come when we'd be crying over a Bradley, and wanting to do everything we can for her? It just shows what strange things life throws at yer. It doesn't do to fall out with someone and say yer'll never speak to them again as long as yer live, because yer never know whether some day yer'll have to eat your words.'

This brought a cheeky grin to Nellie's face. 'Ay, girl, it would be God help you if yer had to eat yer words, what with all those long ones yer use. It would serve yer right, though, for trying to be posh.'

They didn't have long to wait for a tram, and when the conductor came around Molly had the right money to hand to him. 'You can pay for us on the way home, sunshine.' She put her hand in her pocket and brought out two pennies. 'This is for Fanny's fare, I don't expect yer to pay for her.'

Nellie waved her hand aside. 'I'm not taking that off yer! I'll pay for Fanny, I'm not a flipping miser. Put that away and let's hear no more about it.'

Molly slipped the coins back into her pocket. 'I was going to say yer'd get paid back in heaven, but I know yer'll be paid back before then. Victoria is treating us all to cream slices, so yer've something to look forward to.'

'I've got a long life to look forward to as well, girl! At least I hope so. And that's more than Fanny Bradley's got. My heart bleeds for her, it really does.'

'Don't, by word or deed, let her see yer feel sorry for her, sunshine, 'cos that will only make her feel worse. We've got to buck her up, make her feel happy, not sad.'

'I'll do me best, girl, but I can't promise to spend the rest of the day telling jokes to make her laugh, 'cos I don't know that many jokes.'

'A cheerful face should do it, sunshine, that's all.'

Frances Bradley had put one of the wooden chairs by the window so she would have something to hold on to while she waited for sight of Molly and Nellie. She knew they wouldn't be taking her to see Phil today, but at least they'd tell her whether her son wanted to see her or not. Her insides had been churning over since they'd left yesterday in case Phil didn't want to have anything to do with her. She couldn't blame him if that was the message they brought, but she prayed to God it wouldn't be. She did feel better about one thing, and that was Tom being pleased for her. He'd even cleaned the windows last night and made the girls scrub the step and wipe the windowsill down. And Brian had dusted everywhere without even being asked. So she didn't feel as ashamed as she had when they came yesterday. Not that they'd looked down their noses at her, they hadn't. In fact they were really nice and understanding, and their visit had cheered her up.

When she saw them coming, she moved from the chair so quickly she nearly fell over. But she didn't want them to think she'd been on pins watching for them. She patted her hair which had been in pipe cleaners for a few hours, but there was no life in it and no curl. Still, it was neat and tidy and that was the best she could hope for. The knock seemed to be ages in coming and her heart was pounding. She would be able to tell by their faces if they'd brought good news or not, and she was afraid she'd break down if her request to see her son had been rejected.

'Hello, Fanny, how are yer, sunshine?' The smile on Molly's face was enough to send hopes rising. 'I hope ye're ready to go out, are yer?'

Nellie bustled in, a cheery smile on her face. 'Hi-ya, Fanny, ye're looking a bit better today. And yer hair looks nice.'

Fanny was staring unblinkingly at Molly. 'Are yer taking me to see Phil today, Molly?'

'We are that, sunshine, as soon as yer can get ready we'll be on our way. But yer need to get well wrapped up 'cos there's a very cold wind out. Have yer got a woollen scarf for round yer neck and a pair of gloves? Oh, and something for yer head.'

Fanny felt so weak with emotion she couldn't move, and Molly said, 'Tell us where yer things are and we'll get them. I'm not rushing yer, so just take yer time 'cos we're in no hurry.'

Her voice a soft croak, Fanny asked, 'Am I really seeing Phil today? I didn't think it would be so quick. That's if he wanted to see me at all. I wouldn't have blamed him if he said he'd washed his hands of me years ago.'

'Yer've got a lot to learn about yer son, Fanny.' Molly tutted and shook her head with irritation. 'Old Mrs Mitchell said yer were called Frances, so why are yer now calling yerself Fanny when Frances is such a lovely name?'

'It was Tom started calling me Fanny in fun, but it stuck. I hate it, I'd much rather be called Frances. That's if yer don't mind?'

'I'll be happy to call yer Frances, sunshine, so from now on yer get yer full title. Unless yer want to be stand-offish and insist on Mrs Bradley?'

Nellie gave an exaggerated roll of her eyes. 'Will yer just listen to my mate and some of the words she comes out with! Sometimes I think I'm in a foreign country, I can't understand what she means!' She glared at Molly. 'What did yer mean by her being stanfish?'

'Stand-offish, yer silly nit, means being haughty, or the looking down yer nose type. But you being pig ignorant wouldn't know that.'

'Pig ignorant! Well, that's a nice thing to say to yer best mate, I'm sure!' This little exchange was all for Frances's benefit, and it was paying off because there was smile hovering about her mouth. 'I don't know why yer bother with me, girl, yer'd be better off with a mate what spoke as though she's got a bleeding plum in her mouth. Yer wouldn't get no laughs, like, 'cos yer life would be bloody miserable, but it would make yer feel yer were going up in the world.'

Molly winked at Frances. 'Take no notice of her, sunshine, she can't help being daft.'

Nellie wanted to see the smile on that pale face widen, so she stood to attention with her stomach and bosom thrust forward. And the posh accent came into play. 'Hif hi ham so hignorant, girl, would yer prefer me to sit hupstairs hon the tram so no one will know hi ham with yer?'

'Haven't yer forgotten something, sunshine?'

'What's that, then, girl?'

'Yer can't get on the ruddy tram without me there to give yer a hand up.'

Nellie looked dejected as she hung her head. 'I'll walk home, girl, if yer don't want to be seen with me. And I hope yer find yerself a good friend what knows her manners.'

'And leave you, me own private jester! Not on yer life, sunshine, I know when I'm well off.' Molly could see a full smile now on Frances's face, and felt like kissing her little friend. 'Think of all the money I save by not going to the pictures. Laurel and Hardy, Charlie Chase and Buster Keaton . . . they're not a patch on you for being funny.'

Nellie's face acquired a sly expression. 'Yer've given me an idea now, girl, and it's a belting one. Every time I make yer laugh out loud, I could charge yer a penny. And for a titter or a grin I'd only charge yer a ha'penny. That's because ye're me mate, of course, it would be more for them what aren't me mates.'

'That's fine, sunshine, we could both go into business and earn a few bob. I'll charge you a penny for every cup of tea yer have in my house, and a ha'penny if there's a second cup left in the pot. Oh, and what about the custard cream biscuits? I'd have to work out how much each they cost.' Molly cast an eye on the clock on the mantelpiece. She didn't want to get home before Phil, but she didn't want to be late and have him on tenterhooks, either. The clock showed it was a quarter to eleven, so if they started getting ready now, they could take things nice and easy. 'I think yer daft half-hour is over now, sunshine, so we'll start making tracks.'

'But Phil won't be home until teatime, will he?' Frances asked. 'I don't want to impose on his wife and the old lady.'

'Phil's asking off work at eleven o'clock, sunshine, so he can spend more time with yer. They're all looking forward to seeing you, Doreen and Miss Clegg as well, so don't think yer won't be welcome.'

Nellie had taken down a black coat which was hanging on a hook behind the door, and she held it in front of the fire. 'This will be nice and warm for yer to put on, girl, and it's a good heavy coat. Give me yer gloves and scarf and I'll warm them for yer as well.'

'I still can't believe it, yer know,' Frances said softly. 'I feel as though I'm in a dream and will wake up any minute.'

'It's no dream, sunshine, and I know Phil can't wait to see yer. And that's the way it should be between mother and son.'

'I hope I don't make a fool of meself, Molly, and pass out. Even just the thought of seeing him is making me feel dizzy.' Frances put a hand to her forehead. 'I've been such a blind fool, afraid of facing my son over the years and telling him how sorry I was for being a bad mother to him. And such a long time has passed by, I'd given up all hope of ever seeing him again to make amends.'

'No tears now, Frances, this should be a joyful occasion. I know yer'll break down when yer see Phil, it's only natural because emotions will be high, but at the end of the day yer should both be happy at being united. So let me put this scarf around yer neck and we'll be on our way. We don't want to keep yer son and grandson waiting.'

Phil was pacing the floor. 'Perhaps I should go and meet them in case me mam's not well and Mrs B needs a hand.' He spun around and walked to the window. 'They should be here by now.'

'For heaven's sake, Phil, ye're wearing the lino out! Me mam didn't leave here until after ten, so give them a chance.'

'They could have been well here by now, it's turned half-eleven!' Phil remembered the baby sleeping above and lowered his voice. 'I thought they'd be here before I got home.'

'Phil, sweetheart, you're a young healthy man, able to run like the wind if necessary,' Victoria reminded him. 'If your mother is weak, Molly and Nellie will have to take their time with her. They'll be here soon, so be patient.'

'Anyway, yer know what me mam and Auntie Nellie are like for talking, they've probably been sitting having a natter with her to cheer her up. Because her nerves must be the same as yours, if not worse.'

'I can't help having an attack of nerves, love. Yer've no idea what this means to me. You've never had a day away from your mam, so I don't expect yer to understand.'

Victoria saw three figures pass the window. 'They're here now, sweetheart, but remember the message that Molly left. If yer see a big change in yer mam, don't for heaven's sake let her see it because it will spoil what should be a marvellous day for both of yer.'

Phil's head and shoulders moved forward but he couldn't lift his feet from the floor and he could feel beads of sweat running down his forehead. He'd been on edge all day at the thought of seeing his mam again after five or six years, but his nerves had gone completely now and panic set in.

'Phil, will yer hurry up and open the door?' Doreen said. 'It's cold for them out there.'

He shook his head and spread his hands. 'I can't, my nerves are shot to pieces. You open the door while I get myself a drink of cold water to calm me down.' Unsteady on his feet, he made his way to the kitchen and closed the door behind him.

'I don't know, what a performance,' Doreen said aloud before she opened the front door. She had only ever seen Phil's mother from a distance before, and had never exchanged one word with her. So she had no picture in her mind that she could compare to the woman standing between her mam and Auntie Nellie. She looked a lot older than the girl had expected, and she did look ill, as though she didn't have the energy to stand. 'Come in out of the cold.' Doreen put a smile on her face and kissed each of the women as they passed her. 'Ooh, yer faces are freezing. Get in near the fire and I'll take yer coats off yer.'

Victoria pushed herself out of the rocking chair and smiled a greeting as Molly introduced her. Holding out her hand, she said, 'I'm very pleased to meet you, Frances.'

She returned a shaky smile. 'I'm pleased to meet you, too.' But she looked shy, frightened and bewildered. She'd been expecting to see Phil's face as soon as she walked through the door, but there was no sign of him.

Molly was quick to notice her dismay and asked Doreen, 'Is Phil not home yet? I expected him to be here before us.'

'He is, Mam, he's in the kitchen. I think he's got himself into such a state his nerves have gone and he feels sick.'

Victoria, with the wisdom of her years, said, 'Perhaps it would be best if Frances went into the kitchen to Phil. Their first meeting is bound to be emotional and I'm sure both of them would appreciate some privacy.'

'That's an excellent idea, Victoria,' Molly said, cupping a hand on Frances's elbow and steering her towards the kitchen.' She put a hand on the knob, opened the door slightly and gave a gentle push. 'Your son is waiting for yer, sunshine.'

And while tears flowed profusely between mother and son in the kitchen, there were no dry eyes in the living room. Except for Nellie, who kept her tears back by sniffing up every two seconds until Molly said, 'For heaven's sake, Nellie, will yer blow yer nose! That sniffing is getting on me nerves.'

'I can't help it, girl, I haven't got no hankie. I never thought to bring one, and I knew if I used me underskirt yer'd go mad.'

'Don't you dare, Nellie McDonough, or so help me I'll clock yer one.'

Doreen opened a drawer in the sideboard and brought out a freshly washed and ironed handkerchief. 'Here yer are, Auntie Nellie, yer can use that.'

'Thanks, girl, ye're a pal.' Nellie shook open the handkerchief and blew her nose soundly. 'I won't forget to give it back to yer.'

'Yes, after it's been washed and ironed, sunshine! Doreen doesn't want it back today after you've blown yer nose on it.'

Nellie pulled faces at her friend. 'Pig ignorant I might be, girl, but I wasn't brought up in a pigsty. I do know what handkerchiefs are for.'

Doreen was looking anxious. 'I hope they won't be too long, 'cos the steak and kidney might boil dry. And I really want the dinner to be nice today.'

'Another fifteen minutes won't do it any harm, sweetheart,' Victoria said. 'It won't be cooked enough yet.'

'It smells good from here, sunshine, it's making me feel hungry.'

'I'll say it does.' Nellie licked her lips. 'If yer hear a loud rumble, if won't be thunder, it'll be me tummy telling me it's hungry.'

Molly chuckled. 'Nellie, we only have to walk past Hanley's and yer tummy rumbles. And if we see someone eating chips out of a bag, yer dribble like a baby. To be honest with yer, I've even thought of buying yer a bib for Christmas.'

'Nah, don't yer go wasting yer money on me, girl.' Nellie, as ever, had an answer ready, 'Your Doreen must be able to spare one of the baby's bibs, and I don't mind if it's second-hand.' Then came the crafty look in her narrowed eyes. 'But do make sure it's been washed and ironed before yer give it to me.'

'Shush!' Doreen put a finger to her lips 'Isn't that the water running in the sink?'

'Perhaps they're rinsing their faces,' Victoria suggested. 'There's nothing like a splash of cold water to take away the tell-tale signs of crying.'

'Oh, dear.' Doreen jumped to her feet. 'There's only a fiddling little towel out there, not a ha'porth of good for two people. Ay, Mam, you're nearest to the cupboard, would yer pass me a towel out?'

When Molly opened one of the doors of the cupboard which was built into the recess at the side of the fireplace, she smiled with pride. Sheets and pillowcases in neat piles, next to towels and tablecloths. She was a good little housewife was Doreen. 'Here, catch, sunshine!' She threw a fluffy hand towel over. 'Knock on the door and pass it in.'

But Doreen didn't to like knock in case she was intruding, so she called softly, 'Phil, here's a clean towel.'

'It's all right, love, we're coming out now.' And when mother and son came through the door with their arms around each other, it was a sight that had Molly wiping away a tear, and Nellie blowing her nose hard enough to blow a hole through

Doreen's handkerchief. The two friends wouldn't have missed this for the world, and they felt quite emotional that Frances had been granted her wish.

'There's a lovely smell in the kitchen, Doreen,' Phil said. 'Me mam told me it's making her feel hungry.'

'Her and everyone else,' Molly laughed. 'Nellie's been licking her lips.'

'I'm sorry there won't be enough to go round, Mam, unless I put some extra potatoes in the roasting tin.' This had been worrying Doreen. Apart from not having enough dinner for an extra two, there were only four wooden chairs. And she'd never had anyone to dinner before, so she wanted everything to be perfect so Phil would be proud of her. 'Anyway, it won't be ready for an hour because Aunt Vicky has to make the pastry for the pie yet.'

'Oh, me and Nellie won't be staying, sunshine, we've got shopping to do for our own dinner. The family want feeding when they come in from work.'

'I think I'll settle for steak and kidney, girl.' Nellie's chins agreed with her. 'That smell has set me yearning. I'd love a steak and kidney pie 'cos I don't half like them, but I'm hopeless making pastry. Unless me mate offers to make it, then that would be fine.'

'It would also be a ruddy miracle, sunshine, 'cos I've got enough to do for me own family without having to do yours as well.'

'I knew yer'd say that.' Under her breath but heard by all, she added, 'When the mood hits her, she can be a miserable so-and-so.'

'What did yer say, sunshine?'

'I didn't say, nothing, girl!'

'Oh, I thought I heard yer calling me a miserable so-and-so.'

Her mouth open in feigned horror, Nellie said, 'As if I'd say that about me best mate! No, girl, what I said was, that yer were a busy little so-and-so, always on the go.'

'Swear on yer heart that was what yer said. Go on, swear on yer heart.'

'Yer know I don't know where me heart is, it's buried deep in all me fat. Anyway, what d'yer want me to swear for, yer miserable so-and-so?'

Phil was pleased his mother-in-law and Auntie Nellie were there, for they were making light of the occasion with their quips. Without them, things could have been awkward, with conversation strained. His mam had a smile on her face now, and that was a tonic to him. He'd got such a shock when she walked into the kitchen it took him all his time to keep his composure. And when she was in his arms and they were both crying, his tears of happiness were overshadowed by sadness. 'Yer don't have to dash off, do yer, Mrs B? Stay for a while, me mam would like that.'

'Oh, I won't be dashing off until I've seen me grandson, sunshine! I couldn't let a day go by without seeing me pride and joy. So ye're stuck with us until he wakes up.'

'That should be any time now 'cos he's due for a feed. But I'll make a pot of tea to keep us going until the dinner is ready.' Doreen felt ill at ease with Phil's mother there. She didn't know how to address her or how to make conversation. 'Do yer take milk and sugar in yer tea, er, Mrs Bradley?'

'Yes, please, one sugar.' Frances knew how uncomfortable the girl felt, because she felt the same way. Doreen was her daughter-in-law, but it was the first time they'd looked each other in the face. And she was aware the girl would have bad memories of how Phil had been treated and she might not welcome Frances being over-friendly. 'A cup of tea would be nice, thank you.'

'While you're making the tea, sweetheart, I'll make a start on the pastry and get the pie in the oven.' Victoria got to her feet with the help of the arms of her chair. 'The meat should be nice and tender by now.'

'I'll help with the tea, sunshine,' Molly said. 'I may as well make meself useful.' She followed her daughter into the kitchen and whispered, 'Did yer manage to get any cream slices? I promised Nellie, and she does deserve one 'cos she didn't have to come all that way with me yesterday and again today. Not many people would do that and pay their own tram fare.' She winked at Doreen. 'Mind you, she wouldn't have missed it for the world, she's a nosy beggar.'

'She's no more nosy than any other woman, Mam, we all like to know what's going on and if we're up-to-date with the news. I don't get out much, and I don't know all the neighbours because most of them still think of me as a young girl, but I'd do me nut if something exciting happened and no one told me about it. And when our Ruthie starts in Johnson's I'll be wanting to know if any of the old girls are still there that I used to work with, and if so, how they're getting on. If they're married or courting, have they got any children, what do they look like now? You know, like, if they've put a lot of weight on.'

'Blimey, yer are nosy! If yer don't watch out yer'll be ending up like yer Auntie Nellie, or worse still, heaven forbid, Elsie Flanaghan.'

Doreen's chuckle was heard by her husband and he smiled at his mother. 'That's Mrs B for yer. Wherever her and Auntie Nellie are, there's laughter not far away. They are a pair of smashers.'

Nellie, sitting alone at the table, cocked an ear. 'Did I hear yer taking my name in vain, Phil Mitchell? Whatever yer said, it's not true and I never did it.'

For the first time since she walked into the house, Frances spoke before being spoken to. 'He was paying yer compliments, Nellie. Both you and Molly.'

Nellie sat up straight. I mean, you have to look your best when being paid a compliment, don't you? 'That's nice of yer,

Phil. Go on, Frances, what did he say? Yer don't have to worry about me mate, I'll tell her everything on the way to the shops.'

It was Phil who answered. 'I told her that you and Mrs B. are always helping people who are sick or in trouble. And I've never known two mates to be as close as you are.' He saw Molly coming through with the tray. 'And that's all the compliments ye're getting, Auntie Nellie, otherwise yer head will be so big yer won't be able to get through the door.'

'It's not me head I'll have trouble getting through the door with, lad.' Nellie's body began to shake with silent laughter. 'Yer don't seem to have noticed that I've got two ruddy big things in the front of me and have to go out of a door sideways because of them.'

The little woman hadn't seen her mate come up behind her, and she jumped when a loud voice shouted in her ear, 'Nellie McDonough!' Molly placed the tray on the table before glaring at her friend. 'Have yer not got an ounce of shame in yer? I leave yer for five minutes and yer manage to embarrass everyone.'

'Embarrass everyone, girl? There's only Phil and Frances here, and I'm sure they weren't embarrassed by what I've said. Not everyone went to a convent school like what you did, all pure in heart and soul.'

Phil looked puzzled. 'I didn't know yer went to a convent school, Mrs B? It's funny that no one has ever mentioned it.'

'That's because I didn't, sunshine, it's just one of me mate's jokes. She likes to make fun of me because I won't let her tell dirty jokes or swear while I'm around. I've told her that if anyone has to resort to swearing it means they're ignorant and they've lost the argument before they start. With me they have anyway.'

Nellie's face was doing contortions, and she looked so funny Phil and his mother were having trouble keeping their faces

273

straight. 'Don't yer ever get bored, girl, being so bleeding good? I know yer want to go to heaven when yer die, but if I were you I'd be afraid Saint Peter would refuse to let me through those pearly gates on the grounds I'd make everyone miserable.'

It was in that second that Nellie's eyes lighted on the tray, and in particular on the plate which held four cream slices. Her facial expression changed completely. 'But yer know I wouldn't go in without yer, don't yer, seeing as ye're me best mate. I'd try and talk Saint Peter around, and if that didn't work I'd insist upon seeing the top man. And I know God would listen to reason, especially when I told him how good yer've been to me over the years. And that yer go to Mass and light a candle at least once a week.'

Unfortunately for Nellie, and against her will, her eyes strayed to the plate of cakes several times, and Molly was no fool. 'It's amazing what a cream slice will do, isn't it? You'd sell yer soul for one cream cake, Nellie McDonough.'

Biting on her bottom lip, Nellie hung her head in shame. 'I know, girl, I'm no good, am I? I'm bad enough to sell me soul for a cream cake, I'll hold up me hand and admit that. But I would never sell me best mate for a cream cake.'

Molly knew her friend was laughing herself sick inside, so she went along with it. 'Ah, sunshine, what a lovely thing to say. And I'll take yer up on that kind offer and have your cream slice as well as me own.'

Nellie's head shot up so quick her chins split into three and went in different directions. 'What! I never said yer could have me cake, Molly Bennett! Yer can just sod off, that's what you can do. I've never heard nothing like it in me life! Ye're a greedy beggar wanting two cream slices, and I can tell yer I'd be hoping one would choke yer.'

Molly laughed. 'That's more like it, sunshine, I don't trust yer when ye're being nice to me. So we'll be very ladylike in front of the guests and take our time over eating the cakes. We're not going to stuff them down our mouths in two bites, are we? Nor are we going to lick the cream off our fingers, are we?'

Nellie's face was a picture. 'Listen, girl, I was all right up to being ladylike in front of the guests, 'cos I wouldn't want Phil to be ashamed in front of his mam. But I draw the line when it comes to not being able to lick the cream what oozes out of the sides of the cake. And the best part what I like is licking me lips and me fingers. So I hope yer won't take offence at what I'm going to say, Frances, but I intend to enjoy me cake and it's sod the lot of yer.'

'You do that, Nellie,' Frances told her. 'If you lick your fingers, then I can enjoy meself and lick mine.'

By this time Nellie had one of the cakes in her hand, and Doreen ran through from the kitchen with a small plate for her to put it on. 'Here yer are, Auntie Nellie, save yer dropping any cream on yer clothes.'

'Not much chance of that, girl!' Nellie's chubby face held a look of perfect bliss. 'Never yet has any cream got away from me, I'm too quick for it.' And to prove it, she held the plate under her chin while sinking her teeth into the soft icing on the top of the cake and groaning with pleasure when she got through to the cream. 'I hope they have these in heaven, girl, or I'll be real disappointed. But I'll have a word with Saint Peter on the quiet and I'm sure he'll oblige.'

Molly was pouring the tea out when they heard cries from upstairs. 'There's Bobby, Doreen, d'yer want me to go up?'

'No, I'll go, Mam, and I can change his nappy before I bring him down.'

Nellie finished her cake and drank her tea, but while Molly ate her cake, she deliberately left some tea in her cup. And when Doreen came down with the baby and handed him to her mother,

Molly shook her head. 'Let Frances hold him, sunshine, while I finish me tea off before it goes cold.'

Victoria came to the kitchen door, her hands covered in flour. She didn't want to miss this first meeting of Bobby and his grandma. As she watched the very emotional scene she regretted not wiping her hands first because when the tears ran she wiped them away, leaving flour all over her face. But nobody noticed because all the eyes were fastened on Frances and the baby, and all were filled with tears. For the baby was being held close to his new grandma's face as she looked down on the child she never thought she would see. She was filled with love and longing, and regret that she had lost so many years of being a mother to her son and now had little time left to get to know her grandson. But she fought hard not to let anyone see how affected she was to have her son by her side and her grandson in her arms. She'd shed her tears tonight, when Tom and the children were sleeping.

Molly wasn't easily fooled, though, and said casually, 'Ay, I'll take him for a few minutes, Frances, to have me daily cuddle, then yer can have him back again. Then next time yer come we'll share him again. He's a lucky lad having two grandmas.'

Phil had often had cause over the years to be grateful to his mother-in-law, she was always there when you needed her and always seemed to know if there was something bothering you. You didn't have to ask for help, she'd sort out whatever it was without saying a word to anyone. But he'd never felt so grateful to her before as he did now. She had brought about this meeting with his mother for which he would always be in her debt, and had made it possible for her to see Bobby.

After Molly and Nellie had finished cooing and making baby noises, Molly handed the child back. 'He's all yours now, Frances, so yer can spoil him as much as yer like.' She was in a bit of a dilemma because she didn't like asking how his mother was going to get home in case it upset her. But something had to be said. 'D'yer want me and Nellie to take yer mam home later, Phil? We won't mind, as long as we get back for the men coming in, but it's up to you.'

'No, thanks, Mrs B. I'll take me mam home by taxi. You and Auntie Nellie have done enough and I'm very grateful to yer.'

'I'm grateful too,' Frances said. 'Both of yer have been very kind and I'll never forget it.'

'We were glad to do it, weren't we, Nellie?'

'Yeah, we were, girl, and we're here any time yer want us.'

Molly slipped into her coat. 'We'll probably be seeing a lot of yer, Frances, and we'll come for yer whenever Phil can't make it.' She kissed the face which looked lined and weary. 'See yer soon.'

'I'll come to the door with yer, Mam,' Doreen said. 'Then I'll get the roast potatoes on.'

'Okay, sunshine. We'll be seeing yer, Victoria!'

A head popped around the door, and it was hard to see where the white hair started and the flour ended. 'Ta-ra, Molly, ta-ra, Nellie. See yer tomorrow.'

Chapter Seventeen

'I've never been so moved in all me life,' Molly told Jack as they sat having their dinner. 'I know I cried like a baby when th children got married, but they were tears of happiness and joy But seeing Phil and his mam clinging to each other, well, ye would have had to have been made of stone not to feel lik sobbing yer heart out. And don't think it's because I'm soft hearted, because Victoria, Nellie, and Doreen were all the same We calmed down after a while, and me mate had us all laughing But when the baby was brought down and put in Frances's arms it was like seeing a sad film. Except that in the darkness of th picture house yer can cry yer eyes out to yer heart's content an nobody bothers.'

'I noticed yer didn't say anything to Tommy, love, so am I t presume that no one is being told?'

'I didn't tell Jill when she called, either, because like Tomm she's only here for a few minutes and I want to be able to explai everything properly to them, not just blurt it out so they don understand about how ill his mother is. I want them to forge what happened years ago and stand behind Phil now, give hi their support and make his mother welcome and treat her wit respect.'

Ruthie had been listening with eyes wide. 'Is Phil's moth going to die, Mam?'

Molly chose her words with care. 'Listen, sunshine, ye'r

turned fourteen and leaving school in less than a week . . . so ye're no longer a child. I am going to speak to you like I would a grown-up. Mrs Bradley is a very sick woman, but how sick only a doctor could say. She knows herself she's going to die, but when only God knows. So I think it's up to everyone to make her life as happy as possible, never forgetting that she also has a husband at home and three other children who she loves.'

Ruthie laid down her knife and fork. 'I remember them, Mam, and they were horrible. I bet they won't look after her proper.'

'Oh, I think they will, sunshine, because she said they are being good to her. Anyway, I managed to have a word with Phil when the taxi came for him to take his mother home, and asked if he wanted me to tell the families and friends what is going on. He said he did, and would be grateful because he wanted them to know but would find it hard to do himself.' Molly held her daughter's eyes. 'I was going to say they would find out anyway if Frances becomes a regular visitor, but they wouldn't because with the great change in her appearance no one would recognize her. So only family and close friends are to be told, not the neighbours who have reason to remember and dislike the whole Bradley family. And not any of yer young friends, sunshine, even the Corkhills. Now I've treated yer like a sensible grown-up, Ruthie, so I'm hoping yer won't let me down.'

The girl shook her head. 'I won't, Mam, 'cos I love Phil, and I wouldn't do anything I thought he wouldn't want me to. But what about Bella? Mrs Watson goes in to see Miss Clegg nearly every day, she's bound to find out. And if she tells Bella then yer'll think it was me and I'll get a telling off, even though it wasn't.'

'No, yer wouldn't get told off, love,' Jack said, thinking his wife had handled it very well. 'Me and yer mam trust yer.'

That brought a smile. It was nice to be treated like a grown-up, and the girl made up her mind that wild horses wouldn't drag anything out of her about Phil and his poor sick mother. And if anyone had anything bad to say about them, she'd soon put them in their place.

Molly turned to Jack. 'I hope yer won't mind, love, but I'll go out as soon as we've finished eating 'cos I want to call in to see Jill, Steve and Mrs Corkhill. Then I'll go round to me ma's and tell them the news. I think everyone will be pleased that Phil's made it up with his mother, especially the way things are.'

'You get away now, then,' he said. 'Me and Ruthie will clear the table and wash up, won't we, love?'

Molly scraped her chair back with a smile on her face. 'Ye're a pair of smashers, and I know I'm a lucky woman to have yer. If I get away now, I might have time to call next door and see Ellen and Corker on me way home. That's if it's not too late, like. I won't call in now because all the children will be in and the less they know the better.'

'Hey, don't be taking advantage of me generosity!' Jack grinned.' Talk about give an inch and they'll take a yard isn't in it. I don't want any wife of mine coming home at the stroke of midnight.'

When Molly bent to kiss him, she said softly in his ear, 'Yer know my mate Nellie says that only cats and loose women are on the streets at that time of night.'

Jack raised his brows. 'Now I wonder how your mate Nellie would know that, unless she'd seen it with her own eyes.'

Ruthie was collecting the plates, her mind dwelling on the words of her mother when she'd said she was no longer a child but a grown-up. So she wasn't listening to this conversation or she might have asked what her Auntie Nellie had seen with her own eyes.

Molly reached for her coat hanging on the hook behind the door. 'Ay, I'll tell yer what, sunshine, it was a day of tears and sadness today, there wasn't a soul not affected by the goings-on. But if it hadn't been for my mate Nellie, it would have been ten times worse. In the midst of the crying and sobbing, she was still able to tell jokes and make the situation a little bit lighter. Half-a-dozen times she had Frances laughing, and I could tell that Phil, like meself, felt like kissing her. She makes a fool of herself, pretends to be stupid, just to bring a smile to yer face. Yer certainly wouldn't get many like her in a pound.'

'I bet right now she'll be telling George, Lily and Paul all about it.' Jack blessed the day his wife had made friends with Nellie, because they'd been good for each other. 'And I bet she's being all dramatic, like Ethel Barrymore.'

Molly nodded, laughing. 'I'd love to see it, but I haven't got the time. I told her Phil said it was all right to tell families and friends, but she mustn't tell Elsie Flanaghan. And yer should have seen the look on her face. "Elsie Flanaghan! I wouldn't even tell her the time of day!" She said more than that of course, but it's not fit for young ears.'

Ruthie came through from the kitchen. 'Mam, will yer tell us what Auntie Nellie did to make yer laugh when yer were all feeling sad and crying? Not now, I mean, 'cos ye're going out, but when yer come in? I love hearing yer impersonating her 'cos yer sound just like her. I'm very lucky having you for a mam and her for me Auntie Nellie.'

'If I'm too late back tonight, sunshine, then I promise I'll tell yer tomorrow night about the hankie, the bib and the cream slice. And I'll even do the actions for yer.'

'Yer'd better get going, love,' Jack said, not wanting his wife to stay out too late because he liked to see her sitting opposite to him in her fireside chair. The room didn't seem the same without her. Neither did his heart, because it was missing her. 'Try to be home at a respectable hour, love, or yer'll have the neighbours talking.'

'I'll try.' Molly kissed him before holding out her arms to her daughter, who rushed into them. 'Look after yer dad, sunshine, and make him a nice cup of tea. Show him how grown-up yer can be when yer feel like it.'

When Steve opened the front door and saw Molly standing there, he stepped back and threw his hands up in exaggerated surprise. 'Well, speak of the devil and she's bound to appear! We were just talking about yer, Mrs B, and here yer are! Me and Jill were saying we'd walk down later and have a game of cards with you and Mr B.'

Molly tilted her head. 'Steve McDonough, do yer intend keeping me on the step talking, or are yer going to let me inside?'

Steve smiled. His dimples appeared and so did the devilment in his eyes. He had inherited his humour from the mother he adored. 'To tell yer the truth, Mrs B, when the knock came on the door, yer daughter told me that whoever it was, I was to keep them talking while she tidied up and made the place respectable.'

'Who is it?' Jill's head appeared over her husband's shoulder. 'Mam! We were coming down to yours later. Steve said he hadn't seen yer for three days and he was beginning to forget what yer looked like.'

Molly tutted. 'Are you going to keep me talking on the step as well?'

Lizzie Corkhill's voice called, 'Come in, Molly, before yer either freeze to death or they talk yer to death.'

Molly pushed her daughter and son-in-law back and stepped into the hall. 'I was beginning to think I'd been barred for some reason.'

There was a roaring fire in the grate and the room looked warm and welcoming. Lizzie was rocking back and forth in her chair, a smile on her wrinkled face. 'Take yer coat off, queen, and make yerself at home. We weren't expecting visitors and it's a nice surprise.'

Warming her hands in front of the flames, Molly said, 'Me and Nellie haven't been to see yer for few days, Lizzie, and when I'm warmed through I'll tell yer the reason.'

'D'yer want a cup of tea, Mam?' Jill asked. 'The kettle is boiled.'

'Yes, I will, sunshine, 'cos I didn't have one after me dinner with having a few calls to make. I've left Ruthie to make one for yer dad.'

'I'll see to it, love,' Steve told his wife. 'You sit down and put yer feet up.' He fussed over the wife he had loved since he was two years of age and she was a baby in her pram. She was five months pregnant now and really beginning to show. 'I'll be glad when yer finish work at the end of the week, yer shouldn't be on yer feet all day in your condition.'

'I'll be glad meself, love, 'cos I am finding it tiring now.'

'I think it suits yer being pregnant, sunshine, yer look really bonny.'

Lizzie nodded. 'I told her, she's like a rose coming into bloom.'

Jill, always the gentle one, blushed with embarrassment. 'I don't know about a rose, more like a daisy yer see growing wild in the parks.'

Steve didn't care whose company they were in, he never kept his love for Jill to himself. 'I've never seen a daisy as beautiful as you, love, yer put all the flowers in the shade.'

There was real affection on Lizzie's face as she listened. She'd known this young couple since they were born, and when her son Corker told her they'd get married the same day as Doreen and Phil, and make it a double wedding if they had somewhere to live, she'd been quick to offer them her spare bedroom and the run of the house. And not for one second had she regretted it because they became her family and chased away those lonely days when she lived alone and one day was very much like another. 'Make the tea, son, or Molly will be dying of thirst.'

When she had a cup and saucer in her hand, Molly said, 'I have something very sad and very emotional to tell yer, and then I'm going round to me ma's to let them know.'

'It all sounds very cloak and dagger, Mrs B,' Steve said. 'It's not something bad that affects anyone in the family, is it?'

Molly took a sip of her tea before placing the saucer on the table. She was wondering how Lizzie would take the news, because the Bradleys had led the old lady a dog's life. Living in the house opposite, they'd made her life a hell on earth by knocking on the door several times a day and asking to borrow tea, sugar, bread, all sorts. When at first she'd refused they began to threaten her until she gave in through fear. The two young girls were real tearaways and afraid of no one. The old lady was ashamed of her weakness and didn't tell a soul, until one day the youngest girl got into the house and stole money. That was the day Molly noticed there was something very wrong with Corker's mother, and she and Nellie gradually got the truth out of her. They tackled the girls and their mother, who was then called Fanny, and got the height of abuse from them. It nearly came to blows, with Nellie rolling her sleeves up ready for action, but Molly wouldn't lower herself by acting like a fish-wife and settled for warning the mother what dire action would be taken if they didn't leave Mrs Corkhill in peace. And when Corker came home from sea and heard what had been going on, there was hell to pay. Nowadays Lizzie wasn't terrified every time there was a knock on the door and she wasn't afraid of the dreadful family across the street. But how would she react to what Molly was about to tell them?

'I'll be quick about this, and if yer've anything to say I'd be grateful if yer'd wait until yer'd heard the whole story. It concerns Phil and his mother.'

There was complete silence while Molly told her tale, except for the creak of Lizzie's chair as she rocked back and forth. Although she could feel herself filling up again, Molly avoided looking at their faces and carried on until they were in possession of all the facts. She left nothing out, even Nellie's ability to break the ice and bring smiles to faces.

'So there yer have it. Phil knows I'm telling yer, I'm not doing this behind his back. What I would like is for everyone to give him their support and forget everything that's happened in the past. He's found his mother again, but she's a dying woman and he'll need all the sympathy and help he can get. That's how I feel, but ye're all entitled to yer own views and to say what yer think.'

Lizzie was the first to speak. 'What happened is in the past for me, queen. Phil can bring his mother here any time and she'll be made welcome.'

'I'll second that, Mrs B,' Steve said. 'Phil's one of the family now and we should stick by him. But, ay, it's really sad, Isn't it? I've often thought how he must have envied us having all our families together when he had no one. That's until you and me mam found the Mitchells for him. But a mother is the most important part of a family, isn't she? She holds it together, like, and we'd all be lost without ours.'

Jill put her open hands on her swollen tummy and rubbed gently. 'This baby is going to have a good mother, I love the bones of it now and we haven't even met yet. But I remember years ago someone saying his mother and the lad she was going out with adored each other. How must she have felt, losing the man she loved and who she was due to marry just three weeks before he was killed? I know they should have waited until after they were married to have a baby, but the lad was as much to blame. Yet it was Phil's mam who was left to bear the brunt of the worry and shame. So who can blame her for marrying Tom Bradley when he offered, because he was her only chance? It doesn't excuse the way she treated Phil, but it's best not to dwell on that. I for one feel sorry for her and Phil, and if you and Auntie Nellie bring her up again, I'd be happy if yer brought her here. After this weekend I'll be a lady of leisure and home all the time.'

'Oh, we won't be going for her again until after Christmas, sunshine, because we're behind with our preparations and have loads to do and only a few days to do it in. I've a feeling Phil will bring her sometime over the holiday, by taxi, so she can see the baby. But she has a husband and three other children, we mustn't forget that. No matter what we think of them they are still her family, and she says they are good to her.'

'Of course they are!' Steve said. 'We'll be there when we're needed, Mrs B, but we won't intrude. I think it would be nice if me and Jill walked down there tomorrow night, just for a chat and to let Phil see we're behind him all the way.' He squeezed Jill's hand. 'Is that all right with you, sweetheart?'

Her pretty face moved closer and she kissed his cheek. 'You can talk to Phil man to man while me and our Doreen talk about babies.'

Lizzie grinned across at Molly. 'Yer family is growing bigger, queen.'

Molly rolled her eyes to the ceiling. 'And there's our Tommy and Ruthie to go yet. Me and Jack could end up with twelve grandchildren! Still, looking on the bright side, they can look after us in our old age.' She stood up and stretched her arms above her head. 'The trouble with making yerself too warm and comfortable is that yer don't want to move. But I'll have to shake a leg and get round to me ma's, where I'll have to go through it all again. I get upset every time I think or talk about

286

it, but I'd rather get it all over in one night and be done with it. Then me and Nellie can start thinking about our Christmas shopping.'

Steve chuckled. 'And don't forget the Christmas party, Mrs B! Has me mam talked yer into it again?'

'Oh, she's got it all sorted out, son! Even to the guests! But that's only because it's what I want as well.'

Tommy's reception when he answered the door to his mother was very much the same as Steve's had been. 'This is a surprise, Mam, yer never mentioned yer were coming when I called to yours on me way home from work.'

'I've just been to Mrs Corkhill's, son, and Steve kept me talking on the step, too! In fact I was as stiff as an iceberg when he finally let me in.'

'I'm sorry, Mam, I just wasn't thinking.' Tommy reached for his mother's arm, pulled her up the step and gave her a noisy kiss. 'That's two yer've had today, so don't say I never give yer anything. Now come in because they'll all be sitting with bated breath waiting to see who it was at the door.'

'Oh, it's you, sweetheart, so it is!' Bridie's face lit up at the sight of her daughter. 'Me and Bob were only saying today we hadn't seen yer for two days.'

'Get by the fire, lass,' he said. 'Ye're shivering.'

'I know, da! It's only a couple of minutes walk from Lizzie Corkhill's, but by golly yer could freeze to death in that time.'

Rosie, her cheeks as bright as the flames leaping up the chimney, gave her mother-in-law a big hug and kiss. 'Give me yer coat, Auntie Molly, and I'll hang it over the back of the chair so it warms through for when ye're going home.'

'Yer said yer'd been to Lizzie Corkhill's, me darling, but what on earth possessed yer to go visiting on a bitterly cold night? The best place is by the fireside.'

'It's not exactly visiting, Ma, I've come with some news. It's not the sort of news yer want to hang on to, so I thought I'd get it over in one night. When I leave here, if it's not too late, I intend to call and see Ellen and Corker, so all families and friends know.'

Bob, wearing a spotlessly clean shirt and neat pullover, sat forward. 'What is it, lass? Ye're not in trouble, are yer?'

'No, Da, I'm not in trouble.' Molly smiled to allay his fears. 'I never have the blinking time to get into trouble. No, it's nothing to do with the Jacksons, the Bennetts or the McDonoughs. But to put yer mind at rest I'll get it over quickly.' Knowing her mother and Rosie were both as emotional as herself, she said, 'I hope yer've got hankies ready. Oh, I'd better get mine out of me pocket before I start.'

There were questions thrown before she'd had a chance to say very much, but she ignored them and kept her eyes on her hands, which were laced together in her lap. And gradually the questions stopped and there was absolute silence except for the loud ticking of the Westminster chiming clock on the mantelpiece. She tried not to let the words get to her, to pretend she was talking to strangers about strangers, but it didn't work and she could feel herself becoming emotionally drained. However she managed to keep going until the whole tale had been told, even though she felt as weak as a kitten. 'That's it now, yer have the whole story to make of it what yer will. I've told you what I hope will happen, as I told Jill and Steve, but yer have to make yer own minds up.'

'Poor Phil,' Tommy said softly, 'he must be heartbroken.'

'And what about his mother, the poor soul?' Bridie shook her head sadly. 'And did yer say, me darling, that she'd sent that husband of hers to let Phil know she was ill?'

'She did, Ma, but he didn't pass the message on because our Doreen didn't give him the chance, she chased him off. Not that I'm blaming her, because I'd have done the same thing.'

'And what a good job it was, Auntie Molly, that you and Auntie Nellie did yer detective work again.' Rosie's bonny face was dead serious. 'Sure, if it wasn't for you, nobody would have known where they live. It's a gift from God, yer have, and that's the truth of it.'

'I'm not taking any praise, Rosie, because me and Nellie went after Tom Bradley to tell him to keep away from our Doreen's house. We didn't go out intending to do a good deed, but I thank God that we did.'

'I'll nip in and see Phil tomorrow night,' Tommy said. 'Just to let him see his mates are thinking of him.'

'I'll come with yer, my beloved,' Rosie said. 'Sure it's been nearly a week since I saw the baby, and I'd not like him to forget that he's got an Auntie Rosie.'

'Then yer can take our good wishes with yer, me darling, and tell him we're all thinking about him,' Bridie said, while Bob sat beside her, nodding his head in agreement. 'We'll be saying a special prayer for him and his mam every night. And isn't there a tiny voice in me head saying that perhaps getting her son's forgiveness and being welcomed back into his life will give the poor soul something to live for. Then there's her grandson, as well, so she'll not let the good Lord take her without putting up a fight.'

Molly gave a sigh of contentment. 'I knew yer'd all rally around Phil, never doubted it really. And I'm thinking how lucky we are, each and every one of us, to be part of such a loving and loyal family. And that includes me two sons-in-law and me daughter-in-law, who brought more happiness and love with them.'

'We're the lucky ones, Auntie Molly, and that's the truth of it. As me mammy said when she was over for the wedding, she'll never have to worry about me because she knows I'm in good hands.'

Tommy let out a loud guffaw before grabbing his wife around the waist and holding her tight. 'I think your mammy got things the wrong way round, my love. You are not in our hands, and never have been. You've had Grandma, Granda and me eating out of your hands since the day we first set eyes on yer.'

'Not true, Tommy Bennett, 'cos yer didn't like me one little bit when yer first met me.'

'Yeah, I thought yer were a bossy boots who never stopped talking. But yer'd soon woven yer spell around me and I was lost.'

'Blimey!' Molly said. 'Looking at me ma and da holding hands, and you two in a clinch, I feel left out. I'm going home to me husband so he can tell me how much he loves me. And if he's not as soppy as you four, then I'll clock him one.' She picked up her coat from the back of a chair. 'I might go straight there instead of giving Corker a knock, I'll see how I feel when I get nearer home.'

After hugs and kisses all round, Tommy saw his mother to the door. 'Walk quickly, Mam, and yer won't feel the cold. Goodnight and God bless.'

'Goodnight and God bless, sunshine, and I'll see yer tomorrow.'

As she went to walk away, Tommy said, 'Yer know, I wish yer'd let me walk yer home Mam, I'd feel better than letting yer walk on yer own in the dark. But every time I mention it yer turn me down.'

'I'm all right on me own, sunshine, but thanks for the offer. I doubt if anyone will run off with me, not at my age. If they picked me up in the dark, they'd drop me in the light.'

'Ay, that's my mother ye're talking about, so watch it!'

'You go back into the warmth, sunshine, and I'll be fine. But I do love yer for caring about me so much.' Molly pulled up the collar of her coat. 'I'll see yer tomorrow, ta-ra.'

* * *

As Molly passed the pub on the corner of the street she could hear the sound of men's voices and could smell cigarette smoke and beer. Under her breath she muttered, 'They want their bumps feeling, coming out on a cold night to drink cold beer. They'd be better to keep their money in their pockets.'

There was a gas lamp halfway down the street, and in the light from it Molly saw three very familiar figures walking with their backs to her. No one could mistake Corker, six foot five and built like a battleship, and she'd know her own husband anywhere. And she was sure the third man was Phil. What were they doing out this time of night, unless something untoward had happened? That worried her enough for her to take to her heels and run towards them.

'Where have you three been, is there something wrong?'

'Hello, Molly, me darlin'!' Corker picked her up as though she was a toy doll and spun her round. 'Even in the dark I can still see ye're the prettiest woman in this street.'

'Would yer mind putting my wife down, if you please?' Jack said. 'Yer'll have the neighbours talking.'

'Never mind the neighbours,' Molly said when her feet were back on the ground. 'What's going on, has something happened?'

'Nothing's happened, love, so don't be having a heart attack. Yer hadn't been gone long when Corker knocked to see if I felt like a pint. Ruthie was at Bella's, so I didn't have her to worry about, I was all on me tod, and Corker said we wouldn't be out long. And it was his decision to call and see if Phil felt like a pint.'

'Well, it's nice for some people, I must say!' But Molly was delighted. Corker had always treated Phil like a son, and was a hero in the eyes of the young man. Mind you, he was a hero in her eyes, too! After the men in her own family, the gentle giant had always been the closest to her heart. 'I hope they're not taking yer home drunk, Phil?'

'No, I've only had two halves, Mrs B, so I can still walk a straight line. I've really enjoyed meself, and I've been telling Uncle Corker about me mam – how she used to watch for me coming home from work. And how she tried to get hold of me. It means a lot to me, that does.'

'All the family know now, sunshine. If yer mam is up to it sometime, they'd like to see her. And there's a special message from me ma, which I agree with. She said it will do yer mother the world of good to be back in touch with you. Seeing you again, and her new grandson, it will give her the strength and the will to get better. Me ma's exact words, sunshine, were, "She'll not let the Good Lord take her without putting up a fight." And, yer know, I believe she's right.'

Corker thought it best to send Phil home now. He'd been able to talk freely about his mam and it was easy to see he felt proud that she'd never forgotten him. But it was enough for one night. 'You get home to yer lovely wife, son, and I'll get home to mine. If yer want anything and think I can help, then I'm only across the street.'

Jack put his arm around Molly's waist. 'I'll get home with my lovely wife, and I'm sure I'll be treated to a kiss and a cuddle as soon as we're in the front door. She can't keep her hands off, she's so crazy about me.'

Molly pushed him off the pavement. 'Say goodnight to yer boozing pals, then yer can come home and make yer wife a cup of tea. After that, perhaps, yer'll get a kiss and a cuddle.'

Leaving the other two men to laugh at his antics, Jack practically carried his wife across the cobbles. 'A kiss from you, love, is better than a pint of bitter any day.'

Chapter Eighteen

'Where are we going first, girl?' Nellie had a woollen scarf wrapped around her head and it kept falling down over her eyes. All you could see of her face now was a bright red nose and she looked really comical. 'I hope we're not out long 'cos me feet are freezing already and it's only five minutes since we left the house.'

'I thought we'd be best off starting at Tony's and ordering our turkey, and I'm asking him to put a pound of beef sausage and a pound of dripping in my order. With there only being the three of us for Christmas dinner we won't get through the whole turkey, so with the sausage it should be enough for at least three days, if not four.'

'I'll need a big turkey, girl, 'cos Archie and his mam are coming for Christmas dinner. So I'll be cooking for five of us.' Nellie pushed the scarf up over her forehead and out of her eyes, and walked with her head back, hoping it wouldn't fall down again. 'Our Lily will give me a hand, though, she said.'

Molly smiled but kept her thoughts to herself. Lily wouldn't be just giving a hand, she'd be cooking the whole dinner. And she'd have to set the table if she wanted matching crockery and cutlery because Nellie didn't care if a saucer didn't match a cup, or a knife didn't have the same handle as a fork. And Archie's mother, Ida, she was very easygoing too, not the type to inspect what was put in front of her. But Lily wouldn't be thinking along

293

those lines, she'd want everything spot on with it being the first time she'd have cooked for her future husband and his mother. It was only natural, Molly thought, she'd want everything perfect. 'Are yer all right for crockery and cutlery, sunshine? I might be able to help yer out if yer get stuck.'

'Oh, don't worry, girl, our Lily's had me out of me mind about that. I can't help it if a few of the cups have got chips in them, can I?' Once again Nellie pushed the scarf back so she could see her friend. 'I told our Lily that Ida knows she's not been invited to bleeding Buckingham Palace, and she near bit me head off!'

'Come on, sunshine, of course Lily wants everything right, yer should understand that. I bet you were the same with your ma when yer first took George home to meet the family.'

'My old ma, God rest her soul, would have clouted me if I'd asked her to be any different than she was. We thought it was our birthday if we got a cup with a handle on in our house. Don't forget there were millions of men out of work and people were going hungry, so yer were lucky if yer had tea to put in the cup. And my ma didn't stand on ceremony with anyone, she treated everyone alike. If yer didn't like it, then yer could ruddy well lump it.'

'Now that description reminds me of someone I know.' Molly put a finger on her chin and looked thoughtful. 'Who is it? Ooh, isn't it annoying when there's something on the tip of yer tongue and it just won't come. Never mind, I'll remember in a minute.'

Nellie tugged on her arm. 'Is it me, girl?'

'Oh, aren't I stupid, of course it's you! But d'yer know why I didn't think of you right away? Because I can't see yer ruddy face for that blinking scarf, that's why. So will yer stand still for a second while I tie the knot a bit tighter under yer chin? Then I can see who I'm talking to, and you can see where ye're walking.'

'I don't know why my ruddy scarf keeps falling down when

yours doesn't.' Not for one moment did it strike Nellie that while Molly only had one chin, she had several. And it was very difficult for a knot to stay put when those chins were in motion. 'That's better, girl, I can see what I'm saying now.'

'It looks as though we're in luck, sunshine, 'cos there's no one in the butcher's. We should be in and out in no time.'

But Tony had no intention of letting that happen. He'd just been saying to Ellen that they hadn't had a laugh since he'd opened up at eight o'clock. 'Good morning, ladies! I hope you are both well on this crisp winter's day?'

Nellie looked at him as though he was soft. 'A crisp winter's day! How can a day be crisp, yer silly beggar? A piece of toast can be crisp, like what I made for my feller this morning, except he said it wasn't crisp, it was ruddy well burnt to a cinder. But I've never known anyone call a day crisp.'

'Burned George's toast again, did yer, sunshine? It's a wonder he doesn't get up half an hour earlier and make his own toast.'

'I didn't burn no toast, girl, he was just looking for something to moan about. It might have been well done, like, but nothing to kick up a stink over.'

Tony leaned back against the wooden table used for cutting meat on, while Ellen leaned her elbows on the counter, and both of them waited to hear what Molly would come back with.

'Let me try and get this straight in me mind, sunshine. Now, was the toast a nice golden honey colour, or was it dark brown, or was it black?'

'I don't only make toast for George, yer know, Molly Bennett, I have Lily and Paul to see to as well.'

'Oh, so there were no complaints about their toast then? They were able to spread jam on it and enjoy it, were they?'

Nellie looked to the ceiling for inspiration. Why the hell hadn't she kept her mouth shut when Tony said it was a crisp day? She should have agreed with him and then there'd have been no mention of toast. It was her own fault for having a big mouth, she was her own worst enemy. 'Ye're a nosy bugger, Molly Bennett, but for yer information I do all the toast together 'cos me grill is big enough to take four slices. And after I'd put them under the grill, I carried the teapot through and put it on the table. I'd only turned me back for two bleeding minutes and when I turned round the smoke was pouring out of the kitchen 'cos the ruddy bread was on fire!'

In her mind's eye, Molly imagined the scene that could only happen to Nellie. 'Yer didn't put burnt bread down in front of yer family for their breakfast, did yer? Not when they were going out to do a day's work?'

At the expression on Nellie's face, Tony and Ellen had to struggle to keep their laughter back. But if they laughed now it would spoil the ending.

'What else could I do with it, girl?' Nellie's hands were spread in front of her, pleading for their sympathy. 'I couldn't throw it all in the yard for the birds, could I? Everyone knows we haven't got no birds down our street 'cos there's no trees for them.'

'So yer put it on a plate and set it in front of yer husband?'

'I did at first, girl, until he took off on me and called me for all the stupid buggers under the sun. Well, I wasn't going to have that 'cos I'd burnt me own piece of toast as well and I thought he was being bloody selfish just thinking of himself. So I picked the plate up and turned it upside down on his head. And I told him to make his own ruddy toast in future 'cos I wasn't going to be spoken to like I was some skivvy. I've got me pride, yer know, girl, so I held me head high and marched through to the kitchen.'

This has got to be one of her best performances for ages, Molly was thinking. And it was being appreciated by her audience of three. What a pity there weren't more people like her mate. If Nellie could bottle her humour, she'd be a million-aire. 'If I believed all that, sunshine, then I'd be daft enough to think it was a lovely summer's day out there, with the sun cracking the flags.'

Nellie jerked her thumb at Tony, who was doubled up. 'Yer can blame soft lad for it, girl, 'cos if he hadn't mentioned the word crisp, we'd be at the greengrocer's by now.'

Ellen ran the back of a hand across her eyes. 'From now on, Nellie, crisp is going to be one of me favourite words. That little show yer put on has cheered me up and I can face the rest of the day with a smile. No matter how many miserable faces come through that door, I'll not let them get me down.'

'If they're real miserable, girl, then what yer want to do is give them short measure on the scales when ye're weighing whatever it is they're buying.'

Molly gasped. 'Nellie! That's a terrible thing to say!' She was flabbergasted. 'Some people might be hard up with no money for food or one of their kids sick or something. And they'd have good reason not to be laughing or full of the joys of spring. Honestly, the things yer come out with, it's a good job there's no other customers in the shop.'

Tony had an idea of playing Nellie at her own game. His face serious, he said, 'I don't short-change any of me customers that have fallen on hard times, Nellie, 'cos I wouldn't be able to sleep at night. But it's different if I know there's good wages coming into a house. I have to admit I take that into consideration and try and get back the money I've lost on those I've felt sorry for 'cos they're skint.' He looked knowingly at Molly to let her know he was only kidding. 'We've got a two-ounce weight we keep by the scales, and when someone comes in who we know doesn't have any money problems, we put that weight on the scale when we're weighing their meat. We don't let them see us, we're good at being crafty. I mean, the likes of you, Nellie, with three lots of wages coming in . . . well, me and Ellen know yer can afford it. And we know ye're so good-hearted yer wouldn't

297

mind helping out someone not quite as fortunate as yerself.'

Molly put an arm across her friend's shoulders and looked down into a face no artist could paint because it was making the most weird contortions imaginable. 'He's very good is Tony, isn't he? And a fantastic judge of character. He knows how generous yer are, and that yer would be the first to offer help to some poor beggar who was badly off.'

Nellie threw Molly's arm off and at the same time regained her voice. 'Good, is he? And generous, am I? Well, I'll show him how bleeding generous I am! I'll break his bloody neck for him.' She waddled towards the opening in the counter. 'And I'll ram that two-ounce weight where the sun don't shine.'

Molly pulled her back. 'Now, Nellie, we don't want customers coming in to see a fight, do we? So calm yerself down and consider the good things Tony has said about yer. He hasn't said the same about me, has he? And I'm not getting me knickers in a twist even though it's a kind of insult.'

'Well, you're not the one he's bleeding well robbing, are yer? I can tell yer, girl, me blood's boiling now, and yer know what that means, don't yer? Someone is going to get a belt.' Nellie began to roll her sleeves up, and when they wouldn't roll any further than her elbow, she curled her fists and took on the stance of a boxer, with legs apart and fists punching the air. 'Come out from behind that counter, yer thieving swine, and let's see what sort of a man yer are what steals off poor defenceless women.'

Tony couldn't move for laughing. The way Nellie looked now, she'd make a marvellous picture postcard like they sold on the prom in Blackpool and you sent to your friends to have a laugh. She had just the figure for it: mountainous bosom and tummy, and her face creased up as though she was really going to belt someone. Of course the card would have a funny caption underneath, but he couldn't think of one off the top of his head.

'I give in, Nellie, I haven't the strength to fight yer. Ye're a better man than I am any day.'

Molly saw two of Tony's regular customers crossing the main road towards the shop. 'Will yer take our order for Christmas Eve, Tony, please, 'cos yer've got more customers coming? If yer have them ready for us, we'll just have to pick them up and it'll save time.'

'Tell me what you and Nellie want, Molly, and I'll make them up first thing,' Ellen said, reaching for the pencil and order book at the side of the till. 'Me and Tony will be coming in at seven o'clock to get as many orders done as we can.'

'I think I'll have enough in me club to cover what I want, but Nellie wants a turkey the size of a house, so she'll probably have to put money to hers.'

Nellie, her face peering around Molly's shoulder, said, 'Only a little house, girl, it's five I'm having for dinner, not a ruddy army. But yer know how me mate likes to exaggerate. She's worse than I am, and that's saying something.'

'In a pig's ear I am! No one is worse than you, Nellie. In fact no one comes within a mile of yer when it comes to exaggerating. What about that little episode over the toast? No one knows whether yer burnt the toast or not, or if yer put it on George's head, or even whether they got any breakfast at all! The only way I would find out what really happened would be if I asked George or one of the kids.'

Nellie's chubby face creased. 'They wouldn't be able to tell yer nothing, girl, 'cos they'd had a good breakfast and gone off to work before I burned my piece of toast to a cinder. And that was only because I was greedy. I'd already had me breakfast with them, but I fancied another piece of toast. So I put it under the grill and went down to the lavvy thinking I'd be back in no time. But I forgot about it while I was sitting on me throne thinking of the Christmas party my mate's having, and what I could do to help, being deputy hostess, like. And didn't I go and forget the ruddy toast? It was only when I smelt the burning it came to me, and I had to run up the yard with me knickers around me knees.' You could never tell by Nellie's face whether she was telling the truth or having you on, and that's how she looked now. 'I was a bit upset 'cos I was really looking forward to that piece of toast.' She hitched up her bosom. 'Still, there's worse things happen at sea, so they tell me.'

'Is she telling the truth or taking us for a ride?' Ellen asked. 'I can never tell with her 'cos she can sound so convincing.'

'Search me, sunshine, 'cos I'm as wise as you are. We might live in each other's pockets but I still haven't got her figured out. Sometimes I have, but not always. And I think that's part of why we get on so well together. Apart from being as thick as two short planks, we both enjoy a joke and having a laugh. It's better than a dose of medicine any day.'

Molly could hear the sound of voices and turned to find there were four or five customers in the shop. 'Tony will be cursing us, so can we give yer our order for Christmas Eve, Ellen? And we want a pound and a half of mincemeat each to see us over today and tomorrow.'

'Go ahead, Molly, and I'll write it down.'

'A seven-pound turkey for me, with a pound of sausage and a pound of dripping. And Nellie will want a ten-pound turkey with sausage and dripping. We'll pick them up first thing on Saturday morning before yer start getting busy.' Molly reached into her pocket for her purse. 'Get yer money out, sunshine, I haven't enough on me to be lending yer until yer get home. And don't say yer forgot to bring yer purse 'cos I can see it in yer pocket.'

'Bloody hell, girl, have yer got eyes in the back of yer head?' Tutting loudly, Nellie brought her purse out. 'Anyone would think yer didn't trust me.'

'I'm not going to answer that, sunshine, 'cos yer'll get a cob on and sulk. Give Ellen yer money and let's get going.'

Walking towards the greengrocer's, Molly said, 'I've got a good idea, sunshine, see what you think of it. How about us asking Billy to deliver our potatoes, veg and fruit today? It won't go off in this weather and he could get the young lad to deliver it in that cart he's got. If Billy's not too busy and can do it, we could add tomorrow's potatoes and onions to the list, save us lugging them ourselves.'

'Good thinking, girl, good thinking! We wouldn't have to worry about getting out early on Saturday and joining long queues everywhere. We'd have the laugh on them.'

'I don't particularly want to get one over on them, sunshine, I just want to make life easier for us. Mind you, I might get me eye wiped if everyone has the same idea.'

There were a few people in the greengrocer's giving their Christmas order in, but Molly was pleased when she didn't hear anyone ask for the stuff to be delivered. However, when it came to their turn to be served, Billy told them several people had asked for their goods to be delivered. 'I hate to tell yer this, Molly, with you and Nellie being good customers, but I've had to say it'll be thru'pence extra, 'cos I'll have to give the young lad a decent wage. It's hard work pulling that cart, I wouldn't like it, so he deserves to be paid for his labour.'

'That's fine by me, Billy, 'cos I would have tipped the lad anyway.' Molly nudged her mate. 'It's all right with you, isn't it, sunshine?'

Nellie narrowed eyes made her look calculating. 'It will certainly be all right if yer can deliver them today, Billy, I'd be made up. And ye're right, it is a hard job and the lad does deserve a few bob for pushing that heavy cart around.'

'Yer want the stuff today?' Billy asked Molly because he'd

been caught out too often by Nellie to fancy his chances of getting any sense out of her. 'That's fine by me, 'cos it'll be less to do on Saturday. Tell us what yer want and I'll get Tommo to start on it now. He could be at your house with it in an hour. Does that suit?'

'Just the job, Billy,' Molly said. 'If yer've got a bit of paper I can write the two orders out for yer. And when the lad delivers them, yer can put a note in each saying how much the order comes to, and if we've got enough on our club card to cover it.' A pencil and a none too clean piece of paper were handed over and Molly began to write. 'I've done mine now, Nellie, so I'll do yours. Potatoes, veg, and was it a dozen tangerines yer wanted, and a pound of apples?'

'That's it, girl, spot on.' Nellie grinned at Billy. 'Oh, and a piece of mistletoe, lad, so I can catch a few fellers unawares.'

'Okay, Nellie, I'll see it's a decent piece.' Billy was saying a prayer of thanks for his good luck. He remembered one year Nellie had chased him around the shop and stockroom with a piece of mistletoe in her hand. Sacks had been knocked over and spuds rolled down the pavement followed by sprouts and onions. A whole box of oranges suffered the same fate. All the other shopkeepers and their customers were out, in the street laughing their heads off, but at the time Billy didn't see the funny side of it. He did when he got to bed, though. His wife thought he'd gone barmy because he was roaring with laughter over something she thought the police should have been called out for, and the woman taken away in a Black Maria.

Billy eyed the list. 'The boy will have this weighed out and at your house in an hour's time. Will yer be back home by then?'

'I hope so, but give us an extra fifteen minutes just in case.' Molly took a deep breath and smiled. 'Well, that's a load off me mind and chest. We'll be in tomorrow to sort our club cards out.

It we owe yer anything we'll pay up then. If you owe us, we'll spend it on nuts and fruit. Thanks, Billy, ye're a pal.'

When they were outside the shop, Nellie nudged Molly and winked knowingly. 'Ay, girl, d'yer know when yer said it was a load off yer mind and yer chest? Well, did yer notice Billy's eyes go to me breasts? It was as if he was hypnotized, couldn't help himself, like. Mind you, he's no different to all the other men what see me. All their eyes go straight to me bosom.'

Molly knew she was a fool for taking any notice, she should just carry on walking as though she hadn't heard. But she couldn't help herself. 'Nellie, everyone's eyes go straight to yer bust because it's the first thing they see! When you walk into a room, yer bust enters it at least five seconds before the rest of yer body. Anybody that didn't notice it would have to be blind, so don't be making out that Billy fancies yer. Just imagine if someone was walking behind yer, heard what yer said and told his wife. She'd play merry hell with him, and the poor man's done nothing wrong except be as nice to you as he is to all his customers.'

There was a sly grin on Nellie's face. 'I knew that would get yer worked up, girl, that's why I said it. I wouldn't say nothing to my feller, though, 'cos he's like you, very straitlaced. The pair of yer miss an awful lot of fun in life.'

'Listen to me, Nellie McDonough, I've saved yer from many a go-along from someone yer've insulted. Ever since I've known yer I've been pulling yer away from a situation that was going to end up in fisticuffs. I'm surprised yer get away with it as often as yer do, yer've been a lucky blighter.'

'That's 'cos I've got you for a mate, girl, and yer always look after me. I'm hopeless on me own, I don't know what I'd do without yer. Those lists for the butcher's and greengrocer's, I couldn't have written them 'cos I'm hopeless at adding up and spelling.'

Molly chuckled. 'Yer don't have to tell me that, sunshine. I can remember once when yer weren't feeling too good and asked me if I'd get yer something from the butcher's when I was out shopping if yer wrote it out for me. Well, soft girl that I am, I just takes the piece of paper and puts it in me pocket, I never thought of looking at it. And I couldn't make out what Tony was laughing at until he passed it over to me. Yer wanted one pound of sosarge.'

'Well, what was wrong with that, girl? I wasn't asking for much, was I?'

'No, yer weren't, sunshine, only Tony doesn't sell sosarge 'cos he said there's no call for it around here and yer'd have to make do with common or garden beef sausage like the rest of his customers.'

'Yeah, well, we can't all be clever buggers, can we?' Nellie pulled up abruptly. 'What are we walking this way for, girl, where are we going?'

'To the sweetshop. We may as well do as much as we can today and then we can take it nice and easy tomorrow. I know what I want: ciggies for Jack, baccy for me da, a selection box for Ruthie, and as many small boxes of chocolates as me Christmas club allows.'

'Get the same for me, girl, except two lots of ciggies instead of tobacco. We've got the same amount on our club cards, which is good, isn't it, girl? I'm glad yer make me put money away each week, otherwise I'd be in a right state and end up having to do all me shopping out of one week's wages.' Nellie gave a little hop to keep up. 'Are we going to Irwin's as well? If we are, we're going to have to put a move on to be back for the lad coming.'

There were only a few people in the sweetshop, so they weren't kept waiting long. For Molly to get everything she wanted, she had to pay a shilling with her club card, and because Nellie felt like a slab of Cadbury's, she had to fork out one and six. But they left the shop feeling very pleased with themselves.

'Can't we leave Irwin's until tomorrow, girl? Me chilblains are giving me gyp. I need to take the weight off me feet and take these ruddy shoes off.'

'Yes, okay, sunshine, we'll head for home. We've done well for one day, and tomorrow we only need some groceries from Irwin's.' Molly looked down on her friend who was grimacing with pain. 'Let me carry that bag for yer, then we can walk quicker. A warm by the fire and a nice cup of tea will do yer the power of good.'

Even in pain, Nellie didn't forget her tummy. 'Have yer got any biscuits in, girl?'

'Not for eating now I haven't, they're for over the holiday. Anyway, greedy guts, yer've got a slab of chocolate which should satisfy yer craving for sweet stuff. And I know yer won't like me saying it, but yer really should cut down on cakes and chocolate 'cos ye're carrying a lot of weight, sunshine, and it's not good for yer. I'm not getting at yer, it's just that yer are me mate and if I think anything's bad for yer, I'd be a poor mate if I didn't tell yer.'

'I know yer mean well, girl, but I can't help meself. Our Lily had a go at me a few months ago, and she told me to chew gum to take me mind off sweets. She even bought me a packet of Wrigley's Spearmint gum, and honest to God I did try, but I hated the bleeding stuff. Me jaw got tired, the ruddy stuff stuck to me teeth and I ended up throwing the packet in the fire. I didn't tell our Lily that she'd wasted her money, mind, or she'd have gone mad. But I never want to see another stick of gum in me life. And have yer ever watched anyone what does chew gum, girl? I think they look stupid with their mouths going up and down and their faces all shapes. I'd rather be fat and happy than looking gormless all the time.'

'They say it's good for yer teeth, keeps them clean,' Molly said. 'But I have to admit I don't like the stuff. Our Doreen used to chew it when she was at school and she knew I didn't like it, so she'd stick it anywhere I wouldn't see. I found a piece stuck under the dining table once and raised merry hell when she came in. And the cheeky little madam said she didn't know where else to put it, and anyway it was my fault for coming into the room without making a noise to warn her.'

When they reached her house, Molly put her bag down while she took the front-door key from her purse. 'Let's hope the room's warm 'cos I banked the fire down thinking we'd be out longer.' She opened the door and picked up her bag. 'It won't take long to get it roaring, though, sunshine, so come on in and take the weight off yer feet.'

The first thing Nellie did was pick up the carver chair, place it at the table, then groaning with pain, she used her big toes to ease off her shoes. 'Oh, thank God for that! I couldn't have walked another step, girl, I was just ready to drop.'

'Well, you take yer coat off, sunshine, and throw it over the back of one of the chairs. I'll put the poker in the fire to let some draught through to get it going, then I'll stick the kettle on for a pot of tea. And seeing as yer look so sorry for yerself, I'll break into a packet of custard creams. But we're only having one each, and I'm sticking to that even if yer cry yer eyes out. Otherwise all me Christmas goodies will be gone before the day arrives.'

Nellie had a smile on her face as she watched her friend walking through to the kitchen. Things were looking up. One custard cream was better than none, and she still had that slab of Cadbury's for herself. It was too near Christmas to think of giving up sweet stuff, but she would definitely try when the festivities were over, and even make cutting down on sweets and cakes one of her New Year resolutions. Her head and chins nodding, she decided to tell Molly when she came in with the tea. Then her mate could keep an eye on her and make sure she kept to her resolution.

'Here yer are, sunshine, a pot of hot tea and a custard cream each. And the fire's taking off nicely, it'll be roaring up the chimney in a minute.'

Nellie took one look at the two biscuits on the plate and thought how sad and lonely they looked. That's how she'd look if she kept to her resolution. So she quickly made up her mind to forget about making promises she knew she wouldn't keep. There was no point in telling Molly because she'd only nag her, and why should she worry when she was happy? Yer only had to look at Elsie Flanaghan to know that thin people led miserable lives. Nellie wouldn't want to be like Elsie Flanaghan for a big clock.

There was a knock on the door and Molly pulled a face. 'It can't be the coalman or the rent man, and I'm not expecting anyone.' As she made her way to the door, she said, 'Don't you dare touch my biscuit or I'll kill yer.'

Molly opened the door to find the young lad from the greengrocer's standing there beside his cart. He looked frozen, with a cherry red nose, pale blue lips and hands he was trying to rub some life back into. 'Oh, yer poor thing! Haven't yer got a scarf to put on, or a pair of gloves?'

The lad shook his head. He was only just fourteen and should be still at school, but with him having no dad, the Education Authority had allowed him to leave school two weeks early so he could earn some money to help his mother. He had a young sister, and his mother took on cleaning jobs to keep a roof over their heads. After the holiday he would look for a better job, but he was glad when the greengrocer said he'd take him on as long as he pulled his weight. Well, he wasn't afraid of hard work and Billy said he was pleased with him. It would mean an extra fifteen shillings for his mam to buy things for Christmas.

'I'll be all right, missus.' The lad, Tommo, cupped his freezing cold hands to his mouth and blew hot breath into them. It didn't help much, but it was something. 'I've got two orders, are they both for you?'

'One for me and one for a house three doors away. But the woman is in here now, so she'll open her door and yer can throw them in the hall.' Molly looked down into the cart where there were two orange boxes, one on top of the other. 'That one is for me, so will yer carry it through to the kitchen for me? And I'll get me friend's key and open her door for yer. Then ye're coming back for a cup of hot tea and to get a warm by the fire. Come on, son, bring the box and follow me.'

Nellie watched with interest but wasn't about to discommode herself. 'D'yer want me key, girl? It's in me coat pocket.'

'Then get it out, sunshine, 'cos the poor lad's not going to wait around for you, he's like a block of ice as it is.'

When both boxes were in their rightful kitchens, Molly brought Tommo in and stood him in front of the fire. 'I'll bring yer a cup of tea now, lad, and yer can help yerself to one of those custard creams.'

Nellie moved like lightning and one custard cream was off the plate and in her hand without the boy seeing her move. A joke was a joke, she thought. If my mate feels sorry for him, she'll likely offer him my biscuit. But I'm not as generous or good-hearted as she is. I could make a New Year resolution to be more generous in the future, but it's something I'm going to have to consider very carefully.

When the cup of tea was handed to him, the lad held it between his hands, savouring the warmth. 'This tea's good, missus, thanks very much.'

'Ye're welcome, son, you stay there until ye're warmed through.' Molly was on her knees rooting through the mass of odds and sods which kept getting thrown in the sideboard cupboard because there was nowhere else to put them. She'd have to have a good clear out when she had a spare hour, because this was ridiculous. After a few minutes of frantic searching she gave a cry of triumph. 'I knew I'd seen them in there.'

'Who are yer talking to, girl, and what have yer been doing with yer head stuck in there?'

'Looking for these.' Molly scrambled to her feet holding a pair of black woollen gloves aloft. 'These aren't much good, lad, they're donkey's years old. But they'd keep yer hands warm and they're better than nothing.'

'Ooh, thanks, missus, they're great!' The lad's face lit up with pleasure. No one had ever given him anything before and he'd never had a pair of gloves in his life. 'Just the job for keeping me hands warm. And if yer hands are warm it makes yer forget the rest of yer is cold.'

For the first time, Molly noticed the thin coat the boy was wearing, and the scruffy worn-out shoes she'd bet any money had holes in the soles and pieces of newspaper inside to keep some of the cold out. The sight took her back to the days when she was often so skint she couldn't afford to have her shoes mended. 'Have yer got any brothers or sisters, Tommo?' She smiled at him. 'That's what Billy called yer, so I hope yer don't mind me being friendly?'

'I don't mind, missus, 'cos I've always been called that with me name being Thompson. I've got one kid sister at home, and me mam.' He drank a mouthful of tea so they wouldn't hear the emotion in his voice. Big boys didn't cry. 'Me dad died when I was ten.'

Molly had the sense not to show pity. 'You stay there until yer feel warm right through, ye're not in anyone's way.' She glanced over at Nellie and mouthed, 'Kitchen, please?'

Now Nellie didn't like being disturbed once she was in her carver chair, especially when her chilblains were settling down. So she heaved a sigh at the same time as heaving up her body. 'What is it, girl? I was nice and comfy there.'

'That's just too bad, sunshine.' Molly kept her voice low. 'I know yer've got a silver sixpence in yer purse, so will yer hand it over to me without asking any questions?'

Nellie looked puzzled. 'Yer can't expect me to hand over sixpence without asking what it's for. What's the big secret?'

'I want to put it to the sixpence I've got and give it to that boy.' Molly's hand shot out to cover her friend's mouth. 'Take a good look at him. He's half-starved and the clothes he's got on won't keep him warm. And he's got no dad. Now does that answer yer questions, and will yer give me the tanner?'

Nellie wasn't in a position to refuse, not with Molly's hand clamped over her mouth. Although she nodded, her eyes told Molly she wasn't in favour of handing over her sixpence. However, her friend knew how to get round her. She hugged the little woman, kissed her cheek and said, 'Ye're a pal, sunshine, and I love the bones of yer.'

That of course cut off any argument Nellie might have put up. After all, when someone tells you they love the bones of you, you really can't tell them to sod off, it doesn't sound right somehow. But this being generous was getting out of hand. There'd definitely be no New Year resolution, she couldn't afford it. The way her mate was going on she'd be wearing a halo soon.

But Nellie's mood changed completely and she was filled with good will when Molly gave her the two sixpences to hand over to the lad. 'You give them to him, sunshine, and when yer see his face, it'll be all the thanks yer need.'

'Here yer are, lad,' Nellie felt six foot tall and her heart was at bursting point when tears came to the lad's eyes. 'Yer can buy yer mam and yer sister a small box of chocolates to give on Christmas morning.'

Tommo couldn't get over it. He'd been delighted with the cup of tea, then over the moon with the pair of gloves, old as they were. But to get a shilling on top was just unbelievable. 'Thanks, missus, that's very kind of yer. Me mam and our Amy will get a surprise 'cos they won't be expecting anything.'

Molly's mind was working and she thought of another way to help the lad. 'Listen, if yer'd like to call here when yer finish work, I might have some clothes for yer that me son's grown out of. That's if yer don't mind wearing cast-offs? They'll be in good condition, it's just he's grown out of them.'

Tommo's eyes were like saucers. 'Ooh, thanks, missus! I'll come straight from work, but it'll be after six 'cos I've got orders to make up. Will that be all right?'

Nellie would never have thought of that, but now her friend had mentioned it, she said, 'I'll have some for yer as well, lad, 'cos my son's got some he's grown out of too.'

The lad couldn't believe his luck. 'Thanks very much, I'll definitely come after work. And, d'yer know, this is one of the best days I've ever had. That's since me dad died, because when he was alive we used to have good times and lots of fun.'

'We'll be glad to do what we can for yer, Tommo,' Molly said. 'Now I think yer should be getting back to work or Billy will think we've kidnapped yer.'

The boy who walked out of the door was very different from the one who had entered. Pulling on the gloves, and with head held high, he lifted the cart handles and walked down the street whistling.

Chapter Nineteen

Molly came in rubbing her hands. 'That's one very happy lad just left here. His mam probably has trouble making ends meet and they're living on a shoe string. I hope Phil's got some clothes he doesn't wear any more. There's a few inches' difference in their height, but Tommo's mother might be handy with a needle and cotton if we can come up with some trousers. Even a couple of warm jerseys would be a big help. I'll nip over to our Doreen's and ask her to have a root through Phil's things, and Tommy left some clothes here when he got married. He said they were too small or tight on him and I could give them to the rag man, but they're the only things left of his in this house and I hadn't the heart to throw them away. While I'm sorting some things out, you could go and have a look through Paul's clothes. Yer'll know what he doesn't want or won't fit him. They all went into the army as boys and came out men so it's only natural they'd outgrow things. Even their demob suits only fitted where they touched, but they were a godsend at the time.'

'Ah, ay, girl, give us a break! I didn't enjoy that cup of tea because the lad came and interrupted everything. Can't we relax for five minutes and have another cup before rushing round like headless chickens?'

'Nellie, ye're a flaming tea tank! I'm not making a fresh pot 'cos this one's still warm, I'll just add some boiling water to it. And after that I'm going to throw yer out so yer can look for

312

something for Tommo. Yer promised the lad, please don't let him down. After all, sunshine, it is Christmas time, the season of good will.'

'D'yer know, girl, since I've been sat here I've changed me mind half a dozen times over making a New Year resolution to be more caring and generous. I honestly don't think I could keep up with you. I'm sure yer go around looking for people what want help. I'll never be that big-hearted, 'cos we were poor once, remember, and no one offered us help. We just had to get on with it the best way we could.'

'It's because I remember it, I want to help the lad! And don't forget, we both had husbands who were working. They earned lousy wages and we had a hard time coping when the kids came along, but just think how much worse it would have been if we'd had no man behind us?' Molly stood with her hands on her hips, her temper rising. 'In the name of God, Nellie, I'm not asking yer for much, just some old clothes that our kids won't wear again. Can't yer even bring yerself to do that?'

'Keep yer hair on, girl, or yer'll be doing yerself an injury. I promised the lad clothes, and clothes he shall have! But can't I have a cup of tea first to quench me thirst? To whet me whistle before I go rooting through me son's wardrobe? And, for your information, I know our Lily's got a couple of dresses what she won't wear any more, so I have every intention of bringing those to see if they'll be any good to his mother.' A grin spread slowly across her chubby face. 'So yer see, although I might be sitting on me backside looking as though I haven't a care in the world, or a thought for anyone but meself, I haven't forgot me promise to the lad. He'll definitely get something to wear off me, even if it's me fleecy-lined bloomers.'

Molly took a deep breath and smiled down at the little woman who reminded her of a picture she'd seen of Queen Victoria sitting on a throne. Except the Queen was wearing a gold crown with jewels set in it, while Nellie still had a scarf over her head. 'Please accept my sincere apologies, sunshine, I'm ashamed of meself for even harbouring the thought that yer'd let me or Tommo down.'

Nellie waved a hand towards the kitchen. 'Apologies accepted, tea expected. Away and do yer work, girl.'

'Yes, miss, right away, miss.' Molly hurried to the kitchen and turned up the light under the kettle. 'I should have asked him about his mam, but I didn't think,' she called through as she rinsed the dirty cups under the tap. 'Both Doreen and Jill have got dresses from before they were pregnant, they'd be happy to give them to a good cause.'

Nellie slapped an open hand on the table. 'Stop talking and attend to your work, Bennett! Otherwise I'll set the dogs on to you.'

Molly was still chuckling when she carried the tray through. 'Set the dogs on me indeed! And we'll have less of the Bennett! Don't let a few compliments go to yer head, sunshine, or I'll have to withdraw them.'

Nellie waited until her friend was seated and they both had a cup of tea in front of them. 'Ay, girl, has Phil said anything about seeing his mam again?'

'I haven't had much chance to talk to him, so I don't know what he's doing. If I were to hazard a guess, I'd say he wouldn't let Christmas go without seeing her. It's difficult, though, because her husband and kids will want her with them on Christmas Day, which is only what yer can expect. So we'll just have to wait and see what happens. There's no transport on that day, but Phil might bring her by taxi, even if it's only for an hour.'

'It's a pity she can't come to our party, isn't it, girl, 'cos she wouldn't half enjoy it. She'd get a laugh out of me speciality act.'

'Oh, ay, and what are yer going to do this year? Have yer made up yer mind who ye're going to impersonate?'

'I'm having a bad time, girl, trying to think of someone I haven't done yet. I've racked me brains but can't think of no one what would go down well with the audience. Can you suggest anyone?'

'I'm sorry, sunshine, but there's no one who springs to mind. Yer've done Shirley Temple, Al Jolson, Mae West, and the dance of the seven veils. Every film star I can think of is not funny, and yer need someone who'll give us a laugh.'

'There's one I can think of, girl, and that's Betty Boop.'

Molly fell back in her chair. 'Betty Boop! But she's not real, she's a cartoon character!'

Nellie's head started wagging from side to side, a sign she was taking umbrage. 'What difference does that make? Everyone knows her, and it would be a good laugh.'

'I don't believe it, sunshine, even from you! Betty Boop wears skirts up to her backside, she has a deep red Cupid's bow, eye-lashes about six inches long and kiss curls on her forehead. Yer wouldn't have the nerve to let yer friends see yer like that.'

'Who wouldn't!? It's for a bleeding laugh, girl, and I'd be the one making a fool of meself. If I don't care, why should you?'

'George would go mad, and so would Steve, Lily and Paul. They wouldn't want to see their mother making a fool of herself and showing all she's got into the bargain.'

'I'd have yer a bet on that, girl, because I know my George would be the first to laugh. And Steve and Paul would think it hilarious.' Nellie's brow creased. 'I wouldn't have a bet on our Lily, 'cos her sense of humour is a bit dodgy. She used to find everything funny at one time, but since she's been courting Archie she sometimes gives me daggers. Not that he minds, he's usually doubled up laughing and doesn't see the looks she gives me.'

'All I can say, sunshine, is that ye're on yer own in this. It's up to you what yer want to do, but I'll have no part in it.'

Nellie chuckled. 'Ye're not half a bleeding coward sometimes, girl. But if I do Betty Boop, a tanner says yer'll be laughing as loud as the rest of them.'

'That remains to be seen, sunshine, but I'm certainly not going to gamble on it. And now we've emptied the teapot, shall we make a move? I'll slip across to Doreen's, then I'll have a go at Tommy's old clothes. And you can be sorting out what yer've got in yer own house. Give me about an hour and a half, then bring them down.'

The cups were taken out and washed, then the friends left the house to go about their business. But Molly had a thought when she was outside her daughter's house, and called after Nellie, 'Just in case yer feel like a drink as soon as yer put a foot in my house, bring a pot of tea with yer, eh? And make sure the water's boiled properly before yer pour it in the pot.'

Nellie turned the key in the lock. 'Cheeky bugger! Anyone listening would think I was always on the scrounge. And all over a bleeding cup of tea!'

Doreen opened the door. 'What's me Auntie Nellie shouting about?'

Molly pushed past her, eager to get out of the cold. 'I told her when she comes down later to bring a pot of tea with her. She drinks it as though it's going out of fashion and I can't keep up with her.'

'Oh, Mam, that's terrible! She'll think ye're awful tight.'

'Will she hell! My mate doesn't take offence over remarks like that. If she did, we'd have stopped being mates years ago. Anyway, she's already had three lots of tea off me this morning, I can't keep up with her! And the likelihood of her bringing a pot of tea with her is very remote, so don't be worrying.' Molly bent and kissed Victoria. 'Ye're in the best place, sunshine, yer look as snug as a bug in a rug.'

'I'm a very lucky woman, Molly, to be getting so well looked after at my age.'

'It's only what yer deserve.' Molly pulled a chair out from the table. 'Anyway, I've got a little tale to tell yer, and when yer've heard it I'm hoping Doreen will help me out.'

'What is it, Mam? Yer know I'll help if I possibly can.' Doreen walked to the bottom of the stairs to listen for the baby, and when all was quiet she took a seat next to her mother. 'Go ahead, Mam, what are yer after?'

Molly leaned her elbows on the table, cupped her chin in her hands, and began her tale starting at the greengrocer's shop. She was very good at explaining everything in detail, was Molly, and the two women could almost see Tommo in their minds. When the tale was told, Doreen nodded. 'Phil's got a couple of pairs of trousers that are too short and tight for him. He'll never wear them, so ye're welcome to take those for the lad. And there's two white shirts that nearly choked him when he last wore them – they can go, too. And a couple of pullovers. They've all seen better days, Mam, but anyone in need would be glad of them because I wouldn't give yer them if they were rubbish.'

Molly leaned sideways and planted a kiss on her daughter's cheek. 'That's wonderful, sunshine, the lad will be over the moon. I talked Nellie into giving him a tanner, like meself, and yer should have seen the look on his face. Yer'd think we'd given him a hundred pound. He's going to buy his mam and kid sister a box of chocolates for Christmas, and he said they won't half get a surprise.' She sighed. 'We don't know when we're well off, do we? None of us are loaded, but we've got clear rent books, coal for the fire and food for the table. This lad was ten when his dad died, and he's probably trying to be the man of the house. I don't think his job in the shop is permanent, Billy's just taken him on for the Christmas rush and will only be paying him in buttons. That's why I'd like to help him, and his mam into the bargain.'

'I'll give yer a tanner for him, Mam, 'cos every little helps, doesn't it?'

'And so will I.' Victoria said. 'In fact, I could spare a shilling.'

Molly shook her head. 'No, sixpence would be fine. If we overdo it, his mam might think we're doing it out of pity, and if she's anything like me then she'd be ashamed. But I'll find a way of giving him your sixpences without him thinking we feel sorry for him.'

'The baby is due for a feed any minute, he's overdue now. So as soon as he's fed and changed, I'll get the clothes out and bring them across.'

'I know this is going to sound hard-faced, sunshine, but I don't mind being thought cheeky if it's to help some poor beggar. So, have yer got any old dresses yer won't wear again?'

Doreen grinned. 'I can't get into any of the dresses I had before I got married, when I was very slim. Once I got pregnant I put on weight like nobody's business. I've lost some of it, mind, but I'll never get back to being as thin as I was. Ye're welcome to take the dresses, but they wouldn't fit his mother unless she's thin.'

'Tommo is as thin as a rake. I'm pretty good at judging and I'd say he's not thin by nature, more by not getting enough food down him. So I can't see him having a mother who's carrying a lot of weight.'

'I'll bundle everything up and bring it over to you,' Doreen said, 'Did yer say he was coming back about six o'clock?'

'I think it may be after that because the shop is staying open later and he's got to do the orders.'

'Phil will be home before that, I'll bring the clothes over as soon as I've got them ready. I like to have me husband's dinner on the table as soon as he walks through the door.'

Molly smiled. 'I used to be as eager as you, sunshine, when me and yer dad first got married. But when you kids started coming along it wasn't always possible. So you carry on spoiling yer husband while yer can.' She pushed herself up. 'I'll get home and see what I can gather together, and me mate will be bringing her stuff down soon.' Molly chuckled to herself. 'I wonder if she'll bring a pot of tea with her?'

Molly looked down at the neat stacks of clothes on the couch. She'd never expected this much in her wildest dreams. 'I can't get over it, sunshine, I've got more clothes here than one of Mary Ann's stalls. I just hope some of them will fit Tommo and his family.'

'Well, yer know when yer were over in Doreen's talking yer head off as usual, where d'yer think I was?' Nellie bosom was standing to attention which told Molly something of importance was about to be heard. 'I nipped down to the shop and saw the lad again. I asked him about his mother, in a nice way of course, and he said she's very thin. So, don't yer think it was clever of me and that a few compliments are in order?'

'I think yer did blinking marvellous!' Molly gave her a hug. 'Didn't he seem surprised at yer asking such a question? I mean, he wasn't embarrassed, like?'

'Listen to me, girl, I don't spend me life going round embarrassing people. I can be very tactful when I want.'

'I'm all ears, sunshine, so show me how tactful yer were.'

This was right up Nellie's street. So folding her arms and hitching up her bosom, she said, 'I could see him busy in the back of the shop but I didn't go in, I waited until he came out to get a cabbage from one of the boxes on the pavement. And when he saw me, he gave me a great big smile. So I said my daughter had a couple of dresses she didn't wear any more, but which were in good nick, and I wondered whether they'd fit his mam. I told him Lily was nice and slim, and he said his mam was thin, too. He looked as pleased as punch, so I said I'd have them ready for him, and if they didn't fit his mam, or she didn't like them, then there was no harm done.' Nellie was nodding and Molly knew she was congratulating herself mentally. 'So what d'yer think of that, girl?'

'I think ye're one clever, crafty little woman, sunshine, and I'm proud of yer. We've done really well, with six dresses for his mam and three pair of trousers, four pullovers and four shirts for him. I'll have to find something for him to carry them in. I can't wrap them in sheets of newspaper, it would put his mother off and I'd hate her to think we were doing it out of pity.'

Nellie raised her brows and tried to look haughty. 'There's no need to panic, girl, 'cos after I'd spoken to the lad, I asked Billy if I could have one of the empty apple boxes. They're only made of cardboard so it won't be heavy for him to carry.'

'Ay, ye're springing one surprise after another on me! I know what your game is, though, Nellie McDonough, I can see right through yer. This is all to show me why our detective agency should be called McDonough and Bennett. That's what ye're after, isn't it?'

'That never entered me head, girl, which shows ye're more bad-minded than I am. But now yer've brought the subject up, I don't know why your name should come before mine.'

'I'll tell yer what, then, sunshine, seeing as we don't have an office or any official paper, we'll go week about. Me one week, you the other. Now, nothing can be fairer than that, can it?'

Nellie gave this some thought. 'How about it being me one week and you the other? Then I'd say it was fair.'

'I'm willing to go a bit further, Nellie, and say it can be McDonough and Bennett for the next month. You'll be the chief cook and bottle washer all over Christmas and through the month of January. So don't ever say I never give yer anything. But I think it's the least I can do under the circumstances, with yer being so good in helping get things together for Tommo. And now I'd like yer to go home and get the dinner ready for yer family, so I can do the same. And as soon as the lad comes, I'll give yer a knock on the wall. And I'll not say a word to him, or give him anything until you're here. Okay, sunshine?'

'Okay, girl, fair enough.' Nellie got as far as the door before muttering to herself, 'She thinks I've been good and is so pleased with me, yet she couldn't even make me one lousy, bleeding cup of tea.'

'What did yer say, Nellie?'

'Nothing much, girl, just how pleased the lad will be.'

'Oh, it must be me hearing things, 'cos I thought I heard yer calling me fit to burn.'

Nellie turned on the top step, devilment in her eyes. 'Now as if I'd do that, girl! And you me best mate.' She stepped down on to the pavement. 'And me junior assistant for the next four weeks. Yer'll have to clean yer ears out and pull yer socks up if yer want to keep yer job, Mrs Bennett, I expect my staff to be on their toes at all times.'

Molly stood to attention and saluted. 'I shall bear that in mind, sir! Now I request leave to attend to my family's dinner.' She pulled the door closed with a smile on her face. 'Wait for the knock on the wall, sunshine. Ta-ra.'

Ruthie came home from school early, breathless with running and bubbling with excitement. 'I've finished school now, Mam, today was me last day. Yer can't call me a child any more 'cos I'll soon be a working girl.'

Molly gave her a hug. 'I'm so pleased for yer, sunshine, even though yer are wishing yer life away. In years to come yer'll look back on yer school days as the happiest in yer life. I bet Bella's over the moon, isn't she?'

Ruthie grinned. 'Well, she would be if the moon was a lot lower down. But it was a bit sad saying goodbye to all the girls who've been in the same class with us for years, and I nearly cried when we said goodbye to Miss Harrison 'cos she's always been good to us, and she was the one who got us the job at Johnson's. Me and Bella said we'd go back and see her when we got the chance, to let her know how we're getting on. She was really pleased when we said that.' All the while Ruthie had been talking, her eyes kept straying to the clothes on the couch. Now she asked, 'What are all those clothes for?'

'Some are from Phil and Doreen, some from yer Auntie Nellie's family, and some are what Tommy left when he got married because they were to small for him.' Molly had no intention of telling her daughter the truth in case she was here when the boy called and said something to upset him. She wouldn't do it intentionally, but she had a habit of speaking before thinking. 'We had a clear out, and we're giving them to someone who can wear them. It would be a shame to leave them for the moths to get at.'

'That's a nice colour, Mam,' the girl said, fingering a blue crêpe dress of Lily's. 'Can I have a look at it? It might fit me.'

'Indeed yer can't! And don't be pulling at it when they're all folded neat and tidy. That dress was Lily's, and I'm sure yer wouldn't want her to see yer walking round in her cast-offs?'

That was enough to put Ruthie off. 'Ye're right, Mam, I wouldn't.' She lost interest in the clothes then, thinking of her first wage packet. It would be a few weeks off yet because when she started work she had to work a week in hand. But it was something nice to look forward to and dream about in bed at night before she went to sleep. She knew now her mam wouldn't let her wear bright red lipstick, so she'd buy a pale pink one which wouldn't be noticed very much. That would be out of her first week's wages. Out of her second, a bottle of Evening In Paris scent. She got no further than that in her planning before she fell asleep with a smile on her face.

* * *

When Jill leaned forward to kiss her mother, she saw over her shoulder the stacks of clothes. 'Good heavens, Mam, are yer thinking of opening a second-hand shop?'

Of course the story was told again, and Jill was disappointed her mother hadn't asked her. 'I've got dresses I'll never wear, Mam, and I'd like them to go to someone like the family yer've just mentioned. And Steve probably has things he's outgrown as well!'

'I haven't had time to ask yer, sunshine, 'cos me and Nellie only met the boy this afternoon when he delivered our greens and fruit. My heart went out to him because he was freezing in a threadbare jacket, old pants and paper-thin shoes. I never expected to have so much for him. I was thinking if I could get a few things together, he'd be delighted. Perhaps a couple of pair of trousers and a few woolly jumpers or cardigans to keep him warm. I never thought our Doreen would give me so much, or Nellie. And there were a few things of Tommy's upstairs that I knew he'd never wear.'

'Aye, well, I'll let yer off this time. But tomorrow's me last day at work so I'll be seeing more of you and our Doreen. I'll know everything that goes on, what you and Auntie Nellie get up to, and if anything crops up like today, I can get stuck in and help.'

'I know yer'd always get stuck in to help some poor soul, sunshine, and I'm really looking forward to seeing more of yer. So is Doreen, it'll be nice for both of yer to have someone to talk to and have a laugh with.'

'No one will be more pleased than Steve, he hasn't liked me working for a couple of months now. But I'm glad I didn't pack in when he first wanted me to because I feel fine, as fit as a fiddle.'

'And yer look it, I've got to say. The picture of health and as pretty as a rose starting to open its petals. I'd say that working in your condition has done yer more good than harm.'

'I'll tell that to Steve when he comes in, which will be in about fifteen minutes, so I'd better scarper.' Jill opened her purse and took out half a crown. 'Give this to the boy so his mam can buy a bit extra for Christmas.' When her mother began to shake her head, Jill said, 'Mam, me and Steve aren't short of money. We've had two wages coming in and we've been saving up. So I'd be a poor one if I couldn't give a couple of bob to someone in need.'

It was a case of smiling or crying, so Molly forced a smile. 'The way things are going, Tommo's going to have a better Christmas than any of us.' She sniffed up. 'Except he won't have a dad to enjoy it with.'

As soon as Phil came in from work that night Doreen sensed there was something different about him. He acted as he always did, kissing her and Victoria and bending down to smile as he watched the baby's arms and legs punching the air. There was nothing she could put her finger on except that his eyes seemed to be smiling. When he went into the kitchen to wash his hands she followed him. 'Why are yer looking so happy, love?'

'I didn't know I was looking happy.' Phil dried his hands and drew his wife towards him. 'Mind you, I've every reason to be happy, sweetheart. I've got a beautiful wife and baby that I adore, I have Aunt Vicky, a marvellous family and friends.' He chuckled as he held her tight. 'I also have a new job which I start on the second of January.'

Doreen's mouth opened in surprise. 'Yer've got a new job! But yer've been in that place since yer left school, and I thought yer were happy there?'

'I am very happy there, sweetheart, and wouldn't dream of leaving. Especially since I've been made up to floor walker.'

Her arms went around his neck and she rained kisses on his

cheeks. 'Oh, I'm so pleased for yer! That's lovely.' She wriggled free and took his hand to lead him through to the living room. 'Did yer hear that, Aunt Vicky? Phil's been promoted.'

'I couldn't help but hear, love, and I'm so pleased for both of yer. You must be feeling very proud of yerself, Phil.'

'It means a two pound a week rise,' he told them, 'which isn't to be sneezed at. And, yes, I am feeling rather pleased with meself.'

Doreen felt like eating him, she loved him so much. 'Seeing as ye're in a good mood, yer won't mind that I gave some of yer old clothes away, will yer?'

'Which old clothes, love?'

Phil listened to her explanation with deepening interest.

'I'm glad yer gave them to yer mam, sweetheart, and I think she's a smasher for wanting to help the lad.' His hands were folded on his lap and he looked down at them as he asked, 'Did yer say the lad hasn't got a father?'

'That's what he told me mam, that his dad had died when he was ten. Me mam really took a liking to the lad, whose name is Tommo, and wanted to help him. Yer know what she's like for helping anyone not as fortunate as we are. Anyway, she's got loads of clothes for him and his mother. He's got a younger sister but me mam never asked how old she was, so there's nothing we could give that might do her a turn.'

'Molly's not a fool, and she wouldn't be taken in by anybody,' Victoria said. 'She really took a liking to the lad, and is worried because the job he's got at the greengrocer's isn't permanent. Billy only took him on to help over the busy period. He's making up orders and delivering them, that's how Molly and Nellie came to meet him.'

'Will he be over there now?'

Doreen shook her head. 'Me mam said it would be well after six because all the orders have to be made up. Anyway, what made yer ask that?'

'I didn't have a father to help me, remember. I've had to fend for meself all me life. Tom Bradley laughed when I got a job at fourteen, called me stupid because I wouldn't go out robbing with him, so I know how a lad that age will feel having no one to encourage, advise or help him. He probably loves his mother and thinks he should be the one to look after her as he's now the man of the house.' Phil shrugged his shoulders and spread out his hands. 'I'd just like to talk to him, perhaps help if I can. At his age, I would have been glad of someone to talk to and perhaps set me on the right road.'

'I think that's a wonderful idea, Phil,' Victoria said. 'I'm sure the lad would be grateful, because after all he's only a kid and yer can't expect him to know how to make his own way in life. He's probably still missing his dad, and having someone older to talk to would, I think, be heaven sent.'

'I'll put our dinner out, love, then slip over and ask me mam to let yer know when this Tommo arrives. Or shall I ask her to send him over here?'

'No, he knows yer mam and Auntie Nellie, he'd be embarrassed if he was put with more strangers. Just tell yer mam I'll be over as soon as I've had me dinner.'

Chapter Twenty

Kenny Thompson wrapped his arms around his thin body to try and keep the cold wind from penetrating his short jacket. He was shivering inside, but was thankful for the gloves without which he thought his fingers would drop off. They were two nice ladies, that Mrs Bennett and Mrs McDonough. Thanks to them he had a shilling in his pocket and two tangerines Billy had said he could have because they were a bit faded. And the greengrocer had promised him a big bag of fruit on Christmas Eve, all the apples and oranges left over after the orders had been made up. He was a good boss, Billy, easygoing and friendly. But Kenny wouldn't like it as a permanent job, he wanted one that would teach him a skill so he would earn a decent wage when he came out of his time. His mam wouldn't have to go out cleaning so much then, they'd be able to manage much better with his wages.

As he neared the Bennetts' house, Kenny took off one glove to smooth down his wayward ginger hair and straighten his flimsy jacket. As his mam said, they may be poor but that was no excuse for being slovenly. His tummy was churning with apprehension because he wasn't used to talking to strangers. He didn't have much to do with the lads in his street either, because if you didn't have a ball or a decent pair of shoes for playing footie, they wouldn't let you be one of the gang. Not that he'd wanted to be after his father died. He became withdrawn then and spent most of his time in the company of his mam and kid sister. Funny thing, though, he hadn't felt a bit shy or strange with Mrs Bennett or her neighbour, the jolly one called Nellie. They'd treated him nice and he was looking forward to seeing them again. He hoped they'd managed to get him a pair of trousers from somewhere, for no matter how old they were they couldn't be any more shabby or washed out than the ones he had on, which were the only ones he possessed. And he'd die of embarrassment if he had to go looking for a job dressed as he was now. He gave a quick look down the length of himself then plucked up the courage to lift the knocker.

Molly opened the door, and both her smile and welcome were warm. 'Come on in, Tommo, yer must be worn out and freezing.'

As he stepped into the hall he heard men's voices and this made him feel nervous. 'Have yer got company, Mrs Bennett? If yer have I can come back tomorrow.'

Molly closed the door and pushed him forward. 'No, sunshine, it's only me husband and my son-in-law. They won't eat yer.'

The heat of the living room hit Kenny full force. They used to have fires like that until his dad died. Now they were lucky if they had a tiny fire made with wood and a few cobs of coal. There was never any heat from it, but the tiny flames made the room look less bleak.

'Come in, son.' Jack got to his feet. 'Get by the fire and melt the icicles.'

'That's my husband, sunshine, and this is Phil, my son-in-law.'

When both men shook hands with him, the lad grew in stature. Not once in his life had he ever shaken hands, and although no one in that room would ever know it marked the start of his growing-up. These people didn't see his shabby clothes and down-at-heel shoes, they treated him as an equal.

'I've got a pot of tea made, son,' Molly said with her brightest smile. 'Yer'll have to pull a chair out from the table because, as yer can see, there's no room on the couch.'

After a quick glance, Kenny said, 'Yer've been busy washing, haven't yer, Mrs Bennett? And I see yer've got daughters.'

'Only one daughter at home now, son, and she's just left school this very day. She's over at her friend's at the moment, dead excited because they've both been taken on at Johnson's Dye Works. They start the day after Boxing Day.' Molly thought it better not to say she'd practically had to throw her daughter out of the door because the little tinker was nosy and wanted to stay to see what Tommo was like. 'None of those clothes are hers, though. Me and Mrs Mac got them together for you to take home to see if they'll do you and yer mam a turn.'

Phil saw the boy's jaw drop and his eyes widen with surprise. 'Yer don't need to take them if yer don't want, Tommo, but some of them are in good nick. There's two pair of trousers of mine in that lot, and not a thing wrong with them except they won't fit me any more. I won't be upset if yer don't want them, though, so don't worry.' Then he said, 'I know yer told Mrs B that yer get called Tommo, but what is yer full name?'

'Kenneth Thompson. That was me dad's name, and he used to be called Ken so I got the nickname of Tommo. I'd like to be called Ken, though, 'cos I'm growing up and nicknames are only for kids.'

Molly came bustling in with a cup of steaming tea. 'Right, Kenneth Thompson, drink this while it's hot and yer'll feel better.' She put the cup down in front of him. 'As for the clothes, sunshine, if I were you I'd take them home and let yer mam see them. They're all in good condition, we wouldn't dream of giving yer rubbish, and she might be glad of them. I've bought things from Paddy's Market meself before today, and if they don't fit properly I get me scissors, needle and cotton out. The trousers, and there are four pair of them, will need shortening three or four inches, maybe more, but they'll be worth the effort.'

'Oh, me mam's great at sewing!' Ken's heart was thudding so loudly he was surprised they didn't hear it. Four pair of trousers! He bet the King didn't have that many. 'She often cuts dresses down for me kid sister.' He fingered the trousers he was wearing. 'These came from Paddy's Market and had to have some cut off.' For the first time, he chuckled. 'I was in short trousers until last week. I looked a right nit with me being tall for me age.'

'What's yer sister's name, sunshine?' Molly suddenly clapped a hand to her mouth. 'Oh, my God, I was supposed to knock for Nellie as soon as yer came. Oh, lord, she'll have me life. I'd better go and give her a knock.'

Phil was up like a shot and opening the door. 'I'll go, Mrs B, you stay where yer are.'

Molly's eyes went to the ceiling. 'I bet she's been walking the floor waiting for me to knock and I promised I wouldn't say anything to yer until she was here. So when I ask yer what yer name is again, and what yer sister is called, go along with me, sunshine, and yer'll get me out of a load of trouble.'

Nellie came plodding in with Phil close behind. 'I'm going to have a word with that Billy tomorrow, lad, for making yer work till this time of night. A right bleeding slave driver he is.' She grinned at Ken who was now frightened of saying a word out of place, and also of getting the sack in the morning. It was his last day anyway, but he needed the money for his mam. 'What d'yer think of the clothes, lad?'

'Nellie, he hasn't had time to look at them yet.' Molly thought this got her off the hook, and she didn't need to tell a lie. 'I had a cup of tea ready for him 'cos he was freezing right through to the core, and I told yer I wouldn't show them to him until yer were here.'

'And it's a good job yer didn't, or I'd have knocked yer block off.' Smiling sweetly, as though butter wouldn't melt in her mouth, Nellie said, 'I'll let yer off, girl, all is forgiven, 'cos I see I'm just in time for a cuppa.'

'Yer can hang on until we've sorted the clothes out, otherwise the lad will be so late home his mother will be worried out of her mind,' Molly said. 'Did yer bring the box with yer?'

'Yeah, it's just inside the front door, girl, but Phil said it's a bit big for the lad to carry.'

Pretending it was something she'd just thought of, Molly winked at Ken. 'I know yer nickname is Tommo, but what's yer proper name?'

The lad's voice came out in a squeak, but he wasn't too afraid to think properly and he solved the problem of names in one go. 'I'm Ken, me sister is Amy, and me mam is Claire.'

Nellie nodded. 'Three nice names, lad, and you tell yer mam I said so.'

'I will, missus.' His cup empty and feeling nice and warm inside, Ken said, 'Can I have a look at the trousers, please?'

Nellie raised her hand in a regal manner, as though warning servants to await her orders. As they all watched, she marched over to the carver chair and without a by-your-leave picked it up and carried it to the end of the table where her view wouldn't be restricted. 'Go on, lad, pretend ye're at yer grandma's and make yerself at home.'

'Ye're surely not expecting Ken to try a pair of trousers on in here, Auntie Nellie?' Phil didn't know whether she was acting daft as usual, but he wasn't taking any chances. The boy would not only be embarrassed, he'd be humiliated. 'Not with us all looking on? He can go in the kitchen where he'll have some privacy.'

Molly knew her mate well enough to read her mind, and knew that if she didn't speak soon, Nellie would make a remark that might be funny in other circumstances, but not this one. If she said the lad had nothing her feller didn't, then the boy would be so embarrassed it would take all the joy out of being given the clothes. 'He doesn't have to try them on here, I'm sure he'd rather do it at home where he could try them one by one at his leisure. He could put one of the pullovers on now, it would keep him warm and be less to carry, but he'd be best leaving everything else until he gets home and his mam can see what needs doing to them.' She pulled a woollen pullover from the pile and handed it over. It was a thick one, in brown and beige, and would certainly keep the cold from penetrating through to his chest. 'Here yer are, sunshine, put this on and start to make yer way home or yer mam will be worried sick.'

Phil brought in the cardboard box Nellie had cadged off the greengrocer. 'I think this is too awkward to carry on and off trams, he'd be better with two bags. I'll go and get me old army kit bag, that should hold most of the stuff and it will be easy for him to sling over his shoulder.'

'Bang the door after yerself, sunshine, or we'll be blown off our feet.' Molly remembered she had a canvas bag under the stairs that might come in handy, and when Phil came back with his kit bag, all the clothing was packed neatly into the two bags. 'I need this bag back, yer know, son, so will yer bring it with yer tomorrow and I'll call in the shop for it?'

Ken nodded. 'I won't let yer down, Mrs Bennett.' But it was the kit bag that brought a shine to the boy's eyes. He picked it up and tossed it over his shoulder, nearly knocking Nellie off her chair in the process. Oh, boy, did he feel grown-up now! None of the lads in his street had ever had a kit bag and he was only sorry it was dark and no one would see him.

'I'll walk down to the tram with yer,' Phil said, causing Molly's eyebrows to shoot up in surprise. 'Yer seem to have taken a liking to the kit bag, so you can carry that and I'll carry the canvas one for yer.'

'There's no need, I'll be all right!' Ken would never forget this day as long as he lived. He'd never known such kindness outside his own home. 'I don't want yer coming out in the cold just for me, it wouldn't be fair.'

'Ay, lad,' Nellie said, 'there's a lot of things in the world that aren't fair. For instance, me and me mate are never going to see yer in the clothes, or know whether they were any good to yer.'

'Yes, yer will, missus, 'cos I'll come up one day to show off in them. One day in between Christmas and New Year. I'll be out of a job then, so I'll have plenty of time.'

That delighted Nellie. 'Ooh, we'd like that, wouldn't we, girl? You call here and there'll always be a cup of tea and a welcome for yer.'

Molly grinned at the way her friend could take liberties with her house and not think it was out of order. Of course it wasn't really out of order this time, because Molly too would love to see Ken dressed up looking warm and smart. 'Yer'll always be welcome, sunshine. But get home to yer mam now, or she'll be worried. I know I would be if I was in her shoes.'

When Ken walked out behind Phil, Molly followed with the excuse, 'I'll close the door after them.' She had in the pocket of her pinny two sixpences off Doreen and Victoria, and the half-crown Jill had given her. She hadn't wanted to embarrass the lad by giving him the money in front of everyone. In the hall she slipped the coins into his pocket and whispered, 'A little Christmas present off me two daughters and a friend.' Then, after watching him go walking down the street talking with great animation to Phil, she sighed happily and went back into the sitting room. 'That lad is over the moon with himself, and I'm dead chuffed the way everyone rallied around to help.'

'He's a nice young lad,' Jack said. 'He's been brought up properly, not forward or cheeky. Considering the dire straits they must be in, his mother has done a really good job of bringing him up.'

'Hear, hear,' said Nellie, hoping she wasn't going to be sent home without a cuppa and a bit of a natter. 'D'yer know that New Year resolution I told yer about, girl? Well, I've changed me mind again and I'm going to make it.'

'What resolution is that, Nellie?' Jack asked, knowing there was bound to be a laugh come out of a statement like that.

'Well, it's like this, lad. Your wife is very generous with people, always wanting to help the underdog. And I have to admit that there are times I enjoy having me arm twisted into being kind and generous with his. So I intended to make that one of me New Year resolutions: to be generous and pure in heart at all times.' Her eyes narrowed into slits. 'But yer wife isn't always generous. She can be downright miserly too when she wants to be. Take now for instance, lad, I've been here for half an hour and haven't even been asked if I've got a mouth on me! Now there's nothing bleeding generous about that, is there? And the reason for me telling yer all this is because I might very well change me mind and decide I've been selfish for forty-odd year and it's never done me no harm, so why change? And, if yer ask me in a week or two about me resolution, I'll tell everyone I come across that ye're a big liar because I never said no such thing.'

Molly looked at her husband and tilted her head. 'Would yer say it was easier to make a pot of tea than have to listen to that?'

'Oh, without doubt, love! But you sit down and I'll see to it.'

'Are yer staying on at the shop after Christmas?' Phil asked as he and Ken walked down to the main road. 'Or did I hear Mrs B say it was only temporary for the holiday rush?'

'Yeah, I finish tomorrow night. He's been good to me, has Billy, and what he pays me will help me mam out. But I want to get a job as an apprentice if I can, mister, to learn a trade. Me dad had a trade, he was a plumber and a real hard worker. I want to be like him.'

'Have yer thought about what trade yer'd like to be in?' Phil transferred the canvas bag to his other hand. 'And call me Phil, yer make me feel ancient calling me "mister".'

The whole day had been like a dream to Ken, at least from early on when he'd delivered the order to Mrs Bennett's. But he knew it wasn't a dream and couldn't wait to tell his mam all about it. He'd never had a man to talk to and treat him like an equal. 'I don't mind what I do, Phil, all I know is I want to have a trade in me hands when I'm twenty-one. I'll go to the Labour Exchange and see if they can help me.'

'I might be able to help yer. I work in an iron foundry, been there since I left school and I'm quite happy there. I started as an apprentice, had to take two years off because of the war, and worried while I was away that I might not have a job to come back to. But I walked straight into me old job, working with the bloke who trained me. I get on with my fellow workers and the bosses, they're a fine bunch of men, and I'm happy.'

His voice eager, Ken asked, 'Did yer mean it when yer said yer might be able to help me? Like could yer tell me how to go about looking for a job with a skill at the end of it? I don't know where to start, and I don't like asking me mam 'cos she'd only worry if she couldn't tell me what I need to know. And she's got enough to worry about, my mam, so I'm going to have to learn to stand on me own two feet.'

'Were yer good at school?' Phil asked. 'What are yer school reports like?'

'I can let yer see all me school reports going back years, 'cos me mam's kept them all. She's proud of them 'cos on every one I got stars for attendance and punctuality. And my place in class was always in the top four. I've got me mam to thank for that, 'cos when me dad died I stopped going out to play and sat in with her to keep her company. She used to give me sums to do to pass the time, and taught me how to spell properly. I know it sounds as though I'm bragging, mister . . . er, Phil, but I'm not telling no lies, and if I don't speak up for meself no one else will. I really need to find some sort of a job quickly to help me mam out with money, save her scraping from week to week. If I can't get taken on anywhere as an apprentice to a trade, then I'll have to take anything that's going.'

'Yer can read, write and add up, is that what ye're telling me?'

'Yeah, I can, honest!' There was pleading and desperation in the boy's tone of the voice. 'I'll do anything, work me fingers to the bone, if only someone will give me a chance.'

'I'll try and get that chance for yer,' Phil said, remembering himself at this boy's age. 'I'll speak to the boss tomorrow, put in a good word for yer and ask if yer can have an application form to apply for a job as an apprentice.'

Ken felt weak with relief. He didn't doubt for a second that Phil would do as he said because he wasn't the type to talk for talking's sake. 'I don't know what to say, me tummy's turning over. I can only say thank you for listening to me and showing an interest. And I'll be saying prayers in bed tonight, hoping yer boss is in a good mood.'

They were on the main road now and not far from the tram stop. Phil handed the bag over, saying, 'Yer can manage to get on the tram yerself, Ken. I want to get back home because me wife will wonder where I am.' He put his hand in his pocket and took out the ten-shilling note he had folded over, ready. 'Take this, and give it to yer mam to buy a few extras for Christmas. And in case she wonders what sort of people we are, whether yer've got mixed up with a bad bunch, then tell her she's welcome to come down and see for herself. But I'd like you to call to my house tomorrow night after yer finish work so I can tell yer what the position is about the apprenticeship. Our house is right opposite the Bennetts', number twenty-four.' Phil gave a half salute and turned to walk away. 'See yer tomorrow, and I hope I have good news for yer. Goodnight.'

The boy stared at Phil's retreating figure, flabbergasted. He couldn't believe all this was real, couldn't take it all in. But the money in his pocket was real, and what a godsend it would be to the mother he adored. He could hear a tram in the distance coming towards him, but couldn't wait to see what his pocket held so put down the canvas bag. And when the tram stopped, it was a smiling lad who hopped aboard. Fourteen shillings and sixpence he had in his pocket – a small fortune! His mam could stretch fourteen and six a long way. And as he skipped up the stairs to the top deck, he told himself it had been a marvellous day. But the best part was still to come, and that was the look of surprise he'd see on his mam's face when he handed her the money.

Molly had washed the breakfast dishes and put them away, and was wiping down the draining board when she heard the knock. With a sigh of exasperation she threw the cloth into the sink and wiped her hands down her pinny. She'd been feeling pleased with herself. The living room had had a thorough clean out, the kitchen was spotless and there was only the beds to make. They would have been made already if it hadn't been for Ruthie who was taking advantage of having no school to go to and snatching a lie-in. In any case, whoever was at the door wouldn't be wanting to inspect her bedrooms.

As she walked towards the door, Molly was telling herself that if it was Nellie, she'd send her packing and tell her to come back at the usual time of ten-thirty. They didn't have much shopping to do, only a trip to the butcher's to pick up their order and the baker's to buy enough bread to last over the holiday.

However, it wasn't Nellie standing on the pavement, it was a woman she'd never seen before. 'Are you Mrs Bennett?' she asked.

The woman would be in her late-thirties was Molly's guess, very slim with dark auburn hair and a face which looked as though it had been sculpted out of ivory: lovely high cheekbones, perfect nose and beautiful deep brown eyes. 'Yes, sunshine, that's me, but I don't think I know yer, do I? I've got a good memory for faces and I would certainly never have forgotten a face like yours.'

'Yer've never seen me before, Mrs Bennett. I'm Claire Thompson, Kenny's mother.'

Molly stepped back, and with a sweep of her hand, said, 'Come in, sunshine, this is a lovely surprise and ye're very welcome.'

She ushered the woman into the living room and plumped one of the cushions on the couch. Had the cushion been asked, it would have said it wasn't necessary to punch it again, it had been battered once that morning. But no one would ask a cushion its opinion. 'Give us yer coat, Claire, and sit here, near the fire. I haven't long lit it so it's not very bright at the moment, but I'll soon have it up the chimney.' Molly hung the coat up before kneeling down in front of the hearth and taking the poker from the companion set. She slipped it through the bars of the grate to let a draught in, and while she waited for the coals to catch properly, she turned her head. 'I would never have picked you out as Ken's mother in a month of Sundays. I would have expected yer to have ginger hair, like he has.'

'He takes after his dad in colouring and looks. My daughter Amy takes after me, she has my hair and features. Kenny's growing up to be the spitting image of his dad and has the same way about him, kind and compassionate.' Claire leaned forward. 'I hope yer don't mind me calling? Ye're probably busy with it being Christmas Eve, so I won't keep yer long. It's just that I was a bit concerned when Kenny came home with all those clothes last night, and quite a sum of money. I worried about where he'd got it all from, but I have never known my son tell a lie in his life, so in the end I believed his wonderful story. I want to thank you and yer friend and families for all the kindness yer showed to Kenny. It's a long time since I've seen him so happy. I couldn't even get him to sit down because he could hardly contain his excitement.'

The flames were beginning to lick around the coals now and Molly put the poker back on the companion set. She scrambled to her feet. 'If yer don't mind, sunshine, I'll go and bring me friend down. She was here with me when Ken delivered our order, and helped with everything. She only lives a few doors away, I won't be two minutes.'

Nellie looked taken aback when she saw her mate. 'What's wrong, girl? There's nobody sick, is there?'

'No, sunshine, everything in the garden is rosy. I've got a visitor, and I think yer'd like to meet her. She'd definitely like to meet you.'

Nellie looked down at herself. 'Ah, ay, girl, just look at me! I'm not in a fit state to let anyone see me. Who is it, anyway?'

'Ken's mother.'

Nellie frowned. 'Who the hell is Ken?'

'Tommo!'

'Well, why the hell didn't yer say that?'

'It is a bit confusing, sunshine, I agree. When he told us he got called Tommo, he'd only just met us and didn't think he was ever going to see us again. But he did say later he likes to be called Ken after his dad. And it gets more confusing now, Nellie, 'cos his mother calls him Kenny! But no matter, if the lad likes to be called after his dad, then we'll stick to Ken.' Molly rubbed her arms briskly. It was too cold to be standing nattering with no coat on. 'Yer've got a couple of minutes to get yerself down to mine, otherwise I'll have heard everything, you'll have heard nowt, and yer'll have a right cob on. So shake a leg, sunshine, and I'm going 'cos I'm flipping freezing standing here.' As she moved away, she thought of something that would make her friend put a spurt on. 'I'm putting the kettle on as soon as I go in.'

Molly heard the McDonoughs' door close, and grinned. She'd bet a pound to a pinch of snuff that her mate would be running round trying to make herself respectable. But she wouldn't waste too much time on it in case she missed something. Ten to one she'd be banging on the window before the kettle had time to boil. Oh, she'd better tell Claire how Nellie let them know she was coming, otherwise the woman would jump out of her skin with fright.

'Me mate won't be long, she's just making herself presentable. And neither of us is in a hurry because we've got the bulk of our shopping in, so sit back and relax, sunshine, while I light the gas under the kettle.'

And Molly hadn't been far out in her prediction, for Nellie was banging on the window just as the kettle whistled. Molly smiled at Claire as she passed her to go and open the front door. 'I don't know how she hasn't put the window in before now, but she's been banging on it like that for about fifteen years and I think it's come to a war of wills. Nellie's determined not to use the knocker and the window is determined she's not going to get the better of it.'

Claire managed to keep the surprise from showing on her face when Nellie waddled in. The turban she'd tied on her head to hide her untidy hair hadn't been tied tightly enough and had slipped to one side, making her look as though she'd had one over the eight. Her lisle stockings hadn't been pulled up properly and were wrinkled like a concertina around her ankles, not that

Nellie would know that, because she could only see her feet when she was sitting down. But her chubby face and cheeky grin won Claire over right away. Kenny had said the little fat woman was very funny, and it was easy to see her son was right even before she opened her mouth.

When Molly introduced them, Nellie stuck out a chubby hand. 'I'm glad to make yer acquaintance, girl. Yer'll have to forgive me appearance but I had me hand up the chimney when me mate knocked, trying to get some of the soot down so we won't be smoked out over the holiday.'

Molly gaped. 'You big fibber! If you'd had yer hand up the chimney yer would have been as black as the hobs of hell, but there wasn't a speck on yer when yer opened the door.'

'Ah, well, yer see, girl, I thought yer might be someone important, so I got the tin bath down off the nail in the yard wall, and had a quick bath before I opened the door.'

When she saw Claire's face break into a smile, Molly shrugged her shoulders. 'There's no answer to that, is there?'

Nellie's whole body shook. 'I could think of an answer, girl, but I don't see why I should pass me jokes over to you free of charge.'

'The tea's ready, so sit yerself down 'cos yer make the room look untidy.' Molly got as far as the kitchen door, then turned around to see if what she was thinking came to pass. And sure enough, Nellie marched round the table and picked up the carver chair, which she placed as near to Claire as possible. Any nearer and she'd have been sitting on her knee. 'I'll stay and listen to what she's got to say,' Molly said under her breath. 'Yer can't be up to her at all.'

'Ooh, I see yer've got yer own chair,' Claire said. 'And very posh it is, too!'

And of course Nellie had to be as posh as the chair. 'My friend bought hit for me has a present. Hit was ha very

341

hexpensive chair, has you can see, so nobody his allowed to sit hin hit, only me.' Then she reverted to her normal self. 'That means, girl, that nobody else has ever parked their backside on it.'

'That's what you think, sunshine,' Molly said, coming through with the tray. 'But the truth is I sit on it now and again on me way to the kitchen. It breaks the journey, yer see.'

'Oh, very funny!' Nellie saw the tray contained a plate with some biscuits on, and gave a soft sigh of pleasure. Things were looking up, she thought as she turned to Claire. 'Were the clothes all right for you and Ken, Kenny and Tommo?'

Molly chuckled. 'She's pulling yer leg, sunshine, take no notice of her. When we asked yer son what his name is, he gave us his nickname. Then when he lost his shyness he said he'd like to be called Ken. And that's what it'll be, Nellie McDonough, so leave well alone.'

'I'll start again then,' she said, 'and I'd be grateful if yer didn't interrupt this time, girl, 'cos it's bad manners. Even us what were brought up in the gutter knows that.' Throwing her mate a look of disdain, the little woman faced Claire. 'Were the clothes all right for you and Ken, did they fit yer?'

'Yes, they did, and I can't thank you enough. The dresses fit me perfectly, as though they'd been made for me, but I'm going to take one to pieces to make a dress for my daughter out of it. She was looking at me and Kenny with envy, and although she didn't say anything, I think she felt left out. I started unpicking it last night, and with a bit of luck, and staying up half the night, I might just have it ready for her to wear tomorrow.'

'Yer'll never make that, sunshine, not for tomorrow, even if yer do stay up all night.'

'I'm pretty quick with my hands, and if I didn't have to go to work today I'd have a pair of trousers turned up for Kenny, and the dress made for Amy.'

Nellie looked surprised. 'Ye're not going out to work today, are yer?'

Claire nodded. 'I have two cleaning jobs today, but only for two hours each. That's why I can't stay too long, much as I'd like to. I have eight two-hour cleaning jobs a week and have to go, hail, rain or snow, because we'd starve if I didn't. I should have gone to one this morning, but my daughter said she'd go and tell the woman I'd be late. Yer see, I had to come and thank you for everything. And on top of all that kindness, I believe your son-in-law, Phil, is going to try and help Ken in getting taken on as an apprentice?'

'I couldn't tell yer about that, it's the first I've heard of it. Yer see, I didn't see Phil after he left here last night to walk to the tram with yer son, and I haven't been over to me daughter's yet. But if Phil said he'd help, then he will, sunshine, because he is one hell of a nice bloke. In fact I have two of the best sons-in-law anyone could wish for, and I love them like they were my own sons. My eldest girl Jill is married to Nellie's son Steve, and like Phil, he's one of the nicest people ye're ever likely to meet.' Molly noticed Nellie squaring her back and holding her head high. 'Mind you, he had a good mother and father, didn't he, sunshine?'

'I'm far from perfect, girl, and I'll be the first to admit it. But me and George must have done something right 'cos we've got three good kids.'

'All I can say is, I've never known such kindness from people who don't even know us.' Claire was feeling emotional and it could be heard in her voice. 'You took my son at face value and I'll never forget that. When he went out to work yesterday morning I could have cried for him because he looked so pitiful in his old jacket and worn-out shoes. He must have been freezing, there was never a word of complaint. Amy's the same. I've done my best for them since my husband died, God knows I couldn't do any more.

But it's hard to bring up two children on the pittance I get for being a widow. By the time the rent is paid there's little left for food, clothing or coal. But we manage because we love each other. And things can only get better now Kenny's left school. We'll pull together until our fortunes take a turn for the better.'

'If Phil said he'd help, then he will.' Molly didn't want to say any more in case she raised the woman's hopes too much. 'Is he going to let Ken know?'

'Yes, he's asked Kenny to call tonight and says he might have some news for him then. I believe he lives right opposite?'

Molly nodded, and chose her words carefully. There was no need to go into detail, talk of the past and how Phil and Doreen came to be living with Victoria. That was their business and better left alone. 'Phil and my daughter Doreen have a new baby and are so happy it's a pleasure to see them, and they have an elderly aunt living with them who makes their family complete. Needless to say, if my children are happy, then my husband and I are happy. And talking of children, I've just remembered me youngest is still in bed. It's her first day of not being a schoolgirl, and already she's laying down the law.'

Molly pushed herself up from the chair. 'You have another cup of tea, Claire, while I go and wake Ruthie.'

'No, thank you, I'll have to be on my way.' Claire passed her cup to Nellie who was nearest the table. 'I badly need the money from the two jobs today so the children have a present to open tomorrow morning. Thanks to you and your families, it will be a better present than they've had for four years.' She shuffled to the edge of the couch and got to her feet. 'Words are not enough, Nellie, but they're all I have to give.' She kissed a chubby cheek. 'You never know, but one of these days I may be able to pay you back for your kindness.'

'I'll see you out,' Molly said. 'The visit was short and sweet, but I understand the need for yer to work. Me and Nellie know what it's like to be skint, don't we, sunshine? Robbing Peter to pay Paul, hiding from the rent man and getting food on tick, we've gone through all that and survived. And you will, Claire, 'cos yer've got two children to help yer through these lean times. And as yer said, things can only get better. Perhaps, please God, Phil will have good news for Ken when he calls tonight.'

'I'll say a prayer, girl, and keep me fingers crossed for yer. And if I could think of the word what means yer can feel something about the future, I'd tell yer what's in me mind.' Nellie looked at Molly. 'Come on, smart arse, what's the word I'm after?'

'I don't know, sunshine! Yer don't mean to have a premonition, do yer?'

Nellie slapped her thigh. 'That's it! Well, I've got one of those which says the future is going to be rosy for you and the kids, girl. And me mate will tell yer I'm pretty good at these prem . . . er . . . pronto . . . er, well, I'm more often right than I am wrong.'

Molly chuckled. 'Come on, Claire, I'll see yer to the door. If Nellie had her way yer'd be here all day. I hope Ken has good news for yer tonight, and like Nellie said, we'll say a prayer. Wouldn't it be a marvellous Christmas present? The stuff that dreams are made of. Anyway, I'm the one keeping yer back now, so get going. And thank you for coming, it was a real pleasure to meet yer.'

Chapter Twenty-One

Molly was smiling when she came back from seeing Claire out. 'That was a nice surprise, and what a lovely woman she is! Both in looks and nature.' She rubbed her hands in front of the fire. 'I feel as though we don't have to worry about Ken any more, him and his family are going to be all right.'

'We did well there, didn't we, girl? If it hadn't been for us, no one would have known how badly off they were. I really feel chuffed with meself, and at the moment the resolution is back on course again.'

Molly chuckled. 'Yer change yer mind more often than the weather, you do, sunshine, I can't keep up with yer. Anyway, what are yer talking about resolutions for? Yer don't need to 'cos ye're just as generous as the next person.'

'Only when you remind me to be, girl, or shame me into it.' Nellie pushed the turban back into place. 'I've got to admit it makes me feel good when I see how happy yer can make people what are not as lucky as we are.'

'Well, our good deeds are over for this year, sunshine, but no doubt something will come along next year.' Molly looked down at her friend's legs and shook her head. 'It's time we were getting out to the shops, but I hope ye're going to pull yer stockings up before we go otherwise I'll make yer walk behind me.'

'It's not my fault I can't bend down to pull them up proper, and anyway, I can't see me feet so it doesn't worry me.'

'I'm fed up telling yer, sunshine, that yer should bend down more than yer do. Yer could do with losing some of the fat around yer waist and tummy.' Molly secretly worried about her best mate, knowing that carrying so much weight must be a strain on her heart. 'Just try bending down two or three times a day, sunshine, and yer'd soon have a figure like Mae West.'

Nellie's eyes narrowed. 'If I did it four or five times a day, girl, would I get a figure like Jean Harlow?'

'I think that's being a bit optimistic, sunshine, I'd settle for Mae West if I were you, then yer won't be disappointed.' Molly heard a noise from above and then a floorboard creak. 'It sounds as if me daughter has decided to drag herself out of bed. She can get her own breakfast seeing as she was too lazy to get up when I called her.'

Ruthie came down rubbing her eyes and yawning. 'I heard that, Mam! Me first day of luxury and yer won't even make me breakfast.' The girl smiled when she saw the position of the carver chair. 'Good morning, Auntie Nellie, are yer watching for Santa Claus?'

'Yer Auntie Nellie is going home now to get ready for the shops. And you, young lady, can put a move on. Don't forget Uncle Corker is getting someone to drop three Christmas trees off here, and he said it would be in the morning. So look sharp and get yerself washed and dressed before seeing to yer breakfast. Yer've got all day to sit and do nowt,' Molly said, chuckling to herself, 'after yer've made the beds and washed yer breakfast dishes.'

'Make the beds! Ah, ay, Mam!'

'Don't argue with me, sunshine, 'cos they'd have been well done if yer'd come down when I called yer. Anyway, fifteen minutes is all it takes to make two beds and wash a couple of dishes. Then yer can sit and wait for the man to bring the trees.

I've got next door's key, so they can put theirs inside, in the hall. And the same with Auntie Nellie's.'

Ruthie was beginning to brighten up, remembering tomorrow was Christmas Day. 'Can I start to decorate ours, Mam? I'll be careful, honest!'

'Of course yer can, sunshine, it will save me a job. The wooden block to stand it in is on the floor of the pantry, so put that on the little table first, then stand the tree in it.' Molly noticed her friend was sitting comfortably, nodding her head as she listened. 'As for you, Mrs Woman, you can get yerself home, tidied up and back here in fifteen minutes without a wrinkle in yer stockings.'

Nellie lumbered to her feet, calling her friend fit to burn under her breath. 'I suppose you are going to sit counting the minutes till I get back, are yer, bossy boots?'

Molly bent down to put her face close. 'Why, would yer like me to come and pull yer stockings up for yer?'

'Don't be so bleeding sarky, Molly Bennett. And what makes yer think I'd want your hands fiddling around the top of me legs? I might be untidy, but that doesn't mean I'm not fussy about who goes up me clothes.'

We're getting on to dangerous ground here, Molly thought when she heard Ruthie titter. God knows what Nellie's going to come out with next. Best not to give her the chance. 'Come on, sunshine, away home and get yerself ready. We'll only be out an hour at the most, and because I've been a bit short with yer, I'll make it up by letting yer buy me a cream slice.'

'You cheeky bugger! Yer insult me all ends up and then expect to be rewarded for it!' The narrowing of her eyes warned that the little woman's thoughts were devious. 'Our Lily put some of the decorations up last night, but she couldn't do the tree because we didn't have it, did we? So if I was to buy an extra cream slice, would you decorate the tree for us, Ruthie? It's only a case of hanging a few coloured balls and some tinsel on it. I'd do it meself, girl, but I can't stretch up to the top. I tried last year and pulled the bleeding thing down on meself.'

'Nellie, will yer watch yer language, please? The children don't hear it from me and I don't want them to hear it from anyone else.' Molly gave a sharp nod to say she meant it. Then she said, 'If Ruthie wants to do it, it'll have to be when we come back from the shops. I don't want her in your house when you aren't there.'

Ruthie was eager. She loved decorating the tree, and seeing an ordinary everyday living room change to one that looked warm and Christmassy. 'Yeah, I'll do it, Auntie Nellie! Can Bella come and help me?'

'Ooh, yer strike a hard bargain for a young girl,' Nellie said. 'That means I've got to fork out for four cream slices. But go on, I'll let yer off as long as yer promise to make me room look like Blackler's grotto.'

'And you promise to pick out the four cream slices with the most cream in.' Ruthie took after her mother for having a sweet tooth, but where Molly had been forced for money reasons to rein in her craving, her daughter didn't give a thought to the money aspect. 'Mind yer don't squash them, hold the bag straight.'

'Will you two pack it in and let's be getting about our business? It's Christmas Eve and there's loads to do.' Molly gave her friend a not-so-gentle push towards the door. 'I've got everything sorted out in me mind, but you two gabbing is making it hard for me to stick to me plan.'

Putting on a show of weariness, Nellie let out a deep sigh. 'What plan is that, then, girl? All week yer've been saying how well we've organized ourselves this year, and we were going to have a very easy day instead of rushing round like those flies with blue bottoms. We can sit with our feet up, that's what yer said.'

349

'And so we can! We're a lot more organized than other years. All I've got to do when we get back from the shops is peel the spuds and get the veg ready. And I'll clean the turkey and stuff it ready to put in the oven at eight in the morning.'

This gave Nellie an excuse to linger. 'Oh, I knew there was something I wanted to ask yer, girl. When ye're making the stuffing, will yer make a bit extra for me? Yer know I'm bloody hopeless at it, and our Lily wants everything just right with Archie and his mam being there for dinner.'

'Will I do a bit extra for yer?' Molly shook her head in disbelief. 'Nellie, your turkey is twice the size of mine, so I wouldn't have to make a bit extra, I'd have to make three times as much.'

'It's not a lot to ask, girl, so don't be pulling a face. Anyone would think I'd asked yer to cook the ruddy turkey for me! All yer've got to do is use a bigger bowl to mix it in.'

'I'm going to close the door on yer now, Nellie, so I can calm meself down. Just go home and pull yer stockings up, comb yer hair, and by the time yer get back I might be in a better frame of mind.'

'Okay, girl, I'll do that.' As Nellie walked away her bosom was shaking, and Molly knew her mate had something up her sleeve. 'I'll remind yer when we got to the butcher's to buy an extra packet of Paxo stuffing, and I've got an onion I can let yer have.'

When Nellie banged on the window a quarter of an hour later, her scarf was neatly tied under her chin and there wasn't a wrinkle to be seen in her stockings.

'That's better, sunshine, yer look more presentable than I do now,' Molly said, eyeing her up and down. 'It just shows what yer can do when yer put yer mind to it, and how yer can bend down if it comes to the push.'

'Oh, I didn't fix me stockings meself, girl, I couldn't for the life of me bend down far enough to pull them up. I got meself in a right state and all, the sweat was pouring off me 'cos I knew how yer'd carry on if I didn't pass yer test and look presentable.'

Molly was slipping her arms into her coat. 'But yer managed in the end, sunshine, so it was worth the struggle.'

'Ah, but I didn't manage it on me own, girl, I couldn't! Then, when I'd given up all hope, I happened to glance out of the window and saw the coal cart going past our house and stopping at Beryl Mowbray's next door. So before Tucker had time to knock on Beryl's door, I called him in and he pulled me stockings up for me.' Nellie's eyes were bright with mischief. 'Only to me knees, though, girl. I told him above me knees was out of bounds.'

Molly looked at her daughter and they both burst out laughing. How could you fall out with someone who always saw the funny side of life? And how could you not be thankful that you had her for a friend? 'What am I going to do with yer, Nellie McDonough? The only thing I can think of is to stick something in yer mouth so yer can't speak.'

'I'll go along with that, girl, it's a good idea! And if yer stick a cream slice in me mouth, I promise I'll be as good as gold.'

'Oh, dear, oh, dear, oh, dear!' Molly pulled on a pair of navy woollen gloves and reached for her basket. 'Will I ever be able to have the last word?'

'I wouldn't think so, girl, 'cos ye're too ruddy slow to catch cold.' Nellie took a key from her pocket and passed it over to Ruthie who was busy wiping away tears of laughter with the back of her hand. 'Here yer are, girl, that's to let the man put me Christmas tree in the hall. If he's been by the time we get back, yer can come and decorate it for me. With Bella, of course.'

All of Molly's children loved their Auntie Nellie and wouldn't hear a word said against her. And they showed their affection with hugs and kisses. Now, Ruthie flung her arms around her and planted a really noisy kiss on each chubby cheek. 'Blackler's grotto won't have anything on your living room by the time me and Bella are finished with it, Auntie Nellie. I bet Uncle George will stand back in amazement when he gets home from work. He'll think he's in the wrong house by mistake.'

'I'll hold yer to that, girl! In fact, I'll even sell tickets if it turns out as good as yer say it will. A penny for a peep through the window, or tuppence to come in the house.'

Molly pointed to the door. 'Off yer go, Mrs Woman, I don't know who's the daftest, you or me daughter.'

Nellie walked towards the door, but she didn't go without having her say. 'For what it's worth, girl, I'd say this youngest daughter of yours will knock spots off both of us before much longer.' She held on to the side wall while she stepped down on to the pavement. 'She's got her head screwed on the right way, that's for sure.'

The friends were walking down the street when Nellie said, 'Ay, I've sorted the outfit out for me turn tomorrow night. Yer know that black dress I've had for years? Well, I've cut it very short like Betty Boop wears hers.'

Molly lifted her hand. 'Whoa, there, sunshine! I really do not want to know about your turn tomorrow night. The less I know the better, or I won't be able to sleep tonight. But I will ask yer not to go too far, not in front of the men and children.'

'But it's only a laugh, girl, no one is going to take offence.'

'They haven't taken offence at anything yer've done before, sunshine, but there's always a first time. And as I don't want that first time to happen in my house, please keep it clean and respectable, if yer don't mind.' Molly was clicking her tongue. 'How yer expect to look like her I'll never know. Kiss curls, Cupid's bow lips, and a squeaky baby's voice? Yer'll never do it, sunshine, so if I were you I'd think of someone else.'

Nellie kept her eyes on the ground so her mate couldn't see the sparkle in them. Best not to talk about it, just do it! She'd made up her mind now, and had sorted out the kiss curls, thick red lips and baby's voice. She thought she'd go down very well, but perhaps she should let the matter drop now so Molly could get a good night's sleep. 'Where are we going to first, girl? Butcher's or bread shop?'

'Butcher's I think, sunshine, so we can put our bread on top of the turkey instead of the other way round. We shouldn't be out too long, unless you decide to wish every person we meet the compliments of the season.'

'Well, it is the season of good will, girl, when everyone should be happy and friendly. And I can't help it if I know a lot of people and they stop to talk to me.'

'I don't mind the odd person and the odd few minutes, Nellie, but it's every person and it takes yer about ten minutes to wish them well. And some of them are people we've never set eyes on before! They're all pleasant with yer, but I bet underneath they're wishing yer'd let them get about their business. Today is the busiest day of the year and most women are up to their necks.'

Molly gasped with dismay when they reached the butcher's to find it heaving with people who were packed in like sardines. They couldn't even stand in the doorway and Molly groaned. 'Oh, Lord. This was the last thing I expected. It's what we get for spending time gabbing instead of making the effort to be here when the shop opened.'

'We couldn't have managed that, girl. It was Claire coming what upset the apple-cart.' Nellie thought that didn't sound very nice, so she quickly added, 'I'm not saying I'm sorry she came, like, because I'm not, but it has put the timetable out.'

'Not to mention you gabbing away to me daughter and wasting more time.' Molly looked down and grinned. 'And we mustn't forget the time yer wasted getting the coalman to pull yer stockings up.'

Two customers pushed their way out of the shop, carrying heavy bags and sighing with relief to be out in the fresh air. It was no joke pushing your way through a crowd who were more interested in getting to the counter than moving to let you get past. One of the women put her basket on the ground and wiped the sweat from her forehead with the back of her hand. 'It's every man for himself in there – holy murder. And they're an ignorant bleeding lot, wouldn't budge for yer to get past. It's a good job Christmas only comes once a year 'cos I couldn't cope with this too often, it's too much like hard work.'

Now this chatty woman was just up Nellie's street. 'Never mind, girl, yer'll have forgotten all about the worry and trouble yer've had when yer wake up in the morning to find Father Christmas has been and left yer a present.'

'Listen, queen,' the woman said, 'the only thing I'll find when I wake up in the morning is my feller laying next to me snoring his bleeding head off. And as for a present, the only time he bought me anything was when he bought me wedding ring thirty years ago. It cost him five pound, and I get it thrown up at me if I tell him he never buys me anything. He's a tight bugger, only thinks of himself. He'll be out tonight getting blotto with his mates, come home drunk, fall into bed in a drunken stupor and wake the neighbours with his snoring. And tomorrow he'll sit by the fire all day in his slippers and expect to be waited on hand and foot.' The woman picked up her basket and nodded to her companion. 'Come on, Milly, let's go and buy the arsenic we said we'd stuff our turkeys with to teach our husbands a lesson.'

Molly chuckled. This woman was another Nellie McDonough. 'So are you not going to be having any turkey tomorrow, ladies? I'm sure yer don't want to polish yerselves off as well as yer husbands?'

The woman chortled. 'We're not that daft, queen! We live next door to each other and have it all figured out. One turkey has the poison in the stuffing, the other is safe. So tomorrow, just before putting the dinner out, we're going to cut the birds in half and swap them over the backyard wall. We have the safe meat on our plates and the men can have the turkey what's got the poison in, and help themselves. Then we'll be able to live with our conscience because the silly buggers will have committed suicide.'

Nellie was all eyes and ears. 'But what happens if yer get the turkeys mixed up? They all look alike to me, and yer could easy get confused and give them the good bit while you end up poisoning yerselves.'

The smallest of the two women, the one who hadn't opened her mouth up until now, said, 'We have thought about that. Over a cup of tea one day last week, we talked the whole thing through. Looked at it from all angles, if yer know what I mean. And we both decided that even if we did make a mistake and ate the poisoned meat, we didn't care whether we went up or down, as long as we were still together. Even the ruddy devil himself can't be any worse than the husbands we've got.'

'Ooh, there's many a true word spoken in jest, girl!' Nellie didn't think she'd go that far even for a joke. 'It might just come true, and then where would yer be? Shovelling coal on Old Nick's fire for the rest of yer life.'

Their breathing back to normal and their temper even, the ladies put their baskets in the crook of their arms. 'Ye're right, queen,' one said, 'we shouldn't be joking about a thing like that, because honestly we've got the best two husbands in the world.'

Nellie was quick to correct them. 'Oh, no, yer haven't. Me and my mate here have got the best two husbands, haven't we, girl?'

Molly saw another two women coming out of the shop and the doorway was now clear. 'We all think we've got the best husbands, and children, sunshine, that's only natural. Unless ye're unlucky enough to marry a real baddie. I'm quite content with me husband, me kids, me ma and da, and me mates.' She nodded her head to tell Nellie to get inside the shop doorway before somebody came along and got there before them. 'Have a nice Christmas, ladies, and I hope yer turkey is really nice and tender.'

'Yeah.' Nellie was moving forward. 'A merry Christmas to yer.'

'And to you, queen, and many of them.'

Molly gave her friend a gentle push, and they found themselves inside the shop. She could see Tony and Ellen, and said to Nellie, 'They're rushed off their feet, I bet they haven't had a cup of tea since they opened up.'

Nellie couldn't see them, even though she stood on tip-toe. 'We could bring a pot down to them, girl, they must be gasping by now.' And being crafty, she said, 'I'll stand here and keep yer place while you run up and make them a pot.'

'You are many things, sunshine, but daft you are not. If I lose me place now, d'yer think they'd let me come back to it? Not on yer life they wouldn't, they'd lynch me! When we get nearer the counter I'll ask if Tony wants me to go through to the back room and make them a drink. I think that's best.'

It was twenty minutes before the friends found themselves in front of the counter, the crowd behind pressing forward, hoping to find a small space they could slip into. Nellie turned her head to the women behind and growled, 'If yer don't stop pushing we'll be over the counter in a minute. Give us some ruddy space, will yer?'

One woman, a stranger to Molly, sneered in a sarcastic voice, 'Give yer space, did yer say? Blimey, the size of you, yer fat cow, yer'd need the bleeding shop to yerself! So shut up and get served, 'cos when you're out of the shop we'll all have enough room to breathe.'

Nellie couldn't turn around, her tummy was squashed against the hard counter and her basket crushed against her ribs. 'Take me basket, girl, I can't move.'

Molly smelled trouble the second she heard the woman calling Nellie a fat cow. But there was little she could do to stop it, so she took the basket and put it on the counter. She noticed Tony and Ellen had stopped in their tracks, and there was now complete silence in the shop. The women who lived in their street and were friends of Nellie's knew they were in for a treat and shuffled back as far as they could to give their neighbour as much room as possible. They'd been clamouring to be served a few minutes ago. Now they reckoned they could spare some time to be entertained and were no longer jostling to be near the front of the queue. And if Nellie found she'd taken on more than she could chew, they'd get stuck in and help her.

The only person who had never seen Helen Theresa McDonough in her life before was the one who had just insulted her, and she wasn't from around the area. She had come to visit her sister who lived in a street five minutes' walk from the butcher's, and as she was passing, had thought she may as well get her turkey here as anywhere.

Nellie put her two hands on the counter and pushed her body back with all her might. She managed to gain enough room to turn around, and with her hands on her hips and a look in her eyes that said she meant business, she faced the women in front of her. 'Right, which one of yer is it what thinks I'm a fat cow?'

'Don't be looking at me, Nellie, I never said a word,' said Tina Smith, 'and it wasn't Mary either, was it, queen?'

Mary was so sure it wasn't her she nearly shook her head off her shoulders. 'No, Tina, I never opened me mouth.'

Tony pushed his straw had to the back of his head and weighed up the situation. Actually, he was glad of a lull in the storm. A rest from hands reaching across the counter clamouring to be served, saying they were there first and it was only fair they should be served before the woman next to them. He and Ellen could do with a break, they'd been hard at it since eight o'clock without a drink to whet their whistle. 'Ellen, stick the kettle on, there's a love. If yer only half-fill of it won't take long to boil and we might manage a drink before battle commences.'

Ellen's eyes went to Nellie and she asked, 'Are yer not going to put a stop to it, Tony?'

'Not yet, I'm not! It's a very welcome diversion. If I think they're going to kill each other, then I'll step in. But as none of the customers seem to be in a hurry now, let's make the most of it. The wife gave me a couple of packets of biscuits. Open them up and bring some through with me cup of tea.'

Meanwhile, Nellie was eyeing up the women in front of her. 'I know it wasn't you or Mary, Tina, but who was it?' She began to push up the sleeves of her coat. 'Or is the woman too much of a coward when it comes to the push?'

The culprit was a hard-looking woman, a bully with a loud mouth. 'It was me what said yer were a fat cow,' she sneered, 'and I'm no coward, so what are yer going to do about it?'

'I'm going to knock spots off yer, that's what I'm going to do.' Nellie leaned forward and stared into the woman's face. 'Who the bleeding hell are you to call me a fat cow?! Don't yer ever look in the mirror, missus, 'cos ye're as ugly as sin! There's a bulldog lives in our street and he's better-looking than you.'

Now the woman could hear tittering behind her, and even a couple of people laughing out loud, getting her dander up. But she remembered she was in strange territory here and most of the locals would be against her, so she decided she wouldn't be the one to strike the first blow.

Tony leaned across the counter and whispered to Molly, 'Ellen's in the back making a pot of tea. If yer can slip round the counter, why don't yer join her? There's some nice biscuits out there, too! I'll keep me eyes on things here.'

Nellie pricked up her ears. Tea and biscuits, eh? I'd better get this over with or I'll miss out on them, she decided. So, without further ado, and moving like greased lightning, she put her two hands on the other woman's chest and heaved with all the force of her considerable weight. Taken by surprise, the unfortunate victim tottered backward, hoping one of the people behind would break her fall. But, sadly for her, they all moved quickly out of the way and she found herself lying flat on the floor with her opponent looking down at her.

Wiping her hands together as though to rid herself of something unpleasant, Nellie said, 'Ye're not from round here, are yer? Well, keep it that way, girl, if yer know what's good for yer, 'cos if I ever set eyes on yer again yer'll end up with two black eyes and never know what hit yer.' She saw her mate squeeze through the narrow space between the counter and the window. 'Hang on, girl, ye're not going anywhere without me.'

'Yer'll not get through there, sunshine.' Molly spoke very quietly, not wanting to add insult to injury. Her friend would never let anyone see she was upset, but deep down she would be. 'The women will let yer through so go over to the other opening, it'll be easier for yer.'

But that was a challenge Nellie couldn't resist. 'I'll get through, girl, even if Tony has to lift me over the counter.'

He rose to the occasion. Molly and Nellie were his favourite customers. It was always a pleasure to have them in the shop because they never moaned or groaned. You were always sure of a laugh with them and they'd go to the ends of the earth to do anyone a favour. 'Nellie, it'll be a pleasure. I've been dying to get me hands on your body for the last twenty years.'

The little woman was so pleased with the compliment she went all coy. But there was no way she was going to ask for his help, she'd get through that narrow space if it killed her. And by manoeuvring her tummy up and down, she managed it. Anyone would think she'd gone five rounds in the ring with Joe Louis and won on points, she looked so proud.

The cause of all the upset wasn't having such a pleasant time, because when Nellie was insulted several of the customers took it personally. They'd put weight on with each child that came along, and never lost it. They didn't look as fat as Nellie because they were taller and their weight didn't look so out of place. At four foot ten inches, the little woman was as round as she was tall, and there was a lot of sympathy for her. So while she was enjoying a cup of tea with Molly and Ellen, and eating a biscuit from each of the packets, the trouble-maker was getting a lot of stick from right, left and centre. 'I don't have to put up with this, yer stupid cows, I can get me meat from anywhere. Any shop will be glad of me custom.'

'There's a butcher's shop a bit further down,' Tony told her. 'It's on this side, about four blocks down. They'll serve yer.'

At the back of the shop stood Nellie's next-door neighbour, Beryl Mowbray. She hadn't been there for the start of the incident, but had heard enough to want to defend the woman who, two years ago, saw them moving their furniture into the house next door and came out and asked if they'd like her to make them a pot of tea. Beryl wasn't one to forget a kindness. So as the woman pushed her way through the crowd, eager to get as far away as possible, Beryl said, 'Yer won't come back again, missus, if yer've got any sense. Yer picked on the wrong one this time.'

Chapter Twenty-Two

When Molly and Nellie arrived home, the tree had been delivered and decorated. Ruthie and her friend Bella were sitting in the fireside chairs facing each other across the hearth.

'Mam, where have yer been?' Ruthie jumped to her feet. 'Yer said yer'd be home in an hour, but yer've been ages.'

'We got held up, sunshine, the shops are absolutely heaving.' Molly focused her attention on the tree, which really looked lovely. 'Yer've done a good job with the tree, girls, it really sets the room off. We've never had one look so nice.'

The two girls came to stand beside her and eyed their handiwork. 'I did this side, Mam, and Bella did the other. Oh, and Bella put the fairy on top 'cos she can balance better than I can. I did try, but I nearly knocked the whole lot over.'

Ruthie turned to her auntie. 'Well, what d'yer think, Auntie Nellie? Do yer still want us to do yours for yer?'

'Yes, I do, girls, and I've got yer cakes here. I've struggled all the way home with them, carrying the bag as straight as I could so they wouldn't get squashed.' Nellie put the paper bag down on the table. 'The tree looks a treat, better than yer'll see in the shops in town. If yer do mine as nice as that the family will be over the moon.'

Knowing her auntie's tricks, Ruthie put an arm across her shoulders and asked, 'Will yer tell them you decorated it, Auntie Nellie?'

'Everyone knows their own tricks best, girl! If it turns out as good as yours, then yeah, I will probably take the credit. If it looks a mess I'll tell them you did it, and I'll be asking yer for me cake back.'

Bella had been friends with Ruthie since they were able to toddle, and often came into contact with Mrs McDonough. But she was always quiet in her presence because she felt overpowered by her. However, she'd left school now and had to come out of her shell and grow up. At least that's what Ruthie told her. So she took the plunge. 'If we've eaten the cakes, Mrs McDonough, we won't be able to give them back to yer.'

Nellie was as surprised as Molly, because Bella never usually opened her mouth to anyone. 'In that case, yer'd better do a good job on me tree, hadn't yer? Otherwise yer'll be in debt to me for the rest of yer life.'

Ruthie tutted and shook her head. 'Only until we get our first week's wages, Auntie Nellie, so don't be putting the frighteners on Bella. And it won't come to that in any case, 'cos we're going to dress your tree as good as this one. As long as yer've got the tinsel and balls to go on it. I refuse to be stuck on the top 'cos yer haven't got a fairy.'

'We've got all the trimmings, girl, including the fairy. Our Lily got them out yesterday and intended to dress the tree tonight so the place will look nice for Archie and his mam coming tomorrow. But she'll be made up if she comes home tonight and sees a tree as nice as yours.'

'Did yer close the Corkhills' front door after yer let the man in with the tree?' Molly asked. 'And did he leave it in the hall?'

Ruthie nodded. 'I told him to take the biggest in there 'cos it's good of Uncle Corker to buy all the trees. So I wasn't greedy, I didn't pinch the best.'

'Well, put the kettle on for a quick cuppa to have with yer cake, then yer can go home with Auntie Nellie and she can supervise the operation.' Molly raised her eyebrows at Bella. 'Does yer mam know ye're over here, sunshine?'

'Yes, Auntie Molly, and I told her I was going with Ruthie to help her decorate Mrs McDonough's tree.' When Bella smiled, her whole face lit up. Although she could be painfully shy at times and no one really noticed her looks, she was actually a very pretty girl with the same dark curly hair as her mother. 'She said it was a good idea and we'd better make a good job of it.'

Out of the mouths of babes, Molly thought, before chuckling and saying, 'See, Nellie, yer reputation is widely known. But Bella should know by now that yer bark is worse than yer bite.' Then there flashed through her mind a picture of the woman lying flat out on the butcher's floor, and she added, 'Most of the time, anyway.'

Jill looked very happy when she called on her way home from work that night. 'Well, that's me last day over, Mam! I couldn't have carried on much longer, but I'm going to miss the girls. I made some good friends and we used to have a laugh.'

'Oh, yer'll get plenty of laughs off yer Auntie Nellie, sunshine, yer'll not go short of jokes.'

Molly wasn't going to tell anyone about the episode in the butcher's, not even Jack. All the family would think it was hilarious and have a good laugh. They'd think nothing of talking about it to George, and he'd laugh with the rest of them. But Molly had a sneaking feeling that while he would laugh at most of the antics his wife got up to, he might draw the line at her fighting with another woman and flooring her. So best keep it to herself. 'I'll be coming up to yours tonight with yer presents, after I've been to Doreen's. Yer can open them in the morning in peace, which yer wouldn't get if I left them until yer came tomorrow night. Yer know what it'll be like, crowded an' noisy. I won't be staying long tonight, just half an hour to have a little natter to Lizzie 'cos I won't see her tomorrow. She won't come to the party 'cos she says it's too noisy and she's gone past that, so she's keeping Victoria company and they're minding Bobby. If it weren't for them, Doreen and Phil wouldn't be able to come. Anyway, sunshine, from yours I'll nip round to me ma's to give the Jacksons and the Bennetts their presents. Such as they are, like, they're not expensive 'cos me money doesn't run to that. Not with the family growing at the rate it is. We've gone from six to nine, all in a short space of time. In fact it's ten if yer count the baby.'

'Soon to be eleven, Mam.' Jill patted her tummy. 'And yer wouldn't have it any other way, would yer?

'No, sunshine, I wouldn't. I can't imagine life without me family, and the bigger it grows, the better I'll like it. Mind you, the Easter eggs will be reduced in size accordingly.'

'Ay, Mam, yer've made a good job of the tree, it looks marvellous.'

'I can't take the credit, sunshine, because it was Ruthie and Bella who decorated it. They're in Auntie Nellie's now, decorating hers. I've got to say Ruthie has been very good, doing what she's told without any argument. So for a treat I'm going to let her get the presents off the top of the wardrobe and put them under the tree. And she can come with me on me travels tonight, which will please her. She'll feel like Lady Bountiful giving all the presents out. But she deserves a treat for being so good.'

'Are Doreen and the baby all right?'

'They're fine. Doreen's taken to motherhood like a duck takes to water. Oh, and Phil is picking his mam up on Boxing Day and bringing her for a couple of hours. That will really make Christmas special for him.'

'What about his step-dad, doesn't he mind his wife coming to Phil's on Boxing Day?'

'According to what Frances told him, Tom Bradley has changed a lot and he looks after her now she's ill. And I don't think it would make any difference if he did object to her seeing Phil, it wouldn't stop her. Yer can see how happy she is to be friends again with her son, she won't let anyone take that away from her. But Phil refuses to go in their house. The taxi will wait outside until she comes out. He's determined never to acknowledge the man who made his life hell, and under no circumstances will he allow Tom Bradley to have anything to do with his family or Victoria.'

Jill sighed. 'I think it's sad that she left it until she was ill to get in touch. It should have happened years ago.'

'As far as Phil is concerned, it's better late than never. If me and Nellie hadn't happened upon her, she might have died without making her peace with him, and he would have lived the rest of his life thinking she didn't care.'

'I still think it's sad.' Jill sighed again. 'Ah, well, I'd better get off home and see to something to eat for Steve.'

'I'd better put a move on, too, 'cos yer dad and Tommy will be here any minute. Not that Tommy stays long, he's usually in and out, like you.'

'Now I haven't been in and out tonight, Mam, I've been here longer than usual. And from now on yer'll be fed up seeing me. I'll be down here every day and yer'll be sick of the sight of me and me tummy.'

Molly opened her arms and held her first-born close. 'Not on your life, sunshine, I would never get sick of the sight of yer. I've missed you, Doreen and Tommy so much, it'll be like having one of me children home again, seeing yer every day.'

'When yer come to ours tonight, I'll give yer the presents for me grandma and granda, and Rosie and Tommy. And to save me a journey, I'll give yer Doreen's as well.'

'It sounds as though I'm going to need Ruthie to give me a hand. Unless we meet Father Christmas on our way and he gives us a lift. Now that would be something to put Nellie's antics in the shade. Me getting a lift off Father Christmas. The trouble is, she would be bound to come up with something to beat it. I've never in all the years I've known her got the better of her. It's a wonder I haven't got an inferiority complex.'

'Never! It's you that keeps Auntie Nellie in check, Mam, she'd be lost without yer. She wouldn't be half as funny if you weren't there for her to bounce off! Yer need each other, and yer both know it. And I need me husband and don't want to lose him, so I'm off. I'll see yer tonight, with Ruthie.'

It was ten o'clock when Molly got home that night, tired and weary. But Ruthie was glowing with happiness and excitement for in her mind she had today left her childhood behind her and joined the ranks of grown-ups. Her cheeks, whipped up by the cold wind, were rosy red, and her arms were full of wrapped parcels. 'Look, Dad, we've brought back more than we took out.' She let them drop on to the table before picking them up one by one to place under the tree. 'This is going to be the best Christmas ever.'

Jack waited until Molly had hung her coat up before saying, 'I expected yer home before now, love, it's after ten!'

She sighed. 'Listen, sunshine, it's been a long day and I'm absolutely bushed. Since I left here at seven o'clock, I've been over the road to Doreen's, on to Jill's, then called in the corner shop to tell Maisie and Alec to be here about half-seven tomorrow night. After that it was round to me ma's, and I can't just run in and out of the houses, I had to spend some time talking to them. Me last call was next door to thank Corker for the tree. And now, if ye're interested, I'm dead on me feet.' She kicked off her shoes and let out a long sigh of relief.

When his wife sat down, Jack left his chair to kneel in front of her. Lifting one of her feet, he began gently to massage it. 'How does that feel, love?'

'Like I'm floating on a cloud, sunshine, I could take a lot of being pampered. And me foot is telling me to thank yer as well.'

Jack turned to where his daughter was reading the labels on the parcels before arranging them under the tree. 'Make a drink for us, Ruthie, there's a good girl. And when yer mam feels up to climbing the stairs we'll hit the hay.'

Ruthie wasn't a bit tired, her mind was too active. 'There's eight presents with my name on, Dad, I've never had that many before.'

'Then ye're a very lucky girl. I've never had eight presents in one go in all me life. But leave them for now and make a pot of tea while I soothe yer mam's poor, tired old feet.'

'Ay, Jack Bennett, less of the old! Don't forget ye're two years older than me, sunshine, so don't be trying to make out ye're only a slip of a lad.'

He grinned up at her. 'Yeah, I regret those two years. Just think, if yer'd been born two years earlier, we would have had an extra two years together. That works out at about ten thousand lost kisses.'

Molly lifted her other foot and used it to push his shoulder and send him sprawling on the floor. 'Go on, yer sloppy thing! If ye're thinking of asking me for those ten thousand kisses then yer can forget it. Yer've only yerself to blame for coming into the world too early.'

Ruthie was leaning back against the sink waiting for the kettle to whistle, and she had a smile on her face. If anyone had asked her what love was, which they hadn't, like, but if they had, she'd have told them it was what her mam and dad had. And Jill and Steve, Doreen and Phil, and Tommy and Rosie. Oh, and she mustn't forget her grandma and granda because they showed how much they loved each other in the way they looked at each other and held hands. All her family had been lucky in love, and she was going to be the same. She knew three likely lads now, but she had a long way to go yet. By the time she was seventeen, those three lads would be eighteen and might all be courting, while she'd have found the one she knew was for her. At the moment it was Gordon Corkhill one day, Jeff Mowbray the next, and then John Stewart the day after. Gordon came first on the list right now because of his dad. Ruthie loved her Uncle Corker to bits because he was so kind and liked to laugh a lot. She always thought he looked like a film star, with his bushy beard and large moustache, and she'd once heard her mam saying that he was built like a battleship. Though she'd never seen a battleship, she knew they must be big because her Uncle Corker was like a giant.

'Ruthie, what are yer doing while the kettle is whistling away like mad? I suppose ye're standing there daydreaming?'

She chuckled before saying, 'I was just thinking about the boy I'm going to marry. I think I'll hang around until someone rich and handsome comes along.'

It was Jack's turn to chuckle. 'Oh, yer'll have to be lucky, sweetheart, because men like me don't come along very often.'

The girl was pouring the boiling water into the teapot when she heard her dad say, 'Ay, that hurt, that did.'

'It was supposed to hurt, sunshine, for being so big-headed. I've a good mind to take yer present away from the tree 'cos yer don't deserve it.'

'Me present? Yer mean I've only got one present? Me daughter gets eight and I get one, that's not fair. That's enough to bring the workers out on strike, that is.'

'Don't come out on strike now, sunshine, I'm far too tired to fight. Be a good boy and leave it until tomorrow.'

Jack was standing in front of the mirror getting more agitated by the minute as he struggled to get the stud through the hole at the back of his shirt. In the end he gave up. 'Molly, give us a hand with this stud, will yer? Everyone will be here before I'm properly dressed. They're a bloody nuisance these studs.'

'Yer make it worse by getting yerself all het up.' Molly pushed the stud through with ease. 'See, if yer stay calm it's a doddle.'

Jack met her eyes in the mirror. 'Yer look very fetching tonight, love, I could fall for yer all over again.'

Molly waved a hand in the air and bent her leg in a curtsy. 'Thank you, kind sir.'

'Eh, what about me, Dad?' Ruthie did a little twirl. 'Do I look fetching?'

When Jack turned, his heart missed a beat, for his daughter was a miniature replica of his wife. He was always amazed that his three daughters could be so like their mother. And he wondered if they ever realized where they got their good looks from. 'Yer look lovely, sweetheart, just like yer mam.'

Ruthie didn't know that both new dresses had come from Paddy's Market. Molly had washed and starched them, and they could have passed for new. After another little twirl, she asked, 'Will all the lads fall at me feet, d'yer think?'

'If they do,' Molly said, straight-faced, 'make sure they're not near the grate in case they fall on the hearth and split their head open. I don't think Auntie Ellen would be very happy to go home and find the fireside rug covered in blood.'

'Oh, I wouldn't leave it for Auntie Ellen, Mam, I'd mop it up.'

There was a knock on the door and it was Phil. 'I believe I've to help yer carry the table to Mrs Mac's, Mr B. I can't say I'm looking forward to it, not after she took off on us last year.'

'Take no notice of her, sunshine, it's her idea of a joke. I'll slip me coat on and come with yer, I know the very thing to keep her quiet.'

Nellie opened the door. She had her speech all rehearsed in her mind. 'Oh, not again! I told yer last time not to bring it any

369

more, so turn around and take it back from where it came from. Go on, hop it, the pair of yer.'

Molly appeared out of the shadows. 'All right, lads, do as she said and carry it back. It's very sad, 'cos it means there'll be no room for entertaining or dancing, but we'll just have to put up with it. Come on, let's go back.'

Nellie stood on the edge of the top step. 'Hang on a minute, don't be so bleeding quick off the mark, Molly Bennett. Can't we do a bit of negotiating, like we do at the market?'

'Sorry, sunshine, but there's no time for messing about, the guests will be arriving any minute now. Besides, it's too cold.' Molly jerked her head. 'Come on, lads, get the table back.'

Nellie nearly fell off the step in her haste to get to the table and lean her considerable weight on it. 'Take yer hands off before I lose me temper and set me husband on yer. For the last ten years that table has spent Christmas night in my house and I'm not having it upset by two upstarts. So pick it up and get it inside before it catches cold.'

Phil saw Molly make a move to leave, and said, 'Don't go yet, Mrs B, not until the table is safely inside. Yer see, I find Mrs Mac very unpredictable.'

'Move aside, Nellie,' Jack said, 'It's flaming cold standing here, we'll catch our death.'

Nellie went to stand by her friend, and while the men were busy, asked, 'Ay, what did Phil say I am? If it's what I think, I'll marmalize him and he won't be in any fit state to go to the party.'

'What d'yer think he said, sunshine?'

'I can't say the word, girl, and if I knew what it meant I wouldn't be asking you. But you're the brainy one, you'll know.'

Molly gave it some thought. Should she tell a lie for an easy life, or tell the truth and stand here freezing for another half hour? 'He said yer were unpredictable, Nellie, and that means . . . er . . . that means . . . er . . . that ye're volatile.'

'Ooh, that sounds good, girl! Wasn't that a nice thing for him to say? I like Phil, always have done, he's a good bloke.' With that Nellie stepped on to the bottom step and called over her shoulder, 'I'll be with yer in ten minutes, girl, I've only got to pack me costume, then I'll be ready to do me duty as yer assistant hostess.'

Molly was scratching her head, hoping Nellie didn't brag to George that she was volatile, when Jack and Phil came out laughing their heads off. 'Your mate is a nutcase, Mrs B, yer can't be up to her.' With that Phil ran across the cobbles. 'Me and Doreen will be with yer as soon as we get the baby asleep.'

Molly looked around her living room and marvelled that so many people could be crammed into such a small space. Mind you, each of the wooden chairs set in front of the sideboard was occupied by two people, otherwise half of the guests would be sitting on the stairs. Jill was perched on Steve's knee, with his arm in front of her to protect her tummy in case anyone bumped into her. It would only be by accident, of course, but he wasn't taking any chances. Next to them sat Phil and Doreen, then Tommy and Rosie and Archie and Lily. The other courting couple, Paul and Phoebe, were leaning against the wall, arms around each other's waist and a smile on their faces that told of their happiness at being together. Ruthie, of course, was next door with the younger ones who, as they had last year, were having their own party.

There had been plenty of drinks served over the last hour as Corker was very generous with the measures, and Molly thought it was time to liven the party up because the young ones weren't used to drink and she didn't want them to be sick. Corker, being an ex-seaman, could drink until the cows came home and it wouldn't have any effect on him. He thought everyone was the same.

'Who's going to be the first to start the singing off?' Molly asked. 'Come on, let's have some entertainment.'

Rosie pulled Tommy to his feet. 'We'll start off, Auntie Molly, and even though me mammy used to say that self-praise is no recommendation, I've got to say that me and me beloved, well, we make a good team right enough.' Her beautiful face beamed up at Tommy, who amazed his family by putting an arm across his wife's shoulder and saying, 'She's had me practising every night. In fact, last night the neighbours both sides shouted for an encore.'

'What's it to be, Rosie, me darlin?' Corker asked. 'Is it one we can join in the chorus?'

'Oh, yer'll know it, Uncle Corker. Sure, everyone will know it.'

Rosie started off in her clear, sweet voice:

'In Dublin's fair city, where girls are so pretty,
I first set my eyes on sweet Molly Malone.
She rolled a wheelbarrow, through streets broad and
    narrow,
Crying, "Cockles and mussels, alive, alive-oh!" '

When every voice in the room was raised, Molly thought she felt the walls shake. But she joined in with gusto, and that was the start of another of Molly Bennett's successful parties. Bridie and Bob stood in the middle of the room, holding hands and singing another song from the Emerald Isle which, because of their age and their devotion to each other, brought tears to the eyes of all the women in the room. They were followed by Corker, who sang a sea shanty with all the actions of rope-pulling that went with the sailor's hornpipe. And to everyone's surprise, including

er husband's, Maisie pulled him to his feet and they did a nifty
ailor's dance. What they lacked in correctness, they made up
or in vigour.

No amount of coaxing would lure the Bennett sisters or their
usbands to the middle of the floor, their excuse being they
idn't know the words to any of the songs, and anyway, they
were tone deaf.

Corker did his best with Phoebe and Paul. 'You two spend half
er life at dances, so yer can't say yer don't know any songs.'

Paul grinned. 'D'yer want to empty the room, Uncle Corker?
can dance to the music, but I can't sing to it.'

Doreen whispered in Phil's ear, 'Uncle Corker is right, we
hould make an effort like the older ones. And we can't say we
on't know any songs because we know loads of them from
hen we went dancing. So, how about it?'

He would never refuse her anything, even if it meant making
fool of himself. 'On your head be it, love.'

When Nellie saw them walking to the middle of the floor, she
aid, 'Well, I'll be blowed! How about that then!'

Their arms around each other's waist, the young couple sang
song they'd danced to on the first night they met. And as the
une took them back to that night, they even forgot to be nervous.
he romantic 'I'll See You In My Dreams' had Archie pulling
ily on to the floor, Jack reaching his arms out to hold Molly,
ellie cuddling up to George, and Maisie and Alec looking into
ach other's eyes. Corker went one better. He pulled Ellen up
nd danced her slowly around the singing couple. And she
njoyed it so much she even succumbed to his kisses.

'Ay, look at me mam.' Phoebe was amazed. 'I've never seen
er do that before. And look at your Lily and Archie! They're not
alf enjoying themselves.'

'Ay, well, they're not having all the fun,' Paul told her, his
eep brown eyes sparkling and his dimples deep. 'We can't sing,

but we can dance and smooch at the same time, so come on what are yer waiting for?'

At ten o'clock Molly called a halt so they could have something to eat, and there was tea for those who wanted i Molly's girls followed her into the kitchen to give her a hand and Steve, Phil, Tommy and Archie went into the hall to free th chairs so their elders could sit down and enjoy the break. 'Hov long has Jill got to go now, Steve?' Phil asked. 'Is it three months?'

He nodded. 'About that. But the doctor said yer can never te with a first baby, they come when they're ready.'

Corker excused himself and went into the hall to talk to th lads. It was Phil he really wanted to have a word with, but h joined in the general conversation for about five minutes before casually saying, 'I'm glad to know your ma's been in touch, so but sorry to hear she's not well. Under the circumstances, though yer must both be happy to be reunited.'

'Me mam is very ill, Uncle Corker.' Phil tried to keep h voice steady as he looked up at the man who was his hero. Th man who, when he was needed most, had been like a father the young lad who'd had nowhere to go and no one to turn to 'The doctor's don't know how long she's got, but I intend to se as much of her as I can to make up for lost time, and to be ther when she needs help.'

'I hear ye're bringing her down tomorrow for a few hours, that right?'

Phil nodded. 'I'm picking her up at two o'clock in a taxi, ar taking her home when she feels ready to go. I don't want to ti her out, but she's eager to see us all, especially me and the bat who she says looks just like I did at his age.'

'Would yer mind if I slipped over for half an hour?' Cork asked. 'I wouldn't stay long, but I would like to make h acquaintance.'

Phil was grateful for those words. There were people here tonight, including this gentle giant, who had good reason not to like his mother, but not one had said a wrong word about her. He knew the man looking down at him now would welcome her with genuine warmth, and that would please her. 'I'd like yer to come over, Uncle Corker, and I know me mam would like to meet yer.'

Molly poked her head into the hall. 'If there's no food left by the time yer decide to come in, then yer've no one to blame but yerselves. And Nellie is straining at the leash to put her show on, which, I have to say, is something I have had nothing to do with and take no responsibility for whatsoever.'

When Corker laughed, the rafters rang. 'Like that, is it, Molly, me darlin'? Well, I don't think Nellie would let us down, so we must be in for a treat.'

'Your words not mine, Corker, remember that.'

'Can I go up to yer bedroom to put me outfit on, girl? And would yer come up with me to give me a hand?'

'Not this time, sunshine, ye're on yer own. I just hope ye're not going to give everyone a shock, that's all.'

Nellie shook her head and her chins moved as if in agreement with what she was about to say. 'It's a party, girl, so buck yerself up and enjoy it. Just say to hell with everything and let yerself go. I think this is going to be me best performance ever.' Then the little woman asked, 'Have yer got a clean duster I can have? Not a good one, though, 'cos yer won't be getting it back.'

'What on earth d'yer want a duster for?'

Nellie tapped the side of her nose. 'All will be revealed in a short time. So are yer going to give me a duster or not?'

Molly took her elbow and steered her through to the kitchen. From a box on the floor of the pantry she took out a cloth. 'Here, this is clean, sunshine.'

'When I'm ready, girl, I'll shout down and yer can introduce me. And make it good, 'cos me act deserves a big build up.'

Molly was beginning to feel guilty. Every year Nellie was the life and soul of the party and everyone loved her. In fact without her it just wouldn't be the same. So Molly cupped her friend's chubby cheeks and said, 'Ye're a worry to me, Nellie McDonough, but I love the bones of yer and I'll give yer a fantastic introduction. And when yer put in an appearance I just hope me ma doesn't have a heart attack, George doesn't throttle yer, and I don't have to go to jail for keeping a house of ill repute.'

Nellie looked at her with pride. 'Ye're not half good with words, girl, even if yer can be a miserable sod at times. Now let me get on, a true professional never keeps their audience waiting.'

Molly stood at the bottom of the stairs waiting for Nellie to call, and listening to the different conversations going on in the room. When the voice finally came from above, Molly was too afraid of what she would see if she looked up, so instead she clapped her hands for silence. 'And now, for tonight's star turn, I present to you the one and only – Betty Boop!'

There was loud applause, whistling and cheering, until Nellie stepped off the bottom stair and could be seen in all her glory. Molly kept her eyes tightly closed. There was silence in the room. But only for a few seconds. Steve, Paul and Archie started to laugh, and soon they were doubled up. For Nellie had on a black dress which she'd cut short enough almost to show her bottom, and her chubby legs were on full view, pure white and with many dimples. The deep red lipstick she'd pinched out of Lily's handbag had been applied with a heavy hand to make a very exaggerated Cupid's bow, and her mousy hair had been flattened down with black Cherry Blossom shoe polish, which she'd also used to make kiss-curls along her forehead and one b each ear. This was beginning to rub off on to her face, making her look even more comical.

By now the whole room was ringing with laughter, Corker's being the loudest as he slapped his thighs. It was all the encouragement Nellie needed. She lifted her hands, palms towards her audience, and began to move them in circles, singing, 'Boo-boo-be-do . . . boo-boo-be-do.' Then she started to give her version of the Charleston, while boo-boo-be-doing. It was hilarious, and there wasn't a dry eye in the room. But there was more to come. She tried to kick her right foot backwards, with the intention of touching it with her left hand as she'd seen them do in the pictures, and that's where she came unstuck. For when she kicked her foot, a leg of her blue fleecy-lined bloomers appeared from under the short skirt and ended up around her knee. She didn't notice. She was putting all her energy into the dance and her chubby face was alight with pleasure as the clapping and cheering increased in volume. She was oblivious to everything. Even when the other leg of her bloomers came down and people were doubled up or falling about, she didn't twig.

Corker had a hankie to his eyes to wipe away the tears. He said, 'Nellie, me darlin', it's a real treasure yer are.'

'Thanks, Corker.' Nellie might have been breathless but she was a real trouper and kept the hands going round while she boo-boo-be-do'ed.

Molly didn't know whether to laugh or cry. It was the funniest thing she'd ever seen, but she thought she should tell her mate her bloomers were hanging down. In the end her dilemma was solved when Lily called, 'Ay, Mam, don't yer know ye're showing next week's washing?'

But Nellie had got into the swing of the dance now and had no intention of stopping in case she couldn't start again. 'What's that, girl?'

Lily had her head on Archie's shoulder and their bodies were shaking with laughter. 'Ye're showing yer knickers, Mam.'

'They're not knickers, yer daft thing,' Paul said. 'That's a barrage balloon she's been hiding.'

Steve called, 'Mam, yer probably don't care, and no doubt yer'll tell me to mind me own business, but yer knickers are hanging down.'

Nellie slowed down. 'Ah, they're not are they?' She wasn't the least bit perturbed when she looked down and saw a flash of blue. 'D'yer know, I put three pins in the bleeding things and they've gone and let me down. It just goes to show yer can't trust nothing.'

Lily felt quite dizzy with laughing, and wondered if she'd ever have the nerve to be the good sport her mother was. 'And yer can't trust no one, Mam, can yer? Where did yer get that lipstick from, by the way, 'cos it looks remarkably like the one I spent half an hour trying to find before we came out.'

Her mother pulled a face. 'Go on, girl, kick a woman when she's down. I don't care, I can take it. And I'm afraid I can't give yer the lipstick back 'cos it got mixed up with the shoe polish, and that went all over me mate's dressing table. So I'd better go and fix meself up and see what I can do about the mess I've made.' She put on her Little Orphan Annie look and raised her brows at Molly. 'I don't suppose yer feel like giving me a hand, do yer, girl? No, I thought not.'

'Of course I'll give yer a hand, sunshine.' Molly put her arm across her mate's shoulders. 'Come on, up the stairs with yer.'

As the two women made their way up to the bedroom, Bob squeezed Bridie's hand. 'That was some performance, eh, lass? The funniest I've ever seen. She's a hero is Nellie.'

Jack was sitting near by and he nodded. 'Ye're right, Da, she's one in a million.'

Nellie's three children were still laughing at their mother's performance, not the least bit embarrassed by it. Steve, Lily and Paul all loved her too much for that. And her soon-to-be son-in-law, Archie, thought she was one big bundle of love and laughter. They nodded when they heard Corker say, 'Like I said before, George, she's a real treasure is your wife.'

He rubbed his forehead and chuckled. 'She's certainly not a buried treasure, is she, Corker? Everything on show, all in the open, that's Nellie. But I'll have strong words with her if she's used up all me boot polish.'

Chapter Twenty-Three

When Corker left Molly's house on Boxing Day afternoon and crossed the cobbles to the house opposite, he was in possession of all the details he wanted regarding Phil's mother. So when he was introduced, he took the look of apprehension from her face as he shook her hand and said, 'Hello, Frances, compliments of the season to yer, me darlin'.'

In a low voice, she said, 'Thank yer, Mr Corkhill, and the same to you.'

'Mr Corkhill!' his voice boomed. 'I don't very often get called that, all me friends call me Corker! So if I can call you Frances, then I'm sure yer can manage to call me Corker.'

He didn't wait for her answer as he didn't want to appear too gushing, which would sound false, and by the same token he didn't want to appear cool. He'd made up his mind to strike a happy medium and see how things progressed. So he turned to Victoria with his arms wide. 'Victoria, me darlin', yer look as young and as beautiful as ever.' His hands were so huge, you would think his touch would be rough for a frail old lady, but when he cupped her face he was as gentle as a butterfly. 'I think yer must be living a good life, for it's hale and hearty yer look.'

'That's because I'm being so well looked after, Corker. I'm allowed to wash a few cups and dust the sideboard, but that's about it. Doreen watches me like a hawk, and I'll swear she's teaching the baby to keep an eye on me.'

'Where is the little feller?' Corker asked. 'Not asleep, I hope, 'cos it's not often I get a chance to see him.'

'Doreen's changing his nappy upstairs.' Phil's heart was full. To have Corker in the same room as his mother, and on friendly terms, was more than he'd ever dared to hope for. 'She won't be long and then yer can hold him for a while before me mam takes over.'

'Are yer happy with yer grandson, Frances?' Corker lowering his huge frame on to the couch. 'I bet ye're as proud as peacock?'

Frances was so racked with guilt over the way she'd treated her son, she didn't think she deserved to be called the child's grandmother. But now she pushed the guilt aside and when she spoke her true feelings showed. 'I am very proud, I can't find the words to tell yer how much. Phil was so like his dad when he was born, and he's the spitting image now of how Bob looked at his age.' There was a catch in her voice and she faltered for a brief second. 'And now Bobby is so like Phil when he was a baby, it takes me back in time. If it was at all possible to go back to the day Phil was born, I would live my life very differently. But that's not going to happen, so I'm doing my best to make up for a little of that time.'

'There's no need for yer to regret anything, Mam, it's all over and done with. I couldn't wish for a better life than I've got, especially now you're back in it.' Phil took his eyes off her to speak to Corker. 'I went to see me grandma on Christmas Eve, Uncle Corker, and told her about me mam. She wants to see her, and me Uncle Wally is bringing her up this afternoon.'

Frances dropped her head. 'I can't go through with it, son, I'm too ashamed. When her son was killed, I should have told her I was expecting his baby, she had every right to know. But I was a coward and left the area because I didn't have the guts to tell Mrs Mitchell or me own mother.'

'Mam, it's time to set the record straight, yer'll feel much better. And yer don't have to be afraid of the Mitchells because the way they look at it, without you they wouldn't have me or the baby. We are part of the son who was killed, their own flesh and blood, and they're grateful for that.'

Corker leaned forward and rested his elbows on his knees. 'Frances, me darlin', life is too short to be unhappy. If the Mitchells bear no grudges and want to welcome you with open arms, then walk into them. I've met Mary Mitchell and she's as fine a woman as yer'll meet in a month of Sundays. Don't throw her friendship back in her face, because she's yer son's grandma and yer grandson's great-grandma. Yer may feel as though yer having to face the music, but it'll only be a short song, over and done with in two minutes.'

Frances didn't meet his eyes when she answered, 'It sounds easy the way yer say it, Corker, and I know Mrs Mitchell is the salt of the earth. I saw her every day when I was courting her son. But I've carried this guilt around with me for twenty-odd years now, and it won't be easy to wipe away.'

Victoria felt heartily sorry for the woman. 'But won't yer feel a lot easier in yer mind and heart when yer've looked her in the eye and told her that? Confession is a very good way of cleansing all wrongs and putting things right.'

Frances could hear Doreen coming down the stairs. She nodded in answer to Victoria before moving her gaze to Doreen, who had just entered the room with the baby in her arms. At the sight of her grandson, Frances's pale face lit up.

'Hello, Uncle Corker, haven't yer got a hangover?' Doreen grinned. 'Yer shifted enough drink last night to sink a ship.'

'It was a good night, though, wasn't it, me darlin'? We can always rely on yer mam when it comes to having a rip-roaring party.' His loud guffaw filled the room. 'And Nellie never lets us down for entertainment with a difference.' His head dropped back and he roared with laughter. 'I've sailed the seven seas, visited practically every country in the world, but I can say in all honesty I have never seen such a sight as Nellie like she was last night in all her glory.'

'It was dead funny, wasn't it?' In her mind's eye, Doreen could see her Auntie Nellie and it brought forth a deep chuckle. 'I honestly don't know how she's got the nerve, but I take me hat off to her for being such a good sport. If it was left to us young ones, the party would have been a flop.'

'I've been telling me mam and Aunt Vicky about it,' Phil said, 'but being told isn't as funny as seeing it with yer own eyes. But I think Mrs B is just as funny in her own way. I mean, she wouldn't let herself be seen in a Betty Boop dress with boot polish on her hair and a ton of lipstick on her face, that's not her style. But without her, Mrs Mac wouldn't be able to function. They feed off each other, and it wouldn't be nearly as funny if they were both exactly the same.' His shoulders began to shake. 'I can still picture her face when Steve told her the legs of her knickers had fallen down. She didn't rush out of the room in embarrassment, just stood there, as cool as yer like, and said, "Ah, they haven't, have they? And I put three pins in the bleeding things, too!" '

'Don't start me off again, son,' Corker said, 'I've thought of nothing else since I got out of bed this morning and I've got pains in me side with laughing.' He pushed himself off the couch, and when his body unfolded his mop of hair was almost brushing the ceiling. 'Let me hold the baby for a while before his grandma gets her hands on him. I don't want the wee lad to grow up not knowing who I am.'

Corker had never had a child of his own, and when he'd married Ellen her youngest boy had been eight, and Phoebe, the eldest, was thirteen. So when he looked down he marvelled at the tiny hands and fingers, so perfectly formed. 'This little feller is smiling at me, can yer hear him gurgling? He likes his Uncle Corker, don't yer, son?'

'He's coming on in leaps and bounds,' Doreen said with pride. 'I took him to the clinic last week and he'd gained a pound in weight. And he's taking notice of things now, like his rattle and the bell I've tied to the end of the cot. When I ring that he gets very excited.' She grinned. 'I reckon he'll be ready for school by the time he's two.'

Corker held the baby so gently, his bright blue eyes smiling down on a little face that was staring back as though he knew exactly what was going on. 'I can see ye're beginning to take notice, me little man. Another month or so and yer'll know one from the other.'

'He knows now,' Victoria said. 'As soon as he hears Doreen's voice, his arms and legs are going like mad. I wouldn't be the least surprised if he grows up to be a footballer, 'cos there's some strength in that right leg of his.'

Corker was swaying, as people do when holding a baby, and he said, 'If that time ever comes, then we'll have to draw lots. Yer see, little feller, all yer family and friends are in different camps, and it'll be a toss-up whether yer play for Liverpool or Everton. But long before that, it's yer Uncle Corker who'll be asking yer mammy if he can take yer to the park to give yer a go on the swings and roundabouts.' He held the baby for another five minutes before passing him over to Frances. 'Enjoy yer grandson, me darlin', I could see yer were itching to get hold of him. And I hope to see yer again soon.'

'Oh, yer will, Uncle Corker,' Phil told him. 'Mrs B and Mrs Mac have said they'll bring her down one day in the week, and I'll be picking her up every Sunday, after she's had dinner with her family.'

'Then I'll look forward to seeing yer soon, me darlin', and I have to say yer look very happy and contented with the baby in yer arms.' Corker turned to give Victoria the kiss she looked for every time she saw him. Then as he passed, he dropped a kiss on Frances's forehead. 'You take good care of yerself now.'

Phil began to follow the big man. 'I'll see yer to the door.'

Corker waved him aside. 'I'll let meself out, you stay where yer are. But if yer ever need me, yer know where I am.'

It was the day after Boxing Day. Jack and Ruthie had gone to work, and Molly and Nellie were facing each other across the table. 'Did yer get Ruthie out of bed on time, girl?'

Molly nodded. 'She mustn't have slept all night because she was up at the crack of dawn. She was sitting having her breakfast when Jack came down. I hope she keeps it up and I'm not yelling me head off every morning trying to get her out of bed.'

'Ooh, I wouldn't rely on that, girl, it was probably a one-off this morning. She'll be excited and nervous, but give her a week to feel her feet and yer'll be back to straining yer lungs to get her and Jack out of bed.'

'Before yer came, I was sitting here asking meself if it was all worth it,' Molly said, 'putting money away every week in Christmas clubs instead of throwing caution to the winds and going to the flicks now and again. Then there's at least four weeks of running around like lunatics, making sure we've got presents for everyone, then the worrying about the food. And it's all over in two days, forgotten about until it comes around the next year.'

Nellie raised her eyes to the ceiling. 'Ah, it's not going to be one of yer miserable days, is it, girl?' She pushed the wooden chair back and lumbered to her feet. 'If I've to listen to yer moaning, I'm going to do it in comfort. I'm bringing me chair over.'

'Who's moaning, sunshine? I'm only stating facts, that's all.' Molly watched her friend carry the chair from beside the sideboard round to the table. And as she watched, she realized something she'd never noticed before. 'Nellie, how come yer carry that chair without bumping into anything, when yer never worry about knocking other things about?'

Nellie set the carver chair down with care, then parked her bottom on it. 'Because, girl, I've never had a chair so posh in all me life. And as I'll never be able to talk yer into buying me another one, I intend to take care of this. And I hope when I'm not here that yer watch nobody else uses it and knocks it about.'

'When I bought the chair I didn't buy it for your sole use, sunshine, although I admit it might have sounded that way to you. I bought it because yer were going on about how nice it was and in the end I forked out just to shut yer up.' Molly chuckled. 'I do sound like an old moaner, don't I? Let's talk about something that'll liven me up. How did yer get on with George over using his boot polish?'

Nellie lifted her hands. 'Oh, don't ask, girl, don't ask! There's only our Paul talking to me, I'm getting the cold shoulder off George and Lily.' The bosom was hitched and laid on the table so she could lean closer to her mate. 'I called them all the silly buggers going, acting like a couple of kids, they are.'

'Go 'way! I didn't think they'd keep it up all this time. What are they complaining about? All yer did was use a bit of their stuff in yer act, and they can't say they didn't think it was worth it 'cos they were both doubled up with laughter.'

Nellie pulled a face. 'It's probably my fault, girl, me and me big mouth. Instead of keeping quiet when they were going on about it, I suggested that as the black polish was mixed up with the lipstick, we could keep it until next year and I could do me Al Jolson act again. I thought it was funny, they didn't see it that way and now I'm in the doghouse.'

'Are yer upset about it, sunshine?'

'Not in the least, girl, not in the least. If they can't open their mouths to speak to me, then they can't open them to eat the dinner I'm not going to make tonight.'

Molly chuckled. 'Of course yer've got to make them a dinner! If they've done a day's work, yer can't expect them to come home to fresh-air sandwiches. What if it comes to the end of the week and they refuse to hand any money over out of their wages? Yer'd be laughing the other side of yer face, then, sunshine.'

Nellie tapped the side of her forehead. 'I've got it all worked out in here, girl. Archie comes tonight, and we get on like a house on fire. So I'm going to get him on my side and he'll coax Lily into agreeing it was funny.'

'I think he might have a job on his hands, sunshine, if she hasn't had anything to eat and is starving after working all day. It's very difficult to laugh when yer tummy is rumbling.'

'Oh, I'm going to make them a dinner tonight, girl, 'cos I've got stacks of turkey left and I'm not letting it go to waste. I've never had a bird as big as that, it was nearly as big as me. And there's carrot and turnip over from yesterday, so they can have that fried up. Waste not, want not, that's what me old ma used to say.'

'We're having a fry-up as well,' Molly told her. 'So it's an easy day for cooking, thank goodness.'

'Ay, girl, how did it go yesterday when Mrs Mitchell met up with Frances? Was she mad with her for running away without telling them she was in the family way?'

'I can't give yer chapter and verse, sunshine, 'cos I only slipped over to Doreen's for five minutes after I saw the taxi leaving. But from what she told me, it went off very well. Buckets of tears were shed, like, but yer couldn't expect anything else after not seeing each other for twenty-odd years. But Frances has been accepted back into the fold.'

'I'm glad for them, girl, and I bet Frances will feel better now Mary Mitchell knows the whole story. I was lying in bed last night, waiting to drop off to sleep, and thinking that when Phil and Doreen got married, Phil didn't have a soul in the world to call his own. And now he's got a bigger family than any of us.'

Molly nodded. 'It's funny how things work out, isn't it? They say that God moves in mysterious ways, His wonders to perform.'

Nellie gaped. 'Who says that, girl? I've never heard it in me life before.'

'I don't know where the saying comes from, sunshine, except I've heard me mam using it, and other people. I certainly didn't make it up, I'm not that ruddy clever.'

'Ooh, I don't know about that, ye're too bleeding clever for me to keep up with.' Then Nellie thought of something to look forward to. 'What day are we picking Frances up?'

'Thursday this week, because of the holiday. But after this week it'll be every Wednesday, as long as she's fit for the journey.'

Nellie's legs were swinging under the chair. 'The next thing to look forward to is the wedding, and it'll be here before we know it. Is Doreen still going to make our outfits, girl, 'cos there's not much time? Easter will be on us before we've had time to turn around.'

'Ay, give us a break, sunshine, it was only Christmas Day the day before yesterday. Our Doreen will make our dresses, she never breaks a promise. But for crying out loud, give her time to take the decorations down first.'

Nellie cupped her chin and looked thoughtful. 'I can't make up me mind what colour to have, girl, have yer any suggestions?'

'It's no good making up yer mind about a colour without having a look at materials first. We could go down to Blackler's one day, they have a very good selection. And from there we could walk to TJ's to see what they have to offer. It's best to scout around instead of taking the first material that catches yer eye.'

'I still think I should be able to wear me posh hat, girl, 'cos it's just sitting on a shelf in the wardrobe doing nothing. And it's a sin after paying three guineas for it.'

'Nellie, over my dead body do yer wear that hat again! Everyone will remember it from the last two weddings, so it's out of the question. And as Lily is yer only daughter, yer wouldn't want to embarrass her, would yer?'

'All right, girl, keep yer ruddy hair on! Ye're always telling me I waste money on cakes and chocolate, and when I try to get me money's worth out of something yer call me for everything! I can't flaming well win!' Then came the crafty look. 'I've got a good idea. Why don't you wear me hat, save yer buying one?'

'I'll tell yer what a better idea is, sunshine, and that's us getting off our backsides and getting down to the shops. I only need bread, milk and potatoes, so we won't be out long. Then I'm going to have a quiet afternoon reclining on the couch with me feet up and me head on a nice soft pillow. It's years since I took an afternoon nap, there was always something that needed doing. But there's nothing to stop me lounging today, I'm as free as a bird until it's time to make the dinner. And as it's only fry-ups, that doesn't need any preparation.'

Nellie shuffled her bottom to the edge of the chair. 'I'll come and keep yer company, girl, and I'll decline with yer.'

Molly had a struggle to keep her face straight. 'Nellie, two things. First, the word is recline, not decline. Yer see, sunshine, decline means to go down, in health, like, or to fade away. And as for the other thing, you coming to keep me company, well, I'm sorry to tell yer, sunshine, but that's definitely not on. Do you think for one minute that I'd get any peace and quiet with you sitting here talking yer head off?'

'I won't open me mouth, girl, I promise. I'll sit on me chair, with me feet up on one of the old ones, and I'll be as good as gold.'

Molly felt a bit miserable about refusing her friend, but she really did need a rest. It was all right for Nellie, she went home on Christmas night full of the joys of having a wonderful time and never giving a thought to the mess that had been left behind. It had taken Molly and Jack, with some help from Ruthie, all day yesterday to get the house back to normal. And when Jack had seen the sweat pouring off his wife as she mopped the drink and food stains off the lino, he'd made her promise to have a rest this afternoon while she had the chance.

'Nellie, yer know I love yer and wouldn't hurt yer for the world. Nor would I let anyone else hurt yer. But I've got to put me foot down this once and say I must have the afternoon to meself. Yer see, sunshine, I was at it all day yesterday, with Jack and Ruthie, cleaning up and getting the house back in shape. And I need a rest 'cos the tiredness has gone right through to me bones.'

Nellie sat back in her chair. 'Well, why didn't yer send for me and I'd have come and helped yer, girl! All yer had to do was open yer mouth, and yer could have done that when George helped Jack bring yer table back. I was only sitting there doing nowt, I'd have been glad of something to do.'

Molly didn't say they would have taken twice as long if Nellie had been there because even if you told her point blank to shut up, it wouldn't have stopped her nattering away and slowing the job down. What she did say was, 'I know yer would have come, sunshine, but yer can't expect me to give a party one night, then the next day ask the guests to come back and clean up after themselves. It would sound a bit churlish, don't yer think?'

'How can I think when I don't even know what ye're bleeding well talking about! Half the time I think ye're speaking a foreign language just to have me on. I'm not even going to ask yer what the word meant 'cos I've forgotten it already. Anyway, yer won't have to ask me to come and give yer a hand next year, I'll come without being asked.'

Molly smiled at her. 'A lot will have happened between now and then. Lily will be married and yer'll have a new son-in-law who is a lovely bloke and who yer get on well with. And our Jill will have had the baby, making Steve a father for the first time. And you'll be a proud grandma for the first time, and me for the second. So, please God, this year is going to be a happy one for the Bennetts and the McDonoughs.'

Those words brought a smile of happiness to Nellie's chubby face. 'I wonder which will come first, girl, the wedding or the baby?'

'We'll just have to wait and see, won't we? But I won't be worrying on me own for this baby, like I did with Doreen's, 'cos you'll be worrying with me.' Molly turned away to hide a grin. For George always said his wife wouldn't worry if her backside was on fire. 'Now, let's get a move on, sunshine, or the day will be over before we know it.'

Tony and Ellen saw the two friends nearing the shop and immediately moved from behind the counter to the front of it, as they'd planned. When the couple walked into the shop they were greeted by the sight of the butcher and his assistant circling their open palms as they did their best to Charleston while singing, 'Boo-boo-be-doo. Boo-boo-be-do.'

Nellie was tickled pink. She leaned her elbows on the counter, and Tony was to say later that when she began to laugh, the counter moved a few inches. 'Yer daft beggars, ye're not a patch on me! That's because yer haven't got shapely legs and a voluptuous body like mine.'

'Ellen's been singing yer praises, Nellie,' Tony said as he walked back behind the counter. 'She said yer were better than ever, and that's saying something. But she also said it was a good job a policeman didn't see yer, or yer'd have been locked up in a cell in the police station with all the other ladies of the night.'

Nellie stood to attention, as did her bosom and tummy. 'Well, yer cheeky beggar, Ellen Corkhill! We only came in to say hello, we don't want nothing 'cos we've got plenty over, and the thanks we get for being friendly is to be insulted.'

Molly tapped her on the shoulder. 'Excuse me, sunshine, but don't bring me into this. It was you they insulted, not both of us.'

'Oh, blimey, they're all ganging up on me. I might have known it was going to be a rotten day when I saw the cob on me mate's face when she opened the door to me.' Nellie jerked her head at Molly and her chins swayed briskly to show they were on her side. 'Come on, happy girl, let's get what we came out for and then yer can go home and decline in peace.'

Tony and Ellen roared when the two women were leaving the shop and they heard Molly say, 'I've told yer, sunshine, it's recline, not decline!'

'Well, that didn't take us long, did it, girl? Me basket has never been as light as it is now, and we've only spent coppers.'

'That's something to be thankful for 'cos I'm not exactly loaded. We only need a pint of milk and we can get that from the corner shop. I keep meaning to ask the milkman to leave two pints instead of one, but when I'm paying him on a Friday it slips me mind.'

The friends turned into their street and Molly smiled when she saw Doreen walking towards them pushing the pram. 'Ooh, here's our Doreen with the baby.'

'Hi-ya, Mam, Auntie Nellie. Yer haven't been out long, have yer?' Doreen looked the picture of health and happiness. 'It's only about half an hour since I saw yer leaving the house, so yer must have run all the way.'

The two mates were standing either side of the pram looking down on the baby who was so well wrapped up against the cold there was only his nose showing. But it didn't stop the women from clucking and cooing. 'Jack Frost won't get to you, will he sweetheart?' Molly was so proud of her first grandchild she would talk about anything under the sun so he would get to know the sound of her voice.

And while her mind was in a world of its own, Nellie took advantage. 'Yer mam said yer'll be making our dresses for the wedding, girl, and I want yer to know how grateful I am 'cos they don't make nice clothes in my size.'

'You and me mam don't need to buy patterns, Auntie Nellie, because I can use the same pattern but make a few alterations so they look different from the last ones.'

Crafty Nellie screwed up her eyes. 'I forget how much material I bought last time, was it four yards?'

'Five to be on the safe side,' Doreen told her. 'Me mam needs four because of her height. And it's best to have a bit to play around with, to make a bolero or a scarf. Be a change from the other dresses.'

'Ooh, yer make it sound as though they're going to be lovely. And as I'm the mother of the bride this time, I want to look special – stand out, if yer know what I mean.'

'Yer'll stand out, Auntie Nellie, I can guarantee that. The whole neighbourhood will be talking about yer. Even those in the wash-house.' Doreen shivered as the cold wind penetrated her clothes, though she was well wrapped up. 'I'll get on me way, Mam, 'cos I'm freezing standing here, and I don't want to keep Bobby out too long.'

'Okay, sunshine, I'll see yer later.' Molly stood next to her mate and they watched her daughter walk smartly down towards the main road. 'She's getting her figure back again,' Molly said, 'see how slim she is?'

'I was like that when I was her age,' Nellie said, trying to think of a way to say what she wanted without getting told off for it. 'I wouldn't have needed five yards of material for a dress if I was still like that.'

'Who said yer need five yards of material now?'

'Your Doreen did!'

'When did she tell yer that?'

'While you were busy talking to the baby, that's when. Five yards for me, and four for you. And we don't need to buy no patterns 'cos she can use the ones she's got.'

'My God, yer got all that out of her in about two minutes? Yer must have asked her, Nellie, she wouldn't have volunteered the information off her own bat. I hope yer didn't pester her 'cos she's got enough on her plate with the baby, and Phil's mam on the scene.'

Nellie looked all innocent and hurt. 'I wouldn't pester her, girl, yer know that! I wouldn't dream of it.'

'So, out of the blue, Doreen just said you needed five yards of material and I needed four. No talk of dresses or nothing, just how much material we needed. Not for one minute am I falling for that, sunshine.'

Nellie's head quivered. 'Well, I just happened to say how grateful I am that she's going to make our dresses for the wedding, that's all.'

'You are one crafty article, Nellie McDonough, and that's being nice about yer. I told yer Doreen would make the dresses but yer couldn't wait, could yer?'

Nellie took her mate's arm, turned her around and steered her across the cobbles. 'Now we know how much material we want, we may as well start to look around. It doesn't mean to say Doreen has to make them right away. We could go into town on Saturday afternoon after dinner, when the men have been paid, and have a look around.'

'I would only be looking, sunshine, not buying, 'cos I'm stony broke. Next week I'll have enough to buy material, but this week I've got to fork out for Ruthie's tram fare to work 'cos she's working a week in hand. But she'll get her first wage packet next week so money won't be so tight then.'

'Ah, ay, girl, what's the bleeding point of going into town if we can't buy anything we like? I hate window shopping, it's a waste of time.'

'There's nothing to stop you from buying, you've got the money. And I'll come with yer and help yer choose, then next week yer can do the same for me.'

'That might seem a good idea to you, girl, but I've got a better one. I'll lend yer the money on Saturday, you get the material yer like and pay me back next Saturday. That way everyone is happy.' They were outside Molly's house now, and Nellie pushed her towards it. 'Let's go inside and talk it over.'

Molly withdrew her arm. 'Uh, uh, sunshine, we'll discuss it tomorrow. I'm going to decline your offer of company, so I can recline on my couch in peace and quiet.' She bent and kissed the chubby face that was wearing a very crestfallen expression. 'See yer tomorrow, sunshine.'

Nellie, her head bowed, walked slowly away, muttering, 'I don't know why she can't decline and recline in front of me, it wouldn't do her no bleeding harm.'

'Did yer say something, sunshine?' Molly took the key out of the lock and pushed the door open. 'I couldn't quite catch what it was.'

'I was talking to meself, girl, about the bleeding alarm, it didn't go off this morning.'

Molly grinned as she closed the door behind her. Her mate might be slow in some things, but making excuses wasn't one of them.

Chapter Twenty-Four

'Shall we get off the tram in London Road, girl, and go to TJ's, or stay on until we get to Blackler's?' Nellie was in very high spirits. There was nothing she liked better than wandering through the big stores in the city, picking up items with a look on her face that said she might possibly buy, when in reality she had no intention. Or she'd finger a roll of material and remark to her bemused mate that it was very good quality, and to the assistant hovering nearby in the hope of a sale, she would say she'd be back later after she'd been to another department. Needless to say the assistant wouldn't see sight nor light of her again. 'What d'yer want to do, girl?'

'I think TJ's first, sunshine, then we can walk to Blackler's. It's downhill from here, so we won't be puffing and blowing.'

So when the tram stopped outside the very popular store, Molly helped her friend down from the platform before cupping her elbow and leading her to one of the main doors. The store was housed in two buildings, with a street dividing them. Between the two they sold everything imaginable and at a reasonable price for the working-class people who were their main customers. 'Here we are, sunshine.' Molly took her hand from Nellie's elbow because although the main door was wide, it hadn't been built for two women, one the size of Nellie, to walk in side by side. 'In yer go.'

Nellie swept through the doors like royalty, with her hips

swaying, her head held high and a supercilious expression that said she was as good as anyone. And walking slightly behind her, with a grin on her face, was Molly. She was thinking she wouldn't be the least surprised if her mate didn't raise her hand and give a royal wave. 'Where to, girl?'

'The materials are on the first floor, so d'yer want to take the lift or can yer manage the stairs? There's not that many of them.'

'Ooh, I hate lifts, girl, they frighten the bloody life out of me. I feel caged in, like a monkey in the zoo, and I go all funny in me head. That's because I'm terrified of them breaking down and us being stuck halfway between floors.'

'Then we'll take the stairs,' Molly said, 'I can't say I'm fond of lifts meself. I don't think anyone really likes them, if the truth were known, but they're handy for those who can't climb up.'

Nellie pulled herself up by the rail running up the wall at the side, and when she reached the top stood for a while to catch her breath. 'Yer'd think they'd have a chair here for people what aren't so sprightly on their feet. And why can't they have the materials on the ground floor, save all this messing?'

'Yer were smiling all the way here, as happy as Larry, and now yer've got a face on her like a wet week. So don't you ever complain about me being miserable because yer can be a right pain when things don't go exactly as yer want them to.'

Nellie straightened up and the cheeky grin appeared. 'Only having yer on, girl, so yer don't go through life thinking ye're the only one allowed to moan. Now, point me in the right direction, if yer don't mind.'

The materials were at the far end of the department, and it was very quiet. In fact the whole store was quiet, but with its being only a week after the big Christmas spend, most people were probably broke. 'Ay, we've got the place to ourselves,' Molly said. 'No pushing and shoving, we can look around at our leisure.' Several assistants approached them to see if they could help, but Molly told them they were only looking and if they needed help then they would ask for it. 'I hate it when they watch over yer like hawks,' she whispered to Nellie, 'I like to take me time and browse in peace.'

'Take no notice of them, girl, they're only doing their job. They may be getting on our nerves watching over us, but they've probably got supervisors watching them, and they'd get it in the neck if they weren't seen to be helping customers.' Nellie ran her hand over a roll of bright green, shiny satin material. 'Ay, I like this, girl, it wouldn't half make me stand out.'

Molly took a deep breath. Buying material for the wedding was going to be a long and tiring process. 'Nellie, you may like the material, but it certainly wouldn't like you. Oh, yer'd stand out, all right, like a ruddy sore thumb. It's a terrible, common colour, sunshine, one of the worst shades of green I've ever seen. If I let yer go home with that material for your mother of the bride outfit, I'd never be able to look your Lily in the face again.'

Nellie clamped her lips together and without a word moved down the counter. The next roll of material she felt was in a bright, pillar-box red. For a moment Molly thought she was looking at it for a joke, to pay her back for what she'd said about the green. But no, Nellie's face was serious when she asked, 'Well, what about this, girl? It's not satin and it's not bright green. Unless I'm colour blind, like.'

'Yer certainly have an eye for bright colours, sunshine, d'yer want to dazzle everyone at the wedding? Yer want a nice softer colour, one that looks like quality, not something cheap and gaudy.' Molly spotted a roll of crêpe material in a lovely colour between lilac and purple. 'Now, something like this is more like it. It would suit you, and it's an unusual colour which would set you apart. I wouldn't mind it meself, so if you're not fussy, I'll have it.'

'Mmm . . . yer reckon I'd stand out, eh?' Nellie fingered the material. 'It feels nice, doesn't it, girl?' She nodded. 'Yeah, I think I like it. In fact, I can see meself in a dress made of this, and it does suit me. How much a yard is it?'

Molly picked up the ticket hanging at the end of the roll. 'It's three and six a yard, sunshine, so it would 'cost yer seventeen and six, plus, say, sixpence for the cotton. So altogether it would be eighteen shillings. But yer haven't looked around properly, yer might find something else yer like better. Cast yer eye over what they've got here, then we'll walk down to Blackler's and see what they've got to offer. I want to scout around, not grab the first material I see. It's not often I buy a new dress, so I want to take me time and make sure I get something I really like. We might have to pay a bit more in Blackler's, but it would only be coppers. So, what d'yer say, shall we take a walk? We can always come back if we want to.'

'We'll go to the cafe downstairs first, girl, and I'll mug yer to a cup of tea. It'll warm us through and we won't feel the cold so much.'

Molly nodded. 'You pay this week, and if we come back next week it'll be my turn. It will be cold walking down London Road because yer get the full force of the wind off the Mersey. Very bracing and probably good for us, but cuts right through to the marrow.'

It was nice and warm in the cafe and when Nellie picked up a tray Molly walked behind her. 'We don't need two trays for just two cups of tea so I'll let you do the honours.'

Nellie had spotted the glass stand with scones on, and a crafty look appeared on her face. 'You go and sit at a table, girl, I can manage on me own.' There were two women in front of her and Nellie was forced to stick to their slow pace. But she didn't do it without giving them daggers and clicking her tongue impatiently. She didn't take kindly to anyone keeping her away from food, especially two women who weren't sure what they wanted and had brought the queue to a standstill.

When she felt herself being prodded in the back, Nellie turned around. 'What was that for?' she asked the woman behind her. 'Yer want to keep yer hands to yerself.'

The woman was red in the face. 'Will yer tell those two to put a move on? I'm going to miss my train.'

'That's too bad, now, isn't it! Tell them yer bleeding self, I'm not a messenger boy! Do yer own dirty work.' Then Nellie lost her patience. 'Who the hell d'yer think yer are, telling me what to do? I was here before you, and I'll make bloody sure I get served before yer, even if yer do miss yer ruddy train. Wait yer turn, like I have to.'

Sitting at one of the small round tables. Molly could hear what was going on, and was just about to get off her chair and go over to Nellie when the two ladies in front of her mate finally made up their mind and walked away with a pot of tea and two buttered scones. Molly sat back and breathed a sigh of relief. The last thing she needed was to be a referee at a fight between two women in T.J. Hughes's. Especially as one of the women was her friend and the other one a selfish snob who thought the world revolved around her.

Nellie waddled towards the table and plonked the tray down. 'There yer are, girl, a pot of tea and two nice buttered scones.' She pulled a chair out and sat down. 'I was nearly coming to blows there, 'cos some cheeky cow thought she should get served first because she had a train to catch. All lah-di-dah she was, but if she wanted to get in front of me it would have had to be over my dead body. I hate snobs, me.'

'Never mind, don't be getting yerself all worked up, it's sorted itself out. But yer shouldn't have got a scone for me, I could have lasted out until we got home.'

'Oh, aye, have you sitting there with yer mouth watering

while I eat one? No, girl, yer face would have put me off.'

Molly grinned. 'I could have put a hand over me mouth so yer wouldn't have seen it watering. But, I honestly don't think yer'd be put off that scone even if yer had an audience of a thousand people watching.'

Nellie grinned as she picked off the top half of her scone. 'An audience usually has to pay to get in the pictures or the zoo, so I wouldn't mind them watching if they bought a ticket.' Her mouth opened and half the scone disappeared. 'That is bloody lovely,' she said, wiping crumbs from her lips.

'They're only tuppence, so I'm going to have another two-pennyworth. And don't start giving me a lecture on saving for the wedding, 'cos yer look like a school teacher when yer do that, and yer'll only put me off the scumtus taste.'

'Nellie, sunshine, the word is scrumptious.'

The little woman pushed herself to her feet. 'I don't give a sod what the word is, girl, all I know is me tummy is calling out for an encore. So be an angel and pour me another cup of tea out while I go on a message for me tummy.'

When the two friends came out of the store and turned towards the river, the wind hit them so hard it took their breath away. 'My God,' Molly said, 'we'll get blown off our feet. Put yer arm in mine, sunshine, and we'll weight each other down.'

'Holy suffering ducks,' Nellie gasped, 'we'd have been better staying on the tram and going to Blackler's first.'

'It's too late now to say what we should have done. We'll cut down the street at the back of the Empire and be shielded from the wind for a while. Then we've only got to cross Lime Street and we'll be there.'

'D'yer know girl.' Nellie's words swirled in the air before reaching Molly. 'If I hadn't been the one who insisted we come today, I'd be calling yer all the bleeding names under the sun.'

'I was going to remind you it was your fault we're here, but then I remembered yer'd been kind enough to mug me to a scone, and thought better of it.' They turned into a street that ran along the back of the Empire and as they were now sheltered from the harsh wind, they leaned against the wall to get their breath back.

'This is a bloody mug's game, this is,' Nellie said, her hand on her chest which was burning like a fire. 'Next time I suggest anything stupid, tell me to go and take a running jump into the Mersey.'

'Now yer know yer haven't got yer bathing costume with yer, sunshine, so don't even think of going swimming. Take a deep breath, calm yerself down and we'll get on our way.'

'Don't dash across Lime Street like a ruddy whippet, will yer, girl, 'cos I can't run as fast as you can. Yer legs are a lot longer than mine.'

'There's not much point in me running anywhere without you, sunshine, 'cos ye're the one with the money.'

That cheered Nellie up no end. She remembered then why they were here, and told herself she should be full of beans, buying material for a dress for her daughter's wedding. 'Well, don't stand there leaning against the wall looking as though ye're waiting for a tram, move yerself and let's go see what Blackler's has to offer.'

And when they'd eventually braved the wind and made it into the warm interior of Blackler's, the friends looked at each other and grinned. 'Nice and warm, sunshine, eh?'

Nellie nodded. 'I don't know where the warm air is coming from, but I know where it's going – right up to the top of me legs. Ooh, I could stand on this spot for the rest of me life.'

'Well, don't make a meal of it, we've got some serious shopping to do. And, unfortunately, the materials are on the first floor.'

'I might have known.' Nellie plodded towards the stairs, muttering, 'These clever buggers what put the materials on the first floor, they'll be old themselves one day and I wonder how they'll like it then?'

Molly walked slowly behind her. 'I'd hardly call yer old, sunshine. If you're old, what would that make me ma or Victoria?'

Nellie reached the top stair in a better frame of mind. 'It would make yer ma a slip of a girl, and me a schoolgirl in a gymslip. But don't be keeping me talking when we've got work to do. Lead on, Macduff!'

The friends had only been at the material counter for two minutes when Molly spotted a roll of material that she instantly took a liking to. The colour was a golden tan, and the material was crêpe. 'Oh, look at that, Nellie, that's just what I want.' She fingered the material. 'What a lovely colour it is. A pair of light beige shoes and a beige hat, and that would be me seen to for the wedding. Oh, I'm really pleased with meself, over the blinking moon.'

'Give yerself a chance, girl, we've only just got here. There's plenty of different materials and colours yer haven't even looked at yet.'

'I'll go around with yer, Nellie, to look, but as soon as I set eyes on this I fell for it and knew it was what I wanted. But we can come back to it, so let's try and find something for you.' Molly put a finger under her mate's chin and lifted her face. 'Although I still say that light purple in Hughes's would suit you down to the ground. It would make up lovely, the colour is beautiful and so unusual I doubt there'll be anybody else wearing it.'

'D'yer think so, girl?' Nellie knew her friend had better taste in clothes than she did, so she always listened when Molly offered words of advice. 'They might have something like it here, we haven't looked on all the counters.' Then her eyelids came down and her face creased. 'How much is that orange material what you like?'

Molly tutted. 'It isn't orange, sunshine, it's more of a browny tan. And it's three and eleven a yard. So with the cotton it would be just over sixteen shillings. Have yer got enough on yer to lend me that much?'

Her friend nodded. 'Of course I have, girl, there'd have been no point in coming if I hadn't got no money. I've got three pound on me, so that should be more than enough for both of us.'

'Yer'll have a pound over, if yer go for the material in TJ's. In fact, yer would have more than a pound over. But let's look to see if there's anything here that takes yer fancy before we decide.'

Fifteen minutes later they hadn't seen any colour that came up to the purple crêpe Molly had pointed out in Hughes's. 'Lend me a pound, sunshine, and I'll get four yards of the tan for meself, with a reel of cotton to match. Then we'll walk back to London Road. It won't be so bad going back, the wind will be behind us.'

'I was going to say we could get a tram which would take us right outside the shop, but I know yer'll only moan about wasting money so I'll keep quiet.'

'That would be downright laziness, to get a tram for two or three stops,' Molly said. 'And as yer say, a complete waste of money.'

As Nellie opened her bag to get her purse out, she mumbled, 'Yer see, I knew that's what she'd say, I know her inside out.'

'What was that yer said, sunshine?' Molly knew exactly what had been said because her mate always muttered loud enough for her to hear. 'I didn't quite catch it.'

'I said me bag is full of junk, girl, and when I get home I'm going to turn it inside out.'

'Oh, I see,' Molly said. 'If I hadn't asked, I wouldn't have missed much would I? Except another little fib to add to the other two yer've told me today.'

'What other two?' Nellie had the pound note in her hand ready to hand over, but she wasn't parting with it until she had some answers. 'I haven't told yer no fibs today, Molly Bennett, so yer must be thinking of someone else.'

'I haven't seen no one else but you today! And just to prick yer memory a bit, who was it said it was one-thirty when they knocked on me door, when they knew ruddy well it was only one o'clock? And when she was caught out in a lie, who was it told another fib by saying their clock must have stopped?'

Nellie's whole body began to shake. 'It's no good asking me who it was, girl, if you've forgotten. Was it Beryl Mowbray by any chance?'

'Yer know very well who it was, Nellie McDonough. You were the only one who knocked on my door at one o'clock, insisted it was half-past, then made the excuse yer clock must have stopped.'

'It worked, though, didn't it, girl? And I've got to say that yer weren't nearly as bad-tempered as I thought yer'd be. In fact, yer behaved impical.'

'The word is impeccable, sunshine, which means well-mannered. And I was only polite with yer 'cos the coalman was opposite and I didn't want him to think I was brought up in the gutter, as common as muck.'

'He knows ye're as common as muck, girl, 'cos I told him that years ago.'

Molly grinned. 'Oh, well, that makes us even, 'cos I told him you'd been brought up in the gutter.' Her hand shot out and whipped the pound note from Nellie's fingers. 'I'll let you have the pleasure of telling the assistant who has been watching over us that we'll take four yards of the tan material and a reel of cotton of the same colour. And if yer speak nice to her, sunshine, she'll never know about yer being from the gutter and as common as muck.'

'Seeing you've got the money in yer hand, girl, I'll let you do the honours. But I'll be listening to every word, and I'll soon make a show of yer if yer let the side down with yer cursing and swearing. I don't wish to be sosiated with people what are as common as muck.'

'Oh dear, oh dear, oh dear! What am I going to do with yer, sunshine? The word is associated, and I feel like a teacher correcting one of the pupils in her class. All I'm short of is a piece of chalk and a cane.'

Nellie slapped a hand on her forehead. 'Now that's what I could have bought yer for Christmas! I thought and I thought until in the end I had a splitting headache and that's why yer never got no present.'

'But we never buy each other presents at Christmas, never even discussed it 'cos we've got enough to buy for with our families.' Then Molly saw a smile lurking around her mate's mouth and knew she was having her leg pulled. But she saw a chance to turn the tables. 'I'd have been made up if yer had bought a piece of chalk and a cane for me, though, sunshine, it would have been a nice gesture.'

Nellie grinned. 'Ye're learning, girl! But considering ye're learning from a master, yer haven't half been slow at picking things up. Still, as the saying goes, better late than never! And now will yer go and see that assistant before she has a heart attack. She can see yer with a pound in yer hand, and she can't wait to take it off yer.'

When the friends stepped out of the store, the sharp wind hit them full force. 'We want our bumps feeling coming out in weather like this,' Nellie said, clinging to Molly's arm. 'Just think, we could be sitting by a roaring fire toasting our feet.'

'That's what most people must be doing, sunshine, 'cos I've never seen it so quiet in the town. The shops aren't doing much trade. Still, at least we've been able to look around without being pushed or elbowing our way through crowds.' Molly's spirits were as high as the wind, with the bag containing the material tucked under her arm. 'Let's make a run for it, and when we get to London Road the wind will be behind us and help us on our way.'

'Ye're dead happy with that material, aren't yer, girl? I can see it on yer face.'

'Well, your turn is on its way, sunshine, and in half an hour you too will be dead happy, with a parcel tucked under yer arm. And I promise yer, Nellie, that Lily will be very pleased when she sees what yer've bought. Naturally she'll want her mam to look nice on her big day.' After that pep talk, the little woman didn't need any coaxing to make a move, and in no time at all the friends were walking through the doors of TJ's again.

Nellie made a bee-line for the stairs. 'I hope they haven't sold out, girl, 'cos if they have I'll kill meself for not buying it when I had the chance.'

Walking up the stairs behind her, Molly chuckled. 'Don't yer think killing yerself would be a bit drastic, sunshine? I mean, yer don't want to miss the wedding, do yer?'

With her hand on the rail to keep herself steady, Nellie turned around. 'I wouldn't kill meself anyway, girl, and d'yer know why? I love meself too much.' With that, she turned again to climb the remaining stairs, calling over her shoulder, 'I'll love meself even more when I'm dressed up to the nines, there'll be no flies on me.' She stepped off the top stair, took a deep breath, then said, 'I might even make yer walk behind me in future, even though yer are me best mate. You know, yer've seen in the pictures how in foreign countries the rich make the poor walk behind them 'cos they treat them like dirt. And they carry whips to whip anyone who doesn't keep up with them.'

Molly shook her head. 'I don't mind you buying me a cane, sunshine, but I'm blowed if I'm going to buy you a whip. That's unless Jack decides to take me to a foreign country on his next summer holiday. Like China or Japan, are they foreign enough for yer? Or shall we make it New Brighton?'

'Ye're getting sarky again, girl, I can see it in yer eyes, they're shooting daggers. I don't know why, it was only a joke. And the one thing I've always said about yer, to everyone, is that yer can take a joke.'

Molly bent until their noses were nearly touching. 'I only hope my Jack has a sense of humour, 'cos I told him we'd be back by half-four at the latest. However, because of your desire to educate me, it's going to be nearer half-five. So shall we leave my lack of knowledge in the classroom and purchase the goods we set out to buy?'

Nellie's mouth gaped. 'Bloody hell, girl, if I had your brains I'd be laughing sacks. With your brains and my voluptuous body, I'd be as rich as . . . as rich as . . . well, I'd be as rich as Maisie and Alec from the corner shop.'

'Maisie and Alec aren't rich!' Molly never failed to be surprised at some of the things her friend came out with. 'They may have a few bob more than us, but by no stretch of the imagination are they rich.'

'Ah, well, maybe not, girl, but if Alec had your brains and Maisie had my figure, then they'd be loaded.' Nellie wagged a stiffened finger. 'Don't you go and blame me if we're not back for half-four 'cos it's you what's keeping us back and I'll tell Jack that. I know I talk as much as you but your words are longer than mine and that's what takes up the time.'

Molly couldn't help it, she burst out laughing, causing heads to turn. 'Nellie McDonough, you have got more on top than I'll ever have. Who but you could say a person talked more because she used longer words? I wouldn't have thought of that in a thousand years, sunshine, and I think it's hilarious. Just wait until I tell the family, they'll be tickled.'

'Ay, girl, will yer stop talking now, 'cos I don't want your Jack thinking it's me what's making yer late. And I don't know any of the long words yer use, so I couldn't talk meself out of it. Now, if yer don't mind, can we go and buy the material what is going to make me look like a vision in purple.'

Her tummy rumbling with laughter, Molly led her friend in the direction of the material section, and then straight to the roll of crêpe that she thought would make an ideal dress for the mother of a bride. 'Could yer unroll it for us,' she asked the assistant, 'so my friend can get a better idea if it's what she's after?'

The assistant was so eager to have a sale, she would have stood on her head if they'd asked. It had been the quietest Saturday she'd known in the five years she'd worked there and the sound of a customer's voice was like music to her ears. 'Certainly, Madam.' She turned the roll of material over several times until there were at least three yards on show. 'Isn't it a beautiful colour? It's new stock in, and heaven knows if we'll get any more.'

Nellie stroked it gently, and as she did, she fell in love with it. 'It is nice, isn't it, girl? It's a good job yer've got sharp eyes, 'cos I would never have seen it.' She nodded to the woman behind the counter. 'I'll take five yards, please, and a reel of cotton to match.'

'It is beautiful, Nellie, yer wouldn't find nicer anywhere even if yer tried every shop in Liverpool. Yer've just been very lucky. In fact we both have, 'cos I'm really made up with mine, I love it.'

'I've got you to thank for it, girl, 'cos I've got no flipping taste. I would have gone for that green satin if you hadn't stopped me.'

'This is your choice, sunshine, and that's what yer tell Lily and the family. I didn't choose it, you did, and yer deserve the praise.'

It was twenty-past four when they stepped on to the tram platform, and as they made their way down the aisle there were smiles of satisfaction on their faces. 'Give me yer parcel, Nellie, and I'll put it with mine on me knee. Then yer'll know it's safe and won't have to worry about it slipping off your knee.' Molly squashed herself in to make as much room as she could for her mate. 'It's been worth getting tossed about by the wind, don't yer think, Nellie? We've both got what we wanted and I think that's a good afternoon's work.'

'Can we do it again next week, girl, and look for our hats?'

'What! I won't have no money next week 'cos I've got to pay yer back the pound I've borrowed. And don't say I needn't give it yer back until the week after, because I couldn't live in debt like that. Yer seem to forget you've got nearly three times as much coming in the house as I have. And me mam always used to say, Never a borrower or a lender be. She was right, too!'

'Yer'll have Ruthie's money coming in next week, that should help yer out.'

'By the time I've given her money for her fare and dinners, and some for her own pleasure, then I'll be lucky if I'm five bob a week better off. Anyway, what's the rush? There's plenty of time to be looking for hats.' Molly saw her mate's mouth droop, and to cheer her up, said, 'Another couple of weeks won't hurt, and by that time Doreen might have started on our dresses. And when we do go looking for hats, we can get our shoes at the same time. And yer can put the flags out, 'cos it'll be my turn to buy the tea and scones.'

That did the trick, and when they stepped off the tram Nellie was as bright as a button and couldn't wait to get home to show off the material that was going to make her stand out at Lily's wedding. Oh, and it was Archie's wedding, too!

Chapter Twenty-Five

Rain with hailstones as big as marbles and the bitterly cold winds continued all through the month of January and kept most people indoors, except those who had work to go to, and children who went to school dressed in heavy coats, woollen hats, scarves and gloves, and housewives who scurried to the shops to buy food for their families. But the streets were deserted during the day for it was too cold to stand chatting to neighbours.

Molly and Nellie kept their promise to pick Frances up every Wednesday, but now they went by taxi which Phil insisted on and paid for. His mother would never have been able to stand up to the high winds, she didn't have the strength. She was very frail, but as Molly remarked didn't seem to have deteriorated in the last month, no doubt due to having her son back again, and her grandson. Whenever she looked at either of them she was taken back in time to when she was courting Phil's father, whom she had adored.

Frances was getting on well with Doreen and Victoria, too, and seemed to be contented in her son's home. All Molly's children had been to see her, plus Rosie and Steve, and she no longer felt out of place with them. They only ones not to have called were Bridie and Bob, and Molly had put her foot down over them coming out in the bad weather. Although it was several years since her father had suffered a heart attack, both Molly and Bridie were very protective of him. 'Tell Phil's mam that we'll be round to see her when the weather is milder, me darlin',' Bridie said. 'We're really looking forward to getting acquainted with her, so we are.'

Corker never missed a week without calling, and he could always bring a smile to Frances's face. But then no one could help but like Corker, 'cos as Bridie said, he was a broth of a man.

Then in the first week of February, the rain and wind became less fierce, although it was still very cold. But it was what Nellie had been waiting for, and she wasn't going to let the cold keep her indoors any more. Not when she had visions of herself in a very large hat which made her look like a film star.

'Can we go to town on Saturday, girl, now the weather has improved a bit?' When Molly looked like refusing, Nellie went on, 'Don't say yer haven't got the money for a hat, 'cos I know yer've been putting some away each week. And time is marching on, yer know, it's not that long to the wedding. I don't want to leave everything till the last minute.'

'There's no chance of everything being left until the last minute, not with your Lily and Archie having control of things. It would be time to worry if they weren't as organized as they are. They've got it all planned, right down to the last detail.' Molly saw the corners of her mate's mouth turn down. 'But, if it makes yer feel any happier then I'll go into town with yer on Saturday. I'll have an extra pound by then, so I might have enough to push the boat out and buy meself a pair of shoes as well as a hat.'

'Yer are better off with Ruthie working, I said yer would be.' Nellie's eyes narrowed into slits. 'How much better off are yer, girl?'

'Yer've been dying to ask that for the last two weeks, haven't yet? I could see yer were, but yer didn't know how to slip it in so I wouldn't notice.' Molly grinned. 'To satisfy yer curiosity, sunshine, I'm nearly a pound a week better off. That's more than

I expected. And what I'm telling yer is for your ears only, so no
a word to Ruthie. She draws just on two pound a week, and I
gave her two options. She could give me a pound a week, pay
her own fares, dinner money and clothes out of the other pound
Or she could give me more and I would buy her clothes for her
But although she didn't say it, my daughter thought she'd be
better off buying her own clothes and opted for giving me a
pound and keeping the other one for herself. She's very crafty is
Ruthie, 'cos she only buys a pennyworth of chips for her dinner,
and the tram fares come to one and eight for the week, which
means she's left with nearly eighteen shillings a week for herself
At her age, I was lucky to get half a crown after working a full
week. But things were different in those days, I think I only
earned seven and six a week. And praise where praise is due
because Ruthie buys me a slab of Cadbury's every Saturday on
her way home, and her dad gets five Woodbines.'

'Ah, that's nice of her, girl, I must say. At least she's not tight
with her money.'

'None of my children are tight, sunshine, and neither are
yours! We're both lucky in that respect. And with our husbands'
Yer'd go a long way to meet better men than we've got.'

'Oh, I know, girl, I tell meself that every day.' Devilmen
appeared in the narrowed eyes.

'Especially at night, when we're in bed.'

Molly put her hands flat on the table and pushed herself up
'Right, before we go into yer bedroom, sunshine, we'd better ge
down to the shops. I feel safer in the butcher's than I do in your
bedroom. And don't forget we're minding the baby for a few
hours this afternoon to give Doreen a chance to get on with our
dresses. She's cut them both out, and needs a couple of hours
peace and quiet to tack the pieces together.'

Nellie's bottom wriggled on the chair. 'Ooh, I can't wait to
see them, girl, I've never looked forward to anything so much

And your Doreen thinks the material is lovely, doesn't she?'

Molly nodded as she pushed the chair back under the table. 'She thinks it's beautiful, really classy.' And then she thought she'd make her friend more happy. 'In fact, she said she would have liked some of the material for herself. But I told her no one was to have the same as you 'cos it's going to be your big day.'

Nellie's grin was so wide it was a wonder it didn't split her face. 'Go on, tell me more, girl, me head isn't quite big enough yet.'

'Oh, it's big enough, sunshine, believe me. I very much doubt there's a hat in the whole of Liverpool that would fit your head right now.'

'What colour shall I get, d'yer think? I want it to be special, and I've told George if I have to pay three guineas for the right one, then I'll pay three guineas.'

'Don't yer mean George will pay? You'd never save three guineas, 'cos yer can't get rid of money quick enough. I'm sure it burns a hole in yer hand.'

Nothing could dampen Nellie's spirits now, she was on top of the world. 'Well, yer won't be able to nag me on Saturday when I feel like a cup of tea, 'cos it's your turn to pay. And I'll be wanting a scone to go with it.' Her short legs swinging under the chair, she grinned. 'D'yer think yer money will run to two scones, girl?'

'I think not, Nellie McDonough, 'cos I'm not going to pander to greed. And that's what it is. Yer have yer dinner before we go out so yer can't be hungry, it's just this craving yer have. All yer need is a bit of willpower to stop yerself from thinking of food.' Mollie gave the chair a final push under the table, and said, 'Can we go out now, please? And I'm in two minds whether to have meat tonight or a piece of fish for a change.' Her hand cupping her chin, she pondered for a few seconds. 'I think I'll opt for fish, and make some chips to go with it. Jack and Ruthie would like that, and it's an easy meal. So while I put me coat on, you put yer thinking cap on. Is it to be meat, or fish?'

'It'll have to be what you're having, girl, 'cos if me family smell your fish they'll ask why they aren't having the same.'

'How would they smell my fish when yer live three doors away?'

'Well, yer know how fish stinks, yer can smell if for miles.'

'Yer've got some queer notions, sunshine, it's hard to keep up with yer. But would yer mind making a move now, 'cos I want to call to Jill's to ask if she needs anything from the shops. The weather's not as bad today, but still and all I don't like her going to the shops on her own and carrying a heavy basket. She's nearly seven months pregnant, and big with it. I'll be glad when the baby's born and I won't worry so much.' Molly wrapped a warm fleecy scarf around her neck. 'So are yer game to walk up there with me, and we can have a chat to Lizzie at the same time?'

Nellie grinned. 'Yer know I'm game for anything, girl, so lead the way.'

It was Molly's turn to grin. 'Ye're also frightened of missing anything, sunshine, yer can't fool me, I've known yer too long.'

'Yeah, that's true, yer have me bang to rights there, girl. I know if I don't go with yer, I'll never find out what yer talked about, will I? Yer'd only tell me what yer wanted to tell me, I'd never hear the juicy bits.'

'I don't think there's likely to be any juicy bits from a seventy-five-year-old woman and a seven-months pregnant girl, so yer wouldn't miss much.'

'Now yer never know! I mean, the coalman could have run off with some loose woman what lives at their end of the street. And what about Elsie Flanaghan? Her backyard door faces theirs, they must see or hear her and she's always got plenty o' gossip.'

Molly shook her head. 'We haven't seen hide nor hair of Elsie since the day she called here to apologize for what she'd said about Jill and Steve. Except for the day yer wanted to tell the whole world about your Lily getting the date for her wedding, and yer wanted to tell Elsie too even though yer can't stand the sight of her. She ran away because she thought yer were going to clock her one.'

'She didn't give me a chance, did she? I told you I'd be nice to her in future, even though I can't stand the woman, and I will. But I'm not going to be polished with her, so there!'

Molly told her friend to put a move on, and soon they were walking up the street with their baskets firmly in the crook of their arms. Nellie was quiet, deep in thought. It was so unusual not to hear her mate chattering away fifteen to the dozen, Molly looked sideways and asked, 'Cat got yer tongue, sunshine?'

'I was just thinking, girl, about Jill having the baby and you being so worried about her. It didn't click right away, but have yer forgot that the baby is Steve's as well, and I've every bit as much right to worry as you have? After all, I'll be its grandma, same as you.'

'I know that, sunshine, yer don't think I've forgotten, surely? But it's Jill who's carrying the baby, and she's the one who will give birth to it, that's why I worry so much. Like you will when your Lily tells yer she's expecting her first baby. After she's married, of course.'

'Yeah, well, I'll have to wait for that, won't I? So, in the meantime, I'm going to worry with you. Every time I see a frown on yer face, I'll do my bit and put a frown on mine.'

'I would have thought you'd have enough on yer plate with the wedding, Nellie. That will be a big headache for yer, making sure all goes off smoothly.'

'Apart from getting meself all dolled up and at the church on time, there's nothing for me to do. George is wearing the suit he

417

bought new when Steve got married, Paul's seeing to himself and Lily and Archie have sorted everything out. They make a good couple, yer know, girl. They're both organized and they've paid for everything now. Even the Hanleys have been paid for the reception. I bet Edna has never been paid so far in advance in her life. She must be made up with them.'

'You should be proud of both of them, sunshine. Your Lily is a lovely girl, and yer couldn't find a better son-in-law than Archie.' Molly lifted her hand to knock on her daughter's front door. 'So count yer blessings, sunshine. Like me, ye're a very lucky woman.'

Jill looked surprised to see them. 'Well, I wasn't expecting visitors. Come in out of the cold, Mam, and you, Auntie Nellie.'

Molly let her mate go first. 'We've just called to see if ye're all right, and if yer need anything from the shops.' She grinned at Corker's mother, rocking her chair in front of a blazing fire. 'Lizzie, yer look as snug as a bug in a rug. And the weather the way it is, yer couldn't be in a better place.'

'Oh, she hasn't been there long, Mam,' Jill said, affection in her eyes for the woman who had given her and Steve a home when they got married. 'In fact, only about fifteen minutes. She was mopping the floor out before that, and putting a few things through the mangle. I wash every other day now the weather's not been fit to hang clothes on the line, and Auntie Lizzie insist she puts them through the mangle before we hang them on the ceiling rack. I keep telling her I can manage, but she will treat me like an invalid.'

Lizzie tutted. 'All the work I do in this house is harmless, Molly, I get waited on hand and foot by Jill and Steve. But don't think she should be turning that mangle in her condition. So I've put me foot down with a firm hand and I'll do the jobs think she shouldn't do. Don't yer agree I'm right, Molly?'

'I think yer should both only do what ye're capable of, Lizzie.

nd neither of yer is daft enough to overdo it. A few clothes
through the mangle won't do you any harm, but I agree it's a bit
angerous for Jill. And if it's a big wash, like heavy sheets, then
think they should be left for Steve to do when he gets home
rom work. That way, Lizzie, neither of us will be worrying
urselves sick in case Jill does herself an injury.'

Nellie wasn't going to be left out. 'And me, girl, don't forget
'll be worrying as well. Like I told yer before, I've got every
ight to worry 'cos Jill is me daughter-in-law. And she wouldn't
e in this condition if it wasn't for my son proving he was a
1an.'

Molly's eyes went to her daughter. She was expecting the
irl's pretty face to be blushing with embarrassment, but Jill was
huckling as she gazed at the chubby face of her mother-in-law,
reased now in concern. 'Good grief, you lot are worse than
teve, and heaven knows that's saying a lot. If he had his way, I'd
e stretched out on the couch with me feet up, all day and every
ay.' Again she chuckled. 'Wait until yer hear this, it's the best
ne yet. Last night he said, "I'd rather come home to conny-onny
utties than have you going out to the shops with the wind
lowing at a hundred miles an hour." '

Nellie's face was doing so many contortions, her chins
ouldn't follow her. They finally decided that when in doubt, do
owt. So they stayed where they were. 'It wasn't, was it, girl?'

'Wasn't what, Auntie Nellie?'

'The wind, girl, the wind! Wait until I tell George it was
lowing at a hundred miles an hour, he'll be flabbergasted.'

Molly's tummy was shaking, and Lizzie's chair was going
aster. 'I think the wind would be, too, sunshine!'

Nellie frowned. 'What would the wind be, too, girl?'

'Flabbergasted, sunshine, that's what.'

'Ye're not making sense, girl, why would the wind be
labbergasted?'

'When it knew it was blowing at a hundred miles an hour, so
girl.'

'Are you pulling my bleeding leg, Molly Bennett?'

'I wouldn't pull your bleeding leg, Nellie McDonough!
might put a bandage on to stop the bleeding, but I wouldn't pu
it 'cos that would make it bleed more. And I'm sure we don
want Lizzie to have to mop blood off her floor. Not when she
just got herself sitting nice and warm and comfortable.'

'For crying out loud, girl, I'll mop the bloody floor mesel
there's no need for yer to carry on, I don't need a lecture.'

'No, what yer need is a nice cup of tea, Auntie Nellie,' Ji
said, heading for the kitchen. 'It's a good excuse for me an
Auntie Lizzie to have one.'

Nellie grinned. 'That's the most sensible thing I've heard sa
since we came through that front door. And did I hear yer say y
had some biscuits as well, girl? That's what I call a goo
daughter-in-law. I'm glad I talked our Steve into marrying y
when he was two years of age.'

When there was a knock on the door, Molly got to her fee
'I'll go, sunshine. Are yer expecting anyone in particular?'

Jill's head popped around the door. 'I'm not, no, but it mig
be one of Auntie Lizzie's boyfriends. She's got a couple and the
often pop in.'

Molly was smiling when she opened the door, and the smi
widened when she saw the visitor was Doreen. 'Hello, sunshin
what are you doing out? Is everything all right?'

'I saw you and Auntie Nellie leaving the house and turnin
up instead of down, so I guessed yer'd be coming here.'

When Jill heard her sister's voice she was out of the kitche
like a shot to give her a hug. 'Oh, this is a nice surprise, where
the baby?'

'I was changing his nappy when I saw me mam and Aunt
Nellie, and after I'd put him in the pram for his afternoon slee

Aunt Vicky said she'd keep an eye on him for half an hour. It's nice to get out on me own for a while, even though I love Bobby to bits.'

'Sit down, girl, ye're making the place look untidy,' Nellie said. Then she grinned. 'I hope yer won't expect a biscuit with yer cup of tea, 'cos there mightn't be enough to go around and me and yer mam were here first. And yer know the rule: first come, first served.'

'Oh, listen to guzzle guts!' Molly pursed her lips. 'I wouldn't put it past her to steal a biscuit from a baby in a pram. Yer'll have to keep yer eye on her when Bobby's old enough to sit up in the pram sucking on a biscuit, otherwise she'll have it off him.'

Nellie's expression was one of horror. 'I will not! That's a terrible thing to say about yer best mate! I would ask the little feller to give it to me, all nice and polite, and only if he refused would I pinch it off him. And it'd be his own fault for being mean.' The chair beneath her started to creak and groan under her weight. 'If he started to scream because I'd pinched his biccy, I'd stuff half back in his mouth to shut him up.'

'How does she think these things up, Molly?' Lizzie asked. 'Anyone who didn't know her would think she was a real terror.'

'They wouldn't be far out, Lizzie,' Molly told her with a sly wink. 'She can be a nasty piece of work when she feels that way inclined. One minute she's Old Nick, the next she's Florence Nightingale, shedding sweetness and light on all around her, and giving alms to the poor and needy. All she's short of is a lantern.'

'What are you on about, Molly Bennett? How can I give arms to the poor and needy when I've only got two and I need them meself?'

'Not those sort of arms, yer silly nit! Yer've seen and heard of almshouses, where poor people go when they have no home of their own. Sometimes I think ye're having me on, 'cos no one can be as thick as you make out.'

'You'd be surprised at how far I can get by pretending to be thick, girl, you just ask my George.' A chubby hand went to her mouth. 'Oh, on second thoughts, don't ask my George or yer'l spoil things for me. Not until I've got me wedding hat anyway 'cos I've got a feeling I'm going to have a fight on me hands over that.'

'It's coming to something when a woman would diddle her own husband. And don't yer be bringing me into yer scheme Nellie McDonough, 'cos I'm not going to be yer accomplice in telling lies to obtain money under false pretences.'

It took several seconds for the implication of Molly's words to reach Nellie's brain. And then she said, 'People often tell me should be on the stage, girl, but has anyone ever told you ye should be Prime Minister? Yer'd do a good job there, baffling the whole country with bleeding science.'

Jill called from the kitchen. 'Will yer come and give me a hand with the tray, Doreen, please? A cup of tea should put a stop to our mam and Auntie Nellie coming to blows.'

Nellie chuckled. 'Never in a million years would me and me best mate come to blows, we love the bones of each other, don' we, Molly Bennett?'

'I'll agree on one condition, sunshine. That yer drink yer tea up without any more of yer tales of fantasy. We've got shopping to do, and don't forget we're babysitting this afternoon so Doreen can get some work done on our dresses.'

The colour purple came to Nellie's mind and she practically purred like a kitten. 'Oh, yes, Doreen, me and yer mam will take good care of the baby so yer don't need to worry, yer can go like the clappers on yer sewing machine.'

'I won't be using the sewing machine today, Auntie Nellie I'll be tacking the dresses together for you and me mam to try on. It's no use me sewing them and then finding out they're not a good fit. I have started on them, so I should have them ready for yer to try on in a couple of days.'

'Ooh, as early as tomorrow, did yer say? Ye're a quick worker, I'll say that for yer.'

'Oh, dear,' Molly sighed. 'The girl didn't say tomorrow, sunshine, now don't be pushing her. Yer knows we're picking Frances up tomorrow, so Doreen can't have the table littered with patterns, pins, cottons, and material when Phil's mam is there. Try to be patient, yer'll have the dress in good time for the wedding.'

Nellie's mouth drooped and Doreen felt a stab of guilt. Like all the Bennett children she loved the little fat woman who'd always been part of their lives, and who they associated with joy and laughter. 'Give me a couple of days, and I'll have them ready for yer to have a dress rehearsal. Like the posh mannequins do.'

Nellie beamed. 'Did yer hear that, Molly? We're to have a dress rehearsal like proper mannequins do. There's no flies on us, eh? My God, we'll be so proper posh there'll be no stopping us.'

Lizzie was really enjoying herself. It was always a treat when Molly and Nellie came. 'Yer won't forget yer old friends when ye're living the high life, will yer, queen? Fame goes to the head of some people and they forget where they came from.'

Molly sat back with a smile on her face as she waited for her mate to answer. It wouldn't be a quick yes or no, not from Nellie. There was bound to be a laugh in it somewhere.

'Of course I won't forget yer, Lizzie, yer should know I'm not like that.' Nellie was preening herself ready for the rest of her reply. 'If I ever see yer on the street I'll always wave to yer from the big posh car. Or it could be a carriage, yer never know.'

'So, ye're going to have driving lessons, are yer, sunshine?

Well, I pity the poor bloke who has to teach you. And I think all drivers should be warned to stay off the roads because of the danger yer present.'

'Nah, yer've got it all wrong, girl! It shows yer weren't brought up, yer were dragged up. Yer see, I wouldn't be driving the car meself, I'd have one of those fellers who sit in the front with a smart uniform on. I know who I mean, but I've forgotten what yer call them.'

'Yer mean a chauffeur, do yer, sunshine?'

'Yeah, one of them. I might even have two, one with blond hair and one dark. Just in case one makes me sick, like.'

Molly looked from Doreen to Jill. 'If yer want anything from the shops, save yer going out, will yer write it down for us? Yer might think me mate is here for the duration, but I promise we'll be out of here in fifteen minutes flat.'

'I need potatoes and a cabbage, Mam, if yer don't mind.' Doreen looked at her sister.

'Have yer got a bit of paper I can write on, Sis, 'cos I've just thought on I need bread and it's going to be too much for me mam to remember.'

Jill took a pad and pencil from the sideboard drawer and passed them to Doreen. 'I've got enough potatoes in, but if there's any chance of a sheet of ribs I'd be made up.'

'Just write it all down, sunshine, and I'll do me best.' Molly turned to where Nellie was telling Lizzie some far-fetched story about when she was a young girl, and Lizzie was lapping it up with eyes bulging, believing every word. 'I'm sorry to interrupt, sunshine, but will yer put yer coat on and we can make our way to the shops.'

'Okay, girl, I'm ready.' Nellie lumbered to her feet. 'I'll finish telling yer the tale next time I come, Lizzie.' She gave an impish grin. 'I'll have thought of another one by then, 'cos I make them up as I go along.'

'Yer make all yer tales up as yer go along, sunshine. It's hard to tell if anything yer say is truth or fiction.' Molly pointed to the door. 'Off yer go, we can't stay out too long 'cos Jill needs to steep the ribs for an hour to get the salt out before she cooks them.'

Nellie stood to attention, tummy in as far as she could get it, and bosom a yard in front of her. 'Aye, aye, boss! All present and accounted for.'

Getting a taxi was something new to Nellie, she'd only ever been in one in her life until Phil asked them to pick his mother up. So it was a novelty, and one which she wanted to show off to as many neighbours as she could. Much to Molly's amusement, Nellie would watch through the window, and would be out of the door like a shot so she could shout at the top of her voice, 'The taxi is here, girl!' And she would stand beside it, smiling to anyone passing by and watching to see how many curtains twitched. Oh, how she loved an audience. And, oh, how Doreen and Victoria laughed as they watched from across the street. She even made Molly get inside the car first so she could show off for as long as possible.

She didn't worry when they reached the Bradleys' house for Frances was always watching for them and Molly made Nellie stay in the car while she walked Phil's mam down the path. This didn't upset the little woman 'cos she didn't know anyone in the street anyway, so there was no point in swanking.

Molly helped Frances into the taxi before getting in herself. When they were settled, she asked, 'How are yer today, sunshine?'

'Not too bad, Molly. Same as usual, really. The doctor calls to see me every few weeks, and he came yesterday. He said I looked better than he was expecting, but he can't really say much more except I'm to send for him if the pain gets any worse.'

Nellie asked, 'Are yer in much pain, girl?'

'Sometimes it's worse than others. I take painkillers which help a lot, and funnily enough the pain is never as bad on days when I'm going to see me son. It's probably because I'm looking forward to it, so excited it takes me mind off it.'

'Well, Doreen and Victoria are looking forward to yer coming, and of course Phil won't be able to get home quick enough. So yer have a lot of nice things happening in yer life now, sunshine, and I always think happiness is the best medicine yer can get.'

Doreen had the door open before the taxi had stopped, a big smile on her face. 'Come on in, the kettle's on the boil.'

As she helped Frances out of the car, Molly said, 'We won't come in today, sunshine, me and Nellie have got some shopping to do.'

Nellie was puffing and panting as she tried to get out of the taxi. 'We're not going to the shops, girl, we got everything we wanted early on.'

Molly held out a hand. 'Come on, let me pull yer up.' And in a very low voice, she warned, 'Don't make a scene, sunshine, but we are not going in Doreen's today. Just for once, let them have some time on their own.'

Doreen helped Frances up the step and into the living room, then rushed back outside. 'Mam, yer can come in for a cup of tea, surely?'

'No, sunshine, yer've got enough on yer hands. Have a nice quiet afternoon, I think Frances will appreciate that.' Molly gave a little sigh. 'It's taken ages for it to sink in that she's yer mother-in-law, and yer need to get to know each other.'

'I know! I don't know what to call her, 'cos "Mrs Bradley" seems so stiff. And I can't call her Frances, that would be disrespectful.'

'Why don't yer ask her if yer can call her "Mam", sunshine? I'm sure she'd really like that and it would please Phil.'

'I'll see if I can bring up the subject this afternoon. I haven't liked to before, but as yer say, she is Phil's mam and my mother-in-law.' Doreen flung her arms around Molly. 'You're the only mam for me, I do love yer.'

'I know that, sunshine, but if those three little letters, M-A-M, make someone happy, then it won't hurt to use them. Otherwise we may well regret it later.' Molly gave her daughter a gentle push. 'Go in and see to her, sunshine, and I'll talk to yer later.'

Doreen climbed the front step and closed the door. 'Here, let me take yer coat and hang it up,' she told Frances. 'You sit by the fire and I'll make yer a hot drink before Bobby wakes up. He's only been asleep for half an hour so he won't wake for another half hour at the earliest.'

While she was in the kitchen, Doreen could hear Victoria talking to Phil's mam. 'She's a good little housewife in every way. There's nothing she can't turn her hand to. Yesterday she sat tacking together the dresses she's making for Molly and Nellie for the wedding. And she makes my dresses, which are as good as any you'd buy in the shops.'

Listening to the conversation gave Doreen food for thought. When they were sitting with a cup of tea in their hands, she said, 'You could come and see the wedding, yer know – er, yer know – oh, I can't keep calling yer Mrs Bradley, it makes us sound like strangers. What would yer like me to call yer?'

Frances blushed. She really didn't deserve to be sitting here, never mind being asked what name she would like to go by. 'I don't mind, love, whatever yer like.'

Doreen pretended to give it some thought. 'Well, I keep hearing Phil calling yer "Mam", 'cos of course that's what yer are. But would yer mind if I did, too? It would make things a lot easier.'

'Yes, I'd like that.' In fact Frances was delighted. 'As long as Molly doesn't think I'm trying to push her out.'

'Me mam wouldn't think anything of the sort, she knows no one could ever take her place. So that's settled now and I won't be stuttering over what to call yer.'

Victoria had listened with interest, and she would have bet that Molly had had a hand in this. It sounded just like her, always thinking of someone less fortunate than herself. She nodded. 'I think that's a jolly good idea. And, Frances, why don't yer call me Victoria instead of Miss Clegg? It makes me sound like a maiden aunt.'

'As we've now settled things to everyone's satisfaction, can we go back to what started it? And that is Lily and Archie's wedding. The weather will be a lot better by then, and I'm sure yer'd enjoy it 'cos it's going to be a lovely wedding from what I've heard. I believe the bride's dress is out of this world, and the bridesmaid's.'

Frances was shaking her head. The first thing that came to mind was that she might not be here in a couple of months. But she wasn't going to tell them that and make them miserable. 'I'd never make it, love, but it's nice of yer to ask, and I'm sure I would enjoy it.'

'Me and Phil would pick you up and take yer home again, and we'd sit with yer in the church. So I'm not taking no for an answer. It'll be something for yer to look forward to, and I'll make yer a dress so yer can swank with me mam and Auntie Nellie. Now, what's yer favourite colour?'

Looking into the girl's smiling face, alive with anticipation, Frances told herself it wouldn't be fair to take away that smile, it would be cruel. 'If yer insist, Doreen, I'll try and make it to the wedding, but yer don't have to make me a dress, I can buy one.'

Her eyes wide, Doreen said, 'Why, you cheeky beggar! Here's me, a fully qualified, sought-after dressmaker, offering you a masterpiece, and you say yer'd rather have a shop-bought dress! Well, I'm cut to the quick.'

Frances smiled. 'I've always liked beige or a soft green. I'll leave it to you and yer can surprise me. But let me pay for the material and cottons, I don't want you forking out for me, it wouldn't be right.'

Doreen learned forward. 'Mam number two, yer'll do as ye're told. This is going to be my treat so don't spoil it by being difficult.'

Victoria gave a sharp nod of the head. 'Quite right, too! And I'm glad yer didn't want French navy, Frances, 'cos that's what I'm having.'

Chapter Twenty-Six

It was half-past nine in the morning when Doreen knocked on her mother's window. Molly got a shock when she saw her. 'Oh, my God, something must have happened.'

'Don't panic, Mam,' Doreen said, seeing the colour had drained from her mam's face. 'I came over early so yer could organize yer day. I won't be bringing the baby over for yer to mind 'cos he's been sick after a couple of feeds and I'm not taking a chance on bringing him out in the cold.'

'I should think not! The little feller might have got a cold on his tummy, bless him. But with you still feeding him, it could be something you ate that doesn't agree with him.'

'I haven't had nothing out of the ordinary, Mam, I'm careful what I eat. I'd say he's caught a cold in his tummy when I've been changing his nappy in the bedroom. I should have more sense, 'cos as yer know the bedrooms are freezing, but I only do that when there's someone called and it's not very pleasant changing a nappy in front of them. Whatever it is, he doesn't seem bothered by it, he's not crying or anything. But I'll stay on the safe side and keep him indoors until he's stopped being sick. If it carries on, Phil said I've got to call the doctor out.'

'Yes, if ye're not satisfied by Friday, and Bobby's still being sick, yer best bet is to call the doctor out. He won't mind because, touch wood, we've never had to trouble him over the years.'

'I'd better get back because I've left him with Victoria. I'm sorry yer won't be getting the dresses to try on, but yer will explain to Auntie Nellie, won't yer?'

'The last thing yer should be worrying about is those ruddy dresses! The world isn't going to fall apart if we don't get them until the week before the wedding. So you go back and see to the baby, he's your main concern. If ye're worried about him, don't hesitate to give me a call. And if yer want any shopping, write it down and I'll knock when me and Nellie are going to the shops. Now off yer go and see to the baby.'

Molly watched until Doreen was inside her house, then she stepped back and began to close the door after herself. But before the lock clicked into place, the door was flung back, sending Molly crashing against the wall, and in rushed Nellie. She didn't see her friend flattened behind the door in her hurry to get to the living room. 'I saw Doreen come over and wondered what was going on. Where are yer, girl?'

'I'm stuck behind the front door, where yer pushed me. It's no thanks to you that every bone in me body isn't broken.'

Nellie came back out. 'What in the name of God are yer doing there, girl? Yer look as though ye're hiding from the rent man.'

As Molly pushed the door away from her, it flashed through her mind that what had just happened was like a scene from a Laurel and Hardy comedy. She would laugh about it later, but not now because her friend really could have caused her an injury. 'Nellie McDonough, in all the years I've known yer, I've never come so near to belting yer one as I am right this minute. Yer just push yer way in, regardless.'

'Well, how was I to know yer were hiding behind the bleeding door? There's not many things I can't do, but seeing through wood is one of them.'

Molly pushed the door closed, feeling more like Oliver Hardy every second. She had to stop herself from saying, 'That's another fine mess yer got me into.' In fact she would have done if she'd been wearing a tie she could fiddle with, that would have completed the picture. 'What are yer doing here this time of the morning, Nellie?'

'Like I said, girl, I saw Doreen crossing over and wondered what was up.' Nellie went to pull a chair out from the table but Molly put a hand on it and pushed it back. 'What's that for, girl? Can't I even sit down now?'

'No, yer cannot, Nellie McDonough! I've only just started on me housework. And talking of housework, can I ask when yer do yours? Nothing goes on in this street that yer don't see, so I can only presume yer spend all yer time looking through the ruddy window!'

'If we weren't meant to look out of windows, then what the hell do they put them in for? I can't help it if the clever bugger what made them put glass in. Although I've got to admit if he hadn't put glass in we'd have been bumping into furniture and be black and blue.' Nellie was eyeing the carver chair, and wasn't happy at being made to stand. 'Anyway, if I'm not welcome then I'll go home as soon as yer tell me what Doreen wanted.'

'She didn't want anything, nosy poke! She came to say the baby wasn't well and she wouldn't be bringing him over today.'

Nellie's whole body seemed to droop. 'Ah, ay, girl, does that mean we won't be having a dress rehearsal? That's rotten that, 'cos I'd set me heart on it.'

It wasn't often that Molly swore, but she did now. 'That's just too bloody bad, isn't it? Not a word about the baby not being well – all yer think about is yerself. Don't yer realize how selfish yer are?'

Nellie hung her head. 'I know I might seem selfish on the outside, girl, but I'm not selfish inside. And if yer'd tell me what's wrong with the baby then I'll do me best not to think of meself and what I want, and I'll show real, honest to goodness sympathy.'

'Listen, sunshine, when someone has to ask for sympathy then it's not worth having because it isn't sincere and doesn't come from the heart. So don't be putting on a show when I tell yer the baby's been sick a few times, 'cos I'll know it's not genuine.'

Nellie raised her eyes to the ceiling. 'If ye're listening to this, God, will yer do me a favour and take my mate's halo back? It doesn't suit her, and it must be a very tight fit 'cos she's in a real paddy this morning. She won't even let me sit down, and it wouldn't cost her nothing to let me rest me legs. I've been on the go since half-past seven, done all me housework, and I'm worn out. And to top it all, she's got the cheek to say I'm selfish! Now I ask You, is that fair and deserving of a halo?'

Molly knew she was on a loser and wondered why she bothered. She could actually feel herself weakening as she watched the chubby face gazing up at the ceiling. So she decided it would be in her own interest to give in gracefully and she pulled out a chair. 'Yer can sit for five minutes, sunshine, and then ye're leaving, even if I have to carry yer out.'

Nellie was on the chair before her mate had finished speaking. She would have preferred the carver, 'cos then she'd be in with the chance of a cuppa, but she had the sense not to push her luck. 'What's wrong with the baby, girl, is he really sick?'

Molly gave in without a fight, pulled out a chair and sat down. With the best intentions and the strongest willpower in the world, she could never hold out against her mate. 'Doreen said he's been sick after his last few feeds and she doesn't want to take a chance on bringing him out. Which I think is very sensible of her. So, we won't be minding the baby today.'

When a knock came on the door, Molly screwed her eyes up tight. 'In the name of God, who can this be now? It's as busy as Lime Street station here today.'

'D'yer want me to go, girl?'

'No, I'll go, I'll get rid of whoever it is quicker than you would. I'll chase them instead of telling them me life story.'

However, Nellie wasn't going to be left out, and she was behind Molly when she opened the door to find the landlord smiling up at her. 'Mr Henry!' Molly's first thought, like any woman's would be, was that she hadn't even combed her hair and she looked a mess. 'Ye're the last person I was expecting to see.' She chuckled. 'I'm not behind with me rent, am I?'

'Good morning, Molly!' Mr Henry, who owned most of the houses in this street and many others, turned to indicate his car which was drawn up at the kerb. 'I had to come this way so I thought I'd give you a knock rather than asking the collector for some information. I trust you, you see, Molly. Some of the collectors have friends lined up for houses when they become empty, and it's not a practice I'm in favour of.' He could see Nellie peeping around Molly's back. 'Good morning, Mrs Mac! I hope you are keeping well?'

Nellie turned sideways so she could squeeze her body in between Molly and the wall. 'I'm fine, Mr Henry, so are all me family. And you, how goes it with you?'

'Can't complain, Mrs Mac, although the years are passing by and the workload gets heavier, even though I don't collect the rents these days, as you know. It must be nearly a year since I last saw you and Molly, but neither of you seems to have changed very much. You are wearing well, I must say. Anyway, Molly, I came to ask a favour and I hope you don't mind?'

'Not at all, Mr Henry,' she said, and meant it because he was a very good landlord and looked after his properties. 'I'll be only too glad to help if I can.' She jerked her thumb over her shoulder. 'I'd ask yer in, but the place is a mess. I haven't finished tidying up yet.'

'That wouldn't worry me, Molly, not after all the years I've known you and the many cups of tea I've had off you. But I am on my way to a meeting, so I won't keep you. It's just that a house is coming empty at the top of the street, almost opposite Mrs Corkhill's, and the name I've got at the top of the list is a Mrs Higgins. Now I'm trying to make sure that this woman is not a crony of the collector's and is jumping the queue. I don't suppose you know anything about her, do you?'

Because of the close proximity of their bodies, Molly could actually feel her friend getting very excited. So she said, 'I'll leave Nellie to answer that, Mr Henry, 'cos she went to school with Mrs Higgins. Known her all her life, she has.'

Nellie was standing on the pavement within seconds, staring up at the landlord. 'Yeah, I've known Ida since we were both five years of age. And what's more important, my daughter Lily is marrying her son Archie at Easter! So how's that for coincidence, Mr Henry? And I'll tell yer what, yer wouldn't get a better tenant than Ida, she's a smasher.' She glanced up at Molly. 'Ay, girl, she won't half get a shock, won't she? It must be eighteen months, even more, since she put her name down.'

'She'll be made up,' Molly said, before asking the landlord, 'Which house is it, Mr Henry, who's leaving?'

'The Cotterells. I've got to admit I don't know them, but they've lived there for about eight years. They're moving to a three-bedroomed house because the family is growing bigger. Five children, I believe, and most of them in their early-teens.'

'She's a nice woman is Sally Cotterell, and her children are a credit to her. But I've known for a long time she was at her wits' end trying to cope with a large family in a small house. She'll be missed 'cos she's a good neighbour.'

'Well, if you would like to give your friend the good news, you may do so. Or would you prefer I write to her?'

435

Nellie was having none of that. She wanted to know what was going on before Ida did, old school friend or no old school friend. 'No, I'd like to tell her, I want to see her face when I give her the news. She'll be over the moon, Mr Henry. Won't she, girl?'

Molly nodded. 'She will that, I think she'd given up hope. When are the Cotterells moving out, Mr Henry, so we can tell Ida? Me and Nellie can make it our business to see her some time this afternoon.'

'They've paid their rent up to next Monday so they'll have to be out of the house by twelve o'clock. Mind you, seeing as they've been such good tenants we wouldn't keep them to that. Now, according to the collector, the house is clean but in bad decorative order. It would need decorating right through. So before she agrees and signs the tenancy agreement, Mrs Higgins can look the place over. If she calls to the office on Monday, after one o'clock, I'll have a set of keys ready for her. If she finds she is no longer interested in taking the tenancy, then she can return the keys the same day. If she decides to take it, you know the rules, Molly, she'll need to sign an agreement and pay the rent a week in advance.'

'I'll explain everything to her, Mr Henry, so there's no problem. I'm sure the state of the house won't put her off, as long as it's not dirty. Archie and all the men in our two families will get stuck in and help with decorating. And I promise, if she does take it, she'll be the perfect tenant.'

'I'll leave it in your capable hands then. Apart from being pleased that you know and recommend the new tenant, so I have no worries on that score, it has been a real pleasure to see you and Nellie again. And both of you looking so well.'

'I'm a grandmother now,' Molly said with pride. 'My daughter Doreen had a baby a few months ago, a boy. And I know Nellie is dying to tell yer that my Jill and her Steve are expecting a happy event in about two months. So Mrs Cotterell isn't the only one with a growing family.'

'Your Jill and Steve married! Good grief, it doesn't seem that long since they were just old enough to go courting! I always thought they made an attractive couple, with Jill so pretty and Steve with the looks of a film star.' He sighed. 'Ah, listening to this is making me feel very old and reminds me of how quickly the years go by.'

'Nonsense, Mr Henry! As my ma would say, "It's a foine figure of a man yer are, and that's the truth of it." '

'I'm not even going to ask how Bridie and Bob are or I'll be very late for my meeting. But give them my regards and tell them I'll knock on their door one of these days and surprise them.' He backed towards his car. 'Tell Mrs Higgins I'll see her on Monday afternoon.'

Nellie thought she'd been left out long enough. 'We might see yer as well, Mr Henry, if Ida wants us to come with her.'

The two friends waited until he'd started his car up and pulled away. Then they waved to him before going back inside the house.

'Ay, fancy that, girl!' Nellie was over the moon now she had a little excitement in her life. 'Ida will be thrilled to bits. Can we go and tell her when we've finished our housework?'

'I thought yer said yer'd done all yer housework?'

Nellie had the grace to blush. 'Yer know me, girl, it's a duster in me hand, a flick of me wrist, and hey presto, housework done. It's only when the dust meets me at the door that I think about giving everywhere a good going over. I can be ready in half an hour, if that's not too soon for yer, and we can get the tram to Ida's.'

Molly cast her eyes around the room. The trouble with her was, she looked for dust while her mate didn't. And if she didn't dust for one day, Jack wouldn't even notice. 'Half an hour's fine, sunshine, I'll be ready for then.' She leaned forward and looked into Nellie's eyes. 'Ye're made up now yer've got something to do, aren't yet?'

The chubby face creased. 'Yer could say that, girl, yes, yer could safely say that. I hate it when there's nothing going on. I get bored, yer see, that's why I spend more time in this house than I do in me own. George said I should take up a hobby, like knitting or embroidery, but I told him to sod off. If he had his way, I'd sit in the house all day with a knitted shawl over me shoulders going ga-ga and counting the roses on the wallpaper.'

'Nellie, yer don't have any roses on yer wallpaper.'

'There would be if I had to sit in the house all day, I'd go soft in the head.' She lumbered to her feet. 'I'll be back in half an hour, girl, then we'll knock at Doreen's to see how the little feller is before we go anywhere.'

Ida Higgins was just closing the door behind her when she heard her name being called. Surprise written all over her face, she said, 'Well, this is a turn-up, ye're the last people I expected to see. What brings yer to this part of the world?'

'Blimey, girl, anyone would think we lived in Australia to hear you talk. We only live five bleeding tram stops away.' Nellie squared her shoulders and hitched up her bosom. 'My mate and me come bearing good tidings, Mrs Higgins. So I suggest yer open yer door again and let us in. For the news yer are about to receive is worth at least a cup of tea and a biscuit.'

'Take no notice of her, Ida,' Molly said. 'If yer were off somewhere, we'll walk to the main road with yer and tell yer the news on the way.'

'No, yer've got me curious now.' Ida put the key back in the lock and threw the door open. 'I was going to me sister's – yer know, the one I told yer about who doesn't keep good health. I go for an hour every couple of days to do her ironing. But I can go tomorrow, she's not expecting me so there's no harm done.'

Ida's house was like a little palace. Every surface was shining and there wasn't a thing out of place. And she seemed to do everything at the double. She put the kettle on before taking their coats, and within five minutes was coming from the kitchen carrying a tray set with three cups of steaming tea and a plateful of biscuits. When they were seated around the table, she asked, 'Right, now let's have the glad tidings.'

Molly sat back and watched the contortions of Nellie's face as she tried to add drama to what she had to say. 'There's a house coming empty in our street and Mr Henry, the landlord, says it's yours if yer want it.'

Ida put a hand to her open mouth. 'D'yer know, I'd given up thinking about that 'cos it's been so long. I'd given up hope.' She looked to Molly. 'Is it true?'

Nellie got on her high horse. 'What are yer asking me mate if it's true for? D'yer think I'm a liar or something?'

Ida grinned. 'Yer forget I sat next to yer in school for nine years, queen, and it was common knowledge that yer were the best liar in the school. So knowing your weakness for playing jokes on people, isn't it only natural I'd need a second opinion on anything yer said?'

'It is true, Ida, and Nellie didn't half sing yer praises to the landlord,' Molly confirmed. 'He was so impressed with what she told him, he said yer can have the keys on Monday afternoon to look it over, and if yer like it, the house is yours.'

'I take everything back, Nellie.' Ida left her chair to cup the chubby face and plant a kiss on it. 'I'll never again mention yer being the biggest liar in the school, or the number of times I got the cane for something you'd done.'

'Hang on, Ida,' Molly said. 'I don't want to put a damper on things, but Mr Henry did say that although the house was clean, it would need decorating throughout. I'm only telling yer this in case it puts yer off, and to let yer know yer'd have plenty of helpers to decorate. At least six strapping young lads, and three not so young but very capable.'

'Ooh, I've gone all excited. Whereabouts is the house, is it near you two?'

Molly shook her head. 'Yer know where Mrs Corkhill lives, at the top end? Well, the house that's coming empty is right opposite. They're a nice family there now, been there for years, but as the kids have grown up, the house has become too small.'

'Will you two come with me on Monday, to pick up the keys and look over the house? I'm in no doubt I'll take it because I know most of your families by now and I wouldn't feel like a stranger. And if the house needs work doing on it, it'll be a case of rolling me sleeves up and getting stuck in. Wait until Archie knows, he'll be over the moon.'

'Hope yer don't think I'm being nosy, Ida,' Molly said, 'but will him and Lily live with yer when they get married?'

'I hope so, Molly, but it's not for me to say what they'll do. I don't want them to think I'm pushing them into anything. Lily might get the impression I'm going to be an interfering mother-in-law, and I don't want that. I'll wait and see what Archie has to say when he's seen the house and talked it over with her.' Ida met Nellie's eye. 'I hope yer don't try and persuade them one way or the other, queen, I'd rather let them decide for themselves.'

Nellie pursed her lips as she nodded. 'I'll keep quiet, girl, and let them make up their own minds. But I can't see them objecting, 'cos they'll have to have somewhere to live when they get married, and I know for a fact that our Lily doesn't want to move far away from her family and friends because she told me so.'

'Let's talk about the wedding, eh?' Molly knew her mate would sit here all day talking on the same subject if she was let. 'Have yer got yer dress sorted out, Ida? Me and Nellie have, and we're going into town on Saturday to choose our hats.'

Ida nodded. 'I saw a dress in a shop window and fell for it. So I've put a deposit down, and I'm picking it up next week. It's in a nice shade of blue, and I think I'll do my son proud. But I haven't thought about a hat or shoes yet.'

'Come to town on Saturday with us, girl.' In her excitement, Nellie's bottom was polishing the seat of the chair. 'We might all get fixed up.'

Ida did some quick thinking. The lady in the dress shop wouldn't mind if she left the dress for another week, so she could use that money to buy a hat. 'I'd like that. It would be nice to have someone there to give a second opinion.'

Nellie was in her element. 'I'm going to buy one that stands out, being the mother of the bride, like.'

'Well, I'm not going to be upstaged by you, queen, seeing as I'm the mother of the groom. I can't let the side down.'

Molly leaned across to put her cup and saucer on the tray. 'Well, let's say we meet outside TJ's at half-one on Saturday, eh? Three smart girls go shopping.'

'I'll look forward to it,' Ida said. 'I don't get out very much, only to the flicks now and again.'

'D'yer still want to go to yer sister's today?' Molly asked. 'If yer do, we can leave together 'cos we get the same tram. Except we have three more stops when you get off. I'd like to make tracks, 'cos our Doreen's baby wasn't well this morning, and I'm not really settled with thinking about it. He's probably as right as rain, but when ye're a grandma ye're inclined to worry more.' She touched Nellie's arm. 'Yer'll know what I'm talking about in a few months, sunshine, when you become one.'

'In that case I'll be spending more time in your house so we can sit and worry together. When you sigh, I'll sigh, and when you cry, I'll bawl me eyes out.'

'Heaven forbid,' Molly said, pushing her chair back and standing up. 'Don't yer think I see enough of yer as it is? And

441

don't sit there thinking of something to say that'll hold us back, 'cos Ida wants to go to her sister's to help with her ironing, and I want to get home to see how Bobby is. So get yer backside off that chair and let's move.'

Ida grinned as she straightened the chairs under the table. These two were the main reason she'd wanted to rent a house in their street. You certainly would never be bored in their company. 'Come on, girls, the Three Musketeers ride again. One for all, and all for one.'

They were three happy women walking towards the tram stop. Ida would soon be joining their clique and would be a very welcome member.

'I'll come over with yer and see how the baby is,' Nellie said. 'And don't be looking at me like that, I'll be as good as gold. If Doreen doesn't feel in the mood for visitors, then I'll leave quietly, yer won't have to drag me out.'

But when Doreen opened the door she didn't have the worried look she was wearing when she'd knocked on her mother's window. 'He's kept the last two feeds down, Mam, and it's not half a relief.' She held the door wide. 'Come in and tell me what Mr Henry was doing knocking on your door so early in the morning?'

'It was with good news, sunshine.' Molly followed her daughter into the living room with Nellie close behind. When she saw the baby lying on the couch, gurgling and kicking, she made straight for him. The news could wait until she'd made sure her grandson was okay. But she was reckoning without Nellie.

'Guess what, Victoria? And you, Doreen? Yer'll never guess in a million years what the landlord came for.'

'Ye're not going to make us guess, are yer, Auntie Nellie?'

Molly tutted. 'Yer could at least come and see how the baby is before playing guessing games, Nellie McDonough. Yer can't wait to be the first with the news, can yer?'

It was Nellie's turn to tut. 'I looked at the baby as soon as I walked in the room, and there's nowt wrong with him, he's the picture of health.' She pulled a face at Doreen. 'Your mam thinks I'm greedy and selfish, and I know I am, but she doesn't need to keep rubbing it in.'

Victoria had a hand over her mouth. It wasn't often you heard someone admit they were selfish and greedy. Then again, it wasn't often you came across someone like Nellie. 'Me and Doreen are filled with curiosity and eager to hear what your news is.'

Molly stroked the baby's cheek before moving from the side of the couch to pull a chair out and sit down. 'I'm filled with curiosity meself so fire away, sunshine, in case I missed something Mr Henry said.'

Nellie glared at her mate for being sarky, but decided to let it pass because the news she was about to deliver was more important. 'The Cotterells, what live at the top end of the street, well, they're leaving and Mr Henry has offered their house to Archie's mam, Ida. He called to ask me and Molly for advice, and we said Ida would make a fantastic tenant. So on our recommendation he said she could pick the keys up on Monday afternoon so she could give the house the once over before signing a tenancy agreement.'

'Ooh, isn't that marvellous! That means Lily and Archie living just up the street!'

'Hold fire a bit, sunshine, we don't know that yet. Mrs Higgins put her name down for a house in this street nearly two years ago. Long before Archie and Lily started courting seriously. They may have other ideas, so the least said the better.'

'I'll make yer a drink, Mam.' Doreen jumped to her feet. 'And I've got some cheese in if yer feel like a sandwich.'

Molly waved for her to sit down. 'We had a drink in Ida's,

sunshine, and I'm not staying, anyway. I haven't done a hand's turn in the house, and I've got to think of what we're having for our meal tonight. I was up at the usual time of seven o'clock, made yer dad's and Ruthie's breakfast and saw them off to work. Then I had a bite to eat meself, cleared the table and washed the dishes, and that's all I've done all day! Half of the day is gone and I've done Sweet Fanny Adams.'

'Well, relax for a while and have a drink, Molly,' Victoria coaxed. 'Half an hour is neither here nor there.'

But Molly wasn't to be coaxed. 'No, I won't stay, I'll walk up and see how Jill is and have a drink with her and Lizzie. I see a lot more of you, Doreen, with yer living opposite, and I sometimes think Jill may feel I'm leaving her out.'

Nellie, her face serious for once, said, 'I'll walk up with yer, girl, and yer can link my arm and lean yer weight on me.'

Gazing at the chubby face, Molly asked herself why she'd been short with her mate all morning. She'd jumped down her throat at the least thing. And while all this was running through her mind, Molly suddenly realized why she'd had this tight band around her head for the last few hours. It had been caused by the shock of Doreen knocking on her window and sending her heart into her mouth as she thought something awful must have happened, and poor Nellie had been at the receiving end of her temper all this time. 'We'll do that, sunshine, and I'll leave everything else until I get back. And I'll take yer up on the offer of allowing me to link you so yer can take some of the weight off me feet. Ye're a good mate, Nellie.'

She beamed. 'Come on then, girl, let's go. Now yer know the baby's all right, yer don't have to worry no more.'

Doreen went to the front door with them, and stepped down on to the bottom step and watched as they walked up the street arm in arm. What her mam and Auntie Nellie had was true friendship. How lucky they were to have each other.

* * *

'Fancy the Cotterells leaving!' Lizzie really was surprised. 'I don't think she's let on to any of the neighbours otherwise we'd have known by now.'

'I'm not surprised, though, Mam,' Jill said, 'because I don't know how they manage. The four lads are big, especially the two eldest, they're as big as grown men. It must be a tight squeeze, and now the two eldest are working, Mrs Cotterell must have a few bob extra coming in and can afford a bigger place. Good luck to her.'

Nellie nodded her head so vigorously her chins did a tango. 'It's good luck to Archie's mam, she's waited long enough to get a house in this road.' Nellie kept trying to catch Jill's eye, and when she couldn't, she had to ask, 'Ay, girl, will yer make yer mam a cup of tea? She's had a rotten morning. Yer know she's like a mother hen with the family. Well, when Doreen knocked this morning to say the baby was sick, yer mam thought the worst like she always does and it upset her for the day.'

'But Bobby's all right, isn't he?' Jill's pretty face showed concern. 'He's stopped being sick, hasn't he?'

Nellie didn't give Molly a chance to answer. 'Ah, yes, he's all right now, but the damage had been done and yer mam's been worrying herself to death.'

'I'll put the kettle on, sweetheart,' Lizzie said. 'You stay where yer are and talk to yer mam. I won't miss anything, I can hear what's going on from the kitchen.'

Molly sat back thinking if she stayed quiet her head would clear. 'Nellie, I'll let you fill them in with the day's news. And don't forget to say that if Ida does take the house, it'll be all hands to the pumps to help her decorate.'

'Oh, I won't forget that, girl, 'cos Jill will have to warn Steve that we'll be calling on all able-bodied men to give a hand.' Half of Nellie's bottom left the chair as she leaned forward to shout through to the kitchen, 'Lizzie, you'll have a good view of all that goes on if yer move yer chair in front of the window. Yer can be supervisor and tell us if any of the men aren't pulling their weight. Apart from telling them off, we'll dock their wages.'

Lizzie poked her head around the door. 'Oh, if it's paid work, I might apply for a job there meself. I'd be good in the canteen.'

'Sorry, girl, but it's charity work, done through the goodness of their hearts. They'll be getting paid in cups of tea. And that'll be down to me and Molly to keep them going in plenty of drinks.'

Jill was watching her mother, wondering why she was so quiet and looked tired. 'Are yer all right, Mam? Yer look fed up with the world.'

'No, I'm fine, sunshine, yer don't have to worry about me. It's me who should be asking how you are?'

'Getting bigger by the day.' Jill patted her tummy. 'I'll be glad when it's all over and I can lie in bed without being uncomfortable. But apart from that I'm great, Mam, I really am. Eating like a horse, everything that's on me plate.'

'That's what I want to hear, sunshine, and being uncomfortable in bed won't last forever. Yer'll forget the unpleasant things as soon as they put the baby in yer arms. And I promise yer it will all have been worth it.'

Nellie nodded in agreement before going back to the day's events. 'Lizzie, did I tell yer we're meeting Ida on Saturday to go shopping for our wedding hats?'

Molly smiled at Jill. 'It doesn't take much to please my mate and your mother-in-law.'

Chapter Twenty-Seven

When Tommy called in with his dad that night, and Molly told him about the house being offered to Archie's mam, his face lit up. 'Oh, that would be the gear if she takes it. Imagine me best mate living a few minutes' walk away. I'd see more of him than I do now.'

'Aye, well, yer can't expect to see much of him when he's courting, can yer? Besides, son, I'll tell yer what I've told everybody, and that's not to take it for granted that Archie and Lily will be living with his mam after they're married. It's not a foregone conclusion, and I don't think it should be mentioned in front of them.'

Tommy put his arms around her and rocked from side to side. 'I was going to say I'd have a bet with yer, but seeing as ye're the best mother in the whole universe, and I love the bones of yer, I wouldn't cheat on yer. Yer see, Mam, Archie told me once that he would never leave his mother. That his home would always be her home, as she had brought him up single-handed when his dad died, and when times were hard often went without to give to him. And believe me, Mam, Archie doesn't say things he doesn't mean.' He released her and looked down into her face. 'That is strictly between you, me and me dad. I wouldn't want it repeated to Lily.'

'I'll not be shouting it from the housetops, sunshine, yer should know me better than that. Whatever they decide is their own business and they are entitled to choose where they live. Ida would be the last one to stand in her son's way, she idolizes him. She's made up to be getting the house, but I certainly don't think she's taking it for granted that Archie and Lily will be making their home with her.'

'Least said, soonest mended,' Jack said. 'They wouldn't thank anyone for interfering. And as I hear Ruthie shouting goodbye to Bella, I suggest yer drop the subject before she comes in. She is the one person who would see no wrong in repeating anything she hears.'

Tommy grinned when his sister dashed in, cheeks pink from running into the wind. 'Here comes the worker, I'd better go so she's not kept waiting for her dinner.' He ruffled his sister's hair. 'How's it going, Sis? Still enjoying the work, are yer?'

Ruthie gave this some thought before coming out with what her brother decided was a very clever answer. 'I can't say I love the work, Tommy, but I do love being grown-up. And as I can't be one without the other, then I'll stick with it until a rich man comes along who will be able to give me the good things in life.' Then as an after-thought she added, 'Which is only what I deserve.'

'Let's hope he won't be as big-headed as you, our kid, or yer'll never find a house to fit both of yer. Unless, of course, yer have designs on a palace.'

His sister chuckled. 'If I ever get that lucky, Tommy, I won't forget yer. I'll giver yer a job as a footman or a butler, whichever yer want.'

'I think right now his thoughts are more on his dinner, sunshine, so don't keep him talking or Rosie will be waiting for him with the rolling pin,' Molly chuckled. 'Whether it's a palace or Rosie, one way or the other he'll get crowned.'

Jack thought that was really funny and he had a smile on his face as he said goodbye to his son, washed his hands and sat down for his meal. 'You sound in a good mood, love, have yer had a good day?'

Molly's eyes went to the ceiling. Where to begin? 'It's been a very mixed day, so I'd better start at the beginning.'

They were having an easy meal because Molly wasn't in the mood for going to the shops after she and Nellie came away from Jill's. So it was egg and chips with baked beans in tomato sauce out of a tin. And because she felt guilty putting this down in front of a man who'd done a hard day's graft, it was with relief that she saw her husband and daughter tucking in with gusto. After spearing a chip on the end of her fork, Molly began the saga of the day's events.

'You have had a busy day, love,' Jack said. 'It got off to a bad start with Doreen knocking on the window, yer must have got a fright.'

'Yer can say that again, sunshine, I got the fright of me life. In fact I think I was in shock until me and Nellie walked up to Jill's and I sat down and relaxed. I sat back with a cup of tea and let Nellie do all the talking.'

'Baby all right now, is he?'

Molly nodded. 'He was kicking away and really enjoying himself, talking fifteen to the dozen in baby talk. He's a little love, he really is, I could eat him.'

Ruthie had made herself a chip butty and was dipping it into the yolk of the egg when she asked, 'Is our Jill all right, Mam? I haven't seen her for days 'cos yer won't let me and Bella go up there. I understand, like, 'cos she won't feel like a lot of visitors, but I want her to know I haven't forgotten her.'

'She wouldn't think that, sunshine, I'm always telling her yer ask about her. And she never forgets to ask about you. She's keeping well and looks as pretty as a picture.'

Ruthie swallowed the last of the sandwich and ran the back of a hand across her mouth. 'Our Jill really is pretty, isn't she?'

'Ay, are you fishing for compliments?' Jack asked. 'Seeing as you and Doreen are the spitting image of her.'

'I didn't mean it like that, Dad. Our Jill is different in her manner to me and our Doreen. She's more gentle and doesn't have a big mouth like me and Doreen. Yer never hear her shouting or arguing.'

'Then you should have one ambition in life, sunshine, and that's to be more like yer big sister. In fact, yer two big sisters, because our Doreen is a million miles away from the forward girl she was before Phil came on the scene. She has certainly opened my eyes. She's a perfect wife and mother, and the way she looks after Victoria is a credit to her. I never thought I'd see the day when she would be as calm and patient as she is now. I was going to say I'm proud of her, which I am of course, but then I'm proud of all my children. Never brought me a moment's grief, any of them. And that includes you, sunshine.'

A slow smile spread over the girl's face. 'I've only just joined the grown-ups so I haven't had time to make anything of meself. But yer will be proud of me one day, when I'm settled in that palace I mentioned before. I'll make sure yer have servants to wait on yer hand and foot, and I'll have a tiara specially made to fit yer.'

There was affection for her youngest child in Molly's eyes. 'I don't want one with diamonds in, sunshine, I'd prefer rubies, to match me eyes.' She began to collect the empty plates. 'Start as yer mean to go on, sweetheart, and help yer old mother with the dishes.'

The table was cleared in record time and the dishes put away. 'Thank you, sunshine, that was a big help, and now I'm going to be lazy and sit on the couch with me feet up.'

Jack's head appeared over the evening paper. 'You do that, love, and we'll have an early night. Yer know what they say about an hour's sleep before midnight being worth more than two after.'

'What time are yer going to bed then?' Ruthie was draping her coat over her shoulders for the short run to her friend's house. 'D'yer think perhaps I should take the front door key with me, just in case?'

'I wouldn't be going to bed if you weren't in, sunshine, I'd never close me eyes with worry. Yer might be older in the head, but ye're fourteen years of age, far too young to be staying out until all hours. Me and yer dad will wait up for yer, but you make sure, me lady, that it's no later than ten o'clock or I'll need matchsticks to keep me eyes open.'

The girl wasn't going to argue with that, she saw it as further evidence of her growing up. It seemed only weeks ago the time limit was nine o'clock.

'Okay, Mam, I'll be home by ten, I promise.'

Molly kicked her shoes off then slid her legs on to the couch. 'D'yer know, love, me feet are practically talking to me. I think I might soak them in warm water later, but I'll rest them for half an hour first.' She heard Ruthie opening the front door, then her voice saying, 'Hello, Archie! Ay, yer didn't half give me a fright.'

'Sorry about that, love, I should have coughed or whistled. And I would have done, but I got as big a shock as you did. Is yer mam in?'

Molly was off the couch like a shot from a gun, and was squeezing her feet into her shoes when Archie walked in. 'Yer'll have to excuse the state of me, sunshine, but I wasn't expecting any visitors.'

Archie's handsome face was trying to keep a smile back, but it lost the battle when he saw one of her feet being stubborn and refusing to go back into the shoe. 'Leave it, Mrs B, yer don't have to worry about me. In any case, that foot is determined to stay free so I wouldn't bother. I'm sorry to be disturbing yer, but Ruthie said it was all right to come in.'

451

'Of course it's all right, lad,' Jack said, folding his paper away 'Ye're welcome here any time, so take a seat.'

'No, I won't sit, I'm on me way to pick Lily up. And yer know what women are, they hate to be kept waiting. I've known her to sulk for a good five minutes when I've not arrived on the dot. So I won't stay, I just called to say how delighted I am about me mam getting that house. She's thrilled to bits, and apparently it was down to you and Nellie giving the landlord a glowing reference for her.'

Molly chuckled as she remembered Nellie pulling it on to Ida, about how they'd fought for her. 'We did put in a word for her, of course we did, why shouldn't we? She's your mam and a mate of ours. But yer know what Nellie's like for exaggerating.'

'Well, yer've certainly made her happy, and me, too! I'm taking Monday afternoon off to have a look at the house with her. And I'm almost as excited as she is, I can't wait.'

'Did she tell yer it needs decorating right through? It hasn't put her off, now she's had time to think it over?'

'Good Lord, no! That would be the least of our worries. Both me and me mam are good at decorating. After me dad died, she did everything in the house that a man does, until I was old enough to do it for her.'

Molly was dying to ask if he and Lily would be living with his mam, but thought it would sound nosy. And she'd be doing what she'd told everyone else not to do. 'Me and Nellie are looking forward to her being a neighbour, we all get on well together.'

'Yeah, so she told me. I believe she's meeting yer in town on Saturday to go shopping for hats for the wedding. I'm glad about that because she doesn't have many friends that she can go out with, they've all got husbands and families to look after.' Archie glanced at the clock. 'I'd better make a move, I'm ten minutes late as it is.' He grinned, showing a set of perfect white teeth 'Anyone would think I was under her thumb, wouldn't they? It' not like that, we get on fine and no one is the boss.'

'You'd better get cracking then, sunshine, and remember yer've got to go through it all again with Lily's mam. She'll talk the ear off yer if yer let her. She was so excited anyone would think it was her getting a new house.'

'Oh, I can take a lot of Mrs Mac,' Archie said. 'I think I'm dead lucky to be having her for a mother-in-law, we get on great. Anyway, thanks again, Mrs B. I know yer had a hand in all this and I'm very grateful.'

'Ye're welcome, Archie, and if yer mam likes the house everyone will get stuck in and help. She won't be left to do it alone. So poppy off and enjoy the rest of the night.'

'Come on, sunshine, Ida's standing outside the shop.' Molly cupped Nellie's elbow and steered her quickly across the busy road. 'Have yer been waiting long, Ida? Yer must have been early because it's not quite half-one yet.'

'Not long, queen, I was on the tram before yours. But I'll tell yer what, it's not half cold standing here, I'm like a block of ice.'

'Yer'll be all right when we get inside, there's a lovely warm draught as soon as yer go through the door. Last time we came Nellie wanted to stand there until she thawed out. And yer should have seen the look of bliss on her face.'

Nellie's grin told Molly she wouldn't like what was coming. 'Yeah, it was like the look I get on me face in bed on certain nights. And it is bliss, pure bleeding bliss.'

'Let's get inside, Ida, because as long as we stand here, she'll keep on talking about the antics she gets up to in her bedroom. She doesn't feel the cold like we do, she's got plenty of fat to keep her warm.'

Nellie was first through the door of the store, and they had to push her out of the way so they could get in. 'Can yer feel that, Ida? Ooh, it's going right up me legs.'

'Yeah, it is nice and warm in here, queen, it won't be long before I'm thawed out.'

Molly tugged on her mate's arm. 'Come on, let's move, we haven't got all day. I want to be back in time to make the tea, and I also want to walk through me front door with a hat bag in me hand and a broad smile on me face.'

'Would yer like to go for a cup of tea and a cake first?' Ida asked. 'Archie gave me the money to treat yer.'

The look on Nellie's face when she glared at Molly would have been impossible to describe. 'Well, you jammy bugger! It was your turn to fork out for our snack and ye're getting away with it! If yer fell down the lavvy, girl, yer'd come up with a bleeding gold watch.' Her face screwed up, she added, 'And I bet the bleeding thing would still be ticking.'

'What are yer talking about, Nellie?' Ida looked puzzled. 'Archie wants to pay, so why not let him? He'd be upset if I gave him the money back and said yer didn't want to have a cup of tea and a cake on him.'

'Give him the money back! Blimey, ye're as bad as Molly for being daft. Yer never give a man money back, that's fatal, that is, 'cos he'd never give yer any more.' Nellie shook her head as though she couldn't believe anyone would be soft enough to give money back. 'No, it's not Archie I'm on about, it's bugger lugs here. Yer see, I paid last time, so it's her turn today. That's the only fair way.'

Ida wasn't really used to Nellie's ways, and she walked right into it. 'What difference does it make to you, queen, as long as ye're getting tea and a cake and it's not going to cost yer anything? Why worry about who's paying?'

Molly hadn't said a word. She thought it was really funny but managed to keep her face straight. 'Nellie, if yer keep us standing here much longer they'll have sold out of hats by the time we get to the millinery department and we'll end up buying three berets.'

And I'll tell yer this for nothing, I look terrible in a beret and so would you. So to put yer in a happy frame of mind, we'll go down to the cafe now and Ida can pay for what we have with Archie's money. Then, when we've finished shopping, hopefully having bought three hats that any film star would be glad of, we'll go back down to the cafe and I'll pay for what we have. Does that improve yer temper at all?' She jerked her head upwards and tutted. 'With the face on yer now yer'll never get a hat to suit yer, they'll take one look at that sour expression and run a mile.'

As though a magic wand had been waved over her, Nellie's face became the picture of innocence. 'Ah, that's nice of yer, girl.' She turned her gaze to Ida. 'Haven't I been singing me mate's praises to yer? Well, yer can see it for yerself now, yer don't have to take my word for it.'

'Listen, queen, I can still remember our school days. I couldn't believe a word yer said then, and yer haven't changed one bit.'

Nellie beamed. 'Ah, ye're both being so nice to me, paying me compliments. I'm lucky to have not only one, but two such good friends. And now we've sorted all that out, let's get down to the cafe 'cos I'm parched. And I don't give a bugger who pays for it, I'll still enjoy it.'

'You find a table and I'll get the tea,' Ida said. 'D'yer want a cake or a scone with jam?'

'I'll have what you're having,' Molly told her. 'It's not long since I had me dinner, so I'll be quite happy with a cup of tea for now.'

'Yer'll have a scone and like it, queen, even if it's only to make our Archie happy.' Ida turned to Nellie. 'And what about you, queen?'

'I'll just have a scone, same as you.' Nellie could have eaten two scones, but she didn't want to appear greedy. Besides, she'd be getting another one soon when it was Molly's turn to pay. And being in a cafe, she put on her best accent. 'I'll have raspberry jam if yer don't mind, girl, or strawberry. Not marmalade, though, I can't stand that.'

'I'll give yer a hand,' Molly offered, 'it's a lot to carry on yer own.'

'There's a queue, queen, and not much point in both of us standing in it. When I'm served I'll give yer the wire and yer can come and help.'

Nellie was in her element gazing at the people on the tables nearby. And she brought a blush to Molly's face when she said rather loudly, 'I hope you've brought a piece of the material my dress is being made of? I must have it so I can look for a hat that will go with the colour. As mother of the bride, everything must be perfect on the day.'

'I didn't forget, sunshine, it's in my bag.'

'Will yer get it out, please, so I can have a look?'

Oh, no, Molly thought, not on your life! That piece of material would be taken to all of the tables near them and shown off as though no one had ever seen, or had, such quality before. 'No, I'll leave it where it is, I've got to keep my eye on Ida, so when she wants me I can give her a hand.'

Nellie was laughing so much inside she had to press a hand to her tummy to keep it from shaking. 'Ah, yes, Ida, our very new friend and soon-to-be neighbour. What a delightful woman she is, so kind and generous.'

Molly could see heads turning, because Nellie didn't speak quietly. And heaven alone knew what she'd come out with next because it was plain she was enjoying her funny half-hour. So Molly put her bag on the table and stood up. 'Keep yer eye on that, sunshine, while I go and give Ida a hand with the tray. And because all the money I've got in the world is in that bag, don't take yer eyes off it for a second.'

When Molly came back with Ida a few minutes later

Nellie was sitting like a statue with her eyes fixed on the handbag. 'Can I take me eyes off it now, girl, 'cos they're beginning to ache?'

After the tray had been set down, Molly asked, 'I hope yer eyes aren't aching so much yer can't eat your scone? Not when Ida has been kind enough to have butter and jam put on them.'

Nellie, forever the entertainer, rubbed her eyes with the heel of her hands. 'No, they're fine now, girl, I'll be able to see what I'm eating. And seeing as yer've both been good, I'll be mother and pour out.'

If it had been left to Nellie, they would have been sitting in the cafe until it closed, but Molly was thinking of her husband's tea and hurried the proceedings along. Twenty minutes later they were making their way to the millinery department. 'Shall we split up until we see a hat we like, then we'll have a confab to see if we all like it? It would save a lot of time.' She opened her bag and took out the two small pieces of material Doreen had given her. 'Here yer are, Nellie, there's yours. If yer see a hat yer like, give us a shout.'

That had been the wrong thing to say, because Nellie happened to think green, blue and pink would all go with purple, and was calling her two friends over by the minute. In the end, Molly said, 'You look for yer own, Ida, and I'll see if they've got anything that will both suit Nellie and be the right colour.' Within minutes of speaking those words she had spotted a lilac hat that would be the ideal colour. Whether the style would suit was a different matter. The hat was definitely a wedding hat, a lovely colour with a stiffened turned-up brim that wasn't too big. And it didn't have a feather near it. 'It's a beautiful hat, sunshine, the right colour and just the thing for the mother of the bride. Here, stand in front of this mirror and try it on.'

The fit was perfect, the hat moved when Nellie's head moved, the colour suited her and so did the style. 'Oh, sunshine, it looks lovely on yer. Honest to God, yer'll not find one nicer if we walked the length of the city.'

Ida came hurrying over, a pale blue picture hat in her hand. 'Nellie, that hat is perfect for yer. Yer look like a million dollars.'

The shoulders went back and the bosom stood out as Nellie looked in the mirror. She nodded her head, 'Yes, it does look nice, but I'd better walk around in it for a bit to make sure it's comfortable.'

Ida's brow furrowed. 'What d'yer mean, queen? It's a hat ye're trying, not a pair of ruddy shoes! And if yer don't buy it, then yer want yer bumps feeling 'cos yer'll not get another that looks so nice on yer.'

Not wanting to take the hat off if she looked so nice in it, Nellie said, 'Ay, Molly, have a look at the price tag, will yer?'

Molly caught the tab hanging down the back. 'Two guineas, sunshine, and worth every penny.'

Nellie pursed her lips and nodded. 'A guinea cheaper than me other one, eh? Well, as far as my George is concerned, it's three guineas, so watch what yer say in front of him, girl.'

Molly gasped. 'Don't yer be expecting me to lie to yer husband for yer, 'cos I won't! And another thing, Helen Theresa McDonough, you needn't expect to get into heaven 'cos yer don't stand a chance.'

'She's only kidding, queen, she wouldn't tell lies to her husband.'

'Oh, she's not kidding, Ida, she makes a habit of telling George lies,' Molly said. 'But she needn't think she can drag me into it because I've no intention of being part and parcel of her games. Especially as George has a lot on his plate at the moment with the wedding. He needs all the money he can get for that.'

Nellie was still looking at herself in the mirror while all this was going on, and because she was really taken with the hat and thought she looked glamorous, she was in a mood to be agreeable. 'You win, girl, I'll tell George the truth. Not that he'll believe me, like, 'cos he knows I always add a few bob to the price of everything. So I'll tell him what it cost in front of yer, Molly Bennett, 'cos he'll believe you.'

'Right, well now, after all that time wasting, are yer buying the hat or not?'

'Of course I am, girl, because I definitely think it does something for me. And it'll look better still when I have me hair done for the big day.'

'That's one down and two to go.' Molly pointed to the hat Ida was carrying. 'What about you, sunshine, have yer got yer eye on that hat?'

'I haven't tried it on yet, queen, but I'm hoping it suits me because I fell for it as soon as I saw it. And the colour will go well with me dress, which is a darker blue. So, if yer'll move away from the mirror, Nellie, I'll try it on.'

The pale blue hat had a wide brim with a silk flower of the same colour sewn on one side of the crown which really set it off. Ida put it on and twisted and turned to see herself from all directions. 'Well, what d'yer think?'

'It's perfect, sunshine, it really looks good on yer. Don't yer think so, Nellie?'

Nellie was in the mood to be generous. 'Yeah, it really does look good on yer. How much is it?'

'Two guineas, same as yours, queen, and I'm definitely going to buy it 'cos I don't think I'll get one any nicer no matter where I go or how much I pay.'

'That only leaves me, now,' Molly said, 'and see that beige hat on the stand over there? Well, that's taken me fancy.' Then she raised her brows. 'Here comes an assistant.'

'Good afternoon, ladies.' The assistant was middle-aged, and with her hands joined together in front of her, had the air of someone in authority. 'If you don't intend buying those hats, I'm afraid I'm going to have to ask you to put them back on the stands before they get fingermarks on.'

'Oh, yes?' Nellie didn't like the woman's condescending attitude on little bit. Not when she was talking to customers who were prepared to pay two guineas a hat. 'For your information, my friend and I are buying these hats. My other friend has yet to see one that she really likes.'

'In that case, madam, perhaps you and your friend would like to come to the counter and I'll have one of the juniors bag your hats while I take your money and give you a receipt.'

Nellie, who still had the hat on her head, let her eyes travel from the woman's feet to the top of her head. Then she opened her purse, took out three pound notes and handed them to Ida before removing the hat and passing it to the assistant. 'You pay for my hat, Ida, before this woman bursts a blood vessel. I'll stay with my friend until she finds a hat to her liking.' She took hold of Molly's elbow. 'Come on, girl, yer helped me and Ida choose a hat, so I'll help you find one yer like. It's coming to something when ye're buying an expensive hat and are accused of being dirty or a thief.'

The assistant realized she was dealing with someone who wouldn't hesitate to make a complaint at the office, and if this happened she'd be in for a telling-off. It wasn't every day of the week they sold three two-guinea hats. 'Madam, I didn't mean to insinuate you or your friends were either. If I gave that impression then I apologize.'

Molly raised a hand. 'Leave things be, please, and see to the two hats that are definite sales. And perhaps in future you could be less abrupt with customers – and a smile wouldn't go amiss. My friends and I were surprised by your manner, to say the least. Come, Nellie, I'd hate to be the only one who goes home disappointed.'

And she wasn't disappointed because the hat on the stand suited her down to the ground. The light beige colour was what she wanted, the brim wasn't too wide or too narrow. In fact, it was exactly what she'd been seeing in her mind's eye for the last month. So very soon the three friends were back in the cafe, all looking like the cat that got the cream. And when Nellie was all for getting her hat out to show to the people sitting in the cafe, it brought laughter instead of embarrassment. She wasn't allowed to, of course, but she saw the joke herself and there was much laughter from their table, especially when she began to mimic the snooty assistant. Molly was doubled up and Ida was rocking to and fro, thinking how lucky she was to be going to live near these two.

Molly and Nellie stood back on the pavement with Archie while his mother put the key in the door and turned it. Opposite, Jill and Lizzie Corkhill were watching through the window as they had been a few hours before when they waved the Cotterells goodbye. Both of them clapped when Ida pushed the door open. Molly turned and waved to them, then chuckled when Ida jerked her head at her son. 'Come on, Archie, let's go in together in case there's a ghost we haven't been told about.'

As soon as they walked in it was apparent the place was badly in need of decorating. But there was no smell, which was a good thing because that would have been a right put-off.

'What d'yer think, Mam?' Archie asked. 'Are yer still as keen?'

'Of course I am, a bit of hard work won't hurt me. I can start scraping this paper off tomorrow and then wash all the paintwork down, and it'll look a lot brighter. Then all we've got to do is decorate and in no time at all I'll have it like a little palace.' She tilted her head and looked up at her son. 'What do you think, love, would you live here?'

'Mam, wherever you are, that's my home. And I told yer what Lily said, she's over the moon because she won't have to move away from her family.'

'So you and Lily will be living here?' Molly was delighted and it showed on her face. 'I am so pleased, and I know our Tommy will be. And me and Nellie will give yer mam a hand tomorrow, washing the place down and scraping the paper of the walls. But we'll leave the decorating to the men, they're much better at it. There'll be enough of them to have the place done in no time. I'll reel off the ones that have offered, starting with Tommy, then yer soon-to-be brothers-in-law Steve and Paul, Phil and Corker, Jack and George. And yourself, of course, Archie, you'll have to muck in as well.'

'I'll be glad of the help, Mrs B, 'cos the job will be done much sooner. It's me mam's house, don't think I'm taking over from her, but we sat down over the weekend and talked every thing through. When we take the keys back this afternoon I'm going to ask Mr Henry if my name can go on the rent book with me mam's. But my name is only going on in case of an emergency. It'll be her house and me and Lily will be living with her, not the other way round. Lily's meeting me mam in her dinner hour tomorrow and they're going to choose wallpaper and paint. With the wedding being only about six weeks off, I'd like to get us all settled in before then so we can concentrate on enjoying our big day.'

'Oh, I think your co-workers will be prepared to work all the hours God sends to get yer fixed up by then. You haven't seen our gang at work, has he, Nellie?'

'No, he hasn't, girl, he's got that pleasure to come. Like greased lightning they are, and yer can't work faster than that. In yer blink, yer'll miss seeing one of the rooms being decorated, that's how quick they are.'

Archie laughed as he rubbed his hands together. He was very lucky the way things had worked out. He'd always promised himself that he'd look after his mother all her life. It was what she deserved, she'd earned it. And when he'd told Lily, she had

objections and said it was fine by her. And now this house
d come up, making all his wishes fall into place. 'I think we'd
tter go and see Mr Henry, Mam, before the office closes. And
l see you tomorrow night, Mrs Mac and Mrs B.' He put his
m across Ida's shoulders. 'Me and me mam are going to love
ing in this street.'

ne next morning Molly and Nellie went up to the house armed
ith scrapers, a stiff brush, and a mop and bucket. With Ida, they
arted upstairs in the bedrooms and worked non-stop until it
as time for something to eat. They hadn't gone short of drinks,
ll had seen to that. Three times she carried a pot of tea over,
d at one o'clock told them to lay down their tools because
ross the street there was a stack of sandwiches ready for them
eat.

Each day after that fell into a pattern. The women would work
rough the day until it was time to make a meal for their family,
en about seven o'clock the men took over. For the living room,
a and Lily had chosen a light beige paper with just a sprig of
nk flowers on, and white paint for all the woodwork. Archie
d Lily were to have the front bedroom, Ida insisted, while she
as happy with the smaller back bedroom. They bought light
per for both bedrooms, and also for the staircase. The kitchen
as to be painted in a pale yellow, so it looked as though the sun
as always shining.

It was amazing each day to see how much work had been
ne. The men really put their backs into it. Molly and Nellie
pt them supplied with tea, because it was thirsty work, and
ellie never failed to entertain them while they had a ten-minute
eak. They laughed and joked, happy to be in the company of
eir friends, and happy to be helping a young couple who were
on to be married. At the end of the first week it was clear the
use would be ready by the end of the next so Ida gave notice

to her old landlord. Two weeks to the day after they went to view the house, Archie took a day off work and he and his man moved in. Everyone was invited around for a housewarming drink as a thank-you for helping and for being the best friend anyone could have.

Molly, Nellie and Ida stood with a glass of sherry in their hand, gazing with admiration at the brightness of the room. 'Well what d'yer think, queen?' Ida asked. 'The Three Musketeer came through with flying colours, eh? Now, when are we going to buy our wedding shoes?'

Chapter Twenty-Eight

tried me wedding outfit on last night, girl,' Nellie said, putting
er cup down on to the saucer. 'And even if I say it meself, it
ally makes me look good.'

'Yer tried it on again!' Molly's voice went higher. 'The dam'
ing will be worn out before the wedding! And Lily and George
on't give it a second glance on the day because they'll be sick
f the sight of it.'

'Oh, they haven't seen me in it, girl, I'm not that daft. I lock
e bedroom door so they can't get in, even though they have
ied. George can't make out why I won't let him see it, but I'm
icking to me guns and I told him so. It'll be a pleasant surprise
r them when I come down the stairs two weeks on Saturday.'
ellie was sitting pretty on her carver chair, and now she
lished the seat of it with her bottom. 'I'll have to give your
oreen a few bob for making it 'cos I couldn't never have
ught one what suited me so well, even if I'd paid twenty
iineas.'

'Doreen wouldn't take any money off yer, sunshine, she's just
ppy that it looks so nice on yer. She's made a good job of all
e dresses, not only yours. I'm delighted with mine, I'll feel a
oper toff in it with me smart hat and high-heeled shoes. Victoria
more than pleased, and Frances, God love her, is over the
oon. She still doesn't think she'll make it to the wedding, but
ll have a bet with anyone that she will.'

'D'yer think so, girl? I must say I didn't think she'd make until now, never mind the wedding. She must have a stron constitution.'

'And a will to live, sunshine, that's what it is. Because she ha so much in her life now to live for. And I've got to say Tor Bradley is a big surprise to me, he has certainly changed. H really does look after her and seems to love her very much. N that we've seen anything of him but he doesn't stop France from coming, and when she does talk about him, it's always ho good he is to her, she never says a wrong word about him or th kids.'

'Yeah, well, it takes all sorts to make a world, girl, it wouldn do for us all to be alike,' Nellie would never forget how bad Tor Bradley used to be, and if he had changed, well, it was too lat for her. 'I've got to take George's suit to the Chinese laundr today, so that'll be him all fixed up with his new shirt and ti He'll be as proud as Punch walking down the aisle with our Lil on his arm.'

'I don't suppose yer've seen the bridal dress, have yer? I b she wants it to be a big surprise on the day.'

'I never even got a whiff of it, girl, she took it straight up Ida's and locked it in the wardrobe covered in layers of tissu paper. And the same goes for her veil and headdress, they'r locked away, too! Even Ida hasn't seen them, 'cos wherever Lil goes, the keys to the wardrobe go too! A friend from work wer with her to choose the dress and the other things, but no amou of coaxing will change her mind about me seeing them.'

'I don't blame, her, sunshine, because if we all saw what sh was going to wear it would spoil the wedding for everyon We've seen the bridesmaids' dresses, and they're lovely. With ring of flowers in their hair, and their posies, they'll look a re picture. She is very organized is Lily, but I bet she's nervou inside. And as for Archie, yer'd never know if he was nervo

466

ecause for the last few weeks he's had a permanent smile on his
ace.'

'George said that's because the lad is walking around in a
ream. I think I'm more nervous than any of them, I've got
utterflies in me tummy from the minute I wake up until I go to
ed at night.' Nellie was counting the days to the big event,
ecause her reflection in the long mirror in the wardrobe told
er she looked a treat in her glad rags, and she wanted her
aughter and husband to be proud of her as well as Archie. She
dn't want to let him down because he was almost like a son to
er. 'The bridesmaids are going up to Ida's to help Lily get
eady, and Archie is bringing his clothes down to ours and getting
hanged there. That's so he doesn't see Lily until she's walking
own the aisle on George's arm.'

Molly knew all this because Ruthie and Bella were brides-
aids, and she'd seen them in their dresses. Phoebe and
orothy Corkhill from next door were the other two. So really,
he knew as much of what was going on as Nellie did, but she
asn't going to tell her mate that and dampen her enthusiasm
ecause she remembered how she'd felt when Jill and Doreen
ot married. Because Nellie's family had always seemed like
a extension of her own Molly could feel herself getting more
nd more excited as the big day drew nearer. 'Well, I'm looking
orward to the wedding, sunshine, 'cos Lily's like a daughter to
e.'

'Ay, girl, Ida asked us to call for her to go to the shops, and I
orgot to mention it to yer. So shall we make an effort?'

'Nellie, if Ida was going to the shops, she'd have to pass our
ouses, so why would we walk up there just to walk back down
gain?'

'I don't know, girl, I never thought! It's this wedding what's
oming between me and me sleep. Half the time I don't know
hat bleeding day it is, or if I'm coming or going.'

Molly tried to look stern. 'That sort of language isn't going
go with yer posh hat, sunshine, so cut it out. And going back
the subject of calling for Ida to go to the shops, it so happens
won't be an inconvenience today because I'm going up to s
how Jill is as soon as I've rinsed these cups out. She's only go
couple of weeks to go now and I'm keeping me eye on her.
I'll go to Jill's, and you go to Ida's and wait for me.'

'Not on yer blee—' Nellie hesitated, then found a wo
that wouldn't get her into trouble. 'Not on yer blinking li
girl, I'm coming with yer. What you seem to forget is that I'
got as much stake in this baby as you have. So, you go to Jill
I go to Jill's. I'm going to be like yer shadow until the bab
born.'

Molly grinned. 'I'll go along with that, sunshine, during t
day. But I'm sure yer don't want to get into bed with me a
Jack, do yer?' She saw the devil lurking in her mate's eyes a
knew she'd said the wrong thing. 'Okay, yer don't have to answ
that, I'm sorry I spoke.'

Nellie rocked in the chair. 'I bet yer could kick yerself,
girl? Left yerself wide open for me to say that if you and Ja
were behaving yerselves in bed, then yer wouldn't need to wor
about me being there. But I won't say it, 'cos I know h
embarrassed yer get, and because yer are me best mate.'

Tutting loudly, Molly said, 'Take those cups out and rin
them for us. And I can tell by yer face that ye're dying to s
something else, but I'd rather yer kept it to yerself.'

'Nah, it was just something that ran through me head, gi
not worth telling yer.' Nellie waited for her friend's curiosity
get the better of her and for her to ask what it was that r
through her head, but Molly kept her lips together. 'All it w
girl, I just thought I might learn something if I slept with y
and Jack. I mean, my old ma used to say that ye're never too c
to learn, and I'm not too proud to be taught.'

Molly did her best to make her face look like thunder. 'Take those cups out, sunshine, and rinse them. And I hope yer don't embarrass yer daughter by coming out with remarks like that on her wedding day. I can hear the guests whispering to each other behind their hands: "Posh hat, but as common as muck." '

The table rocked with the rise and fall of Nellie's tummy. 'Sticks and stones, girl, sticks and stones. The day I worry what people think of me, well, that's the day yer want to take me along to the doctor's 'cos I'll have lost the run of me senses.'

Molly lifted her coat down from the hook and slid her arms into the sleeves. 'I know, sunshine, yer couldn't give a monkey's what folk say about yer.' She made sure she had her front door key, then jerked her head. 'Come on, let's go. And I don't blame yer for not worrying what other people say. They're not the ones paying the rent or putting food on the table.'

Nellie waited for her mate to step down on to the pavement, then she linked her arm. 'Sod 'em all, girl, that's what I say.'

Molly chuckled. 'Yes, I know yer do, sunshine, but don't say it when yer've got yer best hat on, eh?'

Jill opened the door and was delighted to see her mother and her Auntie Nellie. She was looking forward to having this baby, but she was frightened because she didn't know what lay ahead of her. There were times, especially at night when Steve was snoring away with his arm across her, that she felt the need for the comfort of her mother's arms and a sympathetic ear to confide in.

Molly would have loved to have held and comforted her daughter now, but she was afraid of being thought soppy. And if Jill knew she was worried about her, it would only make her more anxious about having the baby. 'Yer look well, sunshine, but ye're not half a size. I suppose it's awkward and heavy for yer now. Yer don't go to the clinic this week, do yer?'

Jill shook her head. She was booked into Oxford Street Maternity Hospital, where Doreen had her baby, and which was supposed to be the finest in the country. 'The doctor said he didn't want to see me again until I started in labour.'

'How are yer, girl?' Nellie asked. 'Can yer feel the baby?'

'Feel him, Auntie Nellie? He kicks like mad! Steve said he's definitely going to be a footballer 'cos he can feel him too in bed at night.'

'Why d'yer all keep saying he?' Molly asked. 'I'm convinced it's a girl, and it'll have blue eyes and blonde hair, just like her mam.'

'Never mind what it is,' Nellie said, 'as long as it's healthy. Have yer got a case packed ready, 'cos it might come on ye sudden, like.'

Lizzie stopped rocking to say, 'It's been packed for the last month. Jill made a list of what the nurses said she'd need, and she checks it every day to make sure everything is in its place and neatly folded. And for what it's worth, from the look of her I'd say it won't be very long now.'

Nellie leaned forward. 'Ay, girl, do us a favour and try not to have the baby until after the wedding, eh? Tell him, or her, to hang on 'cos me and Molly couldn't cope with a wedding and a birth at the same time.' There was real affection in her eyes because she loved her son's wife dearly. 'I don't want to be running to the hospital in my glamorous wedding outfit, so if yer could have a word with the baby, and yer both time it well, say a couple of days after the wedding, I'll really appreciate yer consideration.'

'If the baby is listening to yer right now, Nellie, I'm sure he or she will do their very best not to discommode yer.'

Lizzie resumed her rocking with a knowing look on her face. 'Yer can talk until the cows come home, but that baby will come when it's good and ready, and not a day before or after.'

'Yeah, I understand that, Lizzie,' Nellie said. 'After all, I have had three of me own. And they all came at a very convenient time, never on a day when there was a wedding.'

'Well they wouldn't, would they, sunshine?' Molly raised her brows. 'I mean, yer had no family to get married, they hadn't been born yet.'

'Oh, aye, I never thought of that!' Nellie grinned. 'Aren't I the silly one? It's a good job I've got a clever mate, otherwise I'd never make it to the shops on me own.'

'Oh, talking of shops, which we weren't, do yer need anything, Jill? Me and Nellie are walking down with Ida, so if yer want anything, sing out. And always be in advance with the shopping, just in case of emergency.'

'I was thinking about that, Mam, with Auntie Lizzie saying she thinks I could go into labour any time. So if yer can carry a loaf, some spuds and a pint of milk, then I'll last out for a couple of days. I'm doing stew for today, and there'll be enough for tomorrow as well. And I've got bacon and eggs in, so we won't starve for a few days. If you get me shopping, Mam, I'll pay yer when yer come back.'

Walking down the street fifteen minutes later with Nellie and Ida, Molly said, 'I would willingly have that baby for her if I could. If she's anything like I was before she was born, she must be absolutely terrified. But I wasn't long in labour, only a few hours, so I can only hope it's the same for her.'

Nellie was walking in the middle and when her head moved from side to side, half her chins went towards Molly, the other half opted for Ida. 'I've got to admit, girl, that having a baby wouldn't go down as me favourite pastime, but yer soon forget about the pain when it's all over. Just as long as she doesn't give birth when the priest is asking, "Archibald Higgins, do you take this woman to be your lawful wedded wife?" '

Ida glanced across at Molly. 'She's all heart, isn't she, queen?'

And the three friends carried on walking with smiles on their faces.

* * *

It was a few days later, on the Friday morning at six o'clock when a worried-looking Steve came knocking on Molly's door. As soon as she heard the knock, she knew what it would be and slid her legs over the side of the bed before leaning back to shake her husband's shoulder. 'Wake up, sunshine, I think Jill's time has come.'

Jack pushed himself up on his elbow and, rubbing his eyes, asked, 'How d'yer know that, love?'

'Because Steve is knocking hell out of our front door.' Molly slipped a cardigan over her nightdress. 'I'll go and open up, the poor lad is probably out of his mind.'

'Jill is having pains, Mrs B, and her waters broke about fifteen minutes ago.' The quaver in Steve's voice told of his fear for his beloved wife. 'She's asking for yer, so would yer go up while I run to the phone box to call a taxi?'

'No, you go back to Jill while I put a dress on, it won't take me two minutes. Maisie will let me phone for a taxi from there. Her and Alec will be getting ready to open the shop now.'

'Are yer sure, Mrs B?'

'Of course I'm sure, sunshine, you go back to Jill. Tell her I'll be less than five minutes, I won't stop to talk to Maisie and won't even get washed. I'll rinse me face and comb me hair in yours. Now go on, Steve, I won't be far behind yer, and I'll have ordered the taxi.'

As he walked away, Molly called after him, 'Is Lizzie awake?'

'Yeah, she's with Jill. And thank God she's there because I panicked and just went to pieces. This will be the first and last baby, Mrs B, I couldn't go through this again.'

'Don't let Jill see ye're upset, act as though it's nothing out of the ordinary.'

Molly closed the door to find Jack standing behind her. 'I'll come up with yer, love, it won't matter if I clock in late for once.'

Pushing him aside, Molly made for the stairs and was pulling

472

dress over her head when he came into the bedroom. 'Are yer ure I couldn't be any use to yer, love? I don't like to think I'm eaving yer with all the worry.'

'Jack, have yer forgotten I've had four children so I know xactly what the procedure is? If no one around Jill gets panicky, hen she won't either. I'm calling to ask Maisie to ring for a taxi, nd hopefully I'll have time to rinse me face and comb me hair efore it arrives. But what yer can do to help is make some reakfast for you and Ruthie, and see she gets off to work at the ame time as you.' She reached the bedroom door, then said, Oh, on yer way out, will yer give Nellie a knock and tell her? 'll be staying at the hospital until they examine Jill, and I'll ask ' the birth is imminent or not. If Nellie wants to come, the tram 'ill drop her off right outside.' She ran across the room to kiss is cheek. 'I'll have to fly now, love, but just think, next time I ee yer we might be grandparents again.'

ill was biting on her bottom lip and near to tears. Wrapped in er mother's arms, she asked, 'Are the pains always this bad?'

Molly held her away so she could look into her daughter's ightened eyes. 'Yes, sunshine, they are. So now yer know how uch I much love me children to have gone through what you're oing through now four times.' She smiled and stroked the long londe hair. 'And d'yer know what, sunshine? I'd do it all over gain. Because after a few hours of grunting and screaming and anting to kill yer dad, the nice nurse put a beautiful baby in me rms. And what I used to do while I lay waiting, I used to think f what I was going to call the baby. I had two boys' names and vo girls' name all ready.'

They heard the taxi pulling up outside, and Steve panicked nce again. So Molly said, 'Steve, take the case out and I'll ollow with Jill.'

Lizzie gave the girl a last hug and kiss. 'They won't let me in to see yer, sweetheart, they only allow husbands in. But I'll be thinking of yer, and waiting for the day when yer step out of a taxi with a bonny baby in yer arms.'

When they got to the hospital everything was done quickly and efficiently so there wasn't time to worry. The nurses delivered dozens of babies every day, and had no time for petting or sympathizing. Jill was whisked away to be examined, and Steve felt lost. 'Won't they let me go in with her?'

'Not on your life, sunshine, husbands would only be in the way and they have very strict rules here. But yer can rest in the knowledge that this hospital is reckoned to be the very best. Jill is in capable hands.'

It seemed an eternity before anyone came to see them, but in fact it was only half an hour. The nurse was brisk, though not unfriendly. 'We're keeping your wife in, Mr McDonough, because the contractions are coming every fifteen minutes. So I suggest you go home and ring up in a couple of hours.'

'Can't I see my wife before I leave?' Steve was in shock. 'Just for a few minutes?'

'I'm sorry, but your wife is in the labour ward, and no one except hospital staff is allowed in there. So as I said, please go home and ring up in a couple of hours.' With a half-smile, the nurse hurried back to her duties. There were ten women in the labour ward; those who were lucky would give birth quickly, but others could be there for many hours.

Molly took Steve's arm and led him though the big double doors into the street. 'Come on, sunshine, we'll go home and have something to eat. I'll come back with yer in a couple of hours and hopefully there will be good news for us then.'

'I'll have to ring work and tell them I won't be coming in. I couldn't concentrate, not with me mind on Jill.'

Molly glanced sideways at him. 'Far be it from me to interfere, sunshine, but I think the best place for you right now is in work.

with yer mates around yer. I'm sure most of them have children, so talking to them will make the time go quicker. Ask if yer can clock off at dinnertime, I'm sure the boss will have no objection when he knows the reason. Yer could go straight to the hospital and me and yer mam will meet yer there.' She glanced at his anxious face. 'I know how yer feel, sunshine, 'cos I feel the same. But sitting at home twiddling yer thumbs would only make yer worse.'

'I think ye're probably right, Mrs B, I'd only make meself miserable sitting thinking and worrying. I'll knock off at half-twelve and meet yer at the hospital. I won't bother going home for me overalls, I'll borrow a pair off one of the men.'

He looked so lost and dejected, Molly squeezed his arm. 'I know ye're worried, and so am I. But think of the little mite who will be entering this world sometime today, and who'll be enriching your lives in all the years to come. And before I go all sentimental and bawl me eyes out, you go that way for your tram, I go this way for mine.'

'Yer should have knocked me up.' Nellie glared at Molly through lowered lids. 'I had every right to be told the same time as you.'

'Oh, yeah, yer'd have been delighted to have been knocked up before six in the morning. And what difference would it have made? Yer couldn't have done anything 'cos it was all one big rush. I haven't even had a proper wash, the taxi came and there wasn't time.' Molly had been expecting this kind of reception and wasn't unduly worried. 'Anyway, as soon as we got to the hospital they took Jill away to be examined and that was the last we saw of her. I've told Steve you and me will meet him there between half-twelve and one o'clock. By that time, please God, there may be some news.'

Nellie still wasn't mollified. 'Yer even told your Doreen before yer told me, that's another thing what's annoyed me.'

'Don't be so ruddy childish, Nellie McDonough. I didn't even go in Doreen's, I told her at the door because I knew yer'd have a cob on. But Doreen had every right to know first, she's Jill's sister, for heaven's sake!' They were sitting at Nellie's dining table, which made it a very rare occasion. 'Anyway, sunshine, are yer going to offer to make me a cup of tea, or shall I go home and make me own? If yer were in my house and I kept yer waiting for a drink, the air would be blue.'

Nellie's head and eyes moved from side to side like an animal being hunted. 'I'll make yer one, but yer can knock it off that one thousand seven hundred cups yer said I've had off you over the years. And don't think I'm not still mad at yer, 'cos I am.' She pushed herself off the chair and swayed towards the kitchen. 'Let's hope a cuppa will put me in a better frame of mind because, seeing as ye're me best mate, I don't want to spend the rest of the day not talking to yer.'

'Ye're not going to have much time for not talking to me, sunshine, 'cos by the time we've been up to let Lizzie know there's nothing to tell her yet, and been to the shops to get something in for our dinner, it'll be time to make our way to the hospital. Which means we're going to be so busy I won't even notice ye're not talking to me.'

Later, when they were out shopping, Molly kept a tight rein on her mate's tongue. Apart from telling Tony and Ellen the news, she didn't want anyone else to know until after the baby was born and they knew everything was all right. Tony showed great interest and Ellen great excitement. 'I hope yer've go good news by the time Corker comes in from work, Molly, 'co yer know he's got a special place in his heart for Jill and he'll b sick with worry until it's all over.'

'He won't be the only one,' Nellie said, feeling she was being left out and that was unfair seeing as her Steve had a hand in thi baby. Well, not a hand exactly, but we all know what she mean

476

'The men will all be up at the pub wetting the baby's head.'

'I'll let yer know as soon as we know ourselves, Ellen.' Molly paid for the sausages Tony had weighed, and put the parcel in her basket. 'Pay up, sunshine, and let's be on our way. We've got a busy day in front of us.'

Steve was pacing up and down outside the hospital when the two women arrived. 'I couldn't bring meself to go in, I'm a bundle of nerves and shaking like a leaf.'

'Oh, dear, you big daft ha'porth.' Nellie seldom showed sympathy. 'Did yer think the nurses might keep yer in, or something?'

'Leave him alone, Nellie, the lad's worried. And he wouldn't be much of a husband if he wasn't. Now let's compose ourselves and hope that when we go in, a nice nurse will come towards us with some good news.' Molly knew she was being optimistic because no nurse would be looking for them, they'd have to find one themselves. 'Steve, see that window over there with Enquiries on? Well, go over and knock and when someone comes to attend to yer, ask if there's any news of your wife. They'll take more notice of you than they would of me or yer mam.'

'I couldn't, Mrs B, I'm a nervous wreck. I've never been in a hospital in me life before and I'd be stammering and stuttering. Can't yer come with me?'

'Come on, son, me and Molly will stand behind yer.' Nellie wasn't a hands-on mother like Molly, who openly showed her love for her children, but that didn't mean she didn't love them to bits and wouldn't fight to the death for them. 'We'll help yer out if yer get stuck.'

The woman who came to the window was smiling and friendly, but wasn't able to help and said they'd have to see one of the nurses. However, as she was about to close the window she noticed the distraught look on Steve's face and it found its way to her heart. 'Look, if you take a seat, I'll see if I can find out how your wife is.' She wrote the name on a piece of paper. 'And you say she was admitted about a quarter-past six this morning?' Smiling again, she nodded to the waiting room. 'Sit in there, please, I'll try not to keep you waiting long.'

The next twenty minutes were the longest of Steve's life. He paced the floor filled with worry and guilt. He'd never put Jill through this again, never. But those thoughts and worries were lifted when the woman from Enquiries came into the room clutching her hands in front of her and wearing a broad smile. 'Your wife had her baby ten minutes ago, Mr McDonough, a little girl weighing seven and a half pound. Both mother and baby are fine. One of the midwives will be along to see you shortly, after they've cleaned the baby and transferred your wife to one of the wards.'

'Can't I see them?' he begged. 'Just for five minutes?'

'I'm sorry, I can't help you there, I only work in the office. Please be patient, there'll be someone here soon who will be able to answer your questions.'

Molly and Nellie waited until the woman had closed the door behind her before pouncing on a bewildered Steve. They hugged and kissed him, patted him on the back, shook his hand, then went back to hugging him. They were filled with delight and pleasure, particularly Molly, who felt weak with relief that the ordeal was over for her daughter. And as the realization began to sink in that he was now a proud father, and his beautiful wife was all right, the smile on Steve's face spread and his dimple appeared for the first time that day.

'Yer were right, Mrs B, yer said it would be a girl. I don' know whether to sing or cry with happiness, and I can't wait to see them.'

Molly, knowing the procedure, thought it best to warn him. 'They won't let yer see them now, sunshine, they have very stric rules. Yer mam will tell yer I'm right, 'cos we went through it with Doreen. We found a very sympathetic nurse, but there's not much likelihood of that happening again. Still, yer'll see them tonight at visiting time, and yer can walk around with yer chest out now, and a smile on yer face, 'cos yer know it's all over.'

'He won't be the only one with a grin on his face, girl, what about me?' Nellie felt like doing a jig. 'A grandma for the first time – I'm entitled to brag now.'

At eight o'clock that night Molly's living room was full, as all the female members of the families and friends had turned up. The conversation was happy and noisy, and they'd all come bearing nicely wrapped parcels and greetings cards which were to be taken in to the hospital to show Jill they were all delighted for her and she was in their thoughts. There was Bridie, Lizzie, Doreen, Rosie, Lily, Ellen, Phoebe, Maisie, and of course Nellie ruling the roost from her carver chair. Molly was really moved as she heard the visitors discussing what was in their parcels: hand-knitted matinee coats, leggings, mitts and hats. Also blankets, embroidered sheets and pillowcases for cot and pram, plus nappies and bibs.

Nellie was so excited she couldn't keep her bottom still. Molly feared there'd be no varnish left on the chair seat by the end of the night. 'Me and George are going half with Molly and Jack to buy the cot. In fact, my feller is so happy at being a granda, he'd buy them anything they wanted.'

'And we're buying the pillows, don't forget,' Molly reminded her. 'I'm dying to see Jill and the baby, and I know when she sees all the presents you've given she'll cry her eyes out.'

'What about a pram?' Maisie asked. 'Has she got one yet?'

Molly shook her head. 'She thought it would be bad luck to buy everything before the baby was born, so all she's got are some matinee coats she's knitted. But Steve will be sorting the pram out in the next few days, and he's going to ask Jill what type of cot she wants, so me and Nellie can have that ready for her.' She waved a hand to the sideboard which was piled high with gifts. 'And yer've all been so kind, she'll have enough baby clothes to last her for the first year.'

Lily brought the only sad note. 'She's going to miss me wedding, isn't she, Auntie Molly? D'yer think there's any chance of her being out by then? I did want everyone to be there for me big day.'

'Steve is going to leave it a few days to ask if Jill will be allowed out by then, because if he asks now, when she's just had the baby, they'll definitely refuse. But if all runs smoothly for her and the baby, and there's ten days to go, I think there's a good chance they'll let her out, seeing as it's a family wedding. Yer can bet yer life, sunshine, that Jill will do her best, 'cos I know she wouldn't want to miss yer wedding, Lily.'

As arranged, Steve went straight from the hospital to the corner pub where all the menfolk were gathered. When he walked through the door, he was greeted by loud cheers and applause. It seemed every man who lived in the street was there, and everyone wanted to shake his hand. He was dazed by it all, but not too dazed to know this would always be remembered as one of the happiest days of his life.

Corker counted the men in their clique, nine including himself and the proud new father. He nodded to the manager. 'Eight pints and one half of bitter, Wally.' Then he put his arm across Steve's shoulders. 'How's my princess, son?'

'She's fine, Uncle Corker, very happy but tired. And the baby . . . well, she's just the most beautiful baby I've ever seen. I know everyone says that about their own baby, and I shouldn't brag, but I can't help it. Seeing her in Jill's arms, well, it took me all me time to keep from bawling me eyes out.' Steve looked from his father to Jack and then to Bob. 'We've got two new grandads here tonight, and one great-grandad. Just you wait until yer see the baby, she's a little beauty.'

Phil grinned. 'I'm an old hand at this, but I know how yer feel. There's nothing in the world like having a child of yer own.'

Tommy said, 'Well, me, Archie and Paul, we've got our time to come. And I suppose we'll be just as smug as you are.'

Bob was on strict instructions from Bridie that he was to have no more than one half-pint, so Tommy found seats for him, his dad and Uncle George, and the four took their glasses and sat at a table. Paul, Phil and Archie were engaged in conversation about work, which gave Corker the chance to talk to Steve. 'And Jill is happy, is she, son?'

He nodded. 'I've never seen her look more beautiful, Uncle Corker, and she can't keep her eyes off the baby. They've put her in a cot at the end of the bed where Jill can see her, and the nurses are very pleased with them because the baby is feeding from her with no problems at all.' He grinned. 'I wasn't the only new father there at visiting time, and we all looked a bit sheepish, but I bet every man there was thinking their baby was the best-looking. I stuck me chest out a mile, 'cos anyone with half an eye could see our baby beat the others by a mile.'

'Have yer thought of a name for her, yet, son?' Corker lifted his glass and in one swallow emptied half of the glass. 'Or haven't yer had time to think about that?'

'We've got a few names, but we're waiting until Jill's home before we make up our mind definitely. And I don't mind telling yer I'm counting the minutes, Uncle Corker, 'cos I don't half miss her and this is only the first day.'

'I rather think she'll be missing you, son, which will make her homecoming all the sweeter.'

Chapter Twenty-Nine

'What are yer doing here at this time, Nellie?' Molly looked down from the top step, her feet planted firmly in the middle so her friend couldn't walk in. 'Surely yer must have plenty of work to do in the house with it being the wedding tomorrow?'

'That doesn't make no difference, girl, 'cos nobody is coming to my house. All the guests will be going straight to the reception from the church.' Nellie didn't like being kept on the pavement, but as she had no intention of going back to her own house her only tactic was to bide her time and sweet-talk her friend. 'And if anyone did come, they're not going to lift me rug to see if I've brushed the dirt under it, are they?'

Molly took a deep breath then blew the air out slowly. 'So, yer think ye're going to sit in my house for the next couple of hours, on yer posh chair, and watch me work, do yer?'

'Something like that, girl, I knew yer'd get the message sooner or later.' Nellie grinned, and before Molly knew what was happening, she'd been pushed aside and her mate was on her way to the living room. 'Yer took yer ruddy time about it, though, leaving me standing on the pavement like a lemon.'

With a sigh of resignation Molly closed the door. When she entered the living room it was to see Nellie lifting the carver chair from its place by the sideboard and plonking it at the table. Before she sat down, the little woman took a crumpled, finger-marked white sweet bag from her pocket and placed it on the table. 'I've brought some tea, so don't say I never give yer nothing.'

'Yer leave me speechless, Nellie McDonough! It's not ten o'clock yet, we don't have to go to the shops because we got our shopping in yesterday, apart from bread which Maisie is going to put aside for us to pick up later, so we've got a couple of hours to spare which I intended to use to do some housework.'

'We can go and pick Jill and the baby up after yer've made us a drink. We don't want to be late 'cos she'll be expecting us and yer know what it's like waiting for someone. Besides which, I'm all worked up with wanting to see me grandchild for the first time.'

'Nellie, I'll swear you only hear what yer want to hear. Anything else yer just let go in one ear and out the other.' Before Molly realized what she was doing, she'd pulled a chair out from the table and was sitting facing her mate. 'She's my grandchild as well, don't forget, and I can't wait to see her and our Jill. But yer must have heard what Steve said? They won't let Jill come home until the doctor has done his rounds and says that she and the baby are fit to be discharged. And as he doesn't usually get to Jill's ward until between twelve and one o'clock, there's no point in us getting there early and having to sit in the waiting room. So, from the looks of things, I'm going to be stuck with you for the next couple of hours and that means me housework doesn't get done.'

'Don't get yerself in a tizzy, girl, it's bad for yer health. I won't be in yer way, yer can work around me. What yer should do first, and it's my recommendation, is put the kettle on, make a nice cup of tea and sit down and relax.' Nellie picked the sweet bag off the table and handed it across. 'Here yer are, girl, yer'll enjoy a cup of tea, seeing as it's me what's given yer the tea leaves to make it with.'

Molly took the scruffy bag between two fingers and held it away from her. 'Couldn't yer have found something better to bring it in than a dirty bag? Honest, the state of this would put anyone off drinking the tea.'

'If ye're so bleeding fussy, girl, why don't yer wash the tea leaves before yer put them in the ruddy pot? Yer must count the leaves, otherwise how would yer know how many cups of tea I've had? So, while ye're counting the bleeding things, wash 'em at the same time.' Nellie shook her head slowly, inspiring her chins to break into a nice slow foxtrot. 'If anyone could hear you, they'd think I was a dirty beggar.'

'No, sunshine, if I thought yer were dirty yer wouldn't be sitting at me table. I'd say the word to describe you was untidy, rather than dirty. Or that yer eyesight isn't what it used to be and yer don't always see things clearly.' Molly could see her mate's brain working to find a good answer to that, so she got in while she had the chance. 'Another thing, Helen Theresa McDonough, yer've used the swear word twice in the space of ten seconds. Now that word wouldn't go with yer posh wedding hat, but it would be a very suitable word for this ruddy bag.'

'For crying out loud, girl, will yer shut up about the bag? Ye're not putting it in the teapot, so why harp on the bl— er, the blinking thing? I'll tell yer what, it'll be a long time before I ever feel good-natured enough to bring me own tea leaves with me again.'

Molly was in fact in a much better mood by now as she glanced at the clock. In two hours' time, please God, she'd be able to hug and kiss Jill and the new baby. And the main reason for the time going by quickly, and her feeling happier, was her little friend Nellie whose facial expressions would be hard to describe and impossible to impersonate. 'There's one way out of all this argument over a ruddy pot of tea, yer know, sunshine, but of course it would never occur to you.'

'Oh, ay, girl, and what's that?'

'Yer could invite me to your house for tea, and perhaps yer could even run to a custard cream biscuit. That would save any cursing and swearing, and it would make the time go quicker.'

'Sod off with yer big ideas, Molly Bennett, I'm out of me house now and I ain't going back in it until I've seen me grandchild and had a little nurse of her.' Nellie's nostrils flared and she glared. 'I'm going to watch you like a hawk, girl, so that yer don't see more of her than I do. I'll make sure she knows I'm granny, just like you.' Once again she pulled a face. 'When I ask her where her grandma is, it's me I want her to run to, not you. You've already got one grandchild, so don't be so ruddy greedy.'

'I'm in two minds now, Nellie, and I don't know what to do.'

Nellie's bosom was laid on the table and her arms encircled it as she leaned forward looking interested. 'What is it, girl? Tell me, I might be able to help yer out.'

'Well, it's a choice between making a pot of tea, or emptying the bag of leaves over your ruddy head! The first proposition would help pass the time and be very enjoyable. The second would be to teach yer not to be so bad-minded.'

Nellie cupped her chin. 'Mmm, that's a hard one, girl, I don't think I can help yer out there.'

Molly chuckled as she pushed her chair back. 'That's passed half an hour away, sunshine, and by the time we have a cup of tea, maybe two, we can start thinking of getting ready for the hospital. I can't wait to see them!'

'No, me neither, girl.' Nellie put her hands flat on the table and pushed herself up. 'You put the kettle on and I'll get the cups ready. And before I go into the kitchen I may as well warn yer I'll be looking in yer pantry for the biscuit tin. Yer never know, there might just be a few custard creams yer forgot yer had, or some broken arrowroot biscuits. I don't mind which, I'm not fussy, just as long as there's something I can put in me mouth to keep me tummy happy.'

Molly moved her aside and stood in front of the kitchen door. 'Keep out of me pantry, sunshine, I'll pass a few biscuits out to yer. If I let you loose in there, there'd be nothing left for Jack or Ruthie. And my feller likes a biscuit to dunk in his tea, especially ginger snaps, they're his favourites.'

Nellie shook her head and tutted. 'D'yer know what I think, girl? I think by the time I get this cup of tea, our granddaughter will be starting school.'

The hospital corridor seemed to be a flurry of activity when Molly and Nellie walked down it hoping to catch a nurse to ask where they could find Jill and the baby. But each nurse they came across seemed to have a definite destination in mind and looked as though she wouldn't appreciate being kept away from the job in hand. Until Nellie said, 'Ay, girl, isn't that the nurse we saw last year, when Doreen was in?'

'Oh, yeah, let's get to her before she disappears.' Molly was just in the nick of time as the nurse turned to enter one of the wards. 'Excuse me, Nurse, but d'yer think yer could help us out?'

There was a smile of recognition. 'You're Jill's mother, I remember you. Only because she's so much like your other daughter. At first I thought it was Doreen, and she was having another baby, until I realized the timing wasn't right. Anyway, I believe Jill is waiting for you in the next ward down on your right. She's all dressed ready for the off, and the baby is well wrapped up.'

'Thank you.' Molly could feel the butterflies in her tummy. ' can't wait to see them.'

Nellie felt she had to say something too or the nurse would think she was dumb. 'We'll try not to make a habit of it, Nurse At least not until next year, and then it might be the turn of my daughter.'

Molly pulled on her arm and dragged her away. 'Nellie McDonough, how can yer say such a thing when Lily isn't even married yet?'

Nellie pulled her arm free. 'She'll be married by tomorrow night, girl.' She was dying to laugh at the look of horror on her mate's face, and couldn't wait for her reaction to what was coming up next. 'And all things being equal, she could be pregnant by Sunday morning.'

'Nellie McDonough, ye're past redemption and I give up on yer. If ye're saying these things to shock me, then yer'll be happy to know yer've succeeded. So will yer give over now because here's our Jill coming out of the ward with the baby and a nurse carrying her case.'

Jill's face was aglow with happiness. 'Oh, Mam, Auntie Nellie, it's so good to see yer. They've been wonderful to me here, and I've made friends with the other women, but now I know what they mean when they say there's no place like home.'

Nellie was fussing around, trying to stand on tiptoe to see the baby, but all she could see was a blanket and shawl. 'Can I have a peep, girl, before we go? Don't forget this is me first grandchild and it's only natural I'll be thrilled and excited.'

'She's asleep, so don't touch her, Auntie Nellie, please.' Jill moved the blanket just a little, and the sight of the tiny face, so perfect, had the little woman wiping away tears. 'Oh, Molly, will yer just look at her, she's lovely! We've done well, haven't we?'

Molly smiled at the nurse before saying, 'I don't know what part we played in it, sunshine, but I agree that Jill and Steve have done well.'

'Of course we played a part in it, girl, what's wrong with yer memory? If it weren't for you and me, Jill and Steve wouldn't be here.'

'Oh, dear, don't let's go into that, Nellie, for heaven's sake.' Molly stretched her hand out to the nurse. 'I'll take the case, sunshine, and will yer thank everyone for looking after my daughter and granddaughter, please? We'll be on our way now, before my mate tells anyone who wants to listen that if it weren't for our parents, none of us would be here today.'

'Before you go, Mrs Bennett, the doctor did ask me to tell you that Jill must take it easy for a while. We know it's a family wedding tomorrow, but it would be very unwise for her to overdo things. However, I'm sure you're quite capable of knowing when to call a halt.'

'You need have no worries there, Nurse, because family and friends have it all worked out. Only immediate family to call to see the baby today, then tomorrow Jill will go straight home after the wedding ceremony. Depending how she's feeling later, she could go to the reception for half an hour because it's only at the bottom of the street, but it all depends on whether her husband and I think she's getting tired. If so she'll be whisked off home right away. We'll not let her take any chances, even if she wants to.'

Moving the case to her other hand, Molly said, 'Thanks again, Nurse,' before taking her daughter's arm. 'Come on, sunshine, let's get yer home where yer belong. We'll get a taxi outside, so yer can ride in comfort.'

There were plenty of taxis driving past, but most of them were taking fares into the city centre. 'There'll be one along in a minute, sunshine,' Molly said. 'All those going into town will be coming back empty.'

'Don't worry about me, Mam, I'm all right. The nurses have you up and about after the first day, so I don't feel weak or anything.'

Nellie had something on her mind and it was worrying her like a dog worries a bone. 'Ay, girl, don't blow yer top at me, but I think my George and your Jack need a mention here. I mean, without them you and me couldn't have had any babies.'

'Nellie, if yer keep this up, we'll be going back hundreds of years to our great-great-great grandparents. And I'm sure that if they're looking down on us now they'll be wondering why they bothered. Come to think of it, in the case of your forebears, if you take after them, then they'll be looking up at us, not down.'

Jill, who loved her mother-in-law, smiled down at her. 'Take no notice of me mam, Auntie Nellie, she's only joking. We all know she loves the bones of yer.'

The chubby cheeks moved upwards as she smiled and almost covered her eyes. 'I know that, girl, but I get a kick out of winding her up. She'd fall for the ruddy cat, she would.'

'Let's discuss the cat another time, here's a taxi.' Molly stood aside to let Jill take her time getting in, while the driver took the case and put it in the space next to the driver's seat. 'You get in now, Nellie, 'cos I'm feeling polite. Age before beauty, and all that.'

'I'll get me own back on yer for that, girl, when me mind is clear. After I've had a cup of tea from the pot I know ye're going to make when we get to Lizzie's.'

'Don't think ye're going to take up residence at Lizzie's, Nellie McDonough, 'cos yer've got another think coming. Jill and the baby want a bit of peace, time to settle down. I'll make a pot of tea because we could all do with one, but after that you and me are going to leave them to it.'

Molly was sitting facing the long back seat, and smiled at her daughter. 'I've made a rota out for visitors, otherwise yer would have had a full house all day because everyone is dying to see you and the baby. So today yer grandma and granda are coming round this afternoon about three o'clock, but they won't outstay their welcome. They were so excited I didn't have the heart to tell them to leave it for today. Then tonight Tommy will be calling to see yer – I couldn't talk him out of it, he's over the moon. But Rosie understood when I said yer'd be tired today, and said to give yer a kiss, tell yer she loved yer and she'd see yer at the wedding tomorrow. And Doreen will be coming on her own.'

'I hope they don't mind, Mam? I'd hate them to think I don't want to see them.'

'Of course they don't! Yer shouldn't even be out of hospital yet, so it would be crazy to overdo things, and the family and friends understand that. And I'm not doing this off me own bat, yer know, sunshine, Steve was a bit worried that the house would be full tonight and yer'd be tired out.'

Nellie patted Jill's knee. 'Don't you worry, girl, none of our gang are bad-minded enough to think yer were turning yer nose up at them. Yer Mam and Steve are right, yer should take it easy for a while. And as soon as I've seen me grandchild without all the shawls and things, and I've had a little hold of her, I'll be off and leave yer to settle down. That's after I've had a cup of tea, like, 'cos yer mam would think I was ignorant if I left without having a drink. And we wouldn't want her to think I was higorant, would we?'

Molly twisted in her seat to talk to the driver. 'It's the second street on yer right, sunshine, and we're going to the top half of the street, number seventy-eight, on yer left.'

As soon as the taxi stopped outside, Lizzie was at the front door. 'Oh, it does me heart good to see yer, queen, I haven't half missed yer.'

'And I've missed you, Auntie Lizzie. I never thought it possible to miss me home as much as I did. I cried meself to sleep the first two nights.'

'You go inside with the baby, sunshine,' Molly said, 'I'll see to the driver.' When she saw Nellie stepping up into the hall, she called, 'Put the kettle on, Nellie, and get the cups ready, me throat is parched.' But after paying the driver three and sixpence for the fare, and picking up the case from the pavement, Molly entered the house to find Nellie sitting on the couch, smiling happily, with the baby lying on her lap looking the picture of contentment. 'Oh, she likes you, sunshine, and your lap must be very comfortable for her.'

Nellie was feeling very emotional and could only manage a weak grin. 'I didn't hurry in deliberately so I could have the first nurse, girl, honest! I would have made the tea but Lizzie had beaten me to it. Come and sit down and you can have a cuddle now.'

Molly shook her head. 'It would be a shame to move her, she looks so happy. I think you two are going to get on well together.'

That pleased the little woman. 'D'yer really think so, girl?'

'Yer can tell by looking at her that she's found a spot she likes. Your lap is going to come in very handy, I can see that.'

'Mam, I've been thinking.' Jill put her cup on the table and leaned over to stroke the baby's face before going on. 'What about me dad and Uncle George? Surely yer haven't told them they can't come tonight?'

'It would have been a waste of breath, sunshine, 'cos nothing will keep the pair of them away. They're both walking around with smiles on their faces and their chests sticking out a mile. Anyone would think they were the only grandfathers in Liverpool. They'll be here about half-seven, but they've got orders not to outstay their welcome. And as for the rest of the clan, yer'll see them all tomorrow at the church.'

'Yer'll get a big surprise when yer see me and yer mam in all our finery. And Archie's mam.' Nellie was thinking how wonderful life was. 'I hope we don't put the bride in the shade.'

'I won't have anything new to wear,' Jill said. 'But I should be able to squeeze into one of last year's summer dresses. And I'll have a coat on, anyway.'

'Would yer like me to come up in the morning to give yer a hand?' Molly asked. 'I could see to the baby while you get yerself ready.'

Jill shook her head. 'Thanks all the same, Mam, but I can manage as long as I take me time. And Steve will be here to help out.'

'Okay, sunshine, but yer know where I am if needs be. Me and Nellie have made the cot up, and it looks lovely. And Steve knows all the arrangements regarding one of the wedding cars coming for yer. So me and my mate will love yer and leave yer now, and we'll see yer at the church.'

Lizzie saw the friends out, and couldn't get back into the living room quick enough. 'Now perhaps I can get a look in. Wait till I settle meself in me chair, sweetheart, then put the baby in my arms. While I'm rocking her, we can get to know each other and it will give you a chance to empty the case and do what yer have to.'

When Jill was halfway up the stairs with the case in her hand, she heard Lizzie talking to the baby and stopped to listen. 'Now I know yer've got two grannies already, but it wouldn't hurt to have another one. In fact, it would be very good. So I'd like to put meself forward as grandma number three. Yer see, yer live here, and yer'll be growing up here. And we can't have yer calling me Mrs Corkhill, can we, 'cos it sounds like we're strangers. So, in the right order, there'll be Grandma Molly, Grandma Nellie, and meself, Grandma Lizzie. We'll all get on like a house on fire, and we'll take good care of yer and give yer all the love in our hearts. And that, sweetheart, is a whole lot of love.'

Molly was awake early the next morning, and rather than lie tossing and turning, she decided to go down and make herself a drink. She slipped her legs over the side of the bed as carefully as she could, so as not to disturb Jack, and crept across the room stepping over the floorboard she knew would creak. Treading softly on each stair, she made her way down to the living room and closed the door behind her. She didn't want to wake her daughter because this was Ruthie's big day and she'd be so full of excitement there'd be no stopping her talking her head off.

Leaning back against the door, Molly asked herself if she should clean the grate out first or make herself a cuppa? The thought of a drink was most appealing, but would she enjoy it while staring at a grate that needed raking out and cleaning? Molly had a conversation with the empty room. 'I could kill two birds with one stone by putting the kettle on and clearing the grate while I'm waiting for it to boil.' Then she answered herself, 'Good idea, Molly, if yer put a move on yer could have the grate done by the time the water boils.'

Fifteen minutes later she was sitting on the couch with a much appreciated cup of sweet tea. And in the peace and quiet she allowed her mind to reflect on the past few years. When the three eldest children were little and at school, she never gave a thought to whether time was passing by slowly or quickly. One day was very much like another. Then Jill left school and found a job, making life a little easier financially. A year later Doreen left school and went to work in Johnson's, and Tommy the year after. Then the war started with years of food and coal shortages, and the dread of air-raids. Steve was called up for the army first, Phil didn't wait to be called up but volunteered to get away from his family, and then her beloved Tommy got his call-up papers and that nearly broke her heart. But all three were amongst the lucky ones who came home safely.

It all seemed just like yesterday, the memories were so vivid. And yet her two daughters and her son were married now, and she was a grandma twice over. It was hard to take in that her girls were now mothers themselves. But she was lucky they lived so close and hadn't moved miles away, she'd have pined something terrible for them if they had.

'Oh, ay, what are yer doing down here all on yer own?' Ruthie asked, sleep still in her eyes and hair tousled. 'Couldn't yer sleep?'

Molly smiled. 'I could ask the same of you, there's no need for yer to be up so early.'

'Ooh, I'm too wound up to stay in bed, Mam, and I bet Bella's up as well.'

'Yer'll never find out if ye're right, sunshine, 'cos there's no way I'll let yer go across to the Watsons' at this time in the morning. So put a light under the kettle and we'll have a cup of tea together. And I think I'll give yer dad a treat and take him one up.'

Ruthie and her friend were to be at the Higgins's house for half-eleven, the same as the Corkhill girls, Phoebe and Dorothy, and half-eleven couldn't come quick enough for Molly as Ruthie couldn't sit still and couldn't stop talking. After she'd waved them off she went back into the living room and heaved a sigh of relief. 'That youngest daughter of ours talks more than the other three put together.'

'She's no shrinking violet, that's for sure,' Jack chuckled. 'No one will ever get the better of her until she falls in love with a lad who can handle her.'

'Let's give her time, eh, love? I couldn't cope with another wedding for a good few years.' Molly put her arm around him and kissed him soundly. 'D'yer think I should go up to see if Jill needs a hand?'

'I know ye're dying to, love, but meself I think yer should leave them be. Steve and Lizzie are there if she needs help. What time have we got to be ready for?'

'Ye're right about Jill, she probably wants to do things for herself. I know I did after I'd had each of the children. And as for what time we're to be ready, the car will pick us up with Doreen, Phil and Frances, between one and half-past. Then it's coming back for Nellie, Paul, Corker and Ellen. So we can relax for an hour or so.'

'Ooh, there seems to be a lot of people here.' Molly stood just inside the church door. 'I can see our Tommy with Archie, and I think we're supposed to sit in the pews behind them because Archie has only got his mam, with her sister and her husband, and we can even the numbers up. There'll be more than enough family and friends to fill the McDonough pews.'

'I see George's sister and her husband are here.' Jack spoke softly as he always did in church because of the sombre atmosphere. 'I think they only see each other at weddings.'

'Let's go and sit down anywhere,' Doreen said, 'the baby is heavy to carry. We can always move later if need be.'

When Tommy saw his parents he went right over to them, his handsome face, as ever, in a smile. 'Mam, yer look lovely, like a film star.' He chucked Doreen under the chin. 'And you look very chic, Sis, it's no wonder Phil's got hold of yer arm so yer can't run away.' He gave Frances a special smile. 'Yer look a picture, Mrs Bradley.'

Archie came across, and considering he was the groom, he didn't look a bit flustered, 'Me last minutes of freedom, Mrs B, I must want me bumps feeling. Mind you, Tommy's been telling me he would definitely recommend marriage to anyone. So long as it's to the right person, of course.' He raised his hand and waved. 'Here's me mam and me auntie and her husband. And, ay, doesn't me mam look posh in her picture hat? I feel real proud of her.'

'So yer should, sunshine, 'cos she's a lovely woman, is Ida.' It was Molly who waved her hand now. 'Here's Jill with Steve and the baby, and me ma and da are behind them with Rosie. So let's sit down 'cos we're taking the whole aisle up.'

When Corker arrived with Ellen, Molly asked softly, 'Where's Nellie? I thought she was supposed to come with you?'

'She did come in the car with us, me darlin', but where she's got to heaven only knows. She was beside me one minute, then gone the next.' Everyone had to move along the pew to make a double space for Corker, and he made sure it was next to Jill so he could see the baby 'Yer'll be coming to the reception, won't yer, princess, so I can hold the baby and get acquainted with her?'

'I'm going to try and get there for an hour or so, Uncle Corker, I really want to be there for Lily and Archie.'

Molly turned her head to see if she could see her mate, and was surprised to find the church was almost full. Apart from all the families and relatives, Maisie and Alec from the corner shop were there, so was Beryl Mowbray and her family. And it seemed half the street had turned out. Then there was a united, 'Ooh, ay, look!' and Molly gasped and signalled to the family to look towards the door.

For Nellie had waited for everyone to be seated before making a very grand entrance on her own. She walked down the aisle with an air of confidence that many a professional mannequin would envy. She looked a real treat in her light purple dress and lilac hat, and you could tell by her swaying hips that she felt like a million dollars. Molly whispered to Jack, 'Look at that smile, it's like sunshine on a rainy day.' And under her breath she muttered, 'She'll be the talk of the whole neighbourhood for the next month, and after an entrance like that, good luck to her.'

Nellie had just taken her seat next to Paul, when the organ began to play and once again all heads turned. There was a murmur of appreciation when they saw Lily on the arm of her very proud father. She looked really beautiful, like a fairy. Behind her, in perfect step, came the four lovely bridesmaids in their full-skirted pale pink dresses, a band of flowers in their hair and carrying pretty posies. Three of them were old hands at being bridesmaids, but Bella's smile looked a little strained until her mother called, 'Yer look wonderful, sweetheart,' and that brought a touch more confidence.

Archie, who had been laughing and joking, showing no signs of nerves whatsoever, now looked stunned when he saw this vision walking towards him. 'My God, she's lovely.'

Best man Tommy said, 'She certainly is, ye're a very lucky man.'

It wasn't a long service, but it was a happy one because the two people being married showed their happiness and love for each other. No stammering or hesitating, just smiles. When it was time for the bridal couple to sign the registers, with George and Ida as witnesses, most of the neighbours left the church to stand outside where they would have a better view. But there wasn't a lot of space between the church and the tall black iron railings that surrounded it, so things were pretty hectic with people pushing and elbowing to get the best speck. When the newly married couple came out on to the top step and posed, as had been arranged, the poor photographer couldn't find space for his tripod to get a good shot. He was only a small man, and too polite for his own good because no one took a blind bit of notice of him, until Corker, Tommy and Paul took over and were quite firm about moving back the people who were their neighbours. It was all good-natured and everyone was in a happy mood as the first photograph was taken, then the bridesmaids were brought out to stand with the bride and groom and all smiled as the camera clicked.

It was then that Corker noticed the group inside the porch. Molly and Nellie, and their husbands, were waiting to have their photograph taken with Lily and Archie. But what caught Corker's eye was Jill hugging the baby close, with Steve beside her. And next to them were Doreen and her baby, Phil and his mother. The crowds outside would be too much for the babies, and for someone as frail as Frances. So Corker had a word with Archie.

'Tommy, Paul, give us a hand.' He waved them over and explained he wanted a clear path making for the girls with their babies, their husbands and Frances. 'I've asked Archie, and he said it's all right to use the wedding cars to take them home. They're only parked in the side street.'

Very soon a relieved-looking group was on their way home so the two young mothers could change and feed their babies, then hopefully make it to the reception for an hour or two. Out of their special group of families and friends, no one had ever missed a party or wedding, and they didn't want to be the first.

Archie, ever thoughtful of others, asked Edna Hanley if she could delay bringing the food in until the Bennett girls arrived with babies and husbands. He'd also brought the photographer to the hall, so every one of their special group would be in their album to look back on over the years. He'd had one taken of the three mums, Nellie, Ida and Molly, outside the church, and hoped it turned out as well as he thought it would. And he didn't forget Phil and his mother. He was sure the lad would appreciate a photo of himself with her, it was something he would always treasure.

As Corker and Tommy kept topping up glasses, conversations between friends and relatives could be heard on all sides. Paul, who was supposed to help, spent most of his time with Phoebe because she looked so pretty he couldn't take his eyes off her. And there was laughter in abundance. It was the laughter Jill and Doreen heard as they climbed the stairs to the reception room, followed by Steve and Phil who had a hand to his mother's elbow to help her up the stone stairs. 'Just listen to them.' Doreen said. 'I bet we'll be the only ones sober.'

As soon as they entered the door, all the women in the hall surged forward to have a first sight of Jill's baby. There was much cooing, and remarks on all sides that she was beautiful and was going to take after her mam. Of course there wouldn't be a show without Punch, and Nellie bragged, 'She's going to take after her Grandma McDonough, look, she's got my eyes.' And when Molly called, 'Then God help the poor child!' her mate was quick to answer, 'Oh, He will, girl, 'cos me and Him are best of friends.'

Doreen's baby, Bobby, was getting a lot of attention, too. He was at the sitting-up stage now, and gazed around with interest and a chuckle when anyone tickled his nose or under his chin. Archie put the cameraman to work on snaps of the babies with their parents, and a special one of Phil with his arm around Frances, who was looking very tired. She felt it, but was determined to get as much out of today as she could. And she was happy that her son and his wife never left her side.

Edna Hanley popped her head in. 'Can everyone take their seat, now, please? There's name cards by each plate.'

Molly found her place was next to Nellie, with Jack beside her on the other side. 'We can't sit at the top table, sunshine, we're not relatives. This is your day, me and Jack are only guests.'

Nellie glared at her. 'I'm not going to swear, girl, not while I've got me posh hat on. But if I didn't have it on, I'd tell yer to sod off.' She pointed a finger to the chair next to her. 'Sit yerself down, ye're me best mate and I want yer beside me. Yer've never left me out of anything and I ain't leaving you out. So sit down and do as ye're told. And Jack as well.'

It was when they were all seated that, on cue, Paul shouted to his sister, 'Ay, Lily, when yer get married aren't yer supposed to wear something old, something new, something borrowed and something blue? I thought it was bad luck not to.'

'I've stuck to tradition, Paul, I've got them all on.'

'Well, let's see them! I'm sure everyone would like to.'

Lily smiled as she pushed her chair back. 'I'll have to stand in the middle of the room, so yer can all see.' She bent down to whisper in Archie's ear. 'Yer've said yer love me about ten times since we got hitched. Well, I hope yer still love me five minutes from now.'

There were three long trestle tables, one at the top and two running down at right angles from it. It left a clear space in the middle, and this was where Lily stood. First she touched a link of pearls around her neck. 'Mrs Higgins lent me these, they belonged to her mother and are very old.' She waved a handkerchief. 'This has never been used, bought 'specially for the occasion, so it's very new.' Smiling, she lifted the long skirt of her dress to reveal a ruched white silk garter around her ankle. 'I borrowed this off one of me mates in work, which is rather swish, don't yer think?' Then, biting on her bottom lip, she lifted the other side of her skirt quite high, to reveal one leg of a pair of pale blue fleecy-lined bloomers. 'And last but not least, something blue.'

The whole room erupted into laughter and guffaws, the loudest coming from Archie and Corker. Every member of the Bennett, McDonough and Corkhill families was in stitches, and Doreen and Jill looked at each other, glad they were here and hadn't missed Lily showing that when she wanted to be, she was a chip off the old block. But it was Steve who noticed his mother's face doing contortions as she tried to take in what she was seeing. And he nudged Jill, saying, 'Watch me mam.'

Nellie jumped to her feet, sending her chair toppling back. Pointing a finger at her daughter, she said, 'So that's where the bleeding things are! It's no wonder I couldn't find them. After searching the house for them, I've had to come out with no bleeding bloomers on.'

This brought forth more laughter, but the rafters rang when Molly tugged on her mate's dress and said, 'Don't swear, Nellie, not when yer've got yer posh hat on, sunshine.'

'Sod me posh hat, Molly Bennett! What would happen if I ge

run over by a tram, taken to hospital and the doctor finds I've got no bloomers on? They'd send for the police and I'd get put in jail.'

There was a fresh burst of jollity when Molly said, 'No, I wouldn't let yer go to jail with no bloomers on, Nellie, not me best mate. I'd scrounge a nappy off Doreen or Jill.'

Lily was bent double in the middle of the room. Oh, it had been worth it to see her mother's face. And of course Auntie Molly bounced off her as usual. It had been a good idea of Paul's, even though she hadn't thought so when he'd first mentioned it.

Nellie leaned against the table as she pointed a finger at her daughter. And as trestle tables are not strong enough to support someone of Nellie's weight, the table did the only thing it could do, it moved forward with her. She grabbed at it for support, her hat fell down over her eyes until she couldn't see, and she was only rescued by George putting his hands around her waist and lifting her off the floor. While Molly tried to sort table and chair out, Nellie's feet were treading the air and she was shouting to her daughter, 'You make sure yer wash them before yer give me them back, d'yer hear?'

When Edna Hanley went into the bakery to pick up some bread, she said to her husband, 'We don't half miss out on a lot. What we should do, is give them the reception for nothing as long as they invite us as guests. They're having a whale of a time up here, as usual. All crying with laughter, they are, the lucky beggars.'

Her husband grinned. 'I thought the ceiling was going to come down a few minutes ago, what was that in aid of?'

'Ah, well, Jill has just informed everyone that the new baby is be christened Molly-Helen McDonough. And the roar you heard was the two grandmas doing a very noisy Irish jig.'

Taking a Chance on Love

Joan Jonker

Ginny Porter and Joan Flynn were born within days of each other in adjoining houses in a narrow street of two-up two-downs in Liverpool. Now that they've left school, Joan finds work at Dunlop's tyre factory, and Ginny's dream comes true when she is taken on as a counter assistant at Woolworths. But things don't work out as she had expected, and for a while she carries around a dark secret.

Meanwhile, a neighbour, Hannah, is devastated at the death of her son, and her future looks bleak until Ginny's mother, Beth, rallies her friends together to help the elderly woman through her darkest days. Then comes news that lifts Hannah's spirits and enables the old lady to laugh once again. And new arrivals in the street affect the lives of everyone.

Taking A Chance On Love is packed with warmth and laughter that will touch the hearts of Joan Jonker's legions of fans. Don't miss her previous Liverpool sagas:

'Hilarity and pathos in equal measure' *Liverpool Echo*

'Packed with believable, heartwarming characters' *Coventry Evening Telegraph*

'Touching, full of incident and tears and laughter' *Reading Chronicle*

0 7472 6797 9

headline

After The Dance Is Over

Joan Jonker

There's never a dull moment when best mates Nellie McDonough and Molly Bennett get together. And there's always something to keep them busy in their Liverpool backstreet, like becoming private detectives to help a loved one – the results of which are funny, warm and wonderfully satisfying.

Then Nellie is walking on air when her daughter Lily hints that she will soon be setting a date for her wedding to Archie. But when news comes that will affect both the families, Molly sheds tears of happiness while her mate Nellie lifts her skirts and breaks into an Irish jig . . .

After The Dance Is Over continues the lively adventures of two of the most entertaining families you'll ever meet.

Don't miss Joan Jonker's previous Liverpool sagas:

'Hilarity and pathos in equal measure' *Liverpool Echo*

'Packed with believable, heartwarming characters' *Coventry Evening Telegraph*

'Touching, full of incident and tears and laughter' *Reading Chronicle*

0 7472 6614 X

headline

Now you can buy any of these other bestselling
books by **Joan Jonker** from your bookshop
or *direct from her publisher*.

FREE P&P AND UK DELIVERY
(Overseas and Ireland £3.50 per book)

The Sunshine of your Smile	£6.99
Strolling With The One I Love	£5.99
Taking a Chance on Love	£5.99
After the Dance is Over	£5.99
Many a Tear Has to Fall	£5.99
Dream a Little Dream	£6.99
Down Our Street	£5.99
Stay as Sweet as You Are	£6.99
Try a Little Tenderness	£5.99
Walking My Baby Back Home	£5.99
Sadie was a Lady	£6.99
The Pride of Polly Perkins	£5.99
Sweet Rosie O'Grady	£6.99
Last Tram to Lime Street	£6.99
Stay in Your Own Back Yard	£5.99
Home is Where the Heart is	£5.99
Man of the House	£5.99
When One Door Closes	£6.99

TO ORDER SIMPLY CALL THIS NUMBER

01235 400 414

or visit our website: www.madaboutbooks.com

Prices and availability subject to change without notice